ALSO BY TOM LOWE

WRATH

An Elizabeth Monroe Mystery / Thriller

TOM LOWE

K

Kingsbridge Entertainment

Library of Congress Cataloging in—Publication Data, Lowe, Tom, 1952

Wrath by Tom Lowe – First Edition, 2017
ISBN: 198122629X
ISBN-13: 9781981226290

1. Mississippi—Fiction 2. Hattiesburg—Fiction. 3. De Soto deaths—Fiction. 4. Burial Mound—Fiction, Klu-Klux-Klan 5. Casinos, card tricks, poker—Fiction – Title: *Wrath*

Wrath is distributed in ebook, print and audiobook editions.

Cover design by Damonza.

Formatting and digital conversion services by CreateSpace.

Wrath, First edition – December, 2017. Published in the U.S.A by Kingsbridge Entertainment.

ACKNOWLEDGMENTS

My deep appreciation and thanks to beta readers Helen Ristuccia-Christensen and Darcy Yarosh. To the wizards at CreateSpace, Ashley Wells and Lance Buckley. To James M. Garrison, Ph.D. retired history professor in Mississippi. To Shawn Cox, specialist in forensic psychology, Phoenix, Arizona, and to Keri Lowe.

Finally to you, the reader. I'm to those who continue the writing journey with me, thank you. A storyteller always needs a great audience. My readers are the best of the best. I hope you enjoy the first novel in a new series featuring criminal psychologist, Elizabeth Monroe.

"*The sad truth is that most evil is done by people who can never make up their minds to be either good or evil.*"

- Hannah Arendt

For Keri Lowe

PROLOGUE

Shubuta, Mississippi -1918

Ll she could think about was the child. A child who had yet to be born. But the time was growing close. "Be here 'fore Christmas," her mama had said. And that was only three weeks away. Maggie, fifteen years old, closed her eyes for a few seconds, standing near the center of the Shubuta Bridge in Southeastern Mississippi.

She tried to block the noise from her mind, the shouts and taunts of the lynch mob. She held her fingers to her ears. But she couldn't block the odor from her nostrils. The dank smell from a gang of sweaty men. The sour stink in their clothes, acrid breaths laced with beer and rye whiskey, the shared and heightened odor of a pack intent on a kill.

Maggie stared out across the river. It was nearly sunset and the light rippled like gold coins on the surface of the Chickasawhay River that flowed beneath the bridge, twisting around the scrub oak in the ravine.

The baby kicked. She looked down at her swollen stomach. She could see the bulge of an elbow or tiny foot moving under her dress. Less than ten feet away stood her sister, Alma May. She, too, was pregnant. By the same man who ran the farm where they lived and worked.

The man had taken them. Taken their innocence—their virginity, and left wounds, deep scars, that would never heal properly. He had them repeatedly. At first, when Maggie was fourteen. She didn't know what was happening as he raped her in his barn. She would stare at an old gray mare locked in her stall across from them. She'd gaze into the mare's sad brown eyes—eyes that looked like they were weeping. *Don't cry, Misty,* she would think. She pretended as if she could talk to Misty just by sending thoughts toward her. It was a way to ease the pain, to deaden the sound of his grunts, to mask the whiskey on his breath, the stench of his rotten teeth.

She had to leave her body because she was not there anymore, at least until he finished and walked out of the barn.

Today, two teenage brothers also stood on the bridge with the girls. The boys openly cried.

The man who owned the farm, a white man, was dead. Stabbed in the chest. The teens, all black, were rounded up as suspects. They claimed innocence and begged for mercy. They were tossed in the county jail for three days to await trial. But then whiskey flowed. Gossip became fact. Anger spewed like hot lava across the small town of Shubuta. Suspicion and innuendo became hard facts. Men, who alone could be civil, became a seething thing of hate in the form of a mob, collectively responsible to no one. Not the law and certainly not the blacks in Mississippi.

There would be no trial.

"They look guilty," said one man they called Preacher. He was tall with a drooping moustache. He wore a Stetson on his head and a Colt 45 on his hip. He was known to have shot and killed a man on a Saturday night and then preached the gospel the following Sunday morning. His eyes were black as coal, and he had a stare that made most men look away and step aside.

Maggie moved her fingers from her ears. The shouting grew louder. "Hang the bastards!" yelled a man with a scraggly beard.

"Gimme a minute," said a lean man, tying four hangman's nooses from four separate rolls of one-inch thick rope.

Almost two-dozen men, all white, stood in a semicircle around the teenagers. Preacher, his hard sole boots loud against the wooden planks on the bridge, stepped over to each teenager. He looked at them like he was inspecting for lice. "Y'all ready for salvation!" he shouted.

None of the teens spoke. Alma May cried, trying to hold back her deep sobs. She placed both hands on her protruding belly and looked over to her sister, Maggie. Both girls wept.

Preacher's lean face was stoic, his eyes hard as rocks. I said, "Y'all prepared to meet thy God?"

"We ain't done nothin' suh," said one of the boys.

Preacher sneered. "Your boss has been stabbed four times in the chest. Each one of y'all take a turn with the knife...that how it happened, huh?"

Maggie said, "We didn't kill nobody. We heard a fight. It was another white man who come through the property."

"Who? Who was this man?" Preacher asked.

"We don't know his name. Never seen him before."

"Liar! Liars and sinners!" Shouted preacher. He turned to the man with the ropes. "You got 'em nooses ready, Buford."

"Yes sir, Preacher Belmont."

"Let's get 'em ready boys!"

The mob yelled, the men laughing, some passing the bottle. Others with lit cigarettes dangling from wet lips. They moved closer. The nooses ready. They tied off the end of each rope to an iron girder and waited for Preacher's command.

Maggie looked over to Alma May and said, "Let's pray like mama taught us." She nodded and the girls began reciting the Lord's Prayer. Preacher looked at every man with a rope in his hand and tipped his Stetson. They placed the nooses over each teenager's head. Alma May's lower lip trembled. She said, "Give us this day our daily bread and forgive us our trespasses as we forgive those who trespass against us...."

Maggie felt her baby kicking, she cried and continued praying with her sister. "And lead us not into temptation, but deliver us from evil...for thine is the kingdom, the power, and the glory, for ever and ever...amen...."

"Throw 'em over boys!" shouted Preacher.

"Nooooo...please...my baby...." begged Alma May.

One of the teenage boys couldn't hold his bladder, urine soaked his pants and his bare feet.

The men picked the boy up and threw him off the bridge. He fell for twenty feet, screaming. Then a loud *whack*. His neck snapped. They picked up the second boy and threw him over. Another terrified scream until the rope crushed his vocal cords and windpipe.

They came for Alma May. "Please don't! We ain't kilt nobody! Please let me have my baby then y'all can kill me if you won't to."

The men grabbed her by the arms, picked her up and dropped Alma May over the side. Her neck didn't snap. She gasped for air. Pulled at the rope with her two hands until they bled. Her strength was gone. Breathing through her nostrils, mucus and the tears. Her arms dropped. Silence. Her body swayed at the end of the rope above the river.

Maggie felt faint. She placed her hands to her stomach, feeling her unborn child move more than it ever had. The baby somehow sensing its mother's trauma, causing it distress. "Let's get the last girl and call it a night," Preacher said.

One man drained the remaining whiskey from a bottle and tossed it over the bridge. Maggie watched the splash, her heart racing. "This ain't right. We ain't done nothin' to Mr. Harper. It's his baby that's inside me! He come to my sister and me and did things to us. This is his child...a white man's baby."

The men stopped their taunts. Exchanged glances. Not sure what to do or say.

"Liar!" bellowed Preacher Belmont. "Let's send this sinner to hell!"

Two burly men picked up Maggie. She kicked and screamed. She scratched, her nails raking down one man's face.

"Bitch scratched me!" he shouted. "You're goin' over." They tossed Maggie over the side. She reached out and managed to grab one of the girders. She held on with all her strength, the noose tight around her neck, the baby wiggling in her stomach.

Preacher Belmont stepped next to the beam. He gripped a steel joist, standing over Maggie. She looked up and said, "Please suh, you're a preacher. Please take my hand and pull me back...please."

"Now, why would I save a sinner?" He stood next to her small hands, lifted his right leg and slammed the heel of his boot down on her fingers. She screamed and removed her hand, hanging on with one hand. He made a sadistic grin, his mouth bent down, black moustache like the limp wings of a blackbird. He raised his leg and brought his heel down on her other hand.

Maggie could hold on no longer. As she fell, she tried to grab the rope. She tightened her neck muscles as hard as she could. The roped sliced into her vocal cords, severing her carotid artery. She dangled at the end of the rope, heard the jeers from the men, one urinated off the bridge, the urine splashing off her sister's dead body, the baby still moving inside the girl.

Maggie held the palm of her hands to her belly, felt the touch of her child and felt her heart racing. She wanted to speak to the baby, but her throat was crushed. Wanted to tell her child how much she loved it.

She dropped her hands from her stomach and stared into the sunset off the still waters of the Chickasawhay River. *It's a pretty river*, thought Maggie. *Like spun gold on the water.* She saw a horse trotting near the riverbank. It was sweet Misty. Suddenly Maggie was next to the river, standing by Misty. She reached out to touch the horse. Misty gently nuzzled her. The old mare's eyes wet and filled with sorrow. Misty lowered her head and wept, tears falling onto the surface of the river like golden droplets

ONE

Hattiesburg, Mississippi – Present Day

Cindy Carter knew she'd made a wrong decision. She looked for an exit. After her date's third drink of Jack Daniels, three shots within thirty minutes, she wanted to leave. Go back to her dorm. *Just walk out. Now.* The fraternity house smelled like beer and sweat. Old sweat from the bottom of a hamper.

Dozens of college students partied in the esteemed halls of Alpha Phi Kappa, a remodeled antebellum house near the University of Southern Mississippi. Rock and rap music blared from speakers. Joints and bong pipes passed in continuous rounds, and marijuana and hash smoke clouded the hot air. Beer flowed from kegs into red plastic Solo cups, and obnoxious laughter echoed throughout the rooms, forcing conversations to be shouted.

Cindy, nineteen, petite with chestnut brown hair and large, hazel-green eyes, set her glass of Pepsi down and approached her date. Alex Davidson, tall, angular face, stood next to the kegs in the kitchen with two other members of his fraternity, telling raunchy jokes and eyeing the new crop of young women. Cindy touched Alex on his shoulder. "I have to go."

He turned to her, face ruddy from the alcohol, eyes slightly glazed. "I thought you were in the bathroom. We've only been here like an hour." The other two guys grinned, looking at him and Cindy, waiting to hear his answer. "We got pizza and wings comin' in a minute. Let's hang out." He knocked back the remains of straight whiskey in his cup, his face blossoming, eyes wet.

Cindy shook her head. "You're already too drunk to drive me home. I'm sick of this crap." She turned, moving through the crowd—some kids dancing—others sitting in small groups, smoking weed, primal howls erupting as two coeds embraced in a slow dance.

Cindy walked by them. A short, thickset guy in a white T-shirt and red boxer shorts, held a tray of beers, grinning. His black-framed glasses slipped down his nose. He said, "One of these is for you."

She didn't answer, heading for the double doors at the end of a long hallway in the colonial house that, for the last fifty years, had been the home of one of the most popular fraternities. Cindy's heels clacked on the hardwood floor, the sound of the party now muffled behind the doors in the bowels of the great house.

Lightning flashed beyond the large windows in the front rooms, rain streaming down the glass. She had no umbrella and no way home. She called her roommate. After three rings, voice-mail. "This is Andrea...at the beep you know what to do."

Cindy waited for the rumble of thunder to subside. "Hey, Andrea, it's me. Things are like too creepy at the Kappa house. If you're out, maybe I can get a ride back to our dorm. Thanks, call me, okay?"

Cindy inhaled deeply, hoping Alex wouldn't enter the foyer and insist that she stay, or worse, insist that he drive her home. *Just leave me alone*, she thought, looking at the time on her phone screen. 9:30 p.m. She glanced at the apps. Uber. Lyft. And a new one—one she never used before—Kars. The first ride was free. *Why not?* She tapped the app, entered her credit card and address at the prompt.

There were five drivers within fifteen minutes of the fraternity house. The next in the cue was a driver named Tim Bledsoe. In his picture, he looked like he was in his forties. Round, happy face. He was seven minutes away. Black SUV, a Subaru. Cindy stood at the front door, glancing out the window, looking for headlights, the rain falling.

Alex walked down the hallway, stopping to brace himself against one wall. "C'mon back, Cindy. The party's just started, okay? I wanna...wanna introduce you to a friend of mind. You'll like her." He slurred his words.

"I'm leaving."

"Was it somethin' I said?" He stepped closer.

2

"You drink too much."

"No shit…but once I get a little food in me, I'm like good to go."

"No thanks. I'm tired.

He licked his red lips, eyes droopy. He approached, reaching for her hand. She pulled back. "No! I'm not going back in there."

"Bitch! What's your problem, huh? You embarrassed me again. I'm tired of it. What's your problem?"

"You're my problem. But not after tonight. This isn't working—we should break up." She ducked around him, opened the door and stepped out on the large wrap-around porch. She slammed the door behind her. Rainwater poured from the gutters, torrents slapping the wide leaves of banana plants to the left of the big porch. Cindy took a deep breath, glad to be away from the smoke that burned her eyes and brought out her allergies. The evening air had a clean smell, washed, the scent of night blooming jasmine in the breeze across the porch.

Car lights approached.

Cindy walked to the edge of the porch, near the steps, peering through the rain, looking at the car that stopped. It was an SUV. Same color. *Was it a Subaru?* She couldn't tell. She clutched her purse. *Would the driver get out and approach with an umbrella?*

The front door to the house opened, yellow light casting Alex in silhouette. He stood in the doorframe, staring at Cindy. She looked over her shoulder at him, turned and ran into the curtain of rain, down the wooden steps, along the gravel path to the car at the curb.

Alex held his car keys. "Bitch!" He would go to her dorm as soon as he could remember where he parked his car.

TWO

Elizabeth Monroe glanced at the center seat in the front row of her classroom and saw something she hadn't seen since the semester began.

The seat was vacant.

In three months, it had never been vacant. The student was always there, most often at least fifteen minutes before class started. Not today. Elizabeth looked up at the large clock on the wall. 9:05 a.m. More than two-dozen students filed into her classroom, each taking the same seat they staked out when the semester began.

Except for one.

And that triggered something in Elizabeth's gut. Anomalies did that to her. Keenly observant since she was a little girl, her sixth sense was an innate ability to see what most others didn't. Deception. Inconsistencies. Things out of place, or things arranged to look in place when they really weren't. The gift was a double-edge sword, good and bad consequences, cutting both ways, personally and professionally.

Elizabeth Monroe, Ph.D. Just shy of her forty-fifth birthday. Her brown hair had yet to yield to any shades of gray. She kept her body in shape by going to the gym often, and she ran a mile ever other day, except Sunday. It was the day that Elizabeth allowed herself to rest. Twice a week she taught forensic psychology classes at the University of Southern Mississippi in Hattiesburg.

The rest of the time she pursued her daughter's killer.

Molly Monroe was found dead in a remote section of the Ocala National Forest in Florida four years ago. She and her boyfriend had been shot. That was when Elizabeth's world came crashing down, hard. The search for Molly's killer went from weeks into months. And then—years.

Elizabeth had earned her doctorate in forensic criminal psychology, a long process of taking courses while supporting her daughter and building her small bakery into a success.

Today, her teaching schedule was sometimes interrupted by a homicide case. She was a forensic psychology consultant. When physical evidence is minimal, detectives look for motive—cause—a *reason* someone was killed. For the criminally insane, a reason can be a fantasy—something no more relevant than the day of the week.

When evidence is scarce, for those with the training and an intuitive gift, there are places to look—inside the dark recesses of the criminal mind. To profile an unknown murderer, especially one without apparent motive, Elizabeth begins with the scattered pieces of a macabre jigsaw puzzle. Looking for dark colors and patterns of evil that intersect. Looking for a potential sequence of psychological actions that may have started the chain of events.

The last student rushed in, late, closing the door behind him. Elizabeth watched the sweep second-hand move for a few seconds on the clock in her classroom, looked at the empty seat. She felt that something wasn't right—checked her email, looking for a notice from the missing student. Nothing. Elizabeth stepped next to the lectern. "Has anyone heard from Cindy Carter?"

The two dozens faces were blank, students looking at the empty seat and then at their instructor. Elizabeth smiled. "I know it's Monday, but did anyone see Cindy over the weekend?"

A girl's hand shot up. "I saw her at the Salty Dog getting a carryout pizza Friday night."

Elizabeth nodded. "Was she with anyone?"

"Her boyfriend, Alex Davidson, and some dudes from his fraternity. It was like really crowded. Want me to text her?"

"That would be great, thanks."

Elizabeth looked from left to right, taking in all of her students. "Some of what you'll learn in this class is why a lot of people are creatures of habit. We notice Cindy's absence quicker because that's where she always sits… front row, center. What do you think that means?"

A male student raised his hand. "Maybe she has a hearing problem." There was a chuckle in the classroom.

Elizabeth smiled. "No, Randy, from what I can tell, Cindy has excellent hearing. You sit in the back row, same seat since the first day of class weeks ago. And the rest of you always take the same chairs. You're not alone, dear students. You see it in staff meetings held on a regular basis. Boardrooms. Just about any meeting area where we gather in a semiformal assembly. The question is *why?* What do you think, Madison?" She gestured to a brunette in the front row.

"Is it because people get comfortable quickly?"

"Yes, that's part of it. Does where you sit in class say something about you?"

The same brunette smiled. "It's one less decision to make."

Elizabeth laughed. "To some degree, you're right. Sometimes it's a familiarity move. The seat you take becomes…." She used her fingers to make the quotes sign. "It becomes your seat—your place of power around the campfire. Territorial. The CEO sits at the head of the table, the people in positions of power are often sitting next to him or her, almost in a line of succession to the throne."

A student sitting near the clock, his baseball cap on backwards, raised his hand and said, "Okay, let's do the throne analogy. King Arthur used a round table, all positions equal, so there wouldn't be any office politics." He grinned.

Elizabeth stepped out from behind the lectern and drew a circle on the whiteboard behind her. She pointed to the image. "The roundtable, designed from the circle—the universal symbol of unity." She drew three figures seated at the table, the one in the center, the largest of the three. "This is King Arthur. Siting to his right is Sir Lancelot, the knight who held the most power. To the king's left, is Sir Galahad, the knight with the second most power, and so on around the table. However, the power diminishes relative to the distance each knight is seated away from the king. A psycho-logical diminishing distance of return, if you will."

Elizabeth placed the cap back on the marker. "Human nature is predict-able to some degree unless we're talking about the dark knight sitting at the table. Who is he, and what does he want?"

The class is silent. No hands in the air.

Elizabeth nodded. "That's where we'll segue in to today's topic—the psychodynamic investigations of the unconscious or subconscious relation-ship between childhood trauma and adult choice."

The same student who earlier had sent the text message raised her hand.

Elizabeth pointed to her, "Yes, Julie?"

"Cindy never responded to my text. That's not like her."

"I'm hoping she's sick in bed and asleep, getting some rest." Elizabeth turned back to the whiteboard.

A male student, shoulder-length hair, glasses, looked up from his laptop. He cleared his throat. "Professor Monroe...."

"Yes."

"I just read a breaking news alert on my computer. Channel Seven is reporting that cops found a body of a young woman. They haven't released her name. I'm hoping it's not Cindy."

THREE

It's only twenty-nine miles south of Hattiesburg, but it might as well be another world. The De Soto National Forest is a land of paradoxes. It's more than a half million acres intertwined with longleaf pines, black water creeks—pastoral serenity and ghosts of the bloodiest war on American soil, the Civil War. Trails, covered deep in rust-colored pines needles, lead to the physical and mystical ecosystem of the Deep South—the share cropper's cabin leaning on the shoulders of time, the rustic barn covered in a cloak of kudzu, family cemeteries buried in milkweed, the silent spirits that speak through the wormholes in time and the landscape.

Elizabeth drove south on State Highway 49, well above the speed limit. Her hands gripped the wheel, knuckles white. Both sides of the road were thick with pine trees; an eagle soared above the tree line.

A whitetail deer bolted across the highway. Elizabeth hit her brakes, barely missing the deer before it vanished into the forest. She used one hand to pull a strand of hair behind her ear. There was no GPS address in the national forest, only natural landmarks, dirt roads and miles of wilderness. She spotted a fire tower a half-mile beyond the tree line.

She sped up, soon slowing to turn off the main road onto an unnamed spur road. It was not much wider than the width of her car. It wound through loose sand and long leaf pines, she followed tracks of other vehicles—some left knotty tread marks in the sandy soil. Limbs slapped the side of her Ford Explorer, wood thrushes squawking and flittering from trees.

She thought about the most horrible day in her life, the day they found her daughter Molly in a Florida forest. Elizabeth's mind played back the grisly images. The gurney loaded into the coroner's van. Molly's body under the white sheet. The pop of police radios. The somber look on the medical examiner's stoic face. Police and emergency technicians wanting to say something comforting, but at a loss for words. The compression of time and space—the twenty years Molly had lived, from her first step as a baby to her final walk on earth. She'd come to the forest to release endangered butterflies for her entomology class.

And she'd met a monster.

Elizabeth bit her lower lip and focused on driving through the sand, intercut with slight gulches from those who were already on the crime scene. Through a gap in the branches and foliage she spotted the first sheriff's cruiser—and then six more. In the mix were three unmarked cars, an ambulance, the coroner's dark blue van and the ME's van. All of the emergency lights were off. Yellow crime scene tape laced through the saplings. In the center was a massive live oak tree, its thick limbs draped in Spanish moss.

At the base of the tree was where someone left horror.

Elizabeth parked, took a deep breath, and got out, the air warm and humid, the scent of honeysuckles and pinesap. A bumblebee hovered above a pink orchid. Elizabeth gently closed her car door; the tree and the girl's body still more than one hundred feet away. She watched and listened for a moment, the medical examiner taking pictures of the body, the coroner speaking with a detective, the staccato clip of police radios.

Off to one side, Detective Mike Bradford questioned a tall man dressed in jeans and a dark T-shirt. He wore a baseball cap and military boots. She watched, staying in the shadows of towering pine trees. The man was animated, palms out, tattoos on both arms, nodding his head as the detective took notes in a small pad. After another minute, the questioning ended. The detective gave him a business card, the man shoving it in his back pocket.

He walked toward a black ATV four-wheeler. Before he got behind the wheel, the man looked back over his shoulder at the body in the distance. Elizabeth could see him mumble something, purse his lips, turn his hat backwards, crank the engine and drive away down a long dirt road, bouncing in the ruts like a cowboy riding off.

Detective Mike Bradford took a call on his phone. He spotted Elizabeth, disconnected and approached her. Bradford, early forties, kept his brown hair short. He wore a sports coat, dress shirt untucked, jeans. "Are you with the press?"

"No."

"This is an active crime scene. You need to leave."

"My name's Elizabeth Monroe. I teach criminal psychology at Southern Miss. I believe the girl killed might be one of my students."

"What's her name?"

"Cindy Carter." Elizabeth looked toward the large tree and the body at the base. "That's Cindy, isn't it?"

Detective Bradford said nothing for a moment. "Why did you come to the crime scene?"

"It is Cindy. I can tell in your eyes."

"What sort of a teacher-student relationship did you have with her?"

"What do you mean?"

"Was she a good student?"

"Yes."

"When was the last time you saw her?"

"Last week in class."

"Where were you Friday evening?"

"Am I a suspect?"

"Do you mind answering the question?"

"Yes, I do mind if I'm a suspect. I came here because I thought I might be of some assistance to you. I knew the victim well. My own daughter was murdered, and she was about Cindy's age when it happened. I have a doctorate in forensic psychology. I've been asked to evaluate mental competency in murder trials where the defense pleas insanity. I've studied criminal profiling with some of the world's top experts. Maybe there's something I can do to help."

Detective Bradfield studied her face for a moment, the crack of police radios in the humid air. "Elizabeth Monroe...now I remember you. You were called in to evaluate the metal competency of Zeke Fisher, the guy who killed two men from the Philippines at a gas station because he thought they were terrorists. The defense pleads innocence by reason of insanity. But after your testimony, the jury came back with a guilty verdict and a recommendation for the death penalty."

"He was no more insane than you. He was mean...had been all his life. A half bottle of Tennessee whiskey was all it took to assassinate those two men as they stopped for directions."

Bradford nodded. "Didn't you do the mental competency evaluation on the guy who was killing tourists visiting casinos in Biloxi?"

"Yes. Now may I look at the body?"

Bradford glanced over his shoulder at another detective watching them. "Thanks for the offer, but we don't need the services of a criminal profiler at this time. We can handle it. Stay on this side of the yellow tape." He reached in his pocket and pulled out a business card. "If you hear any students talking about this murder...maybe knowing more than they should... if you can think of something that might be of value, here's my card. Have a good day, Doctor Monroe." He turned to leave.

"The man you were questioning...did he report the murder?"

"As a matter of fact, he did. Why?"

"Because, at one point in your interrogation, he was lying to you."

"What? How do you know?"

"His hands and feet were contrasting. Once he covered his mouth with his left hand when you asked him a question, the same left hand with the wedding band he fiddled with as you questioned him."

Bradford said nothing. He glanced down at the notepad and looked up at Elizabeth. "You got all that from fifty feet away?"

"Yes. That doesn't mean he killed her. But it does mean something in your line of questioning bothered him. It bothered him enough to be deceptive."

"He's a hunter, out scouting the area for the next hunting season. He said he drove by in his ATV and saw what he thought was some kind of hunter's blind that had maybe rotted out of that tree. He came closer and discovered the body. He called it in and waited for us. He didn't have to do that."

"No, he didn't. But he wouldn't be the first to kill and call."

"What did the killer write on her forehead?"

"Excuse me?"

"The word. I can see the letters but I can't make out the word from here. I can see that he placed some sort of flower crown on her head. He posed her didn't he?"

"It looks that way. I have an investigation to conduct. Goodbye, Doctor Monroe."

"The word on her forehead. It could tell us if Cindy is his first victim?"

"How?"

"If you let me closer, I might have a better idea."

FOUR

The closer she got, the more the revulsion took form. Cicadas droned in the trees, the smell of damp moss, pine needles and death in the air. Blowflies orbited the body. Elizabeth's heart beat faster, her hands clammy, throat so dry she couldn't swallow. She raised one hand to her lips. "Dear God…."

Detective Bradford looked at her. "I've worked a lot of murder cases, but this one has to top the sicko list. I'm sorry you have to see one of your students in this condition."

"She was one of those rare…near perfect students. Eager to learn. Eager to live life to its fullest. Full of everything that's good. Today was the only day she wasn't in the front row—center chair." Elizabeth's eyes were damp. She said nothing for a moment. "I asked her why she first took that seat. She said it was because she wanted to make eye contact with me, to engage in the lesson, to learn."

Elizabeth clenched her fists, bit her lower lip and stared at the small and tortured body of Cindy Carter.

Bradford said, "Coroner says she's been dead for a couple of days. You can see how the killer posed her at the base of the tree. He made the crown out of honeysuckle vine. In the vic's own blood, the perp wrote the word *wrath*."

Elizabeth said nothing, studying the scene. "Do we know the cause of death?"

"He slit her throat, but there's not that much blood in the neck area, which means he may have strangled her earlier because of the dark bruises on her neck. Also, there's…."

"There's what, Detective?"

Bradford stared toward the ground for a moment, shook his head, and then looked at Elizabeth. "There's blood on her clothes apparently from her vagina. If you can profile this sick bastard, and if it leads to him, this pervert might be one of the guys studied like Bundy or Dahmer." He paused. "You mentioned that your daughter was murdered. Was the killer ever brought to justice?"

"Justice? What does that mean in cases like this? To answer your question, no. The case is cold. I'm doing what I can to find him myself."

Detective Bradford was quiet. He cleared his throat. "Is that the real reason you're out here? Are you searching for your daughter's killer? Looking at similar crime scenes, trying to catch him?"

"Right now Cindy is someone else's daughter…and that alone is painful enough." She turned, walked toward the tree. Bradford waved off a deputy who didn't recognize Elizabeth. She waited for the forensic techs to finish. They scoured the area, careful to photograph and bag almost anything that seemed out of place or out of character. "Found a cigarette butt," said one tech, using tweezers to lift it from the ground less than thirty feet from the body.

Detective Bradford nodded and then looked at Elizabeth. "Maybe it'll have detectable DNA."

"Maybe. But unless it's in the database, it means finding a real, live psychotic match." She walked up to the body, studied it, trying to oppress the rising feelings of rage and fury, knowing Cindy as a student and as a person. Knowing her potential and how a killer decided to remove that from the face of the earth.

Bradford let Elizabeth examine the body alone. A second detective, Ed Milton, walked up to Bradford. Milton was in is mid-fifties, black, bulldog jaws and guarded eyes. He lowered his voice. "Who that hell is that?"

"Elizabeth Monroe. She's the forensic psychologist who blew the defense outta the water in the Zeke Fisher murder trial. Remember it over in Natchez?"

"Yeah. Why?"

"She was the expert forensic that pretty much destroyed the plea of insanity. Remember the case in Biloxi…the one where the perp, Justin Morrison, was targeting tourists coming out of some of the casinos. He killed three, almost slit the throat on the fourth before he was caught. Said because the word 'sin' was in casino, he had the authority to stop sinners from compulsive gambling."

"And they say legalized gambling doesn't have a negative effect on the area. It attracts the compulsives and weirdoes like bugs to a light bulb."

"Elizabeth Monroe evaluated the perp and found him competent to stand trial. She teaches criminal psychology at the university."

"A shrink that deals in theory. So tell her to go back to class."

Bradford paused, a mourning dove cooing beyond the tree line. "The victim…she was one of Elizabeth's students."

Milton grunted and watched Elizabeth study the body. "Suppose a quick look can't hurt. We're done anyway. All that's left is for the ME to do an autopsy." He paused and folded his big arms, his face wary. "We'd better watch her like a hawk."

"Why's you're guard up?"

"Because she had a teacher-student relationship with the vic. Maybe it was intimate." He started to smile but stopped. "Sometimes the shrinks are the weirdest of the weird. Look at the peculiar way she's studying the body, like she sees somethin' nobody else sees."

"Maybe she does."

"Maybe she had somethin' to do with the murder, too. I don't trust shrinks. Even a good lookin' one like her. Nobody suspects a pretty woman. That's why it's hard to trap a black widow."

FIVE

Elizabeth was quiet. A blowfly whirred, orbited her head. She looked at the wounds, fingernails, the position of the body, the honeysuckle vine on the girl's head, and a wooden bowl on her lap. She could see dirt at the bottom of the bowl, a small sprig in the dirt, and the smear of dried blood on her forehead: *Wrath*

Elizabeth pulled back the opening at the top of the blouse. She stared at the two raised welts on the girl's skin. Burn marks. Two inches apart. She looked at Cindy's open eyes—locked on the unseen—the thousand-yard stare of terror transformed into a powerless recognition of mortality. One earring missing. Elizabeth drew in a sharp breath, swatted a blowfly from the body and slowly stood.

Wrath, she thought. *The seven deadly sins, maybe?* She used her phone to look up information on the seven deadly sins, reading the screen in the dappled light. She finished and walked back to Bradford. "We've got to find this guy. He'll do it again. Cindy is probably his first victim…or the first we've found. He put her on display."

Bradford said, "Elizabeth, this is Detective Ed Milton. We're working the case together."

Elizabeth extended her hand. "I'd much rather be meeting you under different circumstances."

Milton eyed her a moment, releasing her hand. "So you teach forensic psychology at USM in Hattiesburg?"

"Yes."

"Mike mentioned your involvement in the casino killer case and the crazy shit in Natchez looking for terrorists under every rock. So the crazies can't fake it around you?"

"Some do."

"What do you make of the word he wrote on her forehead, the crown of honeysuckles and the wooden bowl in her lap with the dirt and a leaf of some sort?"

"Give me a second." Elizabeth pulled out her phone and punched numbers, reading the information on the screen. She exhaled deeply and looked at Milton and Bradford. "The crown of honeysuckle flowers may be an attempt to give her an angelic look."

Bradford let out a low whistle. "What do you mean?"

"The word wrath…the wooden bowl. It's handmade. Wrath is listed as one of the seven deadly sins. The others include things like greed, gluttony, lust and so on. If it is connected to the seven deadly sins, and if this is his first kill, there may be six more murders—all with a different sin scrawled on the body."

Milton's jaw line tightened. "Sounds like a lot of mumbo jumbo."

Bradford looked over at the body, the bowl resting on the girl's lap. "If that's accurate, we have one very sick psycho we're dealing with here."

Elizabeth blew out a long breath. "What's perplexing, though, is what you found inside the bowl…dirt and a sprig. But one thing is very clear: this perp has a grandiose authority complex. He wants to make a statement. And he'd relish seeing our reaction to what he did." Elizabeth looked at the CSI techs going about their business, checking faces, body language.

Milton said, "I assure you no one on this team did it."

"I didn't say they did."

Milton's phone buzzed. He looked at the screen. "It's the captain. I gotta take it." He stepped away to answer the call.

Bradford waited a few seconds and said, "You've been watching everyone from the moment you arrived. There are no suspects here."

"Serial arsonists often return to the scene to watch the firefighters' heroic efforts to extinguish fire. It's macabre, but you know it happens. And, although rare, some cops return to a murder they've committed to watch their colleagues work the case, and often to steer those colleagues in the wrong direction."

They stepped out of the way as the coroner and two members of his team approached the body with a steel gurney and a white sheet. The coroner spoke briefly with another detective before nodding and instructing his team to remove Cindy's remains.

Bradford said, "You saw the burn marks. The perp got close enough to the victim to make direct contact."

"So the marks are from a stun gun and not a Taser, right?"

"Yes. Whoever did it, most likely met or stalked the girl, stunned her, and then brought her out here to torture and murder her."

"That means the perp had a car…maybe a van…and maybe he had to carry Cindy to the trunk or the backseat, or front seat."

Bradford nodded. "Wherever she was abducted, maybe there are security cameras nearby. We might find something."

"What if she wasn't abducted, Detective? What if she knew and trusted her attacker? Maybe she was already in his or her car. That would eliminate having to carry an unconscious young woman to a car."

"Since the victim was one of your students, I know this is hard and personal for you. Is there anything more that you can tell me about her to give us a potential lead?"

"One of my students mentioned that she'd seen Cindy at the Salty Dog Friday night with her boyfriend. Name's Alex Davidson."

"That's a start. Next is the part of the job I hate the most, notifying her parents. Although we didn't find her phone, we'll pull her records to see who she texted or called before her death."

SIX

Elizabeth watched as one of the CSI techs poured dirt from the wooden bowl into a plastic bag. Then he placed the bowl and sprig in separate paper bags, marked as evidence. The coroner and his staff loaded Cindy's body onto the gurney, draping a white sheet over her.

Detective Bradford turned toward Elizabeth. "How do I tell her parents what we just saw when they ask how their daughter died?"

"You don't, at least not the details yet. I was on the other side once, too. Cindy's from Hattiesburg. When you speak to her parents, please do it in person. No mother ever expects to bury her child."

Bradford nodded. "I need to head out. Are you going back to the university?"

"For a few minutes. For this killer to write the word wrath on Cindy's forehead...for him to place a bowl on her body—the staging...it sends shivers through me."

"He's a sick one."

"He's beyond that. Scrawling the word wrath on her forehead—is some kind of perverted vendetta. If there is a connection to wrath in the seven deadly sins, this perp has a God complex, maybe a cult leader. Maybe he's an introvert. I don't know the significance of the bowl, the soil, and that small plant or twig. But if this slaughter is somehow connected to a pervert's interpretation of the seven deadly sins...God help us."

Bradford folded his arms. "What are you saying?"

"This could be the first of seven murders. Or maybe the other six haven't been found yet."

Bradford looked beyond the yellow crime scene tape. Three TV news trucks were parking. He said, "The sharks are circling. Everybody wants a sound-bite." He turned to four deputies. "Make sure our new arrivals keep back. There's one reporter from Channel Seven who doesn't seem to think the rules apply to her."

"Yes sir," one of the deputies said, the men fanning out and heading toward the yellow tape around the perimeter.

It took the reporters and camera operators less than a minute to begin recording as the coroner's staff loaded the body into the van. Half a dozen CSI techs still combed through the area near where the body had been found. Two other detectives huddled and compared notes. Within a few seconds, they ended their conversation and both men approached Detective Bradford and Elizabeth. One older detective watched the growing swarm of media and looked at Bradford. "Mike, you want to be the official spokesman today. I don't have the stomach for it anymore."

Bradford consented. "Sure. For the most part, they're harmless. I'll feed them some tidbits. Should tide them over 'til the next deadline."

The older detective nodded. "Tidbits are all we have right now." He glanced at the coroner's van. "What a waste of a beautiful kid. I think that hunter who found her knows more than he's telling us."

"Maybe," Bradford said, walking toward the news media.

Elizabeth followed him, anxious to get into her car and leave. She stood back as he ducked under the yellow tape and met the reporters, cameras rolling, microphones extended. After less than a minute, Elizabeth walked away from where Bradford answered questions. She lifted the tape and stood. Beyond her car she could see a cloud of gnats orbiting in a shard of sunlight through the pines. Elizabeth headed for her car.

"Excuse me," came a woman's voice from behind her.

Elizabeth turned and looked into the lens of a TV camera. The reporter, a tall brunette, smiled and stood next to her cameraman. She extended her microphone. "I'm Debra Petty with Channel Seven News. You're Dr. Elizabeth Monroe. You testified as an expert witness in the competency hearing for Justin Morrison. I remember reading your biography. Are you working with police on this homicide?"

"Did anyone tell you it was a homicide?"

"Let me rephrase my question…an apparent homicide. If you're not working with police, how did you get access to the crime scene?"

Elizabeth said nothing for a moment; she could see her reflection off the dark glass in the camera lens, the cameraman's beefy forearms perspiring. "The deceased was one of my students."

"I'm sorry, but can you tell us how she was killed?"

"Please, you should ask the detectives. Thank you." She turned to walk away.

The reporter followed. "I understand your reluctance to comment on the crime, but if she was one of your students, can you tell us the last time you saw her and what you think happened here today?"

Elizabeth turned to face the reporter. "A monster took the life of a young woman. He's sick—a deeply troubled person who has a God complex. But, because of his depraved way of thinking, he doesn't know how sick he really is. He preys on a petite, young woman in a sad effort to satiate his deflated ego, but his personal weakness is most likely because he's as impotent physically as he is mentally. That's all I can tell you."

The reporter's eyes widened. "Do you think she knew her attacker?"

"That's a question for the police. Please, excuse me." She turned to walk away.

The reporter asked, "Dr. Monroe, a few years ago your daughter was found murdered in a forest. The killer was never caught. Could it possibly be the same person? Is that why you're out here today?"

Elizabeth stopped walking, started to turn around but paused, ignoring the reporter's barrage of questions. She got into her hot car and started the ignition, the air conditioner blowing warm air into her face. She looked through the passenger-side window. Two more reporters and cameramen were approaching, walking fast. One reporter held his hand up to get her attention. Elizabeth put on her dark glasses and drove, disregarding his motion for her to roll the window down. She looked up in the rearview mirror as the pack of reporters watched her leave, one jotting down her license plate number.

SEVEN

Elizabeth approached her dark house, headlights sweeping over the tree line. An opossum darted across the country road. She tried to remember if she'd left the front porch light on as she usually did.

Not tonight.

That's odd, she thought. *Maybe it's burned out.* Occasionally she worked late at the university, usually in the library doing research. She often kept the front porch light on, in addition to a light in her kitchen.

All the way home she could think of nothing but Cindy. The horror Cindy experienced the last minutes of her short life—the point when she knew no one was coming to her rescue, the last moment in the clutches of a psychopath. *Did she fight with her final breath? Did she leave fingernail cuts across a monster's face? Wrath? Whose wrath, yours you sick asshole, or God's?*

Her phone buzzed. She looked at the caller ID. Detective Mike Bradford. She answered. "Hello, Detective."

"When I gave you my card, I said Mike works just fine"

She smiled. "Hello, Mike. Anything new with Cindy's murder?"

"We've given the physical evidence to the lab. Skin cells from under Cindy's fingernails on her right hand. The wooden bowl, that dirt and twig, cigarette butt, as well as a dozen other things."

"Thank you for allowing me on the crime scene. I know you didn't have to do it."

"You have the credentials, hell you have the chops, too. I'm hoping you can help profile this freak and get us closer to finding him."

"I'll do all I can."

He cleared his throat. "Did you catch the evening news?"

"No. I had to go back to the university to pick up some things. Then I bought groceries."

"That interview you did with the reporter, Debra Petty—"

"Yes, what about it?"

"I watched it. Elizabeth you're right to call the guy a monster...but it's as if you tried to drive a personal stake through his dark heart. It was like you were slaying vampires. Please be honest with me when I ask you this question. Okay?"

"I can't be dishonest with you."

"Did you say those things to try to lure this creep...to draw him out? Because it sounds like you want to set a trap for him, and you're using yourself as bait. And that's extremely dangerous. Is it also because of what happened to your daughter?"

Elizabeth stopped at the end of her long driveway. The old home she had bought and remodeled sat in the center of four acres. She angled her car, the headlights hitting her mailbox. "That's two questions. I answered what the reporter had asked in a way that wouldn't compromise your investigation, no details about what you've found. However, I wanted the viewers to know what and who this monster is and the danger he represents, especially to young women. The more observant they are, the safer they'll be. I'm not trying to be some kind of vigilante."

Bradford was quiet for few seconds. "All I know is we're dealing with a psychopath that's off the charts. In all my years as a cop, I've never seen a murder like that. The horrible display, the word wrath, a bowl with its odd ingredients, and the cause of death...all spell a special degree of madness."

"I assure you I'm not trying to lure a violent, psychotic person to come find me. But, you're right, if this guy is responsible for my daughter, Molly's, death...or if he knows something about it, I'd very much like to hear it."

"Me, too. I'll do everything in my power to catch him."

"I just got home. I'm exhausted. Can we talk tomorrow?"

"Yes."

"Goodnight, Mike." She disconnected and got out of her car, stepping to the mailbox and opening it. There was a slight floral scent. She glanced at the bills, started to close the lid and stopped. Something else was inside. She reached in and lifted out a small cluster of white and pink honeysuckle flowers, no larger than a golf ball. She studied them under the headlights. Her heart began to race, her mind picturing the crown of honeysuckle flowers the killer had placed on Cindy's head.

EIGHT

Elizabeth thought about the reporter jotting down her license plate number. She stood next to her mailbox, the sound of crickets in the bushes, dew already forming on the mailbox. She got in her car and drove up her driveway, her palms moist. She pulled onto the driveway's half-circle, closest to the brick steps leading to her large front porch. Her home was wood and brick, a 1940's exterior with a remodeled interior. She turned off the motor, hands still on the wheel, honeysuckles on the seat beside her.

She sat there, the motor ticking, her heart rate slowing.

Elizabeth locked her car and walked up the brick footpath to her porch, baskets of leafy ferns hanging from the eaves, a wind chime tinkling in the night air. She unlocked the front door and entered her home, quickly shutting and locking the door. She moved through her home, turning on lights in each room.

She dropped the mail on her kitchen table, set the honeysuckles next to the mail, opened a bottle of cabernet and poured a glass. She stepped around to her kitchen counter and sat on one of the barstools, the stress of the day tightening muscles in her back between the shoulder blades.

She reached for the glass of wine, looking at her nails, trying to remember the last time she had a manicure. *It's been too long.* She stared at the clump of honeysuckles. *Could they be connected to the honeysuckle vine left on Cindy's head? Was it some strange coincidence? There is no irony, only deliberate action. Why?*

She sipped her wine, thoughts returning to Cindy. She played back the crime scene in her mind, the hunter who found the body, his hand movement while being questioned by Detective Bradford. She thought about the burn marks left by a stun gun, the wooden bowl, the dirt, and the word *wrath* on Cindy's forehead. *God help Cindy's parents.*

She sipped the wine and closed her eyes for a moment. Thunder rumbled in the distance, followed by a flicker of lightning far beyond the glass slider doors leading out to her backyard. Her yard bordered a state preserve. She loved the procession of wildlife that paraded through her lawn, the deer, wild turkeys, a family of raccoons that waddled by at dusk looking for the corn cobs she'd leave for them, the songbirds that flocked to the feeder on her wooden deck, the hummingbirds that fed from the flowers Elizabeth grew.

She could hear a storm growing closer, limbs on the large sycamore in her back yard swaying in the light cast from the floodlight. She glanced at the kitchen clock, picked up the TV remote and found the ten o'clock news. A news anchorman and woman welcomed the audience, promising breaking news. "First up tonight," said the anchorwoman, reading the teleprompter, "Police continue their investigation into the brutal killing of a college coed. The body of Cindy Carter was discovered in a remote section of the De Soto National Forest. Debra Petty has the latest."

The image cut to shots of the coroner's staff loading Cindy's body into a dark blue van, the reporter's voice under the video. "Police aren't saying if they have a suspect in the case. The body of nineteen-year-old Cindy Carter was found today by a man scouting the De Soto National Forest for areas to hunt. Police say he was riding an ATV four-wheeler when he drove up near the body. Although they aren't releasing details of exactly how the young woman was killed, they say this was a brutal murder."

The video cut to Detective Mike Bradford. "This will go down as one of the most heinous and senseless killings most of us in the department have ever seen. The person who committed this crime must be taken off the street and soon."

The reporter continued, "One of the paramedics said when he arrived he saw a word scrawled on the girl's forehead. He said it spelled wrath. Do you have details about this?"

Bradford shook his head, "I can't comment on the specifics of the evidence."

"Was there a wooden bowl left on the body?"

"Again, I will not comment on what we found or didn't find."

"Do you think this is the work of a serial killer?"

"We don't know that yet. Thank you, but I need to get back to the investigation."

The video cut to images beyond the crime scene tape, CSI techs bagging evidence, detectives comparing notes, blue and white lights flashing around the perimeter, death in the forest silencing the birdsong into an eerie quiet.

The reporter said, "Dr. Elizabeth Monroe, an expert witness in forensic cases and a professor at Southern Miss, was on the scene, too. Police aren't saying if she's a consultant. But she did have this to say about the person who murdered the girl." The image cut to Elizabeth and she said, "A monster took the life of a young woman. He's sick—a deeply troubled person who has a God complex. But, because of his depraved way of thinking, he doesn't know how sick he really is. He preys on a petite, young woman in a sad effort to satiate his deflated ego, but his personal weakness is most likely because he's as impotent physically as he is mentally." The video stayed on Elizabeth as she walked to her car.

The reporter appeared on camera holding a microphone. "Dr. Monroe did tell us that the victim was a student in her criminal psychology class. It was four years ago when Elizabeth Monroe's own daughter was murdered, her body dumped in a remote forest as well. Could the similarities in the two crimes be one reason Dr. Monroe was out here today? Police aren't saying, and Elizabeth Monroe had no comment. In the meantime, police are asking anyone who may have any information about this homicide to give them a call. Reporting from the De Soto National Forest, Debra Petty, Channel Seven News."

Elizabeth muted the sound, finished the wine, and sat on her couch, thoughts racing. Lightning cracked in the trees less than a hundred yards from her back deck. Rain pelted the roof, showering the wooden deck. In the floodlight, she watched the rain bounce off the wide green leaves of two banana trees she'd planted last spring.

Elizabeth leaned back on the couch, exhaustion building behind her eyes. She picked up a Southern Living Magazine, leafed though a few pages and set it aside, too tired to read. She felt sleep coming on the borders of her conscious mind, her subconscious sending in shadows of deceptions, the prelude to dreams, and far too often—nightmares.

There was a sound on the front porch.

She opened her eyes, listening.

And she didn't move.

NINE

At that moment, Elizabeth wished she were sitting in the dark. She sat on her couch, trying to hear beyond the drone of the rain. She was perfectly still. The noise sounded as if something fell onto the porch. Something knocked down. *Maybe the wind blew over a potted plant. Maybe I'm so tired I imagined it.* She closed her eyes, drained.

The sound returned.

Different this time.

A scratching at the door.

Elizabeth stood. On rare occasions she wished that she owned a gun. Tonight was one of those times. She tiptoed into the kitchen, removing a steak knife from a drawer. Then she walked quietly down the wooden foyer toward her front door. She knew where the old wooden floor would creak under her weight. She tried to avoid the spots, clutching the knife handle in her right hand, her breathing slow and steady.

One step caused a groan in the wood. She paused, listening. The wind jostled baskets of ferns hanging from the porch eave, creating moving shadows across the curtains.

She stepped quietly and stood next to a window overlooking the front porch. In the yellow light, she could see the rain falling beyond the terrace.

And she could see tracks.

Not human. Animal. Wet paw prints. *Maybe the raccoon had come out of the rain.* Elizabeth cracked open the door a few inches, the cool of the night air blowing against her face. She looked around the porch. A plastic pot filled with red and white petunias was lying on its side, knocked from a wrought iron stand, the dirt scattered across the wooden porch.

Something moved in the subdued light.

Elizabeth gripped the knife.

A large gray tabby cat leapt down from the railing, landing on the porch and letting out a soft mewing sound. Elizabeth lowered the knife. She smiled. "Where'd you come from in the night?"

The cat looked up at her, its yellow-green eyes wide, intelligent, and somehow welcome on a chilly rainy night. Elizabeth said, "You don't seem so intimidating after all." She looked up, scanning the long front yard. She could barely see the lights from her closest neighbor's home, more than a hundred yards down the road. "Are you lost or just making the rounds tonight?"

The cat tilted its head and mewed.

Elizabeth opened the door wider, stepping on the porch, the washed scent of a fresh rain in the night air. She looked at the cat, its light gray fur marked with dark rings, large eyes passive. A breeze came across yard and tickled the wind chimes. Elizabeth looked up and the cat darted around her, entering the house.

"Whoa!" she said, turning to chase the cat. Elizabeth shut the front door and followed the cat into the kitchen area. It jumped up on one of the leather barstools and waited. Elizabeth paused, not able to hold back a smile. "So, you want a drink?"

The cat slowly turned its wide head, surveying the lay of the land.

Elizabeth stepped closer. "Well, you're not wearing a collar, so you don't have an ID on you. I can tell you're not a kid. Been around the block, eh? You look like a survivor. You have to belong to somebody. Or maybe it's the other way around, somebody belongs to you. Let me dry you off."

Elizabeth set the knife down on the kitchen counter, the cat watching her, rubbing its chin on the edge of the counter. She pulled a cloth towel from a cabinet, stepped up to the cat and began drying its fur. The cat purred. She smiled, "You just make yourself right at home, don't you? You look well fed. Either you're a master moocher or you just got caught in the rain doing your thing at night. Regardless, you can't stay here."

She looked closer. "Ah, you're a male cat. The last time I had a cat was when my daughter Molly got one as a little girl. He was black and white.

She named him Oreo. Molly said he reminded her of the cookie. Oreo slept on her bed until she went off to college." Elizabeth bit her bottom lip, her daughter's death still just beneath the surface of her emotions.

The cat sat back on its haunches, tail slightly moving. Elizabeth stepped to the refrigerator and opened it. "I don't have any milk, although you look like you'd prefer a beer." She smiled. "Don't have that either. But I do have some turkey rolls. I'll fix you a plate…maybe it'll be a carry out, no offense, but my life is complicated enough. When the rain stops, my hospitality ends. It's hit the road, Jack." She smiled. "I'll call you Jack for the time being. Okay with you?" The cat blinked. Elizabeth said, "I could call you Bob as in bobcat. I had an old boyfriend named Bob. But he acted more like a tomcat. Chased all my girlfriends, caught most of them. Listen to me—I'm rambling on and on, talking to some cat I've never seen before…and inside my house. This is a little crazy, don't you think?"

The cat stared at her, purring. "Don't look at me like that, Jack, with those big eyes of yours." She smiled, opening a package of turkey meat, tearing and placing pieces on a paper plate. When she turned, the cat jumped up on the counter. "What a minute, Jack. We don't walk or sit were we eat. So you can just hop right back down."

The cat ignored her, yawning and stretching. She walked around the counter and set the plate on the floor. Then she picked the cat up and set him near the food. "Jack, maybe I shouldn't be feeding you. You're heavy. What size are you, a ten? Maybe you should be thinking about the Mediterranean diet, lots of lean fish in that plan."

She watched the cat eat. Elizabeth walked over to a bookcase, picked up a picture of Molly and her cat. She looked at it, Molly age six wearing a princess dress, her unflappable cat sitting next to her in bed, a fairy costume on its hips. Elizabeth set the framed picture down, her eyes moist, and turned back toward the cat. He finished eating and strolled into the living room like it was part of his routine. The cat jumped up on the couch, stretched out and licked its front paw.

Elizabeth sat down on the couch and picked up her magazine. She turned a few pages and cut her eyes over to the cat. He was staring at her. She sighed, scooting along the couch, reaching out to stroke the cat's fur. She watched the rain falling through the floodlight near her back deck. She looked at the cat. "Soon as the rain stops you gotta go, Jack. No offense, I'm just not good company. But you're a cat, so does that really matter? Of course it does, that's why you're purring right now. You like affection, but I'm running low in that category."

The cat lowered his head to her lap, his eyelids half closing. Elizabeth smiled. "You're certainly the big charmer. Jack, you seem to be a good listener. I am going to a funeral soon. A young woman, she was really just a kid, was murdered. On TV tonight, I called him a monster. He's out there in the dark. Somewhere in the night, this freak roams. I know he'll kill again. I'm going to do my best to stop him." She leaned closer. "On your rounds earlier, did you see anyone at my mailbox? There was more than mail in there." She scratched the cat behind his ears. "I feel that someone is playing cat and mouse with me. But there's no mouse, only a fiend in the dark."

Elizabeth let out a long breath, her hand on the cat's back. "Maybe I can be more like you and take a cat nap. Real sleep is elusive these days. It's usually interrupted by a word from the sponsor of terror…some dark entity that exists in the borderland of the subconscious." Her voice dropped to a whisper. "And I don't have a night light for those times."

Lightning cracked near her property, and the rain fell harder. Elizabeth sighed. "Doesn't look like the storm is going to break soon. Okay…you can stay the night, Jack."

She leaned over and turned out the lamp next to the sofa. Her eyes grew heavy. She pulled a small blanket from the side of the couch, wrapping it around them. They sat there together in the dark, Elizabeth and Jack the cat. Watching the rain falling, waiting for morning and the promise of light and a new day.

Their eyes soon closed, Jack's purring harmonizing with the sound of pouring rain.

TEN

The next morning, Elizabeth waited until the last minute before dealing with the cat. She showered, put her makeup on, light colored lipstick, dressed for work, and then picked the cat off the sofa. She carried him in one arm, scratching his neck. She stepped out onto the front porch and set the cat down. "I can tell you don't do mornings well, Jack. Maybe that's why you walked into my life in the middle of the night. But it's time for you to go back to your real home. I'm sure somebody's missing you. Go on, okay? Someone loves and needs you. Bye, Jack."

The cat simply sat there, looking at her. She turned and picked up the spilled petunias, setting the pot back on the wrought iron bench. She took a broom from the corner and swept up the dirt. When she finished, the cat hadn't moved. Elizabeth shook her head, smiling. "Don't make me take this broom to you. I really don't want to sweep you out of here."

The cat blinked, turned and walked off the porch, down three steps into the yard, disappearing behind the house. Elizabeth blew out a long breath. She whispered. "I'll miss you, Jack." She turned, locked the door, and walked to her car. She put on sunglasses and drove down her driveway. When Elizabeth glanced up in the rearview mirror, Jack was back. Sitting on the top step, staring at her car with the hopeful eyes of an old friend content to watch and wait for her return.

Elizabeth sighed, looking away from the mirror. "You don't know jack, Jack. Go back to where you belong...but I'd be lying if I said I wouldn't miss you." She gripped the wheel with both hands and drove down the rural road, staring straight ahead.

— —

Detective Mike Bradford was never a fan of fraternities. And, today, he felt a slight taste of distrust as he walked under a live oak and stepped up on the front porch of the fraternity house. The setting sun, sidling through the oak tree, cast deep purple shadows across the antebellum house. *Frat boys*, he thought. *Squeeze in a little education between the parties, coeds and beer.*

He walked across the wide porch, philodendrons growing on both sides, the scent of camellias in the breeze, bass music coming from the Alpha Phi Kappa house. He knocked on the door and stepped back. Nothing. No indication of movement inside. He knocked again, louder.

Thirty seconds later the door slowly opened. A sleepy-eyed student stood in boxer shorts and a tank top, his arms chiseled in muscle, dark scruff dotted his face, eyes red. He said, "Dude, why the poundin' at the door. We're not like deaf. If you're selling something, this isn't the place." He started to close the door.

Bradford opened his sports coat, revealing the badge on his belt. "I'm not selling anything. I'm Detective Bradford, homicide. Can I come in?"

The student made a dry swallow, a small red patch suddenly on his chest. "Um...sure, I guess." He opened the door wider, and Bradford entered the foyer. The floor was polished hardwood. The foyer led off to half a dozen rooms. Stairs went up to the second floor.

Bradford could hear music coming from upstairs, the smell of burnt toast and beer in the foyer. He said, "I need to speak with Alex Davidson."

"I'm not sure if he's here."

"He's here. A car registered to him is in your lot. Go get him."

"Sure dude. I'll check his room. No need for hostility." The student took two steps at a time running up the stairs. Bradford looked around, poking his head into the great room, a beer keg on an oak mantle above a century-old fireplace with a dark, yawning mouth.

Alex Davidson came down the steps alone, the other student nowhere to be seen. Bradford stood in the center of the foyer, watching as Davidson walked without touching the banister but his body slowed by trepidation. He wore jeans and a dark blue hoodie with the words *Southern Miss Golden Eagles* across the chest. Bradford kept his arms loose at his side, looking for any quick move. "Are you Alex Davidson?"

"Yeah, what's this all about?"

"I'm Detective Bradford with the Forrest County Sheriff's Department. I'd like to ask you a few questions."

"Is this about Cindy?"

"Let's step out on the front porch to talk."

ELEVEN

Elizabeth sat behind her desk in her small office, grading papers. Her phone buzzed. She answered and a receptionist said, "Professor Monroe, this is Kristin. A news crew from Channel Four is here in the lobby. The reporter asked if he could see you."

"They didn't call for an appointment. I have a class to teach in twenty minutes. I really don't have time to speak with him."

The receptionist lowered her voice to a whisper. "That's what I told them when I asked if they'd made an appointment. I know how busy you are. The reporter, it's Bill Keelson, the guy who does all that investigative stuff; anyway he's a smooth talker. They're still here. What do you want me to tell them?"

"There's no reason you need to play defense for me. You can put him on the phone."

"Are you sure?"

"Yes, Kristin. Thanks."

A moment later, the deep voice of Bill Keelson said, "Hi Professor Monroe—I appreciate you speaking with us. I missed doing an interview with you at the crime scene. I know the victim was one of your students. My deepest condolences."

"Thank you, Mr. Keelson. How can I help you?"

"If you have a few minutes, we'd love to do a quick, on-camera interview with you. Not only due to the fact that the victim was one of your students, but you teach criminal psychology, and we've watched you testify before as an expert witness in trials. I won't take much of your time. The main questions I'd like to ask are what's your professional assessment of the crime? Whether you've profiled the killer and whether the people in this part of Mississippi should be even more vigilant and cautious as they go about their daily lives?"

"Mr. Keelson, I have a class to teach in a few minutes. I can't address any of those questions because I don't have the answers. I'd suggest that you call Detective Mike Bradford. He's the lead investigator on the case. Thank you for stopping by the university. I'm sorry I can't be of more help to you."

"Doctor Monroe, I'm on deadline. Detective Bradford can't—"

Elizabeth disconnected and looked at the framed picture of Molly on her desk. When it was taken, Molly was a senior in college, studying botany and entomology. *'Bugs rock,'* Elizabeth remembered Molly saying when she was releasing endangered butterflies. In the picture, Molly is grinning and holding a Giant Swallowtail butterfly in the palm of her hand.

Elizabeth picked up her laptop and class notes and stood at her desk. Her door opened. No knock. James Harris, Ph.D., the Chair of the department walked in and closed her door. He was in his early sixties, thinning white hair, trimmed snowy beard, and a sports coat. No tie. He cleared his throat. "Elizabeth, I need a word with you."

"Good morning, Dean Harris. What is it?"

"The university is getting calls from regional news media and some of the cable networks. They all want to speak to you about this horrible death."

"There's nothing I can say. I just spoke to a reporter with Channel Four and directed him to talk with the police investigators working the case."

"Good. This is a tragedy, and the fact that it happened to one of the university's students, hits particularly hard. I've spoken with Mr. and Mrs. Carter, offering them whatever they may need in this time of sorrow." He let out a deep breath. "Maybe it'll be a good idea if you keep a low profile, let the police do what they do well, and you can concentrate on the academics of forensic psychology within the boundaries of the classroom and the campus." He paused, glanced out the window behind her, and then looked at Elizabeth. "When they interviewed you on CNN and Fox news about the psychology of Neo-Nazis and white supremacists after the protest rally at the Confederate Memorial downtown, the university received bombing and death threats. I had mentioned this to you when we received them because they were all directed toward you. All I'm asking is that you refrain from media interviews."

Elizabeth set her laptop down. "I knew Cindy Carter well. She sat in the front row in my class, less than ten feet from my desk. She was a special, bright, hardworking achiever. She came to my office sometimes just to talk. She maintained a perfect GPA. So it was never about grades. It was about what made her curious. About what made others tick. She was intensely interested in people—why they do what they do. And she cared about them. If I might be able to assist in the investigation, and have it not interfere with my job here, I don't see that as a problem."

Elizabeth glanced out her window to the parking lot below her second story office. The Channel Four news truck was still there. The reporter and cameraman were setting up a live shot in front of the university campus.

Dean Harris stroked whiskers on his chin. "The department always encourages its professors to do outside work, if possible. It promotes the interest of both the administration and the faculty by enriching the class-room experience for students by giving the professors current and real world experience." He looked at the photo of Molly and the butterfly on her desk. "Elizabeth, the passion you have to find justice in the death of your daughter is admirable. However, please don't let it cloud your sense of judgment. The university isn't interested in publicity that draws attention to what one newspaper suggested, that you're a vigilante motivated by revenge. Those aren't my words."

"They might as well have been or you wouldn't bring it up. That's hurtful, Jim. I will continue to search for the man who killed Molly. It's no different from how the parents of Cindy Carter feel. In the meantime, I'm a damn good teacher, and you know it. My class surveys are some of the highest in the university. Unless you have something else, you're in my way. I have a class to teach."

He stepped aside and Elizabeth walked out the door. Her phone buzzed with an incoming text. She read it as she walked down the hall. It was from Detective Mike Bradford. He wrote: *Elizabeth, call me when you can. Reference to seven deadly sins and a profile. Mike.*

TWELVE

Detective Mike Bradford liked the silence before the interview. It gave the person more to think about. He stood on the wide front porch of the Alpha Phi Kappa house, finished his text, slipping his phone in his pocket. Alex Davidson stood on the other side of the porch, right hand on a banister, shoulders slouched, looking at the street where two frat members rode long-boards. He turned as Detective Bradford stepped closer. "How would you describe your relationship with Cindy Carter?"

"She was my girlfriend. Hey, am I like a suspect? Because if I am, I wanna call my dad. Do I need an attorney?"

"That's up to you. Either way, I will ask you questions, here or downtown."

Davidson said nothing, glancing at a woman walking her dog up the street.

Bradford said, "Before coming over here, I did a brief background check on you."

"Why? I haven't done anything."

"No, but you were Cindy Carter's boyfriend, and she's dead."

"Does that make me a suspect?"

"It makes you a person of interest. And you do have an interesting background. Raised as the only son of a minister. Seems your family traveled when you were a kid…doing missionary work. I guess it's tough to make friends when you move a lot."

Davidson said nothing, his jaw tight, hand gripping the porch banister.

Bradford continued. "Maybe that's why you got into a fraternity. Make a lot of friends?"

"I had lots of friends as a kid. My dad stopped overseas mission work when I was fourteen. He got his own church. And he built up a descent congregation from scratch."

"Didn't you want to follow in his footsteps?"

"No."

"Why's that?"

"He's old school. Like he's living in the fifties. My sisters and I weren't raised Amish, but it's like the same thing. Pretty strict."

"Do you know the Bible well?"

"Yeah, some parts." Davidson shook his head, crossing his arms.

"When was the last time you saw Cindy?"

"Saturday night. She was here at the house. There was a big party goin' on. She wanted to leave after an hour or so."

"Did she leave in her own car?"

"No. I'd picked her up earlier."

"How'd she leave?"

"I don't know. I think somebody drove her."

Bradford stepped a little closer. "What do you mean...you *think* somebody drove her? Don't you know? Wasn't she your girlfriend?"

"We'd had a big fight. She walked out. I was like drunk, so things aren't real clear. It was raining hard when she left the house. I came out on the porch to stop her, but she just ran off, like she walked into a waterfall. I believe she got into somebody's car."

"Describe the car."

"Man, I can't remember."

"Did you try to call her?"

"Yeah, but it was late at night. Tried texting her, too. But she wouldn't answer." He shoved his hands in his jeans pockets, glanced around the front yard. "Detective, I feel real bad about what happened. I keep thinkin' it's my fault. If I hadn't been drunk, I could have driven Cindy back to her apartment. I gotta live with this the rest of my life. I don't know if I can stand to go to her funeral."

Bradford watched him closely. Davidson looked away, the sound of a car door shutting. "Did Cindy have any enemies?"

"No. Cindy got along well with everybody."

"Maybe it was a simple case of an argument that escalated to a bad accident. Stuff happens, unfortunately, right? Did your fight with Cindy just simply blow up? You had too much to drink…one thing led to another, and she's dead. Why take her body into the national forest? What's the stuff with the bowl and the crown?"

Davidson eyebrows rose. "I don't know what you're talking about. Was that stuff there when you found Cindy?"

"I've spoken with Cindy's parents. They tell me she was deeply religious, not the type of girl to leave the roots she held sacred."

"We went to church one Sunday, when we first started dating."

"Any of your frat brothers into the dark stuff?"

Davidson raised his shoulders. "What do you mean?"

"You know…guys that played Dungeons and Dragons as kids and sort of followed that theme…got darker. Maybe followed it all the way into Satanism."

"None of the guys here are into that stuff. We had a pledge, a guy who always dressed in black—a real smart dude, like he'd create the next billion-dollar social media company or whatever. We let him hang around, thought he'd do some of our math homework." Davidson made an awkward grin. "He came to a few parties…didn't hang out with anyone. That was two semesters ago. I still see him on campus sometimes."

"Did he meet Cindy?"

"Yeah. She didn't say anything, but I could tell the dude creeped her out."

Bradford jotted in his notebook. "What's this guy's name?"

"Larry Tucker."

"How'd you meet Cindy?" The detective watched Davidson's eyes as he followed someone coming up the sidewalk.

"One of the guys here at the house dated her for a while. They sort of drifted apart, and I just asked Cindy if she wanted to go out with me."

"What's the brother's name?"

"Um…Gerald Simpson." He paused and looked at his hands, nails chewed short. "I can't believe she's…she's gone. It's like a horrible nightmare."

"In case I need to reach you, what's your number?"

Davidson gave it to him just as another student walked up the steps to the porch. Bradford watched Davidson lick his dry lips, his eyes darting. The student looked like an athlete, tall, wide shoulders, neatly trimmed hair. He nodded and started to walk around the detective and Davidson.

Bradford looked at him. Same height. Eye-to-eye. He stuck out his hand. "I'm Detective Bradford."

"I'm Gerald Simpson." He smiled and tried to walk around them.

"I understand that you used to date Cindy Carter."

Simpson glanced at Davidson, tried hard to bury anger that surfaced in his eyes for a millisecond, then looked back at the detective. "I'm glad to answer your questions but you mind if I go inside and pee. I had three cups of coffee."

Bradford glanced around the property, the stately oaks, the smell of beer on the damp welcome mat at the front door. "Hey, that's a big ol' house. You could get lost in there, and I'd have to come back with a search warrant. I'd have to bring my bulldog of a partner, he has no sense of humor, and we'd take you downtown to chat. So why don't you step off this porch and pick any of those oaks to take a piss under it. You won't be the first or last frat boy to do it. When you're all done, we'll talk."

Simpson swallowed his anger, walked off the porch and began urinating at the base of a tree.

Alex Davidson turned, looked the other way and lit a cigarette.

THIRTEEN

Detective Bradford's phone buzzed. He looked at the caller ID. It was coming from his partner, Detective Ed Milton. He asked, "Mike, you still questioning people in the vic's inner circle?"

"Yeah, I finished with the boyfriend, and I'm about to start with another guy that dated her."

"You might want to make it brief."

"Why? We get a DNA hit?"

"No, but the hunter who found the body, Paul Heller, he's dead. Looks like suicide. I'm heading that way. He was found in his car, parked in a cemetery. Single pop to his temple. His gun. First responders said it was still in his hand when they found the body."

Bradford mumbled, "She was right."

"What? Who was right?"

"Elizabeth Monroe...she said Heller was lying to me when I questioned him."

"It's not rocket science."

Bradford watched Gerald Simpson walk back up the steps. Alex Davidson stood off to the side, relieved the questioning had moved to his friend.

Bradford lowered his voice. "My gut's telling me that Heller wasn't the perp. He may have lied, during part of the questioning, but that doesn't mean he killed her."

"Then why'd he shoot himself? A heavy guilt trip?"

"Maybe he didn't kill himself. Maybe Cindy's killer popped Heller."

"Heller had reason to do it. He served twelve on a twenty for rape. He'd twice violated his probation. His next infraction would have sent back to Parchman Farm."

"Call you back in a minute." He disconnected and stepped up to Simpson. "So, you dated Cindy. Why didn't it work out?"

Simpson grinned. "Who said it didn't work out? Doesn't make any difference now. That was like a lifetime ago. Freshman year, I think."

Bradford smiled. "Why'd you two stop dating?"

Simpson ran his tongue on the inside of his cheek. "We never got the girlfriend and boyfriend kinda thing goin'. We like hung out a few times. Cindy was cool, but we just didn't have much in common." He made an awkward smile at Davidson. "And then along came my best bro, Alex. And they clicked. Least for a while."

"Where were you Saturday evening?"

"Here at the house. You can ask him."

Alex crossed his arms. "He was here."

"Did you leave anytime?"

Simpson shook his head. "Only to go to work."

"Where do you work?"

"All over the county. I drive for the three ride-sharing companies. Good pay. Doesn't cut into my studies or football, and I work when I want to." He nodded and put his hand on the doorknob. "Unless you have another question, I need to hit the books."

"When is the last time you saw Larry Tucker?"

Simpson grinned, glanced at Davidson and looked directly at the detective. "He doesn't hang around anymore. Somebody said he got rolled coming outta Walmart one night waiting for a ride-share. I'd never pick him up. He like hardly ever showers. He's probably locked in a dark room of his house playing the most twisted video games on the planet."

"Where does he live?"

"I heard he lives on the west side of town." He grinned. "Can I go?"

"Here's my card. Call me if you can think of anything that might aid in finding out who killed Cindy Carter."

"No problem, Detective." Gerald Simpson flashed a wide grin and entered the Kappa house; the setting sun reflecting off the dark glass window resembled a smoldering torch in the back of a cave.

When Bradford got in his car, he called his partner, Ed Milton, and said, "I just finished questioning both students. The first was Alex Davidson—the kid we ran the background check on—the vic's boyfriend."

Milton spoke from his unmarked police car. "Does he come across as the son of a preacher man?"

"He's nervous. Says the last time he saw Cindy, he was drunk at a Kappa frat house party. She got fed up and caught a ride home. Doesn't know with who, but I'm thinking, whoever it was…is our perp, the last guy to see her alive."

"Anybody else see her leave?"

"Not that I can find. I questioned another kid—one of their football players. Name's Gerald Simpson."

"Name rings a bell. It was at least three years ago, before you started here. He was the jock facing rape charges. The vic came forth a couple months after it happened. That's never a good move. No evidence. No witnesses. Nothing. He said the sex was consensual. The girl said it wasn't. His family hired some big time lawyers out of Jackson. It quickly became a he-said-she-said battle. Charges were dropped. The girl transferred to another school, and Simpson led the team in rushing that year."

"Maybe the expensive lawyers set the family back because Simpson's working part-time as a ride-share driver."

"Or maybe his daddy, a guy who made some of his money in the lumber business, got tired of bailing junior out of shit holes. You comin' to take a look at Paul Heller's body? Maybe you're right. Maybe he didn't kill himself. If so, we got a helluva serial killer workin' overtime in southern Mississippi."

FOURTEEN

When Elizabeth's class ended, she dismissed the students, and turned to erase the white board. One student stayed. Julie Lassiter, shoulder-length brown hair and large hazel eyes, said, "Professor Monroe... can I talk with you?"

Elizabeth turned to face the girl. "Of course." She set the eraser down. "What would you like to talk about?"

"One of the reasons I love your class so much is how you make the human psyche more understandable. I know that's sort of a broad statement considering our minds are diverse and complex, but your class helps me put things in better prospective."

Elizabeth smiled. "Good. I'm glad to hear that." She said no more, sensing that the girl wasn't done.

"When I tell my friends I'm a psyche major, the first thing they ask me is if I want to analyze them. When I tell them my real interest is criminal psychology, they sort of don't know what to say. Does that ever happen to you?"

"All the time. It's a natural reaction."

"Cindy and I used to talk about that a lot. She said the guys she dated used to make a big deal out of it. One guy, a jock at the Kappa house, told her she could never have a normal relationship with a man because she would always put people in some clichéd box, like he might be a narcissist or a dependent personality, or whatever."

"It sort of goes with the territory. The more you understand the complexity of people and personalities, the less illusions you'll have. It's

46

sometimes a trade-out for innocence and naiveté, but I believe you receive far more than you lose when you learn to recognize deception. That doesn't mean you should always have your guard up, on the contrary, it should open more doors, let the fun in and help you establish boundaries with people who'd manipulate or take advantage of a person or situation."

Julie smiled, adjusting the backpack on her shoulders. "Thank you."

"You're welcome. Is that all? I have a feeling there's something else. Do you think this jock you mentioned may have had something to do with Cindy's death?"

"I don't know, but Cindy was like really scared of this guy. She said he changed after they dated a few times."

"Changed, in what way?"

"He got like rough. When she refused to have sex with him, she said he punched his fist into the wall, knocking a hole in it. I don't like saying something that might be taken negative about her, but Cindy was someone who always wanted to have a boyfriend, always wanted to have someone love her. There's nothing wrong with wanting to be loved, but when you're always looking for it, seems harder to find."

Elizabeth smiled. "You are a wise young woman, Julie. This student you mention, the jock…do you know his name?"

"Yes. It's Gerald Simpson."

Elizabeth said nothing for a few seconds. "I know who you're talking about now. Thank you for telling me this."

The girl turned to leave and stopped. She looked back, her thoughts deep. "Cindy's funeral is tomorrow. I don't think I can go. I want to remember her when she was alive. I want to remember her smile and how she laughed at my dumb jokes." Her eyes welled. "I hope that doesn't make me seem selfish by not going to the funeral. I know Cindy's parents. What if they're hurt because I didn't go?"

"One thing about psychology I want you to remember."

"What?" She pulled a strand of hair behind her ear.

"The psychology of self-awareness, overall, is a good thing. It increases your perception in dealing with others, power of observation, and it can give you a better insight into situations. The general goal, of course, is to help you make better decisions. Sometimes people, more often women like us, have a tendency to overanalyze some things. It's as if our emotions are black and white piano keys, but rather than play a soothing melody, we strive for a concerto when it's really a solo we should be playing."

Julie smiled and nodded. Elizabeth handed her a tissue and said, "When all the wrong notes are playing in our head, not only does it affect our senses, such as listening, but our vision is more narrow. I don't mean that literally. What I mean is your best vision, your best insight, is when you look into your heart. That's the only place to see who you are and to find your compass—your personal direction."

"Thank you…I won't attend the funeral, but I will visit Cindy's grave. I should be leaving now. I have to go to my shift at the restaurant. Three days a week, tips are good. I really need the money now because my car's in the shop. It has to have a new transmission."

"Sorry to hear that. Can I give you a lift to work?"

"I can take a ride share. It's not much, and I can do some homework in the back seat."

FIFTEEN

Elizabeth thought about Detective Bradford's text as she left the classroom. She locked her office door and walked down the long concrete steps leading to the parking lot. She headed to her car just as another car entered the lot, the driver parking next to Elizabeth.

The driver lowered his window, flecked sunlight breaking through the branches of maple trees. Elizabeth could see it was Detective Bradford. He said, "I figured you might be too busy to answer a text. I called your office and your assistant told me you were leaving right after class. I was in the vicinity so I thought I'd drop by. And, for your safety, your assistant shouldn't be giving out your schedule."

Elizabeth studied him in the soft light for a moment, two sparrows fighting over a piece of bread in the lot. "Hello Detective Bradford. If I didn't know, I might think you're stalking me."

"I told you, Mike works better. And if I'm stalking you, it's only because something came up that I think you could help me with. At I least I hope you might." He reached over and lifted two paper cups out of a holder. "I even brought coffee. I had them put cream in one. The other's black. Figured you took it one of the two ways. Which is it?"

"Black."

He smiled. "Doesn't surprise me." He handed her the cup and got out of his car.

Elizabeth took a sip. "It's good, thank you. In your text, you mentioned the seven deadly sins and a profile. Are you talking about a criminal profile?"

"Yes. I made some calls, checked on Cindy's boyfriend, Alex Davidson. He's the son of a fundamentalist preacher. His father is the head of some sort of a primitive church near Jackson. Their dress is very conservative, especially with the women. Some members of the congregation speak in tongues." Bradford paused. "I guess you know where I'm going with this."

"You want to know if Alex Davison may fit the profile of a kid who's been immersed in religious trauma. Maybe been a victim of heavy guilt trips."

"Yes, that's what I'm wondering and whether it pushed him to becoming a killer."

"That will depend on a lot of things. But in those severe situations, children are often told they're not worthy of God's love until they prove it. In some situations, psychological symptoms, injuries if you will, aren't just exacerbated by a harsh form of cult-like or religious doctrine, they are actually caused by it."

"Brainwashing can happen in any cult. That's when they drink the Kool-Aid."

"It's never about the redeeming and real spiritual comfort found in a loving relationship with God or religions per se. It's about how children, and some adults, can be negatively influenced by toxic teachings that interject eternal damnation, punishment—a vastly skewed mindset of guilt if that person doesn't follow the cult leader's absolute commands. And the really charismatic and corrupt leaders are the ones who convince their followers that they—the leader—were handpicked by God to carry out his wishes on earth. A prophet syndrome."

"I've seen this kind of stuff in my years on the force. Kids rescued from cults where they were sexually abused. I've seen wives beaten and convinced by their abusive husbands that they're ugly and no one would want them. It's sad."

"In terms of abuse by extreme religious doctrine, some psychologists have labeled the condition as religious trauma syndrome, or RTS, similar to a form of PTSD. But it's really about the mental abuse a child receives during the formative years under the strict patriarchal authority in a family where childhood insecurities are fed by telling kids they'll go to hell if they break the rules."

Bradford chuckled. "My old granddaddy used to call them charlatans, and he was a deeply religious man. I'm going to question Alex Davidson again down at headquarters, maybe two other students, all males."

"Who are the other two?"

"Gerald Simpson, he dated Cindy Carter for a while before Alex Davidson stepped in the picture. I'm not sure about the dynamics between those two guys. The third is a kid named Larry Tucker. Apparently lives in the world of dark and twisted video games. He was more or less used by some members of the fraternity to help them with homework. Let him hang out at their parties, look at their girlfriends, but told they're off limits. Maybe you could watch the interviews from behind the observation glass. Let me know who you think is lying."

"Why not just see if they'll submit to a polygraph? You may get a more accurate read than what I might be able to do."

"Because I've seen people beat the polygraph. Maybe there's something you'll see that they can't hide."

"I make no promises, but I'll do what I can."

"Maybe I can pay you back by buying dinner."

"No payback needed, thanks." She smiled. "I would like some advice, though."

"Oh, what's that?"

"When I was a teenager, my grandfather taught me how to shoot a gun. He was an excellent teacher. I became very good at it. Pistols mostly, although I can use a pump shotgun and rifle, too. I want to buy a gun and spend time at the range. What pistol do you recommend?"

"Before I answer, tell me more. Do you want it for target practice or self defense?"

"Maybe assurance is a better word."

He smiled. "Okay." He lifted his sports coat, pulled out a pistol and handed it to her.

She took it and held it for balance, using both hands. "So you use a Smith and Wesson."

"Yes, a few of the officers do, too. Also, the entire LA police department uses it. If it's good enough for a force that size, the M-P 9 is good enough for me. How does it feel?"

"Fine. I'll buy one. Maybe one day I'll see you at the range."

"Elizabeth, can I ask you why you feel the need to be armed?"

She glanced back at the university office building. She saw Dean Harris standing at his third floor window, arms folded, looking down at her in the parking lot. She handed the gun back to Bradford. "I don't know where life is leading me. My department Chair doesn't like my side work—appearing as an expert witness, doing television interviews when one of our kids is killed."

"Understood, but why the gun? Do you want to shoot him?"

Elizabeth smiled and shook her head. "In some way, I believe Cindy's death may be connected to me, and I don't mean because I was one of her teachers." She paused and looked across the parking lot, watching her student, Julie, get into a ride-sharing car, the Kars decal present in the window, the driver hidden behind the tinted glass. Elizabeth reached into her purse and lifted out the Ziploc baggie with the clump of honeysuckles inside.

Bradford sipped his coffee. "What's that?"

"These honeysuckle flowers were left inside my mailbox. Cindy was wearing a crown of honeysuckle vine when you found her. I think these may have come from the same vine. Maybe the state crime lab can do a DNA test to see."

Bradford took the baggie, looking closer at the honeysuckles. "Why would Cindy's killer taunt you?"

"That's a good question."

"Could be he saw your interview on the TV news and took great offense. You hit him above and below the belt, which is exactly where the pervert needs to be pummeled."

"Maybe it's because of my profile in the news from two high profile criminal trials. Perhaps he's the same person who killed my daughter. If so, I'll find him—"

"You need to let us handle this. We'll find who killed Cindy. You don't have to set a trap for this pervert. You—"

"Please...Mike. I hope to God you do catch him. And I prayed to God that they'd find the man who killed my daughter. He's still out there. And now a kid who sat in the front row of my class—a young woman who personified everything good on this earth had her sweet life snuffed out by a soulless ghoul. Tomorrow her parents will bury her. I'll be at the funeral, and there's not a damn thing I can think of to say that will lessen their pain and sorrow. Thanks for the coffee." She stepped toward her car.

"I'll find this guy. Don't let a piece of scum define your life."

Elizabeth looked at him for a moment, not responding. She got in her car and drove through the parking lot, the Chair of her department, Dean Harris, watching from his corner office like a predator in a glass cage.

SIXTEEN

The last time Elizabeth attended a funeral she buried her daughter. Today she watched as another mother and father buried their child. The casket containing the body of Cindy Carter sat on a shiny metallic lowering device over the grave. Soil, the color of wet coffee grounds, was piled to one side. Elizabeth stood under a moss-draped live oak, watching mourners gather around the grave. She looked at the faces and body language.

She looked for deceit hiding in the shadows of sorrow.

Dozens of college students, some with tear-streaked faces, stood in a large semi-circle, many more than could fit under the green awning erected by the funeral director's staff. Elizabeth watched as Cindy's mother and father, both weakened by emotional pain, took their seats at the front in plastic folding chairs. Various family members, including two young girls who resembled Cindy, sat next to them, filling the first two rows.

Jean Carter, Cindy's mother, bowed her head for a long moment and then looked up, variegated light falling across her grief-stricken face. She stared at her daughter's coffin, the call of a crow in the distance, the tender sobbing of friends and family punctuating the sticky air. Jean folded her hands on her lap, clenching her fingers together, knuckles white, a sporadic tremor moving across her small shoulders. Her husband, Ron, face haggard behind dark glasses, reached over, wrapping one of his large hands around his wife's knotted fists.

The minister moved through the crowd, stopping to comfort family members. He stepped to the front of the assembly, his eyes scanning the mourners, a soft breeze flapping the canvas eaves hanging from the sides of the awning. Reverend Stewart Martin had the pious, drawn look of a man who'd spoken at more funerals than he could count. Bony face. Thick, gray hair and large hands holding a tattered black Bible.

"Dearly beloved, we are gathered here for two reasons. One is, of course, to grieve the passing of Cindy Carter, a young woman taken from us long before her time. The second reason is to celebrate the life that Cindy led…and she led by example. As I look out into this congregation, it's not by chance that so many of you are here to pay your respects. You're all here because, in some way, some loving way, Cindy touched you, too. She was an old soul, a loving soul."

Tears spilled down Jean Carter's face. She searched in her purse for a fresh Kleenex, dabbing her eyes and staring at the large framed picture of Cindy. It was secured to a wooden easel near the casket, Cindy sitting on a picnic table in the summer, her smiling face filled with light. Ron Carter wrapped his right arm around his wife's shoulders, their pain as palpable as the scent of the flowers beside the casket.

Elizabeth bit her bottom lip. Her scars resurrected as she watched Cindy's parents in their own quiet desperation, knowing they wanted to scream from a cliff.

Reverend Martin opened his Bible. "Before I read from Psalms twenty-three, let's have a moment of silent prayer for Cindy and her family." He nodded and bowed his head. Elizabeth didn't bow her head. Instead she used the opportunity to observe. She scanned the faces. In the distance, she could hear the wail of a siren fading down the highway. A baby cried once, its mother stood in the back row, rocking the child on her hip. The air smelled of approaching rain and damp earth.

All heads were bowed except one.

He stood out above the lowered heads. He was tall. Elizabeth watched him though the throng of mourners. He had the look and build of an Ivy League quarterback. Handsome. Dark hair. Hands in his pockets, rocking slightly on the balls of his feet. His expression indifferent, a trace of amusement behind the poker face.

Elizabeth knew that people grieved in different ways. But he wasn't grieving. He stood next to five other young men. Elizabeth looked at each one, students most likely. Maybe one of them was Cindy's boyfriend. Maybe he was the tallest. Elizabeth would find out.

Reverend Martin slowly lifted his head. He cleared his throat. "Jean… Ron…and members of the family, I invite you to approach the front before Cindy is laid to rest."

Jean and Ron stood. He held her by the arm as they slowly stepped closer. They reached for two white roses from a large bouquet. Jean, hand trembling, placing one long stem rose on her daughter's casket. "Cindy… we love you so much sweetheart. Your birthday is just a few days away… happy birthday…." Jean's voice cracked. She kissed the casket, a tear falling alongside the rose.

Ron set his rose next to that of his wife, both standing there for a moment. Cindy's two younger sisters, weeping, also laid roses on her casket. A mockingbird sang from the top of a sycamore tree. Cindy's roommate openly wept in her seat. Reverend Martin nodded and others stood, forming a line to place flowers on the casket. The minister turned the pages to the book of Psalms and began. "The Lord is my shepherd…I shall not want. He maketh me to lie down in green pastures…he leadeth me beside still waters." As he continued, Jean and Ron and their younger daughters returned to their seats.

Elizabeth made eye contact with Jean, and for an instant, sharing the universal pain of mothers who've lost a child to a killer.

Reverend Martin continued. "Yea, though I walk through the valley of the shadow of death…."

A black woman in a dark blue dress stood as the minister finished and nodded at her. She began singing *Amazing Grace*, people joining in, standing, holding hands, tears falling.

Elizabeth moved slowly around the mourners, most now standing as the service was coming to an end. Within a few seconds, Elizabeth walked beyond the last row of people. She could hear the preacher say a final short prayer, the turns of a handle lowering the casket into the grave. People crying. Elizabeth stood behind the tall man in the sports coat and black tennis shoes. He leaned over to the young man next to him and said, "Let's get outta here. This is the part I hate. The church service was enough."

"Maybe we outta hang out and say somethin' to Cindy's parents."

"They have more than enough grieving people to give condolences."

The two turned to leave. Elizabeth looked at both of them. She cut her eyes up at the tallest and said, "What a sad day."

He nodded. "Yeah. It's like the worst. The only funeral I've ever been to was when my grandmother died last year."

"How'd you know Cindy?" Elizabeth studied his face.

"I used to date her. Didn't work out. But we stayed friends. She was dating a member of our fraternity."

Elizabeth smiled. "Would that be Alex?"

"Yeah, how do you know him?"

"I teach at the university. Cindy was one of my students. Where's Alex?"

The other student gestured toward the parking lot. "He went back to the car a few minutes ago. Said he felt sick."

Elizabeth extended her hand. "I'm Elizabeth Monroe."

The taller of the two said, "My name's Gerald Simpson. One of my friends is in your forensic psyche class. He really likes it."

"That's good to hear. What's your friend's name?"

"Cameron Bosky."

The other student smiled. "I'm Carson West." He looked up at Simpson and said, "We gotta be going. Nice to meet you, Professor Monroe."

They walked toward the parking lot, Elizabeth watching them. The students got into a Ford Explorer. The tall one sat behind the wheel, the shorter in the back. A third student sat straighter in the front passenger side. As they drove by, Alex Davidson looked out the open window, lighting a cigarette and staring back at the gathering. His face caught in a flash of light, as fleeting as the white belly of a fish escaping through the crest of a sunlit wave. Elizabeth filed his expression away in her mind.

She turned back as the service ended, the people slowly disbanding, making their way back to their cars. Cemetery workers moving in to cover the grave, friends and family offering final condolences to Cindy's parents. Elizabeth knew that time would really never lessen the grief. Time was a placebo, a thief prolonging sorrow for the rest of their lives. She watched as Ron and Jean Carter walked slowly from the gravesite, coming towards her, and at that moment she had no idea what to say to them.

SEVENTEEN

Elizabeth could already see the change. Ron Carter's shoulders were a little more rounded as he walked. Jean searched the ground, taking small steps, avoiding anything that may interfere with the sense of balance she still retained. Ron cupped one of his hands under his wife's elbow to help steady her. They stopped a few feet from Elizabeth. Jean looked up, searching Elizabeth's face for a moment, taking the time to carefully choose her words. "One of Cindy's friends said you are Professor Monroe."

"Please, call me Elizabeth."

Jean inhaled deeply. "Cindy spoke often of you. She said you were the best teacher she ever had."

"She was an extraordinary student and person. I am so very sorry."

"Thank you, and thank you for being such a good influence on Cindy."

"She was an influence on me, too. In some small way, perhaps, I share your grief."

Ron Carter cleared his throat. "How might that be?"

"My daughter was killed…murdered. She was a little older than Cindy when it happened."

Jean stood straighter. "We're sorry."

Ron tilted his head, looking at Elizabeth as if he was trying to recall her face. "Did they find the person who did it?"

"No."

Ron coughed, a small wheezing sound deep in his throat.

Jean added, "It's because of you that Cindy wanted to continue her studies in psychology, eventually doing something to help abused children."

Elizabeth smiled. "You raised her well. She was a remarkable young woman."

Ron adjusted his weight, shifting from each foot, his tired eyes scanning the parking lot. "We've spoken at length with detectives looking for our daughter's killer. One, Detective Mike Bradford, told us you went out to the crime scene."

"Yes, I thought I might be able to help in some way."

Ron nodded. "Cindy used to tell us that none of the students in your class would even think about trying to be deceptive or to snow you over in some way because she said your instincts, maybe it's intuition, were so good."

Elizabeth smiled. "I'm not so sure that's the reason. When you teach long enough, you hear all the excuses for late homework, lame essay ideas, tardy...whatever. I just try to set reasonable expectations with my students and hold them accountable."

"Detective Bradford said you helped profile the bastard who murdered our little girl."

"I offered some suggestions. I could be wrong."

Jean stepped closer. "But you could be right, too."

Ron asked, "Who do you think killed Cindy?"

"I don't know that. I do feel that whomever did it will do it again. He probably has a history of cruelty." Elizabeth was quiet a moment. She could hear the sound of a diesel—a backhoe—digging another grave in the cemetery. "How much did the police tell you about Cindy's death?"

Ron folded his arms. "Everything. At least I believe they told us everything. Detective Bradford told us you said this guy has a God Complex... deciding who will be punished...." Tears welled in his eyes. "The killer should be shot like a rabid animal."

"Punished?" Jean said. "What do you mean by punished?"

"Jean, we'll talk later," Ron told her quietly, rubbing her back.

Jean used the palms of her hands to smooth a wrinkle from her black dress. She looked up at Elizabeth. "You knew our Cindy well. You were her mentor. I have dropped down on my knees and asked God to help make sense of this. All we have left is emptiness so deep it aches every beat of our hearts." Jean extended her hands, reaching for Elizabeth, grasping her hands. "Can you help us? Can you help the police find our daughter's killer?"

Elizabeth held the woman's hands, looked at the last traces of hope in eyes red and swollen from days of crying. "I can't make promises, but I'll do whatever I can. I know that's not what you two want to hear. It could be a long road."

Ron rubbed his gold wedding band with two large fingers, looked at the cemetery workers covering his daughter's grave. "We appreciate anything you can do. Maybe you can help us find closure down that road."

"I hope so."

Jean slowly released Elizabeth's hands, stepping back. "Thank you." She looked up at the sky and lowered her eyes to meet Elizabeth. "You touched Cindy in a way none of her teachers had ever done. In some way beyond our understanding, I think you can still touch Cindy. No parent should ever have to bury a child. And when the hand of a murderer takes your child… the sorrow is felt so deep it aches your soul. As a mother, I know you've felt that pain, too. You might be able to prevent another mama and daddy from going from this."

Jean tried to smile but could not. She turned, waved for her two daughters to come, then walked with her husband to their car, his hand bracing her small shoulders.

Elizabeth watched them for a few seconds, almost everyone now gone from the cemetery. She heard a twig snap, the shadow of someone approaching her from behind. She turned and Detective Mike Bradford walked up to her.

"You got a minute?" he asked. "I'd like to buy you a another cup of coffee. We should talk."

EIGHTEEN

They entered the 1960's style diner in downtown Hattiesburg and made their way to a back table. The diner carried the smells of burgers and a deep fryer belching spent cooking oil. Red checkered tablecloths. A few eyes looked up from the counter where people sipped coffee and passed gossip like slices of hot apple pie. The dozen booths were filled with late lunchtime customers, courthouse workers, attorneys, and construction workers. Two sheriff's deputies sat at the counter, one finishing a Coke and cracking ice between his teeth, his eyes following Detective Bradford.

Bradford took a seat so he could see the room and front entrance. Elizabeth sat with her back to the door, placing her purse at her feet. A middle-aged waitress whirred by, a tray of food in one hand. She said, "Howdy Mike. Be with y'all in just a sec." She moved to the next table.

Elizabeth smiled. Bradford said, "If you're hungry, we can get a bite to eat."

"No thanks. Not much of an appetite. Were you at the funeral the whole time?"

"Yes."

"Do you usually attend a murder victim's funeral?"

"That sounds like a question a psychologist would ask. I haven't had a lot of opportunities, but I have attended a few."

"Why do you go?"

"I think you probably know that answer."

The waitress stopped at the table and whipped out a pad and pen. Dyed black hair tied back, one eyebrow drawn slightly higher than the other. "Where you been, Mike? I haven't seen you in here in a couple of weeks," her eyes catching two more customers arriving.

"It's been hectic. Doesn't take a full moon to bring out the crazies anymore."

"That's for darn sure." She smiled at Elizabeth and leveled her green eyes at Bradford, lowering her voice above a whisper. "I heard about that college girl found dead. I hope you catch the guy…might not be a guy but, most likely, it'll turn out to be one. Somethin' in the gene pool." She looked at Elizabeth, nodding. "Anyway, the devil's got a special place for somebody who'd do that to a girl." She sighed. "What will y'all be havin' today? We got a blue plate special on catfish and hushpuppies."

Elizabeth said, "Coffee would be great."

Bradford leaned back in his chair. "Just coffee, thanks, Lucy."

"I know you take your coffee with cream, Mike. How about you, ma'am?"

"Black, thanks."

The waitress smiled and left. Elizabeth looked at Bradford. "Why did you go out there today?"

"Something you said at the crime scene."

"What?"

"You mentioned that peculiar fact that sometimes the perp circles back and returns to the scene. Morbid, no doubt, but the same principle applies to the killer attending the funeral of his victim. I don't know the psychological terms…it's rare but it can happen."

The waitress brought the coffees and set a cup in front of Bradford and Elizabeth, then left to greet a table. Elizabeth held the large ceramic cup in both hands and sipped. "It is rare. It's mostly serial arsonists because it becomes a sexual deviancy for them. Not so much with a serial killer."

"But we don't know this guy will do it again."

"He will, if he hasn't already. The key is to find something to ID him before his urge to kill recycles."

"And you think he will, right?"

"Yes. He's too meticulous in his handiwork. The FBI calls them organized killers. There are usually three crime scenes, if you will—the place where the victim is abducted, the area where she or he is killed, and the place where the killer chooses to leave the body. When he puts it on display, like he did with Cindy, he's making a chilling statement."

"What's he saying?"

"That I'm in total control. I can do anything I want. And I can do it because I'm connected to a higher authority than you."

"You mean God?"

"Not necessarily. The perpetrator sometimes believes he is God or some kind of a superior deity accountable to no one. And to question him is to result in a deadly fight."

"We'll find him."

"Maybe—or later rather than sooner. These psychopaths cover their tracks because they usually don't leave tracks. They're often savvy in the use of forensics, and they think they're smarter than any investigator."

Bradford stirred his coffee. "Is that what happened in the case of your daughter? You mentioned that the perp was never caught. Please excuse me if I'm getting too personal. You said the case is cold. If I might ask, what happened?"

Elizabeth used her index finger to trace along the lip of the cup. "Molly was a graduate student at the University of Florida at the time. She and her boyfriend went into a national forest in search of a plant called the coontie. It's the only plant that the rare Atala butterfly uses in its life cycle. Molly was so happy when they found the plants. They planned to return to release endangered butterflies." Elizabeth looked up at Bradford and half-smiled. "When she and Jeff returned to the forest they were both killed. Police found their bodies in a grave buried under the carcass of a deer. The killer did that to throw off the scent so police cadaver dogs couldn't find the bodies."

Bradford leaned forward, placing the palms of his hands on the tabletop. "I'm sorry. Do you know why they were killed?"

"They'd innocently stumbled across a large-scale drug operation in the deep forest. Police thought they got the killer—shot him. He was a hit man tied to a Mexican drug cartel. Months later I received the most haunting call of my life." Elizabeth paused, pushing a strand of hair behind one ear. "He left a voicemail. Just above a whisper. He said the person police thought killed Molly and Jeff wasn't the real killer. He said he'd done it, and he had one of Molly's earrings as a souvenir. He said Molly was not his first victim, and there would be more to come. Police reopened the case, chased down dead-end leads and eventually Molly was another cold case."

"Did you ever hear from the perp again?"

"No."

"Maybe he was just some freak who wanted to ruffle your feathers."

"No. He was too composed…too matter of fact. As if he was telling me about the weather, and he knew there was only one earring on Molly's body."

"And so you're looking for the killer."

"Yes."

"It's got to eat you alive. Reading obituaries. Following up on murders of young women to trace similarities. I feel so bad for you—"

"Don't, Detective Bradford. Don't feel sorry for me. Grieve for Molly, Cindy Carter and thousands of young women kidnapped, abused and often murdered around the world every year. Me, I'll survive." Elizabeth leaned back in her chair, the waitress stepping over to refill their cups. "Thank you, but I've reached my caffeine limit."

The waitress smiled. "Mike, how 'bout you?"

"Sure, I'll take a warm up."

She filled the cup and left. Bradford said, "I'm sure Molly's father was devastated, too."

"I don't know. He left when Molly was ten months old. He chose not to be part of Molly's life. It was just my daughter and I for twenty years until she was murdered. After that, I sold my bakery and turned an interest into a determination by finishing my doctorate in criminal forensic psychology. Up until then, I was leisurely working on my degree, picking up the pace some when Molly went to college, when I found I had a bit more time on my hands. It turned frenetic when I lost Molly. Now I'm looking for her killer. One day I'll find him."

"In the meantime, you teach at the university and are called in to occasionally serve as an expert witness in criminal trials."

Elizabeth smiled. "That pretty much sums it up. How about you? What's your story?"

"Not too exciting. I always wanted to be in law enforcement, always wanted to fight for victims of crime, or families of crime victims. I started my career in Jackson. After five years, I heard of a detective's position opening in Natchez. I applied, got the job, but lost the marriage."

"I'm sorry."

"Don't be. We didn't have kids. She's happier not being married to a cop. The long hours and always dealing with the dark side typically doesn't lend itself to a storybook marriage."

"I still would like to believe in the concept of marriage. But after I was left alone with Molly, all my effort went into raising her. I didn't want to explain new boyfriends and all the concessions that go with his, hers, their place, and our place. For Molly, it was always her place with me. She came first."

Bradford started to say something when his phone buzzed. He lifted it from the table, squinted looking at the caller ID. He looked up at Elizabeth. "I'd better take it. Cindy Carter's mother is calling." Bradford answered and greeted Jean Carter.

"Detective Bradford," she said in a strained voice.

"Yes ma'am, Mrs. Carter."

"My husband and I were driving home after the funeral when he realized he'd left his phone back at the cemetery…."

"Yes…."

"Well, sir, when we got there, everyone was gone, of course. All the chairs were removed, but we walked up to where we'd sat earlier. He looked around and didn't find it. And then I walked over to Cindy's grave, just to say a prayer and tell her again how much we miss her. That's when we saw it."

"Saw what?"

Her voice cracked. "It was on top of the fresh earth, in the center of her grave."

"What was there Mrs. Carter?"

"A wooden plate. And in the center of the plate was an earring. It was one of Cindy's earrings."

NINETEEN

When Detective Bradford ended the call, he stared at his phone screen for a moment, almost as if he were reading a text. He looked up at Elizabeth. "I need to go back to the cemetery."

"Why? What did Cindy's mother say?"

"She and her husband returned to the cemetery to look for his phone. They said a wooden plate was placed on top of the grave. Apparently after everyone left, including the cemetery workers."

Elizabeth looked closely at Bradford. "What else was there?"

"How'd you know there was something else?"

"What was it?"

"An earring. Mrs. Carter says it was one of Cindy's earrings." Bradford looked away from Elizabeth's burning eyes. He shook his head. "Maybe it's a coincidence…but the message the guy left on your phone…knowing about Molly's earring. What if this is the same man…the same killer?"

Elizabeth said nothing. She pushed the coffee cup to one side. "What this means is that the killer was probably there during the funeral services for Cindy. Watching. Listening. Something inside his black heart getting darker, if that's possible."

"I'm calling dispatch, have them send the closest officer out there until I can get to the cemetery. Maybe we'll find some physical evidence. Prints on the plate or the earring. Something." He made the call.

When he finished, Elizabeth said, "I didn't spot you in the congregation at Cindy's funeral. When did you arrive?"

"Before the mourners. For the most part, I stayed in my car and observed, watching people as they entered into the cemetery. Looking for anything that seemed out of place."

"I'd say a monster with a wooden plate is out of place."

"I wish I'd seen him."

"You probably did. So did I. The guy simply kept the plate in his car until everyone left."

"Toward the end of the service I stood at the back. I waited to speak with Cindy's parents…wanted them to know the department is doing everything we can to bring their daughter's killer to justice." He took a long sip from his coffee cup, eyes scanning the diner.

"There were students from one of the fraternities. All guys. One was Alex Davidson, Cindy's boyfriend. I only saw him when they were leaving. The other students said Alex spent part of the service in the car."

"As I mentioned, I questioned Davidson and another kid, big guy. Name's Gerald Simpson. I drove out to the frat house and interviewed them. I spotted Simpson there today. Looked like he was doing his pal Alex a favor to attend the funeral."

Elizabeth nodded. "Not a lot of empathy on his face, maybe because he's incapable of real empathy."

"He was that way on the porch of the frat house. Charming, but didn't appear to have a whole lot of compassion for Cindy. Alex told me that he and Cindy had a blowout argument the day she went missing. Cindy wanted to leave the party at the Kappa house and go home. Alex said he was too drunk to drive. The last thing he allegedly remembers was watching her walk into the rain. He thinks she got in a car."

"A friend?"

"I questioned her roommate. She said she got a call from Cindy, but didn't hear her voicemail until much later that night. So she didn't pick up Cindy."

"Then who did?"

"That's the question I don't have an answer for, but I will."

"Whoever it was might have been the last person to see Cindy alive."

"Are you suggesting the killer gave her a ride?"

Elizabeth put her cup on the table, leaned closer. "You saw the stun-gun marks on the body. Maybe the attack happened in the car."

Bradford said nothing, his mind working the possibilities. "Alex Davidson said a student by the name of Larry Tucker used to hang around the house. Although he wasn't a member of the fraternity, they sort of kept him around because of his brains. Someone to help with homework."

"Not good enough to be a member, but good enough to do their homework. That's the very definition of being used."

"Being a brainy sometimes comes with nerdy baggage. Davidson said the guy always dressed in black. Like a comic book character."

"What if Cindy got a ride with someone she knows? Have you had a chance to check her cell phone records and logistics?"

"The last call she made was to her roommate. Nothing after that, and it looks like her phone was shut down, maybe the battery removed. No GPS record. Nothing after she left the fraternity house."

"What if she had a ride-share driver, Uber or one of the others, pick her up? There would be no record of a call because you don't call. You touch an app, enter in the pick up information, and get a response from the closest driver. If you check with the ride-share companies, there should be a record if that's how she left."

Detective Bradford's jaw line stiffened. He interlaced his fingers together. Elizabeth asked, "What is it? What are you thinking?"

"The big guy, Gerald Simpson. He's a part-time driver for three ride-share companies."

"Plus he knew Cindy well. And she knew him. For some reason, she'd stopped dating Simpson, but did she feel comfortable enough to get in a car with him?"

Bradford stood. "I'm interviewing Gerald Simpson again with the other two, Alex Davidson and Larry Tucker. This time I'll do it at the station."

Elizabeth stood from her chair. "When I observe, there will be at least one thing I'm looking for."

"Tell me what it is, and I'll ask the question that might prompt it."

"Ask them if they had a pet as a kid…and how it died."

"Okay."

They walked through the diner, a few heads turning, tongues wagging. In the parking lot, Elizabeth said, "I know I'm not an investigator. I won't touch the plate, but I'd like to see exactly how and where he placed it on the grave."

Bradford nodded. "I'm sure there is a psychological read into that. Let's see what it might be."

TWENTY

A lex Davidson walked into his room in the Alpha Kappa house and pulled out his phone to text Cindy. He punched three letters, and shook his head. "What's wrong with me? She's not here anymore." He read the last text she'd sent him, whispering her words, "I'll be ready in ten minutes. Luv you." He looked at the framed photo of Cindy on his nightstand, stepping across the room to pick up the picture.

He stared at her face behind the glass, the sound of a touch football game in the yard. "It never should have happened. You didn't deserve this." He set the picture down, turned and left his room.

Alex walked through the sprawling fraternity house, his mind replaying snippets from the funeral, the arrival of Cindy's parents and sisters, Mrs. Carter looking a lot older, Mr. Carter helping her to the seating area, the girls with tear-stained faces, looking lost. He knew how Cindy always looked out for her younger sisters and how they looked up to her.

Alex entered the rec room. Gerald Simpson and another student were shooting pool. Simpson made a shot and looked up at Alex. "Hey Davidson, you look like you came from a funeral." He grinned.

"That's not even fuckin' funny."

Simpson motioned toward a corner pocket and sank the eight ball. "Didn't mean to run the table on you, Devon."

The student put his cue stick on a shelf and said, "I got to go to class anyway." He left the room.

Simpson stepped over to a large cabinet behind the bar. He picked up a bottle of tequila and two shot glasses, poured tequila in the glasses and set one in front of Alex. Simpson said, "This will take the edge off. It's been a helluva last few days, bro." Alex stared at the shot glasses. Simpson lifted his, slid the other closer to Alex. "Let's toast to Cindy."

Alex lifted his glass and Simpson said, "To an extraordinary girl, Cindy Carter, we'll miss her." Simpson knocked back this drink. Alex did the same and Simpson immediately poured two more.

Alex lifted his hand. "I'm done."

"No man, we're just starting. If we ever need a reason to get trashed, it's the death of the one girl we both knew well. There will never be another person like Cindy...beautiful and intelligent. To her memory." He drank his shot. Alex exhaled deeply and did the same, slamming his glass down on the bar.

Alex looked Simpson in the eye. "Man, I don't know what it is, but you don't really seem too upset that Cindy's dead. Is it 'cause she dumped you?"

"Dumped me. Is that what she told you? C'mon, Davidson, it was more like the other way around." Alex looked at him with doubt in his eye. Simpson smiled. "I don't want to talk trash about the dead, but that wasn't how it happened little brother."

He refilled the shot glasses. "Cindy and I had a good thing going 'till I got tired of trying to be her ideal man. She was looking for husband potential. In that category, unlike my classes, I failed. But you, bro...you seemed to excel in that area. Except for the last party when you more or less ignored her while you pounded down a few too many—at least for her taste anyway."

Alex could feel the alcohol in his system, his guilt and anger over Cindy's death rushing through his veins, Simpson's sardonic comments punching him in the gut. He lifted the glass, knocking back the tequila. "Fuck you, Simpson." Alex started to leave and stopped, turning back around. "You know what, I don't remember you around? You weren't in the kitchen. I don't remember you even in the house that day."

"Like you could remember. Dude, you were shit faced. Another thing, you already told that detective I was here. And I was. So keep your story together or the next thing you know the cops will be sniffing back around and questioning you again. Think about it, you aren't sure what happened to Cindy. You say she just walked into a thunderstorm and vanished. Maybe she was abducted by aliens." He paused and used his thumbnail to peel back the label on the tequila bottle. "Maybe you lost your shit and you and Larry Tucker took her out in the woods and did some crazy fuckin' sacrifice—"

Alex recoiled, swinging his right fist hard at Simpson's head. Simpson ducked and hit Alex in the nose. He grabbed Alex's arm, pulling it behind his back, inching close to his right shoulder blade. Simpson sneered and said, "You know how long it'll take you to heal from a twisted arm. Don't fuck with me! You be a good little bro and I won't tell the cops that you and the weird Larry Tucker play video games *Hit Man* and *Primal Death* in a dark room."

Blood tricked down Alex's face, dripping on the bar. Simpson released his arm and threw one of the shot glasses into an open fireplace, glass shattering. He turned and walked out.

Alex pulled a paper towel from behind the bar, holding it to his bleeding nose. He used a second towel to clean up the blood. He missed Cindy terribly, believed that she would have taken him back. But now he would never have the chance to prove how much he loved her and that he wasn't a jerk.

He thought about Cindy the day of the party and then the casket at the church, people sobbing in the pews. Somehow Alex didn't cry at the funeral, but now the tears of guilt fell, smearing with blood and dark thoughts across the bar.

TWENTY-ONE

etective Mike Bradford approached the cemetery with a degree of restraint. He parked and waited for Elizabeth to arrive. From the parking lot, he could see Cindy's grave in the distance, the plate perched on the mound of fresh earth. *Was the perp still around? Looking from a condo balcony, a church window, or in his car?* There were three vehicles in the lot. One was a squad car. One was a pickup truck.

Elizabeth parked and approached, looking at the grave near the trees. Bradford motioned for her to follow him over to the squad car. The officer, early twenties, flushed face, sat inside, motor idling, driver's side window down, the police radio a low staccato of brief communications.

Bradford stepped up to the car. "Thanks for waiting."

"No problem, Detective. When you stake out a grave, not a lot of movement." He smiled. "The dish is still there." He pointed through the windshield.

"Good. Did you see anyone when you arrived?"

"The parents were here in the parking lot...pretty shaken up. I sent them home, telling them I'd wait for you. There were a couple of other people on the grounds. A groundskeeper was one. He had an ATV four-wheeler, rakes, weed-whackers and whatnot."

"Did you speak with him?"

"No, I was told to watch the dish until you arrived—to make sure it stayed put. I can see it easily from here. I wasn't told to question anyone about it. What's the deal with a dish on a grave anyway? Maybe one of the funeral-goers dropped it off." He looked over to Elizabeth, the sun behind her.

Bradford asked, "When did you last see the groundskeeper?"

"About a half hour ago, not long after I arrived."

"There's a car and truck in the lot. Who else did you see?"

"An elderly woman was arranging flowers on a grave not too far from the fresh one, the one with the dish in the dirt. I haven't seen her leave."

"How about the other vehicle? You know who's driving the pickup."

"No. But I'd bet a pizza that it's not the grandma." He grinned.

Bradford straightened up, looking across the immense cemetery, the sun setting over the tree line, the pines and oaks casting plum colored shadows in the twilight, a screech owl sounding like the whinny of a horse in the purple haze.

The officer said, "Wish I'd more to give you. Want me to stay?"

"No thanks. As you said, not a lot of movement in a cemetery."

The officer drove away. Bradford and Elizabeth walked toward Cindy's grave. They both scanned the cemetery, the elderly woman sitting on a concrete bench less than one hundred feet away, her head bowed. "Look over there near that big tree," Elizabeth pointed. In the distance, Bradford could see a man standing next to a grave near a lone live oak. From one hundred yards, there was nothing distinguishable, just a tall man with his back toward the parking lot.

Bradford said nothing as they approached Cindy's grave. The detective put on rubber gloves, carrying paper bags in one hand. When they came closer, Bradford stopped walking for a moment, taking in the scene. Elizabeth stared at the plate. She walked carefully around the grave, looking at the angle the plate was positioned in relation to the headstone, the slight mound of earth, the way the plate was tilted to the east.

Bradford said, "It's handmade and appears to be of similar wood to the other handmade bowl found with the body." He leaned over, looking in the indented area of the plate. A blue earring sat in the grooved section like a small bird's egg in a shallow nest. He squatted down, lifting the plate, studying it, removing the earring.

Elizabeth stared at the earring in the palm of his hand. Her mind racing to images of Molly's body under the coroner's white sheet in a dark forest, the squeak from the wheels as the metal gurney rolled over pine straw. Then she heard the abrasive sound of the caller's voice from the message he'd left, *"I took it from her as a souvenir..."*

Bradford looked up. "Elizabeth, are you okay?"

"Yes. Considering the circumstances, I'm okay."

"It seems to match the one Cindy was wearing when we found her body." He placed the earring in a separate, smaller paper bag. Then he set the plate in the bottom of the larger bag. "There are a few shoeprints. They all look like they were made by the mourners approaching the grave."

Elizabeth said nothing, her eyes looking at the small details in the fresh soil. "All look like shoes, men's and women's...." She pointed to a single print. "Except that one. It's a boot print. Look at the pattern."

"Could be a construction boot, maybe worn by one of the cemetery workers."

"I don't think so. There were three workers. One on the backhoe and the other two had shovels and rakes. They all wore the same job-issued blue shirts, khaki work pants, and black lace-up, low cut shoes."

"I'll get a photo of the tread pattern." He knelt down, focused, and snapped a picture. There was the sound of a motor starting in the parking lot. Bradford and Elizabeth watched as the pickup truck was leaving. They looked at the grave in the distance by the lone oak.

The man was gone.

TWENTY-TWO

Detective Bradford glanced across the grave to Elizabeth. He said, "I didn't see or hear that guy go by us. We must have been so focused on the plate, earring, and the boot print, we didn't hear him."

She shook her head. "He didn't walk by us...he walked around us."

"Did you see him leave?"

"No, but from where he was standing to the parking lot, the shortest route would be to walk along the edge of the woodlands to the lot."

There was the sound of a small motor in the distance. Within seconds a man on an ATV was coming through the cemetery, careful not to drive over the graves. As he got closer to them, Bradford stepped away from Cindy's grave, signaling for the man to stop.

The groundskeeper was in his late thirties, ruddy outdoor face, coppery whiskers, faded baseball cap. He wore overalls and a denim long sleeve shirt, the top button fastened, work gloves the color of a decaying pumpkin, and scuffed boots. A small flatbed trailer with gardening tools was attached to the back of the ATV, a bottle of weed-killer capped and strapped down.

Bradford smiled. "Got a minute?"

"Sure do," the man's accent was southern with a touch of Cajun.

"I'm Detective Bradford with the Forrest County Sheriff's Department. This is Doctor Monroe."

He looked over at Elizabeth, his eyes impassive. "Pleased to meet y'all. Most folks call me LT. Kinda like lieutenant. I served in Iraq, but I damn sure wasn't a lieutenant." He looked at his gloved hands and then cut his eyes up to Elizabeth. "I recognize you. You did that live interview on Fox News about that protest rally next to the Justice Center."

Elizabeth nodded. "Yes, I did."

He looked at the two bags Bradford was holding.

Bradford asked, "Did you see a wooden plate that was placed on the grave behind me?"

"No, sir, can't say I did."

Elizabeth watched the man closely.

Bradford looked in the direction the groundskeeper had come. "You always work until sundown?"

"Depends on the time of year. And it depends on what needs to be done in the cemetery. We got every bit of three hundred acres. And there's still room for new folks." He glanced down at Cindy's grave and then looked up at Bradford. "There are gravestones in here that go back to the Revolutionary War."

"Is that right?"

"Yes sir. We got a mound in the center where a hundred Confederate soldiers are buried. All died from wounds in battle. This cemetery is one of the most historic in Mississippi. I worked at the National Cemetery in Vicksburg, but overall this place is more representative of Mississippi folk, even the gypsies that came through the state and found a home here." He leaned back, heat rising from the ATV motor.

Elizabeth stepped closer to the groundskeeper. She pointed to the grave near the lone oak and said, "That grave near the big tree. Do you know who's buried there?"

He looked over his shoulder, the long shrill quiver of a screech owl coming from the deep shade in woodlands. "That's not one grave, it's six. Hard to see from here. The dead are from an old Mississippi family. The patriarch was a cult leader in Mississippi after the Civil War."

"What kind of cult leader?"

"Name was Zachariah Belmont. From what people told me, he was a preacher who preached from the Old Testament. They called him a prophet. He lived and breathed Deuteronomy. Mississippi's original fire and brimstone sort of fella. He developed quite a following. Lots of folks wanting to adapt his ways. He had a commune goin' on, too."

Elizabeth asked, "What do you mean by prophet and…adapt his ways?"

"They say he had visions. Made uncanny predictions. I don't guess he was that much different from some of today's cult leaders, takin' multiple wives, sayin' that you get to God through him. Sort of a charismatic gate-keeper to heaven. Least that's what I heard." He half smiled. "When he wasn't in front of the pulpit, he wore a white robe. Led the Klan in this part of Mississippi."

Bradford glanced toward the lone oak. "Looks like preacher Belmont still has family here. Someone visited the grave."

The groundskeeper lit a cigarette, taking a long drag, blowing the smoke through the ATV handlebars. "Maybe that's so. I couldn't tell you. The man buried in that grave does have followers, or admirers, to this very day. They visit the grave and sometimes leave stuff."

"What kind of stuff?" Elizabeth asked.

"Wooden crosses. Candles. Bible verses. Shell casings. It runs the gamut."

"How about wooden bowls or plates?"

The groundskeeper took a deep pull from the cigarette, the smoke trick-ling out of his nostrils. "Maybe. I ain't seen any. But I haven't been over there today."

Elizabeth looked at the boots the man wore, trying to see a tread pattern.

The groundskeeper removed one glove and scratched the stubble on his face, his fingernails long, black dirt under the nails. "Unless y'all got some more questions, I'd better get goin' before I hit overtime for this week. Management isn't too forgiving about that sort of thing."

Bradford handed the man a card. "If you can think of anything, or see something peculiar, don't hesitate to give me a call."

The man grinned, spitting a piece of tobacco from his tongue. "Lot's of weird stuff happens in a cemetery as old as this one. We got a voodoo high priestess buried out here. Her grave attracts all kinds. They do some kinky stuff on top of the grave." He grinned, pulled from the cigarette. "I know 'cause I got to pick up after those heathens the next morning."

"Isn't the cemetery gate locked at night?" Bradford asked.

"That won't stop crazies from comin' over the old stone wall, especially during a full moon or a lunar eclipse. Be seein' y'all." He shook his head, cranked the ATV and pulled away, tools bouncing across the trailer bed. Elizabeth watched him leave, scrutinized his body language as he wound the ATV around the graves.

Bradford blew out a long breath and glanced over at her. "I'll get this dish and earring to the lab. Maybe we'll find prints or something."

"Did you find prints from the bowl left where Cindy's body was found?"

"No. But criminals make mistakes."

"Not this one. At least not yet. Where's he getting hand-carved wooden bowls and plates? Is he making them or buying them from someone?"

"Who knows? Lots of guys have woodshops all over Southern Mississippi."

"Yes, but I bet very few can make items of this consistent quality. Maybe if we can identify the source, the tree the bowl came from, it'll get us closer."

Bradford grinned. "Sort of like peeling back the bark. Looking for tree ring history."

Elizabeth stared at the lone oak in the distance. "Let's go see that tree and the people buried near it."

TWENTY-THREE

The gravestones were old, dark pewter, weathered from time, nature and visitors. Elizabeth and Detective Bradford looked at the ground surrounding the six graves and read the headstones. The dead were all from the Belmont family. Wife. Daughters. Sons. Elizabeth reread the oldest marker.

Zachariah Belmont
1855 – 1927
God's Prophet of the South

Bradford said, "God's prophet. Makes you wonder if he was hand-picked for the job or maybe worked his way up." He shook his head and set the paper bags on a grassy area.

Elizabeth stepped closer. "Looks like the other graves are those of his wife and children. One, a daughter, died at age seven."

"I wonder if the guy we spotted from a distance standing here is part of the Belmont family?"

"Maybe." Elizabeth leaned down for a closer look, pointing. "There's a wooden cross somebody set against Zachariah's headstone." She studied it, waving gnats out of her face. "Mike, take a look at his."

He knelt down beside her and she said, "It's hand-carved. And it appears to be made out of the same kind of wood used for the bowl and plate."

"Let's see." He put on gloves, lifting the wooden plate from the paper sack. He picked up the cross, holding it in his left hand while holding the

80

plate in his right hand. "You have a sharp eye, Elizabeth Monroe. I'm no expert in woodworking, but this looks like the same wood, maybe the wood from the cross is older. Check out the striation in the grain, the slate gray color pattern. As much as I hate removing a cross from a grave, I'll take this to the lab, too."

Elizabeth nodded. "There's a boot print. It looks like the tread pattern is similar, if not identical, to the print we saw near Cindy's grave."

Bradford moved closer, knelt down and studied the impression. He used his phone to take a picture. "It definitely looks the same. I'll have the lab compare prints."

"Is this the kind of thing where you'd pour a mold?"

Bradford stood and smiled. "I do think you have what it takes to be a detective."

"Just curious."

"Right now the photos will do for comparison purposes. If we'd found the boot print at the actual crime scene, that would be a different story. And if it matched the one at Cindy's grave and these old graves…pay dirt."

"Then, most likely, we'd have our killer. But, we have some evidence just as good, maybe better."

"What's that?"

"The wooden plate and earring in those bags. The plate definitely looks like the same wood as the bowl left at the crime scene. That's probably Cindy's missing earring. The killer is taunting us. He's bold. Brazen. And I bet he was one of the people who attended Cindy's funeral and burial. There were more than one hundred fifty people here. I believe he was one of them."

"Maybe he's the guy we saw standing by these old graves."

Elizabeth looked down at the boot print. "The groundskeeper wore boots, but he said he hasn't been by this grave recently. It rained two nights ago. That's a fresh print."

"I can get a court order to pick up the groundkeeper's boots. But even if his boot pattern matches this, it doesn't mean he killed Cindy. He's all over this place. His boot prints would be here."

"He seemed almost too calm talking to you."

"Do you believe he was being deceptive?"

"In some areas. I think he saw that dish on Cindy's grave. Maybe he didn't want to tell us because he doesn't want to be called in as a witness."

"I can bring him in for further questioning."

"We do know that whoever was standing by these graves left in that pickup truck."

"I'll look at vehicle registration records. I could get lucky and find a pickup truck registered to a man with the last name of Belmont in the area."

They walked back to the parking lot in silence, Elizabeth lost in her thoughts, Bradford not wanting to encroach. He stopped at his car, opened the trunk and put the paper bags inside. He turned to Elizabeth. She had her back to him, hugging her chest, viewing the sunset as it reflected its fire into the bellies of the clouds.

Bradford moved closer to Elizabeth. He watched her follow the profile of an eagle in flight. Elizabeth felt his presence, but she didn't turn around. He remained quiet allowing her to stay in the moment as long as she needed. After the eagle melted into the crevices of a twilight sky, Elizabeth turned to Bradford. She inhaled deeply through her nostrils and said, "The earring placed in the center of the wooden dish…"

"Yes, what about it?"

"Molly's killer removed one of her earrings as a souvenir. But he hasn't displayed it, at least not in public…this guy did with Cindy's earring."

"What are you saying?"

"Besides the earrings, and the deaths of two girls—Cindy and my daughter, Molly, what's the common denominator?"

"What?"

"Me. I don't think the man who killed Molly is the same man who killed Cindy. But I think there is some sort of a connection."

Bradford took in a deep breath, the smell of rain in the distance. "If that's true…why? Unless some sick loser has a helluva vendetta against you."

"I don't know. I wish I did."

"Maybe we can discuss it over some food. I'm starving. I think a tad better with food in my stomach. Hopefully, we'll come up with something."

"Thanks, but I can't tonight. It's Wednesday. I have to meet an old family friend, someone I've known since I was a little girl." Elizabeth smiled at him. "Go on, Mike, get something to eat. You've had a long day. It's Cindy

Carter's first night in a place she should not have been for another seventy years. My heart is so heavy right now. I just want to stand here for a few moments, alone."

"Don't stay out here too long. Like the groundskeeper said, lots of weird stuff happens in a cemetery as old as this one. Something else, if Cindy's killer and Molly's killer are somehow connected, you aren't safe."

"I'll be okay."

"You don't have to—"

"I'll be fine, Mike. I just need a few minutes. Talk with you tomorrow."

"All right. Just be careful." Bradford turned and walked to his car. He got behind the wheel and watched her for a few seconds, and then he slowly drove away.

Elizabeth looked at the historic cemetery, thinking about Cindy and what a delight she was to have as a student. The tall headstones were silhouettes in the dwindling day, a low-hanging sky squeezing drops of blood orange pulp from the sunset. Moss hung from old oaks like lamb's wool drenched in halos of light—the fabled Golden Fleece at twilight in a Mississippi graveyard. Some of the oaks had been standing when bodies of Confederate soldiers were buried nearby.

Elizabeth walked back toward Cindy's grave. Within seconds, following some hushed call of the wild, fireflies arose in unison from the pine straw and milkweed. Their nocturnal flight was a slow waltz above the cemetery grounds, the night chorus of crickets and toads in a singsong harmony. Elizabeth stared, almost without blinking, as shadows moved.

A face.

It was as fleeting as a shooting star. Gone before truly perceptible. Not a human face, but rather the way shadows stirred across the trunk of an ancient oak. For a moment, Elizabeth thought she saw a face in the gnarls and pits of aged bark. A somber face that seemed carved from the collective sorrow and pain of young soldiers who were torn in half from minie balls fired into their dreams, of families decimated by the death of a child. A parent's sorrow from the untimely death of a child had no expiration date. That she knew well.

Elizabeth looked at Cindy's grave and whispered, "He's out there, Cindy, and we'll find him."

There was the sound of a rustling in the trees. Elizabeth stepped back from the grave, squinting in the leftovers of light. A great horned owl flew from a low branch in a pine, alighting on the shoulders of an angel statue next to an old grave. The angel sculpture was on one knee, head bowed, wings folded, a mist rising around the graves.

Elizabeth watched the owl, it's head turning slowly, yellow eyes almost the size of egg yolks, blinking once. She said, "Don't be afraid, ghosts…it's only me." She smiled and walked back to the parking lot.

Standing next to her car, Elizabeth turned around and watched the fireflies play tag, reminding her of childhood—summer games of hide and seek at twilight with her brother. Tonight the pale orbs of light moved across the faces of aged tombstones, timeworn inscriptions faded, chiseled long ago by ghostwriters.

TWENTY-FOUR

Elizabeth checked her rearview mirror more than she wanted to. She drove though Hattiesburg, warm food boxed in the seat beside her, the scent of meatloaf and sweet potatoes. She glanced in the mirror, watching headlights, looking at cars behind her. When one turned off, she felt a slight release of tension in her chest. She made the drive every Wednesday, but tonight she went a different way, taking a few extra streets, checking the mirror.

Finally there were no cars behind her as she navigated her way beyond the Hattiesburg city limits. She thought about the funeral, Cindy's parents, the college boys she'd spoken to, the plate on Cindy's grave, and the cross she and Bradford had found on Zachariah Belmont's grave.

She whispered, "You sick shit."

The small, 1960's clapboard house was on the outskirts of Hattiesburg, a single yellow light burning above the front door to the screened porch. Elizabeth pulled into the gravel drive, parked under a sycamore tree and walked to the door. A wisteria plant grew on one side of the house, pendulous lavender flowers swaying in the breeze, the sweet fragrance of vanilla in the night air. She entered a screened porch, stepped to the front door, knocked and waited.

"Be right there." The voice came from inside the old home. The door opened and an elderly black woman stepped out in a wash of creamy light from her house. She flipped on a porch light and grinned. Nellie Culpepper had streaks of gray hair showing near the red bandana she wore. The wrinkles on her round face disappeared for a moment when she saw Elizabeth and grinned, her dark eyes beaming. "Baby girl, I thought you done forgot all 'bout me t'night." She hugged Elizabeth.

"Nellie, I've been coming to your house almost every Wednesday since you turned seventy-four and that was four years ago." She held up the Styrofoam package. "I brought us dinner. One of your favorites—meatloaf, gravy, sweet potatoes and green beans."

The old woman grinned. "Thank you, child. It's a lovely evening. Let's sit out here on the porch and eat." The wooden floor creaked. Baskets of ferns and begonias hung from the eaves. "You sit in your favorite rocker. I'll get us some tea. Then we can eat." Nellie set the food down on a small wooden table and went back inside.

Elizabeth trailed in the house a few seconds later, calling to Nellie, "While you grab the tea, I'm going to wash my hands." Passing through the living room, she stopped and looked at the framed pictures on the table. One was of Martin Luther King. One was an artist depiction of Christ, and a smaller photo was of Elizabeth as a girl and her older brother, Nathan, in their back yard near a large weeping willow tree, Nellie standing next to them. Big smiles.

Back outside, Elizabeth stood for a moment, crickets chirping in the night, a dog barking one street away. Elizabeth licked her dry lips and looked at a quarter moon through the wisteria.

Nellie returned with two canning jars filled with ice and sweet tea. She handed one to Elizabeth and said, "Food smells good. You get it from the sto'e—Sam's market?"

"They make the best meatloaf and pot roast." Elizabeth opened one of the Styrofoam boxes and handed it to Nellie. "Here you go. It's still warm."

Nellie slowly unfolded a white paper napkin, tucking it under her collar, the knuckles in her fingers the size of walnuts, joints swollen from arthritis. They sat in the rockers, food on their laps. Nellie reached over, took Elizabeth's hand, and bowed her head. "God, we sure 'nough thank you for this food and providin' for us. Thank you, Jesus, for keepin' this precious child, Liz'beth, safe. Lord, we love you. Amen."

Elizabeth squeezed Nellie's hand and said, "Amen." They dined in silence for a moment. Nellie ate a fork full of green beans followed by a bite of cornbread. Elizabeth asked, "How was your day, Nellie? You get your last insurance check?"

"I did. Sho'nough took 'em a long spell to get it to me. God called my husband Rudyard home 'bout a year ago." She took a small bite of meatloaf, chewing slowly, her thoughts veiled.

Elizabeth found it hard to eat. She glanced at the old woman. "The first funeral I ever attended, you were there with me, Nellie. I attended another one today." Elizabeth glanced at her brother in the framed photo she had carried from the living room and set on the small table. "You held my hand when they buried Nathan. My own mother didn't have near your strength. But then again, she'd just lost her son. You were always a rock for Nathan and me. I've never forgotten what you said to me the day of his funeral. You leaned down and whispered in my ear." Nellie looked over at Elizabeth as she continued. "You said, 'Lizzy, the car may have killed your brother, Nathan, but he's just learning to live in God's little playground. You said tears from the heart are never wasted, and you don't ever rust shedding them for others. You allowed me to grieve."

Nellie nodded, looked up at the moon shining through the screen. "I thank the Lord I had a chance to help take care of you and Nathan when y'all was growin' up. After your daddy started comin' home less and less, your mama just seemed to get worst with her sickness."

"You can call it like it was. She was mentally ill. Looking back, she had all the classic systems. I thought her spiral down was caused when Nathan was killed. But that was one of many things." Elizabeth set her food aside. "When Mom took her life, I knew she'd been hurting bad. I just didn't know how to help her."

"You were a child, Liz'beth. There was nothin' you could have done."

"I still resent her for doing it. It was too easy. Just take handfuls of pills, followed by half a bottle of vodka and close your eyes." She paused, looked over at the old woman. "I found her on the couch. She actually seemed at peace, almost as if a slight smile was on her lips. Sometimes I wonder if there are really happy endings. At times the start, even the middle of a journey, are both blissful...but the endings are often brutal. Ugly."

"What happened, Liz'beth? What happened to you that have your feathers flyin' today? Was it on account of the funeral you tol' me about? Who died?"

"One of my students, a girl, was murdered. She had such promise, such a big and compassionate heart. Someone tortured and killed her. I spoke with her parents after the funeral. Nellie, I wanted to comfort and assure them that their daughter didn't die in vain and that her killer would be brought to justice. But the words didn't come easy, and I don't know if they rang true for them."

"Just you bein' there spoke to their hearts. I s'pect you are feelin' this way 'cause of what happened to Molly, too."

Elizabeth set her tea on the table. "You were like a grandmother to Molly. She loved walking around the yard with you, filling the bird feeders. She was mesmerized the day you stood near your sunflowers. You held out your hand and a butterfly landed on your finger. I remember you slowly reaching for Molly's little hand and placing the butterfly on her finger. I wish I'd had a camera when it happened."

"But you got the picture in your mind 'cause it's in your heart. That means you can see it anytime you wont to. I know you still grieve for Molly. You will forever. My grandmother tol' me life is like the ocean. Sometimes it's choppy. Sometimes the water is flat. Whatever it is, you just got to keep your head above water. You're a strong swimmer, Liz'beth. Always was."

"I remember you talking about your grandmother. She lived in Waynesboro. You said she picked cotton until her fingers bled."

"She grew up in the shanties, quarters, not far from a big plantation. She picked cotton, beans, and sweet taters. I look at the tater on my plate and remember how hard she had to work." Nellie glanced at her sweet potato and then looked over at Elizabeth. "You ever heard of Mississippi's hangin' bridge?"

"No, Nellie. And by the expression on your face, I can tell it's something close to home for you."

"My grandma had to learn how to swim against the current. Her older cousins were two of four people they hung from a bridge over the Chickasawhay River near Shubuta. Called it the hangin' bridge 'cause some black folk were lynched there. The first time was in nineteen hundred and eighteen. Anyway, as I was saying, the two girls were my grandma's cousins. They also kilt two teenage boys that first time. All on account of an angry mob, blamin' 'em for a killin' they didn't do. There was no trial. They just hunted 'em down, carried 'em out to the bridge and lynched 'em. Both the girls were pregnant. So those men really killed six people that day."

"I'm so sorry. Why didn't you ever tell me?"

"It was such a long time ago. When Old Death eventually come callin' for the men that did the killins', he musta had a big grin on his face 'cause the devil was callin' his due. The men traded their souls to Satan. And sooner or later, he gets what's owed him."

"What ever happened to your grandmother?"

"She met a fine fella, a man who was a stone mason; he could lay bricks and build big houses. He was my grandfather. They lived on a little farm south of Waynesboro. They had six chillens. And one of 'em was my mama. The hangin' bridge been closed down for years and years. I heard it's all rusted out. Funny thing, though."

"What's that, Nellie?"

"The county caught a fella takin' out some of the wooden planks. I heard he was makin' little crosses out of the wood."

Elizabeth sat higher in the rocker. "Crosses? What was he doing with them?"

"Some folks say he was puttin' them on the graves of the people who done the lynchin'—one cross at a time. My brother, James, heard 'bout it. I think the po'leese ran the man off. But lots of peoples go out on that o'l bridge, 'specially at Halloween time. Some folks got no respect for the dead."

"Do you remember the man's name?"

"No, don't want to neither. What kind of a man puts a cross on the grave of men who hung pregnant women? The babies died kickin' in their mama's stomachs as those girls hung from ropes over a river."

TWENTY-FIVE

On the drive home, Elizabeth thought about what Nellie had told her. The image of pregnant women hanging from a river bridge wasn't one that easily faded. She drove and instinctively touched her own stomach, envisioning Molly's face as a toddler. Elizabeth deeply inhaled, rain beginning to fall. She called Detective Bradford. "I know it's getting late, Mike, but you gave me your number and said call anytime."

"It's not late. Anytime means just that."

"I had dinner with an elderly women who was my family's housekeeper, more of a nanny actually, when I was a girl. Her name's Nellie Culpepper. She practically raised my brother and me. During part of the conversation, she was telling me about her grandmother and mentioned a bridge near Shubuta, a place where some people were lynched many years ago."

"I'm familiar with the bridge, and some of its history. The county closed it decades ago. Nothing much left, except a rusted and sad testament into Mississippi's past."

"Nellie told me that someone, a man—had removed wooden planks off the old bridge and carved them into crosses. She said he'd left them on the graves of the men responsible for the lynching. Maybe we can do some research and track down this guy."

"Do you know if he was arrested?"

"She said he was given a warning, probably for trespassing on condemned property."

"I'll see what I can dig up."

"Mike, what if the cross we found on Zachariah Belmont's grave came from that old bridge? What if this guy is the one leaving the wooden bowl and plate? And what if Zachariah Belmont was one of the people in the lynch mob? Nellie said it happened in 1918. According to Belmont's gravestone, he was very much alive and kicking during that period."

"If all this has some bearing on Cindy's death, I'd be surprised. It'd be a hell of a coincidence—your former housekeeper-nanny talks about her family history and mentions the bridge and some nut who stole wood to make crosses. It's worth a look, but right now I have a strong suspect."

"Who?"

"You met him. Gerald Simpson. We checked his credit card records. He recently bought a stun gun, about a week before Cindy was killed."

"Really? Okay…what do you do next?"

"Bring him in for questioning again. As I mentioned, I'd like for you to observe. Also, I'm going to find Larry Tucker wherever he lives. I want to see if there are signs of any evidence of satanic stuff around his place. He's the kid that hung around the Kappa house long enough to become persona non grata. I hear he's about as Goth as they come, wears clothes like Henry Ford painted cars—all in black."

"When do you want me to come by the station?"

"Monday. Should be around one o'clock. Can you be there?"

"My class ends at noon. I'll be there as soon as I can after that."

"Another thing…Cindy requested a ride-share, Kars. When the driver got there, he said he received a cancellation. Just in case she changed her mind, he said he waited outside the Kappa house for a few minutes. He said it was raining so hard he figured she'd decided not to go. He left, never seeing Cindy."

"At least that's what he's telling you."

"Guy's name is Tim Bledsoe. We're running background checks. So far, he's clean. Not even a traffic ticket. Probably makes him a good ride-share driver. We'll get a court order to impound his car to check for forensics."

"I'm almost home. It may sound a little paranoid, but do you mind staying on the line for a minute. Just give me long enough to make sure there's no surprises in my mailbox."

"Absolutely."

"Good." She parked at the end of her drive, checked her mailbox. Nothing. Got back in her car. When she pulled in her driveway, she saw it. Her headlights swept across the front porch, and there on the top step, sat Jack the cat. He was motionless, staring out into the night like a bronze statue of an ancient Egyptian cat, poised, ready to be adored, maybe even worshipped.

"Damn, Jack's back."

"What? Who's Jack? You need me to drive to your place?"

In spite of her unease, Elizabeth smiled. "No, it's okay. Jack's a stray cat who wants to hang out at my house. He's reminds me of Garfield."

"Elizabeth, I've got an emergency call coming in. I gotta go. Call me anytime. And I mean anytime, day or night, for anything. Okay?"

"Okay…thanks." She disconnected, parked in her driveway and walked up to her front porch. Jack watched her, eyes contented, his head turning just enough to follow her approach. When she stopped at the bottom step, he mewed once as if he were saying hello.

Elizabeth moved her purse strap to her shoulders. "So, you're back. Maybe Jack isn't the best name for you. How about freeloader? Moocher? Don't you have some better place to be than on my front porch? Don't you miss your happy family?"

The cat was motionless, slowly blinked its big yellow-green eyes. Elizabeth shook her head. "Okay, Jack, but this is your last night. I'm taking your picture and plastering it everywhere. I've already eaten, thank you, but I think I can throw together some turkey bites for you."

She unlocked the front door, Jack trotting inside, walking around her, jumping up on the same stool next to the kitchen counter. Elizabeth set her purse down and stepped into the kitchen, Jack's eyes following her every move. She opened the refrigerator and removed the package of turkey meat, tore off several pieces and placed them in a bowl.

"Okay, Jack. Dinnertime." She set the plastic bowl on the floor. The cat dropped down, took his time approaching it, looked up at Elizabeth and began eating. "You'll never be accused of eating your food too fast."

Elizabeth poured water into another bowl for the cat, filled her glass with red wine, and sat at her kitchen table watching him eat. She placed her palms down flat on the table, looking at her nails. She closed her eyes for a brief moment. The day's events, like a time-lapse movie trailer, played at rifling speed behind her eyes.

Jack finished eating and jumped up on Elizabeth's lap, purring. "You're a charmer, mister Jack. I wonder how old you are. Old enough to know better I bet. Somehow I can't see you bothering to chase a mouse. I have to find the family that you belong to. You can only couch surf here for a little while and then it's back to your former life, got that?"

Jack looked at her through sleepy eyes. Elizabeth opened her laptop. "I need to do some research. Going all the way back to 1918 in South Mississippi, a bridge over the Chickasawhay River and people who were hung from that bridge." She keyed events and dates, stopping to read and following key words. She read eyewitness accounts of the group lynching, an NAACP report, and news stories. The more she read, the more outraged she became.

"Jack, this is awful. Four people, two teenage girls—both pregnant and two young men, were hung from the bridge. They were suspects in a murder, but they never had a trial. An angry mob took them from the small jail in Shubuta out to the bridge and hung them, putting the ropes around their necks and throwing them off the bridge. It says one teenage girl had to be thrown off twice because she grabbed a steel girder preventing her from falling to her death at the end of a rope. One of the girls was two weeks from delivering her child. A worker at the funeral house said after the teenager's death, her unborn baby was still moving in her stomach."

Elizabeth had to look away. She closed her eyes for a second, her palms moist. She inhaled deeply and continued reading, clicking further into the history of the old bridge. "Jack, if the lynchings in 1918 weren't enough, two teenage boys were hung from the same bridge twenty-five years later in 1942, never given a trial. Hence the name, the hanging bridge."

She paused, eyes scanning the pages. "Going back to 1918, it looks like one of the leaders of the lynch mob was a fire and brimstone preacher by the name of Zachariah Belmont. Bingo. It says Belmont was a leader in the Ku Klux Klan up until his death in 1927. So now we know something about the man buried in that grave. What we don't know is where the wood came from to make that cross lying against his tombstone…and who put it there. I'll dig further into the past." She keyed in cross-reference words, phrases and read, her eyes moving quickly across the screen.

Elizabeth's phone buzzed. She stared at it next to her untouched glass of wine. Somehow the buzzing sounded alien, out of sync with Jack's purring sounds. She reached for the phone, looked at the caller ID. Nothing there. She looked at the text message.

Did you find the earring? He left it for you.

Elizabeth sucked in a breath, her heart pounding. She looked for the phone number connected to the message. There was nothing. Untraceable. Anonymous sender.

As if it had been sent from a ghost.

TWENTY-SIX

The next morning Elizabeth awoke early to do something she hadn't done in twenty-five years—shoot a gun. She showered, brushed her wet hair, applied minimal makeup, lipstick, and found Jack sleeping on her couch. The cat barely lifted his head when she came down the steps and entered the family room.

Elizabeth smiled. "See, you are a couch surfer. Are you hungry?" Jack yawned and came to his feet. "First things first." Elizabeth used her phone to snap a picture of Jack. "So you don't like having your picture taken in the morning. I can relate."

She emailed the image to herself, opened her laptop on the kitchen table and used Photoshop to design a flyer. "Found cat and my number ought to do it." She glanced up as Jack slithered down from the couch and slowly made his way into the kitchen. Elizabeth smiled. "Don't look at me like that. You won't be here long enough for me to buy a litter box for you. It's outside, Jack."

She looked back at her computer, hit print and heard the printer in her home office printing copies. She walked in the room, picked up a dozen colored flyers and returned, Jack now on this favorite stool, staring at the bowl on the floor.

Elizabeth opened a cupboard. "You're probably getting tired of turkey. How about some tuna? It's white albacore."

Jack lifted his head, staring at the can she held. She opened it and spooned some tuna into his bowl. He picked up his step, almost hustling to the food. "Ahhh, looks like I found something that gets your pulse up. Such a guy thing—begins with the stomach." She smiled, watching Jack eat. When he finished, she picked up her purse, the flyers and Jack under one arm. She set him on the top step of the front porch, locking the door behind them.

Jack sat and looked around the yard, paying no attention to a cardinal in a dogwood tree a few feet from the porch. Elizabeth said, "Okay, this is it. No roaming the neighborhood, playing Tomcat and coming back to my place to rest between your romantic rendezvous. Go home. I'm going to spread your most wanted poster to pet stores, convenience stores, and maybe the post office right up there with the FBI's most wanted. So if you come back, I hope your rightful owner will be a phone call away to come pick you up."

Elizabeth stepped around Jack, got in her car and started down the driveway. When she looked in her rearview mirror, Jack was gone. Then she looked at the flyers on her front seat. "You do take a handsome picture. Maybe I'll keep one of these just for old times sake."

— —

Detective Bradford and his partner, Detective Ed Milton, approached the small home with caution. It was a 1970's ranch style, sitting a hundred feet off a cul-de-sac in a Hattiesburg's neighborhood—one that was stuck in a time warp of tattered homes and unkempt, weedy yards. The detectives parked near the drive, leaving their car in the street, walking up the driveway. Bradford spotted an older Toyota Prius near the house. He said, "That's Larry Tucker's car. He shares this dump with two other guys, all students."

Detective Milton said, "I can almost smell the meth cookin' from out here."

"Maybe they're just typical college kids scraping by, working shitty jobs and trying to figure ways to pay off student loans for careers somebody else picked for them. But we do know that Larry Tucker was arrested once for battery on a girlfriend. Reason enough for a search warrant, at least in my book."

"Back at you. We've got to find this sick prick, whoever he is. Not a lot of people want to do this job. It's certainly not about the pay. Nobody in my family said go for it son. Go make a difference."

"You've made a difference, Ed. You've taken a lot of bad dudes off the street."

"But some judge who couldn't cut it as a lawyer, sits in a robe and releases them for time served."

The side door to the house opened. Both detectives stopped, Milton reaching inside his coat, his hand on the grip of a .44 sidearm. Larry Tucker stepped outside, didn't see the two detectives. He was dressed in black—a black Australian bush hat, ninja pants and a hoodie, unzipped, alabaster white chest and flat stomach. Skinny enough to see ribs. No shoes. A small teardrop piece of glass hung from a necklace around his neck. Inside the glass was a dark red liquid, the appearance of blood.

As Tucker carried a plastic trash bag to a garbage can, the detectives approached.

Bradford said, "Good morning."

Tucker jumped and whipped around toward them, still holding the bag, his eyes guarded, narrow face flushed. "Who are you?"

"I'm Detective Bradford. This is my partner, Detective Milton. We'd like to ask you a few questions. Let's start off with your name. Are you Larry Tucker?"

"Yeah…."

"Anybody in the house?"

"No." He looked at the house and back at the detectives.

"Where are your roommates?"

"At work."

"Do you work?"

"When I can. School keeps me pretty busy."

Detective Milton nodded, his eyes scanning the yard, ragweed and dandelions growing from parched crabgrass, cigarette butts on patches of hard ground. "We're investigating the death of Cindy Carter. You knew her, didn't you?"

Tucker lowered the trash bag to near his feet, toenails long, curved and dirty. "I hardly knew her. Met her at the Kappa house once. Saw her at school a couple of times."

Bradford smiled. "Was she all about the Greek thing…you know, sorority and fraternities all the time?" He looked at a tattoo of a coiled cobra, on

Tucker's right forearm, the snake's eyes blood red. A mosquito alighted on the head of the snake tattoo.

Tucker slapped his arm and said, "I don't know. I probably didn't say more than a few words to her."

"Is that because she is one of those girls who believe they're too good for regular guys who have to work at Pizza Hut to pay their way through school."

"How'd you know I worked there?"

"That's what we do. We know the fellas at the Kappa house only kept you around because they wanted you to help them with their studies. But they're just a bunch of dumb jock types. Somehow, though, they always get the pretty girls, know what I mean?"

Tucker said nothing, staring at the detectives, black flies buzzing around the loosely tied garbage bag.

The detectives stepped closer, watching Tucker's hands. "What do you want? Like I told you, I didn't know Cindy Carter very well."

Detective Bradford nodded. "But as a student, you hear stuff. What's the story? Maybe a pissed off boyfriend? What have you heard?"

"Nothing. Nobody tells me anything. And that's cool. I don't give a crap anyway."

"Where were you last Friday?"

"Umm, I was here doing homework and then went to work."

"Anyone with you?"

"No."

Something caught Detective Milton's eye. He looked over Tucker's shoulder. A curtain moved. He said, "You said nobody was home. Who's in the house?"

Tucker said nothing, a vein pulsing in his neck.

Bradford held a piece of paper close to Tucker, the smell of burnt marijuana on his clothes. "This is a warrant to search your place. Now, do you want to tell us who the hell is in there? If not, we'll have the house surrounded by heavily armed officers in a matter of minutes."

TWENTY-SEVEN

Elizabeth held her purse in one hand and a carried a bag with a gun in the other. She wore dark glasses as she approached her car in the parking lot of a sporting goods store. She unlocked the door and got inside. She placed the Smith & Wesson in the glove box and called Detective Bradford.

— • —

Bradford glanced at his phone as he and Detective Milton walked behind Larry Tucker to the door of the house. Elizabeth Monroe calling. He answered and said, "Elizabeth, I'm serving a search warrant. Can I ring you back in a minute?"

"He sent a chilling text message to me."

"Who?"

"The man who killed Cindy…maybe Molly. In the message, he asked if we found the earring—Cindy's earring. Then he wrote *he* left if for us, but he wasn't referring to himself. He was referring to someone else, as if he'd told someone to do it."

Bradford looked at Larry Tucker who quickly shoved his hands in his ninja sweats, a trace of perspiration above his lip. Bradford asked, "When did you receive it?"

"Late last night."

"Where are you?" He glanced at Detective Milton, impatience growing on his partner's face.

"I'm heading to a gun range."

"You bought a handgun?"

"Yes. Mike, somehow I think this is connected to that old bridge with the horrible history. Maybe this guy has a follower or followers—someone who carries out his bidding. I did some research—the grave we found, Zachariah Belmont, he was one of the mob leaders who hung four people, two pregnant, off the bridge near Shubuta. He was a Klan leader during that period up until his death."

Bradford's jawline hardened, his eyes darting from his partner to Tucker. "Elizabeth, I'll call you back." He disconnected and glared at Tucker. "Let's go inside. We'll chat and have a little look around. Probably be smart if you didn't made a sudden move. Anything much beyond a sneeze makes me anxious."

Milton tapped Tucker on the back. "Lead the way, and tell your girlfriend to stand in an open room with her hands where we can see them."

Tucker shook his head. "This is like some Nazi crap."

Milton said, "Go inside. I'm not going to say it again."

They followed Tucker into the kitchen. He said, "Caitlyn, the cops are here. They want you to come out of the bedroom."

The detectives looked around the kitchen, glasses and plates piled on the counter. Sink full of dishes, the smell of rotting garbage and marijuana. A pizza box was opened on the small kitchen table—a brown roach crawled across a hard piece of crust, the insect's antenna lively.

Bradford could hear someone walking from a bedroom into a TV room. He stepped around Tucker and saw a girl wearing a long black turtleneck shirt, ripped jeans, dark red lipstick, heavy black eyeliner on a sickly pale face, pink hair the color and coarseness of cotton candy. He motioned for her to step into the kitchen. He could see her pupils were dilated. Sunlight from the opening in the curtains seemed to bother her eyes.

"Caitlyn, I'm Detective Bradford and this is Detective Milton. We're investigating the murder of Cindy Carter. Did you know her?"

She stared at him like she was watching fish in tank. Then she shook her head. "No, I never hung out with her?"

"But you knew her?"

"No, I knew of her. Larry said he heard one of the students was murdered."

"What else did he tell you?"

She glanced at Tucker and then looked at Bradford. "Nothing. If you think Larry is in some way responsible…you're so totally fuckin' wrong. He's a pacifist and a vegan. He wouldn't kill a fly."

Detective Milton said, "Or a roach."

Bradford said, "Let's all step in the living room and sit." Tucker exhaled and complied, walking with the girl into the larger room, sitting on a cracked and worn leather couch. "Detective Milton is gonna chat with y'all while I take a look around this lovely place."

Milton nodded. "Try not to catch anything."

TWENTY-EIGHT

Elizabeth aimed for the chest. The paper target was twenty feet away from her. She paid her fee and stood in the last shooting lane in an indoor gun range, ear and eye protection on, her target in sight. She remembered back to a summer on her grandparent's farm—her grandfather setting up more than two-dozen cans. He'd fought in WWII. Never talked about the war, but Elizabeth had a feeling he'd seen heavy combat. His eyes were steel gray, the color of a gun barrel. Behind those eyes was a padlocked tragedy that was not to be shared.

He'd been patient. Coaching her. Getting Elizabeth used to guns. Teaching her respect and how to use a pistol like it was an extension of her hand. By the end of that summer, she'd become an expert.

On the range today, she took a breath and held it, remembering what the old man had taught her. *'Liz, never pull a trigger. Always press it. And hold the gun as still as possible while you're doing it.'*

She fired. Lowered the pistol, took a breath and fired again. Shooting five rounds, each bullet hitting the black-silhouetted target in the chest area.

Three men, friends, stood a few lanes away preparing to shoot. One man watched Elizabeth firing, her expelled brass hitting the glass partition between the adjacent unoccupied shooter's lanes. The man, whiskers like steel wool, mid-forties, baseball cap low over his eyes, said to his pal, "She's got a good eye. Looks like her pattern is pretty tight."

The friend, large and fleshy, grinned. "She's got a tight ass, too. Hate for her to get pissed at me. She'd shoot your balls off."

"You gotta grow a pair first." He grinned.

Elizabeth lowered her pistol, setting it on the bench near her. She removed the earplugs and glasses, hitting the button to retrieve the paper target. Within a few seconds, the target moved up the lane toward her. She removed it, holding the target toward an overhead light, the five bullet holes all within six inches of the center.

She placed a new target in the holder and hit the button to fire at a greater distance.

— —

Detective Bradford walked down a hallway, wooden floor creaking. The AC was off and the house smelled of sour air and smoked pot, dust on the furniture. He entered a bedroom, the bed unmade, pillowcases stained tobacco yellow from sweat and hair oil. Socks and other clothes were strewn about the room. A pentagram hung on a wall. He poked around the room, looking in corners and the closet. He did the same in the next two rooms, all in need of a deep cleaning.

He stepped over to one side of the last room, a video console on a table, monitor on with an image of a flying dragon stationary on the screen. Some of the games were scattered over the table, condensation on a can of Monster Energy, the water droplets pooling at the base of the can and soaking into the wood. He looked at the labels of the video games: *Bioshock, Manhunt,* and *Wrath of the Gods.*

Bradford heard a movement.

He whirled around. Nothing.

The sound came again—from the opposite side of the bed, facing the wall. He placed his hand on the grip of his pistol and walked around the bed. Something, maybe a box, was hidden under a dirty sheet. He reached down and slowly lifted the sheet. It covered a cage. Bradford stared at the creature, not sure if it was dead or alive.

A bat hung by one foot from the top of the cage. It turned its head, chocolate eyes looking directly at Bradford, blinked once. The bat was about the size of his hand, feces splatted on a newspaper in the bottom of the cage.

Bradford placed the sheet back on the cage and exited, walking to the living room.

When he entered the room, Larry Tucker said, "There's like nothing here. Sure, the place is a little messy, but three guys live here, and we're all really busy."

Bradford said, "Who's the batman in your house?"

"The bat's mine. I caught him in our garage. Thought I'd keep him as a pet."

Bradford shook his head. "Bats don't make good pets. They can carry disease."

Tucker smiled, "People can carry more diseases."

"Oh, geez…you have a greater chance of getting rabies from a bat bite than a people bite. You need to get better at playing your odds. Looks like we interrupted your video game. Your energy drink is getting warm on your game table. Do you play often?"

"Not as much as I used to."

He half smiled, glancing at the girl. "I see. What's your favorite… *Bioshock, Manhunter* or *Wrath of the Gods?*"

"You really wanna to talk to me about video games, why?"

"Why not? Some of the guys at the Kappa house play them with you?"

"I know my rights. You may have a search warrant, but that doesn't mean I have to answer your questions."

"No, but if you don't here, you will at the station, and you'll stay down there until we're done. Now, you can either talk to us here or there. Which will it be?"

He blew out a hard breath, looked at his long fingernails. "Here, I guess."

"Good. Did you play video games with any of the guys at the Kappa house?"

"I played a few times with Alex Davidson. But it's been awhile."

"I'm betting *Wrath of the Gods* is your favorite."

Tucker cut his eyes up at Bradford, a bemused expression on his face. "I like them all." He scratched at the mosquito bite on his tattooed arm.

Bradford sat in a hardback chair across from Tucker and the girl. Detective Milton's phone vibrated. He looked at the caller ID, stepping back near the front door. Bradford leaned closer, shifting his gaze from the girl to Tucker. "Are you two Satanists?"

Tucker smiled. "Just 'cause we don't dress like you, and I have a pet bat, you think we're Satanists? That's freakin' weird."

"No, what's weird is what I've seen around here. Pentagram posters on walls, an inverted cross on the cover of one of your video games, a vial of blood hanging from your necklace, a tat of a snake with red eyes on your arm, and a caged bat in your room. These things, added up, are what I'd call unusual."

"You're making a judgment."

Bradford leaned back. "I just follow the evidence."

The girl shifted her weight on the couch. "There's no evidence in here 'cause we didn't do anything."

Detective Milton stepped over to Bradford. "Mike, let's chat a second in the kitchen."

Bradford nodded. They walked toward the kitchen, stopping near the open entrance. Bradford could see Tucker and the girl in his peripheral vision. "What do think? Are we done here with these two?"

"He knows more than he's willing to tell us."

Milton shook his head. "He even speaks in staccato, almost like a character in a damn video game."

"How would you know that?"

"My son's fourteen. Oh, by the way, the lab's got a report back on that honeysuckle found on the vic and the flowers found in Elizabeth Monroe's mailbox. The pollen matches."

TWENTY-NINE

Elizabeth drove south on Interstate 110, toward Biloxi, when Bradford called her. She answered and he said, "I hate to open a conversation with a good-news-bad news scenario, but this is one of those times."

"Can I hear the good news first?"

"Sure. The crime lab has access to some very good forensic botanists. The good news is that they matched the pollen from the flowers found on Cindy Carter's body. The bad news is that it's from the same bunch in your mailbox."

Elizabeth said nothing, driving over the I-110 Bridge across Biloxi Bay, water cobalt blue, the shimmer of the casinos in the distance, her thoughts racing.

"Are you there?" Bradford asked.

"Yes."

"This perp is playing mind games with us. The fact that he murdered one of your students could be a random kill. But when he leaves honey-suckles in your mailbox, pollen that matches what he left on Cindy's body, he's baiting us."

"He's baiting me. For some reason, he wants to punish me. And I don't know why—the text message. The bastard had Cindy's earring. The inference was that he'd directed someone to leave it on her grave. Mike, could the man standing at Zachariah Belmont's grave—in such close proximity to us that day—actually be Cindy's killer? And like Belmont, does he have some kind of cult following that'll do his malicious bidding?"

"If he does, Larry Tucker might be a candidate." Bradford told her about questioning Tucker and what he found in the house. He added, "Tucker is weird. Probably into some kind of satanic or vampire rituals, but he just doesn't seem the type to follow anyone. Cindy's boyfriend, Alex Davidson, is a possibility, considering his strict evangelical upbringing. But the big jock, Gerald Simpson, is by no means a dumb jock. He's got ice water in his veins, and he's deceptive. So who knows? Maybe none of them are connected to the sicko who sent the text message or maybe one of them did it."

"Speaking of the text message, it wasn't linked to a number."

"There are apps that allow anonymous texting. Some freaks use what they call a ghost phone over Wi-Fi, and its essentially untraceable."

"But is this psychopath a college student, or someone with great influence, enough to have others do his bidding?"

"Jilted lovers do some sick stuff. Guys like Larry Tucker, with the proverbial sand kicked in their faces, whisper revenge under their breaths and figure out ways to even the score. Jocks, like Gerald Simpson, can get away with date rape and still be a college football champ the same season."

"But none of that parallels or seems to have a connection to the wooden bowl, the soil in it, and the word wrath. Or even the crosses, if they're part of this. There's something deeper. I still believe it's associated with wrath, as in one of the seven deadly sins. I'd love to know if the cross we found next to Belmont's headstone matches wood from that bridge."

"I don't see how that's linked to Cindy's death. We're talking different counties and historical timelines to a bridge."

"Maybe it's not connected. But psychopaths can stretch or forge the oddest links together. We just have to key into the pattern of behavior. At this point, we shouldn't rule anything out until it reaches a dead end. Oh, did the boot prints we found by Cindy's grave and Belmont's grave match?"

"I sent the boot images to the lab. I should get something very soon."

"Then are you going to the old bridge to see if the planks match the bowl or the cross?"

"It's on my bucket list."

Elizabeth smiled. "You mind if I join you?"

"I don't have a problem with that. I'll simply take a plank from the bridge and test the wood. I doubt if it's on the National Register of Historic Places."

"I'd like to see the bridge."

Bradford said nothing for a few seconds. "Elizabeth, maybe this perp's only connection to you, beside the fact that Cindy was one of your students, is somehow related to your testimony as an expert witness in two of the state's high profile murder trials. He could have researched you, the death of your daughter, and is trying some kind of mimic kills to make you think he was the person who killed Molly."

"What if he was? Maybe, in his twisted mind, it makes sense to come back for me. I just don't know why."

"Can you come meet me for coffee or a light bite? The interrogations are tomorrow. It might be smart for us to talk about it beforehand."

"I can't. I'm almost to Biloxi."

"What are you doing down there? You don't strike me as the gambling type."

"I'll take risks, but not with my money. I'm doing research here."

"Biloxi is where they finally caught serial killer Justin Morrison. It was just a couple of years ago when you were an expert witness at his trial. He tried to fake insanity using the '*I'm hearing voices in my head* defense'."

Elizabeth thought about the wordplay a twisted psychopath used to justify murder. Justin Morrison roamed the Gulf coast along Highway 90 from Biloxi to Gulfport, browsing the casinos, hunting for victims. He looked for high rollers, big winners.

Morrison had lost his house and family due to his addiction to gambling. He blamed the casinos and said the word '*sin*' in casino entitled him to scare people away from gambling. After selecting victims from the casinos, he'd wait, sip bourbon, and then follow them to their cars with a ten-inch serrated knife in his hand.

One victim who survived testified that right before Smith stabbed him in the chest he said: '*You gotta know when to hold them and know when to fold them. Luck runs out sooner or later.*'

Bradford interrupted her thoughts. "You've gone silent again."

"I'm sorry, Mike. I was just thinking about Morrison. I put him through two mental competency interviews. He claimed to have heard voices telling him to *'slaughter the wolves.'* A background check revealed no previous treatments for mental illness. Smith said he was schizophrenic. I drew him in with questions that led to vast inconsistences in his attorney's case for insanity. The fact that Morrison wiped prints and blood off the murder weapon and hid it in the trunk of his wife's car indicated clear thinking with criminal intent."

"And now Justin Morrison is the forty-eighth person on Mississippi's death row. I wonder if it's the high-profile cases, like his and the Zeke Fisher one you testified in, that attract the crazies."

She smiled. "Crazy? Rarely. Mean and narcissistic…just plain evil, most often."

"You mind if I ask what kind of research you can do in a resort—a beach town full of casinos and clubs?"

"The best because places like those entice people from all walks of life. Casinos offer the bells and whistles and the adrenaline rush that some people get when waging real money for the possibility of fantasy money. For some it will go beyond an occasional game of blackjack or roulette to a compulsion and then to a full blown addiction."

"Sounds like a meth user, but there are no drugs."

"The adrenal rush produces dopamine in the body. And that's like a drug."

Bradford pinched the bridge of his nose, slowly exhaling. "So, you're really going to do some people watching in Biloxi?"

"My uncle works at one of the casinos. In his day, he was a legendary gambler. One of the few banned from poker tables in Vegas and Atlantic City. He's semi-retired. Works security at Harrah's."

"It's good to catch up with family."

"I'm here to get a few pointers from him. He has fifty years of reading people, and these are people who try very hard not to be read. I'll be back early tomorrow or late tonight."

"Be careful, Elizabeth. This perp has some extremely warped vendetta problem. As long as he's out there, you're not safe."

THIRTY

As Elizabeth drove past the Hard Rock Casino, Beau Ridge, bars and clubs, she remembered the last time she'd seen her father's brother, Uncle Hal Monroe. It was a year after Molly's funeral. A decade earlier, he was winning more than he was losing in high stakes poker. His luck ran out, and he was mugged in Atlantic City—a parking garage, beaten badly and in rehab for nine moths. A chunk of his winnings paid for his medical bills.

Elizabeth parked beneath one of the bright lights in the casino parking lot. She spent a few seconds looking around the lot, hundreds of cars in a sea of light. She removed the pistol from the console between the seats and placed it under the driver's seat.

Elizabeth got out of her car, looking for security cameras on the light poles. She spotted one of more than a dozen. She looped her purse strap, cross body, from her left shoulder to hold onto with her right hand and walked quickly across the parking lot, checking her watch as she went. She was five minutes early as she glided through the casino doors.

Uncle Hal, dressed in a white shirt with gold cufflinks, blue sports coat and charcoal gray slacks, met her near the entrance. His hair was cotton white, neatly parted. Handsome, tanned round face, smiling blue eyes—he could still turn heads at age 70. They hugged and she said, "Thank you for meeting me."

"It's been too long. How are you Liz? On the phone, you sounded stressed."

She smiled. "You were always excellent in picking up the subtle things. I guess that's what made you a good gambler."

Hal grinned. "Good is a relative term. Luck is really about the law of averages. But skill separates the consistent winners from others." He looked away, the moving lights from the casino twinkling in his eyes. "That's what your father never seemed to grasp. He wanted to one up me, his older brother, but he didn't know when to walk away from the tables. Unfortunately, it took him into a dark place."

"Uncle Hal, I didn't come here to talk about Dad or what happened to him. There's nothing more to say that hasn't been said. You are one of the best in the nation at reading poker players. With knowing the poker tells, you're exceptionally quick to pick up the signs of deception. I've become pretty good at spotting fakes, most on the clinical psychology level and some just by living."

"It's in your DNA, too, Liz. Even as a little girl, you always had amazing powers of observation, especially in areas of human nature."

"Tomorrow, I'm going to be watching detectives question suspects or persons of interest in the brutal murder of a college coed. The killer left her body on display. He placed a wooden bowl on her stomach and scrawled the word *wrath* on her forehead."

"I read about it. Awful, just plain awful."

"The victim was one of my students."

Hal shook his head. "Oh, honey, I'm sorry to hear that."

"So I thought it was worth the short drive down here to spend a little time with you watching some high-stakes poker and hearing some of your commentary about the players."

"We have a couple of big games in session. It won't be a problem to stand in the room and observe. Besides the players, others are in there. Friends or family of the players. Cocktail waitresses, a few employees and, of course, casino security."

"Where are the games held?"

"On the second floor. Some of the high rollers are whales. Some are guys that work the circuit. They're all good. A half-hour in that room, and you'll see why."

THIRTY-ONE

The room was opulent. It had the look and feel of big money. Original Renaissance oil paintings adorned the walls, some of semi-nude women. Near the paintings were framed photos of celebrities and sports stars that had played poker in the room. Soft lights glowed from polished crystal chandeliers. Two ornate poker tables, each with seven lavish chairs, were in opposites ends of the room.

One table had only men in the game. They ranged from guys in their late twenties to old pros in their sixties. A woman, brunette, hair pinned up, high cheekbones, was the dealer. At the other table, six men and one woman were playing, and the dealer was a man.

Elizabeth followed her uncle as he softly walked over the blue and white carpet, stopping about fifteen feet from the table of men. Scantily clad cocktail waitresses brought trays of drinks. Most were fine scotch and whiskey in heavy glassware.

The woman playing at the table sipped red wine. The game was just starting, the dealer quickly moving cards to each player. One man wore a black Stetson. One had a Yankees baseball cap on, diamond stud earring, sports coat with a black T-shirt. Another man had a Van Dyke beard, wore a western shirt and diamond rings.

Hal studied the players. He motioned for Elizabeth to come closer. He leaned in and whispered. "Its important to carefully watch their first look at their hand and the dealer's flop. That will be the most real part of any round.

It's in the eyes, and it's only a millisecond. You blink—you miss it. From then on, poker tells are real and false."

"What do you mean?"

"Some players try to become actors. Some are damn good. Others, well not so much. They'll use physical body language to throw off the other players. The art of the game is reading the bluffs, figuring the odds, and betting accordingly. Some players will toss chips into the pot with a forceful move. He'll keep his hands close to the action. Is it a bluff of a big hand?"

"I wouldn't know."

Hal smiled. "It could be either. So you have to watch the eyes, watch the moment a player looks at the other players right after he sees his hand. Most long or drawn out poker tells are false. There are no rules, but there are patterns. A show of weakness usually means a strong hand. A player portraying strength often means the exact opposite."

"Everything is an act."

"And that's the exciting part of the game. You just have to quickly decide how much merit to give the poker tells from a dealt hand. I'll give you an example."

Elizabeth followed her uncle as he moved around the perimeter of the table. He glanced up at one of the security cameras, his slight nod was less obvious than a poker tell. Elizabeth wondered who was watching the monitors in a secure room and how carefully they watched poker tables compared to blackjack tables.

Hal stopped, observed the betting, and the movement of chips. He whispered to Elizabeth, "Keep an eye on the guy with the Van Dyke beard. See him glance away at the waitress and then look back at the table?"

"Yes."

"That's a tell that indicates a strong hand. He's trying to seem that he's less interested in the game than the girl. Sort of I'm bored, but I'll play."

"Interesting."

"Now, here comes the flop. Watch the guy in the Stetson. See him glance out of the corner of his eye at the other players?"

"Yes."

"See him look at the chips—figuring his bet. Look at the way he quietly, almost methodically, slides his chips into the pot. Next, he'll sit back in his chair. Can you see him moving his tongue on the inside of his cheek?"

"Yes."

"He's got a strong hand. It's a subtle display of swagger."

Elizabeth watched the betting and the calls. The win came from the player wearing the Stetson. He pulled his chips closer, adverting his eyes from the players. Hal said, "Let's walk to the other table." They moved to the second table, standing near a date palm and a bonsai plant. The first round just ending, then new cards being dealt.

Hal gestured with his head. "Watch how the players buy into the game. You'll see tells before the real action begins. If a player is more flamboyant in his buy, waving money, he will, most likely, play the game that way. On the other hand, if you see a quiet, conservative approach at this stage, chances are the player will take a conservative tactic to the game. Watch the woman. I know who she is, and I know she's got an uncanny, intuitive feel for the game. I'll try to show you how she does it."

THIRTY-TWO

Charlie Lehman looked at his watch as he had sex with the woman. Purple neon poured through the slats in the motel blinds, jagged light strips pulsating across her contorted face as she faked an orgasm, her third since noon.

Lehman made a final thrust, his loins quivering. He rolled over in bed and stared at the ceiling tile, yellowed through the decades of floating cigarette smoke. *Seven o'clock*, he thought. *Got a half-hour*. Lehman, mid-forties, slight beer belly, bald spot the size of a fried egg, stood and began dressing.

The woman, firm body, tanned, auburn locks below her shoulders, sat up and pursed her lips. She looked across the room at a mirror on the dresser, hand combing her hair. "Twice this month big boy. That makes you one of my regulars. Once a week, you get a discount."

Lehman grinned. "And I was hoping I wasn't a regular guy, maybe someone you actually like fuckin' occasionally."

"Oh, sweetheart, I do or I wouldn't be in this business. Speaking of business, that's a hundred fifty you owe me."

He looked at his watch again. The woman said, "What's your hurry? I'm betting it's the little wife." She licked her bottom lip and pulled her knees up to her large breasts, wrapping her arms around her legs "Happens to all the guys, you get kids, a wife—"

"Hey, don't bring up my wife, okay? None of that talk when we're together."

She smiled. "Oh, so damn sensitive. What a pretender."

"That's enough!" He opened his wallet and counted out the money in twenty-dollar bills, tossing them on the bed beside her. "I need to call a rideshare. Left my car at the office."

"I'd drive you there, lover, but I gotta be in the opposite end of town, and I need to take a shower."

Thunder rolled and rain began to pelt the motel window, the droplets rolling down the window creating rivulets. The purple neon rain seemed to crawl across the prostitute's face, like eels in shallow, moonlit water.

Lehman hit the app on his phone. Looked at the time the driver would be there, checked a second service and did the same thing.

— —

Elizabeth watched the only woman at the poker table, shoulder length brown hair, mid-thirties. She didn't seem to blink as the hands were read. Hal said, "She's won here more than she's lost. I spoke with her once after she won. Her name is Glenna. She's fairly candid. Not only does she know how to read most tells, she knows how to fake her own very well. More importantly she's trained herself in reading the subconscious moves of players. Most of the conscious moves are an act—the player trying to throw off the others. It's the subconscious ones that give way to deception. Maybe this area will be of help to you."

Elizabeth watched the woman. "Can you give me an example?"

Her uncle said, "I'll give you a few."

— —

Charlie Lehman saw the headlights rake across the motel window. He looked through the blinds. The prostitute stood with a short white towel wrapped around her body, stepping toward the small bathroom, the shower running. She turned and said, "Same time next week or do you want to become a frequent flyer?"

He shook his head. "No, I'll call you."

She smiled. "I have your number. I could call you. Unless the wife checks your phone, it's our secret." She blew him a kiss. "Goodbye, Charlie.

And no, you're not a regular guy. You're actually pretty darn good, maybe four stars."

Charlie grinned and stepped out of the room. He stood under the motel awning, the rain thumping the canopy, the V in the neon *Vacancy* sign burned out. He looked at the car and saw the ride-share logo in the window. But it wasn't the one he'd called. He glanced at his watch. *Got to get home.* He waited a few seconds to see if another driver would enter the motel lot. Under the awning, three doors down, a man stood smoking. No shirt. Beer gut over his ripped jeans. Blue tats on both forearms and across his chest.

Charlie stepped out and tapped on the front seat window opposite the driver. The window lowered a foot. He said, "My driver hasn't shown up yet. I really need a ride."

The driver was a silhouette in the purple neon, his face unrecognizable. "Are you Matthew Zimmer?"

"No." He glanced back at the man smoking under the awning. "Look, I'll give you a fifty dollar tip. I'm trying to meet my wife. You know how it is, right?" He grinned. "So I gotta move quickly."

The driver was silent for a few seconds. "Get in."

"Thanks!"

"You're welcome to ride up here in the adult seat if you want."

"Sure." Charlie opened the door and got inside the car. The dome light didn't come on when he opened the door. He turned to pull the seatbelt over his chest when the shock hit him. The stun was just below his throat. It struck him the same time he looked out the front windshield and saw lightning strike a power line, sparks flying.

Charlie was thrust back against the seat. It was as if a mule had kicked him. His body momentarily paralyzed. He tried to speak, the words not coming, his head swimming. Arms like concrete. There was a second burst from the stun gun, and Charlie's heart raced, his hands felt like bird claws, curling backwards, his lips rubbery, darkness descended as the rain pelted the roof of the dark car.

Charlie Lehman's weakened bladder gave way and urine soaked his pants.

THIRTY-THREE

Elizabeth followed Uncle Hal as he stepped a little closer to the poker table. He glanced up at one of the many discreet security cameras; two large screen monitors mounted on the walls, football games on the screens. A blonde cocktail waitress brought a glass of scotch to the man wearing the brown sports coat.

Hal whispered to Elizabeth. "Glenna watched the guy in the red shirt look three times at his hand. She knows he has a weak hand. It's almost like the guy's trying to change the face value of the cards by staring at them. A pro memorizes them and doesn't make a second look. See the guy in the brown sports coat use his right hand for half a second to cover his cards?"

"Yes."

"Glenna caught that, too, and she knows the guy most likely has a good hand, but not always. It's the other subconscious moves that add up or they don't. The guy in the red shirt is touching his chips." The man stood and sipped his drink, sitting back down. Hal said, "He just went from subconscious to a conscious move. The stand up thing is to telegraph a bluff." Hal smiled and looked at his niece. "It's always in the eyes, Elizabeth. And it's there like a shooting star. Gone before you can point to it. In life, when a liar is asked a direct question, the poker tell is the pause. The honest person usually doesn't hesitate. It's a knee jerk honest response to a direct question. Beyond the eyes, the give away is when they start a sentence with the word, 'well,' it's a hesitation. Liars have a hard time answering yes or no to a straightforward question. If they have to tell you they're an 'honest person,' they probably aren't."

Elizabeth watch the players bet. The woman moved a stack of chips into the pot. The man in the brown coat followed. Four players folded. When his hands hit the table, the dealer nodded at the only woman at the table who slowly slid the winnings toward her.

Hal turned to Elizabeth and winked.

— ▪ —

An hour later, Elizabeth stood in the casino parking lot with her uncle. He said, "I don't think I told you or showed you much more than you already know, Liz."

She smiled. "Yes, you did. Thanks for the refresher course." She glanced around the parking lot, many of the cars gone, the moonlight breaking through fast moving clouds. "Good night, Uncle Hal. Love you."

"Why don't you stay here tonight? It's late. I can get you a good discount on a room."

"Thanks, but it only took me about ninety minutes to drive down here from Hattiesburg. I have to go. Big day tomorrow."

He sighed and smiled. "I wish your daddy had lived to see what a fine woman you turned out to be."

"Both Mom and Dad went down their separate rabbit holes." She pushed a strand of hair behind her right ear. "No one knows for sure whether Dad committed suicide that night. There were no other cars involved. No witnesses. It was a straight road. He managed to plow into a tree at ninety miles an hour. It was less than a month after the bank foreclosed on us. If he did kill himself, how screwed up is it to have both parents committing suicide? What's that say about my gene pool?"

"He was drunk and probably tired, Liz. But, anyway, you're stronger than they were."

"I've had to be, Uncle Hal. I wasn't going to raise Molly in some state of depression or self-pity. And then she was taken away from me. Guess what…you're all the family I have left."

He reached out and took her hand. "We need to spend more time together, Liz. What do you say I drive up to Hattiesburg and take you out to dinner."

"I'd like that."

He touched her cheek. "You have grit. I have it. So don't think for one damn minute you don't have the right stuff, because you do. You're a professor at a big university. You testify in the trials of some bad hombres." He paused, looked at the moon over the Gulf of Mexico, lowering his eyes to Elizabeth. "If I were a bettin' man, which I'm not anymore, I'd bet you have a helluva motive in earning your doctorate and working with police."

"I'm trying to make a difference. I enjoy teaching."

"Do you enjoy looking those cons in the eye and trying to figure out if they're fakin' insanity?"

"When I look the victim's family in the eye, that gives me what I need to sit across the table from a murderer. I know how each victim's family feels—grief-stricken, hurt, confused, angry…helpless."

"You're hunting for Molly's killer, aren't you, Liz?"

She said nothing for a moment, staring into her uncle's thoughtful blue eyes. "Yes, I am. I need some closure to all those feelings. Something to say I'm not powerless."

"What if you never find him? Can you find peace for you?"

"I don't know, Uncle Hal. But I do know I can't stop thinking about what he did to my Molly and her boyfriend. Innocent kids killed and buried in the woods under a deer carcass." She moved her purse from her left shoulder to her right. "I may not have to find him, he might have already found me."

"What do you mean?"

Elizabeth told him about what happened thus far. She added, "So I'm not sure if the killer is doing this by himself or if he has followers or a follower."

"My daddy, your grandpa, saw something in you that brought out the good in him. Maybe it was because you were a Tomboy and liked following him around on the farm. I remember pa teaching you how to use a gun. He was thrilled at how your hand and eye coordination developed." He paused, and looked at her caringly. "Penny for your thoughts."

"Do you remember the housekeeper Mom had for years until our family did a slow disintegration?"

"Yes, a delightful lady. Can't recall her name, though."

"Nellie…Nellie Culpepper. I take dinner to her one night a week. We usually sit on her porch and just talk. You've lived in Mississippi a long time. Have you ever heard of the hanging bridge, it's near the small town of Shubuta?"

"I heard someone mention it years ago. All I know is that it was a remote place where some of the state's notorious lynchings were carried out."

"Nellie told me about a man—someone removing wood from that old bridge, probably right where the victims stood before they were hung. He was taking the wood someplace and making or having someone make small crosses. And he was placing them on the old graves of the men who hung those people that day."

"Is this recent?"

"Yes. Going back to 1918, a man by the name of Zachariah Belmont was the leader of the lynch mob on the bridge that day. He was one of the heads in the Klan at that time. His grave is in the same cemetery where we buried Cindy Carter, the murder victim. I was there, with a detective, when we found a wooden cross propped up against Belmont's headstone."

"Did it come from that bridge?"

"I don't know. Police are going to test the wood." Elizabeth watched canary palm fronds quiver in the breeze and then shifted her gaze to her uncle. "Two of those hung were pregnant teenagers."

He looked across the lot at a car starting, slowing pulling away. "I recall reading how they convicted the man who kidnapped the Lindbergh baby. The kidnapper used a ladder to reach the child's window in the Lindbergh home. Police traced the wood from the ladder to wood the kidnapper had in his attic. And that was in 1932. It shouldn't be too hard to match the crosses with the old wood on that bridge. Let me walk you to your car." He placed her hand in the crook of his arm, and they walked across the lot. A shuttle bus pulled behind them and stopped near the entrance to pick up tourists and gamblers.

At her car, Elizabeth said, "Tomorrow I will watch detectives question young men—all students at the university. Two dated Cindy. Did one of them kill her, and if he did do it, was it because someone coerced him?"

"If one of them did it, just like the poker players, Liz, the one with something to hide will be conscious of it and react accordingly. It's the subconscious signs you need to watch. And it always begins in the eye. But, sometimes, if you blink, you won't see it. So don't blink, Liz."

"Thank you, Uncle Hal."

He bent forward and kissed her on top of her head. "Do me a favor… when you get home tonight, call me. I don't care what time it is…call me. Just let me know you made it safely."

THIRTY-FOUR

Elizabeth pulled in her driveway at 12:45 a.m. She drove slowly, her headlights panning the front porch. She squinted in the dark, insects orbiting the porch lights. No sign of Jack, a touch of sadness welling in her heart. *He's better off,* she thought. She parked, reached for the pistol. She chambered a round, picked up the only remaining flyer with Jack's picture on it, locked her car, and walked to the front door. She carried her purse on one shoulder—the Smith & Wesson in her right hand. The air smelled of night blooming jasmine and something else.

Honeysuckle.

Elizabeth froze on her front steps, listening. Toads chirped in the adjacent woods.

She inhaled through her nose, smelling the cool night air. *Maybe it's just my imagination. Tired. No, exhausted.* The breeze blew in and the scent left as quickly as it arrived. She stepped on the porch, keys in her hand, looking for signs of honeysuckles on or near the porch. Moths circled the lights causing shadows to dance. She couldn't see any honeysuckles.

Elizabeth opened her front door and entered her home, locking the door behind her, listening for any sounds in her house. The air-conditioning kicked on, causing the lights to dim for a split second, blowing through the vents in the ceiling, the cool air falling on her damp face. She stepped into the kitchen and set her purse and the flyer on the table. She kept the gun in her hand and quietly moved through her home, turning on lights and looking in bedrooms. Nothing seemed out of place. She turned on the floodlights, illuminating most of her property. She peeked out the curtain into the back yard.

Nothing.

She returned to the kitchen and set the gun on the table. She picked up the flyer, staring at the photo of the cat. "I didn't get any calls today, Jack. Is that because nobody wants to claim you?" She walked over to her refrigerator and used a magnet to hang the flyer on the door.

Elizabeth poured a small glass of wine and turned back to the image of the cat. She sipped the wine and half-smiled. "You can't really be lonely if you like the person you're with, right, Jack? Maybe you're out there now, stalking under the moonlight, living all of your nine lives. My Molly only had one. But I like to believe she really lived life in her twenty years."

She sipped her wine and walked back toward the kitchen table. "Oops, I was supposed to call Uncle Hal." She unzipped her purse, looked in it. "Where'd I leave my phone?" She set the wine glass down. "In the car."

Elizabeth picked up her keys and started for the door. She stopped, turned and looked at the pistol on the table. She got the gun and walked out the front door.

Elizabeth almost stepped on it.

In the center of the porch was a small circle of honeysuckles, shaped like the crown found on Cindy's head. Elizabeth griped the gun with both hands. Her heart pounding, breathing through her nose, the odor of honeysuckles suddenly like sewer gas.

She looked at the flickering shadows cast by orbiting moths around the lights, the sound of crickets and the drone of toads in the deep woods. She wanted to yell—to challenge her stalker. She moved the pistol in the direction of shadows under the bright floodlights. Nothing moved.

There was a shape on her driveway. Something coming.

In the silence of the night, the cat mewed.

Under the lights, she watched Jack saunter down her driveway near her car. Elizabeth stepped off the porch, eyes searching her yard, holding the gun in both hands. She stared at Jack for a moment, looked behind him. He casually glanced up at her and sat on the pavement, tail slightly moving.

Elizabeth approached him, whispered. "Jack, where the hell have you been? Jeez…I wish you could talk." He blinked, large eyes as mysterious as the stars above. She opened her car door and quickly got her phone, locked the door and walked to her porch, the pistol held upright in her hands. She stepped over the honeysuckles.

Jack followed her inside. She locked the door and turned the deadbolt, pulled all of her curtains tight, and went into her kitchen. Jack jumped up on his stool, purring. Elizabeth let out a pent-up breath. "Jack, did you see some creep out there? Or did you happen to leave a daisy chain of honeysuckles on the porch? It's one in the morning. You think I should call Detective Bradford to tell him I received another unwanted flower delivery?"

Jack looked away. "You're right. I have a gun that I know how to use, and we have each other tonight. Right, Jack?" She scratched him behind his ears, his tail moving slowly, back and forth, like a pendulum in an unhurried grandfather clock. "Look at the fridge. I hung up your wanted poster. But there was a slight problem. No one called. Does that mean you're not wanted?"

Jack cocked his head, his left ear turning slightly toward the driveway. Elizabeth smiled. "Or maybe you've never belonged to anyone…just kind of walked your own path in life. I can relate to your need for solitude. You seemed to be okay in your own fur. Hungry? I think I have some turkey left." She took the food out of the refrigerator and put it in his bowl. Jack dropped down from the stool and began eating.

Elizabeth picked up the pistol. She walked to the front window, peeked out between the curtains. The bright floodlights lit most of her yard. She watched an opossum waddle across the grass. She returned to the family room, peering between the curtain panels into the backyard. Nothing. Elizabeth sat down on the couch, her palms moist. "Maybe I should call to see if a sheriff's deputy could patrol here." Jack jumped up beside her, licked his lips, purring.

Elizabeth sipped her wine and petted him. "Jack, it's okay that you don't belong to someone. The question I want to ask you is this: which of your nine lives are you on tonight? Is it number seven, eight, or is this it…number nine?"

Jack licked his left paw. Elizabeth said, "Some people live long lives, and at the end of the road, they come to a frightening discovery. They find they've never really lived all of those decades. It's when you realize it was all borrowed time; and at that moment, the things you own won't make it through the eye of the needle with you. Maybe that's the worst nightmare because you grasp that you've been sleep walking through life, going through the motions but never making traction to do what you really wanted to do. Who would you have cheated in the end? Only yourself. So I think I'd rather dive for pearls to string a necklace than to buy one."

Jack rubbed his chin against her leg, his eyes half closing. "Okay, sleepyhead. I know I sound like an idiot—sorry I'm being so philosophical tonight. I'm just tired of evil hiding behind the cover of compassion when it's really the mask of madness." She set her glass down. "I'm getting security cameras tomorrow. Oh, shit…Uncle Hal."

Elizabeth picked up her phone and started to call her uncle. "One missed call," she mumbled. "It's from Mike Bradford." She pressed the play button.

"Elizabeth, it's Mike. There's been another murder. Same MO. This time the victim was a man. Another wooden bowl. This one had a seashell in it. I know you're in Biloxi. Call me when you get this. Doesn't matter what time it is, thanks."

THIRTY-FIVE

After Elizabeth called her uncle, she stood from the couch to do something she hadn't done in a long time. She stepped across the room to her bookcase, reached up and took down a Bible. She returned to the couch, Jack watching her. She sat down and opened the Bible, going to the back pages and finding the Book of Revelation.

"Jack, I may have been wrong about the seven deadly sins. The bowl found on Cindy's body had dirt and a twig in it. And the bowl found on the next victim had a seashell in it. I attended a Catholic school, and I remember something one of the priests said, and maybe I can find it in the Book of Revelation."

She quickly thumbed through the pages until she came to Revelation 16. She read, moving her index finger under the words, whispering. "The first angel poured out his bowl on the land. Sores broke out on the people who had the mark of the beast and worshipped its image."

Elizabeth blew out a breath and continued reading. "The second angel poured out his bowl on the sea. It turned into blood like that of a dead person...and every living thing in the sea died."

She looked at Jack. The cat's eyes now wide open, purring stopped, as if he had understood every word she'd read. "Jack, now I know what this psychopath is doing. Dear God. She made the call to Bradford. He answered after one ring. "Elizabeth, are you still down in Biloxi?"

"No, I'm back home. I just heard your message. What happened?"

"A woman found the body when she was walking her dog a few blocks from her home tonight. We just left the scene. The body was in a field next to some rather upscale homes in the Rawl Springs area. The vic is Charlie Lehman, forty-three. Lives in West Hattiesburg. He works for the newspaper—an editorial writer. He has or had a wife and a couple of kids. It was tough getting anything cohesive from her. She pretty much lost it when told what happened. She said her husband said he had to work late. We found his car at his office lot. We'll be checking security cameras."

"You said a seashell was found in this bowl."

"Yes, the kind of conch shell you can hold to your ear and hear the sea."

"Any signs he'd been hit with a stun gun?"

"Yes, preliminary exam indicates at least three burns on his neck and chest. Forensics team will be back at first light. Body's at the ME's office."

"Mike, I was hoping this perp would not repeat what he did to Cindy. Now I believe he'll kill at least five more times if he's not stopped."

"You thought the perp might write one of the other sins on the body, like greed, lust or something. The word *wrath* was on this victim, too."

"That's because I got it wrong. The part I think I got right is the number seven."

"What the hell are you talking about?"

"At first I thought the word wrath had to do with one of the seven deadly sins, and it does. But now I think the perp is using it in another area of the Bible where the number seven is prominent."

"Where?"

"Revelation 16. It has to do with the seven bowls of God's wrath. Basically it deals with God's patience—the time when he's finally done with how deeply screwed up the world has become. So he sends down his wrath to earth—to put and end to the incorrigible sinners. In terms of the apocalypse, it's the real deal. He sends down seven angels, each with a bowl in his hand to pour something on earth."

"What's in the bowl?"

"Something different in each one. In Revelation 16, here's what the third passage reads…*the second angel poured out his bowl on the sea. It turned into blood like that of a dead person…and every living thing in the sea died.*"

"So that's what the seashell represents in the bowl found on Lehman's body?"

"Probably. In the bowl he left on Cindy, dirt was in the bottom of it with a twig. Hold a second." She read from the Bible. "Again, in Revelation 16, it says…*the first angel poured out his bowl on the land*. Mike, we have two bowls—the first with soil—or land. And in the bottom of the second bowl is a seashell. Let me see what it says about the third bowl." She paused and read. "*The third angel poured out his bowl on the rivers and springs of water…and they became blood.*"

Mike exhaled into the phone. "Who the hell are we chasing?"

"A very cunning and diabolical killer, someone who may believe he has the ultimate calling. A predator who thinks he's sanctioned by God to deliver all seven bowls of God's wrath. Mike, growing up Catholic and attending a Catholic school for many years, I remember one of the priests speaking in mass about the eighth angel—the angel of apocalypse. He came right after the seven angels. I have a dear friend who's a priest. He recently retired. I want to visit with him, maybe get his insight into this."

"When it comes to Revelation in the Bible, does anyone have a good insight?"

"He made it interesting when I sat in mass as a girl. Now, all these years later, maybe he can help put a puzzle piece together for us."

"When this is done, when we catch this guy, this one will be studied by the behavioral profile unit of the FBI, right up there with the worst of the worst."

"We have to find him first. He could be on my property right now for all I know. I found another ring of honeysuckles on my porch."

"What! When?"

"Not when I first got home. It was later, when I went back outside to get my phone. I had left it in the car."

"Give me your address, I'm coming over there. You're not safe."

Elizabeth smiled. "I have a very powerful handgun that I know how to use. It's locked and loaded. And I have Jack here to help me."

"The friggin' cat."

"Don't say it too loud. He might hear you."

"Text me your address. If nothing else, I want to look around your property. You can go to bed if you want. I just need to make sure no one is lurking around outside."

Elizabeth started to protest, but Detective Bradford was off the line.

THIRTY-SIX

Elizabeth sat in partial darkness and watched for the headlights. It didn't take long. Within fifteen minutes, Detective Bradford was pulling into her driveway. He parked directly behind her car and got out. She stood and watched through the curtains, the gun in her right hand.

Bradford held a bright flashlight walking around the big yard, looking at the grass now covered in heavy dew. He looked in the flowerbeds, down by her mailbox, opening the box, peering inside. He walked up the opposite side of the driveway, a slight fog dancing, the powerful flashlight pushing a long cone of light through the mist. He stopped next to a tall red maple tree, shining the flashlight at the base of the tree. Then he knelt down and took a picture.

Elizabeth stepped onto her porch. Bradford saw her under the porch light and approached. When he got to the first step he said, "There's a print next to the maple tree. I took a picture. The lab will do an analysis."

She pointed to the ring of honeysuckles near her feet. "No need to do a lab analysis on this latest delivery of wildflowers. I know they are from the same batch found on Cindy and in my mailbox."

Staring at the flowers, Bradford said, "They'll go to the lab. Never know…we might find something else useful." He looked up, the yellow porch light cutting through the mist. His face shiny, eyes burning, sleeves rolled up, his tie loose, gun belt near his badge. "We'll find this pervert. He'll be the forty-ninth asshole on Mississippi's death row." He looked at the gun in her hand. "You say you know how to use that?"

"If I see this guy coming into my house, you'll see that I know how to use it."

"Stay here or go back inside. I want to look around the rest of your property."

She waited a moment before responding and then nodded. "There's a deck on the back. When you're done, I'll meet you at the backdoor."

Elizabeth went inside, turning the deadbolt lock. She walked into the kitchen and set the gun down on the table. Jack watched her from the adjacent family room where he'd settled down on the couch, then turned his head following the movements of the flashlight in the backyard. Elizabeth said, "Don't get too excited, Jack. We have company. That's Detective Mike Bradford in the yard." Jack turned his head toward her and yawned.

She could hear Bradford stepping up onto her wooden deck. She opened the backdoor. He walked into the glare of the floodlights, came to the door and said, "No signs of anyone out here. The grass is pretty wet with dew. I see a fresh set of deer tracks, but nothing human."

"This guy's not human. Or he's a soulless human. I suppose those exist, too. Please, come inside."

"I can't stay long."

"I'd like to hear more about the crime scene."

"All right." He entered the home. Elizabeth closed the door and locked the dead bolt. He set his flashlight down on the kitchen table near her gun. Bradford looked around and said, "I like your home. It looks very comfortable." He glanced into the family room. "Is that cat the infamous Jack?"

She smiled. "The one and only. If you'd like to make his acquaintance, you'll have to go to him. Jack likes to keep a low resting pulse."

Bradford smiled and walked over to pet Jack. Elizabeth said, "I put flyers out in shops and the nearest vet's office. So far no one has called to claim him. In the meantime, Jack sort of comes and goes as he pleases. I think he has a girlfriend nearby, but he's not the kiss and tell type."

Bradford stepped back into the kitchen, glanced at the wine in her glass on the counter. She asked, "Can I get you something to drink? After the kind of day you've had, maybe a glass of wine? I also have vodka, scotch and gin."

He smiled. "I could use a whiskey, but I like red wine, too."

"It's a cab. St. Michelle. One of my favorites." She took a glass from the cupboard and poured some wine for Bradford, handing it to him. And then she picked up her glass. She said, "Let's toast to finding this guy quickly."

They touched glasses and sipped the wine. She said, "Please, sit. How close did the second murder parallel Cindy's death?"

They sat at the table. Bradford said, "Almost identical. The word *wrath* scrawled on the vic's forehead. Slit throat. The stun gun burns, the wooden bowl. The body wasn't displayed in a deviant sexual kind of way, as Cindy was, but everything else matched up."

"Did you find any boot prints?"

"Although it was dark, we had some heavy-duty lights out there. The field was mostly grasses and weeds. No indication of shoe or footprints. The team will be back out in the morning. I've been in law enforcement a while now…never seen anything like this. In criminal forensic psychology, you might not even have a profile for this guy unless you're looking for the devil himself."

"Maybe the devil impersonating an angel." She moved her gun to one side. "When you asked me if I could use this, and I told you that he would be a dead guy if he got in here…I wasn't kidding. This freak is playing games. He's letting me know that he knows who I am and probably the fact that I've given crucial testimony that's helped result in convicting two heinous killers. It's as if he's saying…you'll never be at my trial because I'm smarter than you and the cops. I can kill at will. And I can do it because I have a higher calling with God because I'm the eight angel incarnate."

Bradford sipped his wine. "I've hunted so many bad guys, but never one that believed he could kill because he'd been hand-picked by God as some kind of messenger."

"It may be a complete ruse, something this psychotic killer designed to throw us off, but it has all the earmarks of a psychopath riding this pretentious divine role until he gets caught or maybe makes the ultimate sacrifice…takes his own life on some place he considers an altar. Let's join Jack. The seats are softer. And I want to show you what I think we're dealing with in the criminal mind of this killer."

THIRTY-SEVEN

There was a noise on the back deck. A *thump*. Bradford raised his index finger to his lips. *Silence*. Elizabeth nodded. She glanced at her pistol on the table. Bradford stood and stepped over to the curtains. He barely parted them, looking out at the deck, the fog now thicker. He removed his gun from the holster, slowly opening the door and stepping out on the deck, keeping to the shadows behind the floodlights. A slight breeze jingled the wind chimes, and then the gust died, the fog drifting beyond the deck railing.

Bradford leapt over the railing to the ground a few feet below. He turned on his flashlight and spotted three deer. They bolted off, swallowed by the fog. He scouted, looking for shoe or boot impressions in the dew. He could find none. Then he walked back three steps to the deck, crossing it, stepping on a large pinecone. He picked it up and entered the house.

"I think this made the sound," he said, holding up the pinecone.

Elizabeth let out a long breath. "I have a tall pine tree about twenty feet to the right of the deck. It produces some of the largest pinecones I've ever seen."

He set the pinecone on the table and said, "I read somewhere that pine-cones have existed on the planet more than three times longer than any flowering species of plant. How's that for endurance?"

Elizabeth smiled. "For most of recorded history, pinecones have been the poster children of human enlightenment. We even named a gland after it. The pineal gland, which resembles a small pinecone, is in the center of our brains. It helps us distinguish light. Some in psychology call it the Third Eye, meaning it's where our perception or intuition is found."

Bradford smiled. "I have a gut feeling your pineal gland has been to the gym."

"And that gut feeling you just had is tied to your pineal gland. Let's join Jack."

They walked into the family room and sat on the couch, Jack in the center between them. Bradford sipped his wine and looked at her bookcase across the room. "Do you read a lot?"

"Sort of comes with territory as a college professor. I read mostly non-fiction for work. I use fiction to escape once in a while."

"You might want to try a road trip." He grinned and petted Jack.

"It's been too long."

He nodded. "I can relate. This family room has a nice feel. Fireplace. Bookcase. Comfortable furniture. Widescreen TV. Lots of green plants. But I don't see pictures of family."

"Maybe family room as a designation doesn't apply to me. My family, even extended family, is down to one uncle. The only pictures I have out are of my daughter, Molly." She got up, walked across the room to get a framed picture of Molly dressed in a graduate cap and gown, holding a high school diploma, wide smile, long brown hair. Elizabeth sat back down and handed the photo to Bradford. "That's Molly. It was taken the day she graduated from high school. Not only was she excited to be graduating, she was even more excited to be going off to college. Her college years were, for the most part, wonderful."

"She's beautiful. I know how proud you must have been of her."

"Very much so. Her mind was like a sponge, and her sense of adventure, exploring, helping wildlife, was off the charts. One of the reasons that Cindy's death hits me so hard is because I saw a lot of Molly in her. And when I see this senseless killing happen again, I have a very difficult time with that." She sipped her wine.

Bradford set the picture down on the coffee table. "I wish I could have met Molly. She sounds like a remarkable young woman."

"She was. It was just the two of us for years. We had great times. Being a single parent had its challenges, but they never really came from Molly. It was from juggling the responsibility of doing it all alone."

"Her father never offered to help?"

"He never offered anything. He took. It was always about his needs. He was charming when he wanted to be. But he was self-centered and usually in some form of denial. He walked out when Molly was a baby, and we never saw him again. I could have petitioned for child support, but that would have given him leverage and a negative influence in Molly's life. Sometimes it's better to cut your losses and let go for good."

"I understand. But that was a long time ago. Do you get lonely sometimes? Maybe want to go out to catch a movie or have to dinner with someone?"

She tilted her head and smiled. "I'm not a hermit, I have friends. We play cards and have dinners occasionally. But between my teaching schedule, grading papers and sporadic work with prosecutors in insanity competency hearings, I don't have a lot of time."

Jack stood, stretching. He plopped off the couch and strolled into the kitchen.

Bradford sipped his wine, set the glass on the coffee table and turned more toward Elizabeth. "You're a striking woman. Smart. Caring and you have a sense of humor. I'm sure, over the years, guys have come calling many times."

She chuckled. "A few, perhaps. As long as Molly was home, there were no guys in the house. After she went off to college it was different, but I'm old fashioned. Before I go out with a man, I need to feel we have something in common. Some initial attraction, too. I don't get that combo very often. Maybe it's just me. My friend Beverly says I'm too picky. But what's wrong with that?" She set her wine on the table.

Bradford nodded. "Nothing. But sometimes you have to take a risk or two to see just how much you might have in common." He touched her right hand on the couch.

She smiled, looked at the framed picture and then at Bradford. "I used to tell Molly that, if it wasn't right—the situation or relationship, she had the power to write within her heart how the story would or could end. I told her that when she became old and could look back on her life to understand the times when she thought she was being rejected from something, she really was being redirected to something better but may not know it at the moment." Elizabeth paused, lowered her voice. "And then she was mur-dered. I still believe these things, Mike, but maybe not as much anymore."

He nodded. "Maybe in time, and under the right circumstances, your original convictions will be restored. I know we can never make sense out of the senseless in the midst of the horror we've witnessed. But I think the principles you mentioned are worth fighting for." He gently touched her hand, squeezing it for a moment. Then withdrew.

"Thank you for coming over here tonight. You didn't have to do it."

"Yes, I did."

She nodded and reached for the Bible on the coffee table. "Here's what I think we're dealing with in terms of evil and misdirection." She turned to the Book of Revelation. "In reading the seven bowls of God's wrath, it deals with seven angels. But after all those bowls are delivered, there emerges an eighth angel. This angel mixes the prayers of all martyred saints with burning incense and hurls it to earth. The passages in Revelation seem to depict the eighth angel as the most powerful—the one doing God's final and ultimate bidding—hurling fire to earth, the annihilation of irredeem-able sinners."

She set the Bible on the table, pulled a strand of her brown hair behind one ear. "Of course, I could be completely wrong. It might be a ploy on the part of the killer. But why commit murders with the parallels to Revelation 16 if he didn't have some intense, but warped personal conviction to it?"

Bradford took a deep breath and shook his head. "I don't know. I've never dealt with this kind of sick criminal. That's where you come into the picture. You can try to profile this type of crazy shit. For me, as a detective, murders are usually about money, lust, jealousy or revenge. I follow clues not passages from Revelation."

"I understand, and those same clues and evidence are what help me profile these murderers. I try to anticipate what he'll do next. I try to get in or at least see things from his severely skewed perspective. And, hopefully, you can hunt him down before he does it."

"So where do you think he'll try next?"

"I don't know where he'll get his next victim. But if we don't catch this…this debauched executioner, I think we'll find his next victim by water. Maybe a lake, stream or a river. And that clue comes straight from Revelation."

Bradford pinched the bridge of his nose, his eyes red and tired.

Elizabeth said, "You're exhausted. It's foggy out there. Please, stay the night. Get some rest. You came over here to keep me safe. I want to return the favor."

"I don't know. I have to—"

"You have to take care of yourself to find the bad guys." She smiled. "This couch is comfy. Trust me. I've fallen asleep on it many times. You can stay here. There's a downstairs bathroom beyond the kitchen. You'll even find a new toothbrush and toothpaste in the drawer on the left side. I'll get you a blanket and a pillow. But, there is one thing you should know."

"Oh, what's that?"

"You'll have to share the couch with Jack. He likes sleeping at the end. Maybe he'll keep your feet warm."

Bradford smiled. "Thanks."

"You're doing those interrogations tomorrow afternoon. I hope I can help."

"My money is on the jock, Gerald Simpson."

"He's definitely a cold narcissist. But is he the killer? Maybe tomorrow we'll have a better vision."

"If we do, it's probably going to be because you have a highly developed pinecone gland." He smiled.

Elizabeth laughed. "Pineal gland. Our third eye—the place where we distinguish light…and sometimes…dark."

THIRTY-EIGHT

Elizabeth awoke to an odd smell. At least for her home it was not a common scent. The smell of bacon, eggs, toast and coffee—together. And in her home. She looked at her bedside clock. 6:15 a.m. She quickly got up, stripped out of her pajamas and stepped into the shower.

Less than thirty minutes later, she'd finished with her makeup, curiosity making her take less time than usual. She dressed in dark pants and a long sleeve white blouse. She applied lipstick and made a final check in the mirror, brushing her hair once more. She left her bedroom and walked down the steps to a full breakfast on her kitchen table, Bradford just taking the eggs off the stove.

She smiled. "Wow. And you cook, too. Sorry, that just slipped. Like some line from a silly romantic comedy. This is so sweet and thoughtful. Thank you for making breakfast."

He ladled eggs onto a plate and said, "You're welcome. I figured that you have more than enough on your mind to worry about cooking or even food for that matter. I saw what looked like a lifetime supply of energy bars in one of your kitchen cabinets. I enjoy cooking. Worked as a cook to help pay my way through college. Sit down, let me serve you."

Elizabeth smiled, surprised and pleased at the same moment. She tried to remember the last time someone cooked for her, and in her home. She couldn't recall. He set the plate in front of her. Bacon, toast with jam and butter, fresh cut oranges and bananas, were piled on separate plates in the center of the table.

Bradford poured her a steaming cup of coffee and set it on the table. He sat down. "I know you like it black."

She smiled. "Yes, I do. You are an astute observer, Detective Bradford."

"I'm just paying attention, ma'am." He grinned and motioned toward the pinecone on the table. "However, if my pineal gland were the size of that thing, they'd call me Nostradamus. No need to observe, I'd just predict the future. "

She laughed; somehow the sound of her own laughter this early in the morning was almost foreign. "If your pineal gland were the size of the pinecone, they wouldn't call you Nostradamus…they'd call a brain surgeon for you. Maybe do a nip and tuck." She sipped her coffee. "I know what you're facing returning to the crime scene. You didn't have to spend the time to make breakfast. I hope in the daylight you might find some additional evidence."

Bradford's face turned somber. "Me too. I think I'll have some results back from the lab today, results from the photos of the boot prints. And now, after last night, I have another one. You mentioned installing security cameras. I can help you do it."

Elizabeth sipped her coffee. "Thank you. I appreciate that."

Bradford ate some eggs, looked out the back window onto the deck, leaves on a large maple tree jostling in the breeze. "The lab should have the result back on the type of wood used to make those bowls. I hope it's something that only grows in one area of Mississippi so we're able to narrow down our searches. Wouldn't it be convenient if that specific tree only grew in the De Soto National Forest. Maybe we could set up trail cameras and catch some guy with a chain saw cutting the trees down. Are you going to class today?"

"Yes. Should be done around noon. I'll be there at the sheriff's office before you begin the interviews. Just show me to the observation room so I can sit and take notes."

Bradford nodded. "I don't want to stack the deck, but I'm betting that the jock, Gerald Simpson, will show body language that indicates everything he has to say about Cindy Carter, his relationship with her, and his whereabouts at the time of her death and that of the last victim, Charlie Lehman, will all be a lie. We know Lehman didn't take his car after work. My partner,

Ed Milton, called about a half-hour ago and said there was a witness at a no-tell motel who believes he saw Lehman meet a prostitute at the motel. We'll interview the witness today. Lehman's car was at his work, the newspaper."

Elizabeth shook her head, looked at the surface of her black coffee. "Maybe the perp is targeting people he considers diehard sinners. But that wouldn't explain why he killed Cindy. If his car were left at his company, how'd he get to the motel? Did the prostitute pick him up? Or did he hire a ride-share like Uber or one of the others?"

"I hope to find that out today."

— —

Elizabeth sat behind her desk in her small office at the university, grading papers, preparing for her nine o'clock class. Her office phone buzzed. She answered and recognized the deep voice before he said his name. "Professor Monroe, good morning. This is Bill Keelson with Channel Four News—"

"I'm sorry, Mr. Keelson, I have to teach a class in fifteen minutes."

"I'll take less than thirty seconds. I wanted to follow the university protocol and not just show up again hoping to get an interview—"

"This is not a good time."

"There was another murder last night. It appears to have a lot in common with the murder of Cindy Carter—the word *wrath* also was on the victim's forehead and the wooden bowl set on the body. With your experience as a criminal profiler and testifying as an expert witness in two of Mississippi's most notorious recent murder trials, we'd really like to sit down and do an interview with you—"

"I'm sorry, Mr. Keelson, but—"

"Please, I go by Bill. The prime question I know our audience would like an answer to is this: What type do they need to be on the lookout for in terms of possibly spotting this person? Is he the guy next door, someone running a cult, or just a loner you'd never suspect in a million years?"

Elizabeth looked up and spotted Dean Harris walking by her open door. He looked at her a moment, his eyes superior, a slight nod, turning to enter another hallway.

"Mr. Keelson. I will do an interview with you. I'll answer the first question you proposed, but no more. I don't want to do anything that might compromise the police investigation."

"Okay. When shall I come by your office?"

"Let's not do it here. I'll meet you at 12:15 in the Walmart parking lot a few blocks away from the university."

"How do we find you in the lot?"

"I'll find you. Should be easy to spot a TV news truck. Bye." She disconnected, picked up paperwork and walked to her classroom.

THIRTY-NINE

Sometimes Elizabeth forgot to pass around the class attendance sheet. Not today. Not ever again. She wrote on the white board as the students filed into the classroom. She closed her eyes a few seconds before turning around, before doing a head count—fearful that another vacant desk would connect with the death of another student.

Elizabeth turned, capped the marker, watching as the students took their seats, her role as a college professor infusing with her maternal instincts. The murder of Cindy Carter hung over Elizabeth's class like a dark cloud. It could be felt in the body language of her students, the distrustful look in their eyes—the shared loss and the grief that soldiers feel for fallen brothers. The deer-in-the-headlights dread that one of the students could be next, not knowing whether death hid in a dimly lit parking lot or right next door.

Who is the predator?

Who's next in his sights?

Elizabeth leaned back against the edge of her desk as the last few students arrived. Coming of age wasn't supposed to be a stifling of spirit. And now news of the second victim quickly spread throughout the university. Elizabeth smiled, making small talk as the stragglers set book-bags by their feet, but kept anxiety close to their chests.

She remembered a philosophy class she had in graduate school, the topic that day dealt with the resilience of the human spirit, the will to live and fight against great odds. She thought about how Cindy must have fought. Elizabeth knew that almost every person has a breaking point, a fault line—a crack in the shield, the Achilles' heel that is the cumulative emotional effects of shock and trauma to the spirit.

Wars are won and lost but at what sacrifice to the ground soldier? Charging through fire and fumes, the deafening explosions, the cries and screams shifting to groans, the grisly smell of charred flesh and wet death as heavy as artillery smoke.

"Professor Monroe, did you give us an extension on the essay because of what happened to Cindy?" asked a lanky student with sleepy eyes, soft reddish whiskers and ear-buds hanging like wet pasta from his shirt pocket.

Elizabeth turned to face him. "Yes, Anderson, you have another week." She stood and stepped in front of the white board. "Did everyone hear that? You have another week to finish your essays on the mind of a terrorist. In your work, write a contrast and comparison using analogies to the 'angry mob' syndrome and the lack of personal accountability. How and why can otherwise normal people change behind the veil of a terrorist cause? Is this mindset really any different for a lone serial killer? Name your sources, write APA style, check your syllabus, and be mindful of the grading rubric. This paper must be between five hundred to seven hundred words. No more. No less. Is everyone on board?"

Elizabeth looked around the room, heads nodding affirmatively, no one raising his or her hand. "Good." She took a deep breath. "I know that Cindy's horrible and senseless death is weighing heavy on all of us. I teach criminal psychology, and I have a difficult time sorting this out into something with reason because the very definition of what happened has nothing to do with rational thought, but rather evil motives. Before we begin today's topic on genetics and the criminal mind, I want to just chat...to have some open dialogue and to hear your thoughts and feelings about what happened to Cindy. We all could use a good dose of group therapy, including me, your instructor. Who wants to go first?"

A girl, hair in a ponytail, raised her hand.

"Yes, Katherine."

"This latest murder, the horrible stuff that happened to the guy...does this mean the killer isn't just preying on college girls? And if so, what do you think it says about this form of criminal insanity?"

"Insane, by the true definition of mental illness, most likely won't come into play with this person. Antisocial behavior? Yes, a high probability of that, certainly. Please keep in mind that murders from serial killers are about one percent of all murders in the U.S. every year. We average fifteen thousand murders a year. The FBI estimates that out of that number, approximately one hundred fifty are victims of serial killers. The FBI believes that at any given time in this country, between thirty to fifty serial killers are operating each year. So, in the big picture, there are very few out there."

A male student raised his hand. "Yeah, but we happen to have one of them killing people right here in Hattiesburg."

A female student said, "I wonder if he's from here...or just some creep drifting through and thought this would be a good place to do bad things?"

Elizabeth nodded. "That's a good question. Most serial killers are not drifters. Some, like Ted Bundy, are, but they're in the minority. Bundy killed more than thirty people in at least six states. Also, Tiffany, not all serial killers are men. Most are, but there are exceptions. And unlike the Hollywood version of a serial killer, such as Hannibal Lecter, most aren't brilliant criminals. They're usually of average intelligence, obsessive behavior in some areas, meticulous in planning, and all are psychopaths with blood colder than ice water."

She paused and walked slowly across the front of the room. "By the way, I've invited a friend of mine to come speak to you guys. He's retired from the FBI; but when he was there, he helped train the agents in the Behavioral Analysis Unit or as it's more commonly known, the BAU."

Elizabeth fielded questions and concerns for the remainder of the class. Dismissing her class early, she felt the time spent was beneficial. As the students left, they walked with a renewed sense of purpose, and there was some laughter and good-natured kidding between them.

One student stayed behind.

Julie Lassiter took her time shutting off her laptop, shuffling papers more than she had to, glancing over her shoulder as her classmates filed out of the room.

Elizabeth knew something was on Julie's mind. She waited for Julie to approach.

FORTY

J ulie Lassiter was the last student in the classroom. Elizabeth sat behind
the small wooden table near the white board, sensitive to Julie's languid
exit, and the tactics she used to delay her departure. Elizabeth looked up and
smiled. "Julie, are you okay?"

The girl stood, gathered her book bag and a file folder. She approached
the desk. "I'm all right, I guess. I just can't stop thinking about Cindy. I sat
right beside her in two other classes. We didn't always hang out, but we
were like good friends. I could share personal stuff with her, and she knew
she could tell me something and it would stay with me. That's why I knew
about the crap Gerald Simpson gave her. And she was having a real shitty…
sorry, a real difficult time with Alex Davidson. She said he drinks too much.
His favorite is tequila. Three shots and he's like a different guy. She said
you could see the changes in his eyes, even the color changed from gray to
green. Cindy said it was like watching the hulk turn green. And Alex would
sometimes quote the Bible."

Elizabeth listened closely. "What kind of quotes?"

"I don't exactly know, only that Cindy said he knew a lot about the
gospels and Revelation; and when he drank, she said he talked about the
Four Horsemen of the Apocalypse." Julie looked out the large window,
ashen clouds swelling in the sky. She cut her eyes to Elizabeth. "Professor
Monroe, do you think that Gerald Simpson or Alex Davidson could be a
serial killer…or could both of them be involved, killing as a team? I hate
to even think that, but when the police found another person killed, the

wooden bowl and the word *wrath*, just like with Cindy, my mind starts putting scenarios or possibilities together. I guess that's why I'm so interested in a career in forensic psychology."

"You're curious, Julie. That's the mark of a good investigator or a criminal psychologist; you look for cause and effect. But sometimes the obvious is deceptive, too easy, a ploy or not relevant. However, when it comes to separate events linking to a crime, often that will pass the scratch and sniff test. A former detective friend of mine used to tell me there are no coincidences when he was investigating a murder."

"Do you think he was right?"

"Yes, I do."

Julie thought about that for a moment, and then she handed Elizabeth a file. "This is my paper. I know you said we had and extra week, but I finished it already."

Elizabeth smiled. "Why does that not surprise me?"

"Cindy started on her paper the same time I did…" Julie's words got caught in her throat by way of her heart. She looked away, her eyes welling.

Elizabeth reached out and hugged her, the girl's small hands clutching Elizabeth's shoulders, as if she didn't want to be released.

After a moment, Elizabeth said, "I know I'm your teacher, and that doesn't end in the classroom or my office. Shoot me an email if something is bothering you, okay?"

Julie wiped away a single tear, nodding her head. "Thank you." She smiled. "Are you giving extra points for early delivery of the paper?"

Elizabeth grinned and said, "I would work that into the syllabus if it would entice all of the students to turn their homework in earlier rather than later."

They had a laugh together and Julie started for the door. She stopped and turned around. "Professor Monroe, it might not be anything…"

"Yes, what is it?"

"You mentioned how your detective friend said things that seem to be a coincidence in a crime, such as murder, usually aren't coincidental, right?"

"That's true. Usually there's something else."

"This may be nothing, but when you said that, it reminded me of something Cindy said a few weeks ago."

"What?"

"Last month there was a rally downtown, the third time it was held in Mississippi, and each time in three different cities. The one in Hattiesburg was near the courthouse. A group was protesting, demanding to have that Confederate memorial statue removed. A lot of other people were there…I guess you could call them counter protesters, white supremacists and some neo-Nazis. The police managed to keep the two groups separated. Cindy and I were there, too. She was very vocal when it came to removing what she said was a reminder of human oppression and slavery."

"That sounds like Cindy."

"I wasn't standing right next to her when it happened, but she told me that a man, someone from the other side, walked up to her and smiled a strange kind of creepy grin. She said he told her that it was because of people like her that the Confederate cause isn't appreciated. He said the Civil War wasn't about slavery. The guy said it was about a Southern way of life. Cindy said when she tried to give her opinion, the man told her to shut up or the wrath of God will take her down. I don't know if what he said about the wrath of God has anything to do with the word *wrath* left on Cindy and the man who was killed…or is it coincidental?"

"That's a good question. I'll mention it to the detective working the cases."

Julie nodded. "I need to get to class." She lifted her backpack and left the room.

Elizabeth stood from behind her desk, glancing out the window, dusky clouds forming. Her mind raced, picturing the word *wrath* scrawled on Cindy's forehead, the jagged lettering seared in Elizabeth's memory, bright as a serrated lightning bolt, splintering across the face of a darkening sky.

Elizabeth thought back, remembering the words the cemetery grounds-keeper had said after she and Bradford found the wooden cross on Zachariah Belmont's grave, *'The man buried in that grave does have followers, or admirers, to this very day. They visit the grave and sometimes leave stuff.'*

Elizabeth left the classroom and headed quickly to the university's history department. She had a question for a tenured professor that she hoped he could answer.

FORTY-ONE

Professor Atticus Ward sat at his desk and opened the latest copy of *Smithsonian Magazine*. His thin white hair looked like wisps of fine cotton fibers on a mostly shiny baldhead. He was in his forty-fifth year of teaching and was less than two months before his final retirement. He'd retired once before, but returned to a limited teaching schedule when boredom and domestic chores stifled him.

His small office, with its framed etchings of the Roman Coliseum, Parthenon, and many iconic destinations and landmarks, was deep in the recesses of the university's history department. He'd kept the same office for more than four decades. And it showed.

As Elizabeth approached his open door, he glanced over the tops of his smudged bifocals. "May I come in?" she asked.

He stood in his customary bowtie and a tweed jacket and grinned. "Absolutely. Come in, Elizabeth." He gestured to an empty chair next to his cluttered desk, cardboard boxes stacked in three corners. "Please, sit. What do I owe the honor of your visit to our humble history department?"

"I've always had a deep interest in history, international and U.S.—and, of course, the history of Mississippi. So I've come to pick your brain, and I deeply appreciate your vast plethora of wisdom and knowledge."

He laughed, placed his palms down for a moment on the top of his desk, brown age spots the size of dimes on the back of his hands. "So, aren't we bubbling with flattery today?" He grinned. "I know we've briefly spoken about history in the university coffee shop not long ago. With your background, the psychological nuances of history, the why factor is of keen interest to you." He cocked his head, a sparkle in his eyes. "Why did people do what they did at the time that, often, subsequently had a bearing on us? For example, how was British philosopher John Locke's influence on Thomas Jefferson a contributing factor in how the Declaration of Independence and the Constitution were written? We hold these truths to be self-evident...and we the people of the United States...."

Elizabeth smiled. "Isn't history about human nature and psychology about the nature of humans?"

He chuckled and laced his fingers together. "I've seen you on the news recently. In all my years in education, I can't remember a more sorrowful time at the university. The murder of Cindy Carter is something that I think about daily. I had her in one class. She was an exceptional student and a lovely person."

"Yes, she was." Elizabeth looked at a replica of the Magna Carta framed on the wall. "Atticus, what do you know about the history of the Klan in our area?"

"You mean Forrest County or the surrounding counties as well?"

"Yes, the surrounding counties, too."

"This is Mississippi and, of course, we probably have more historical markers representing the separation of the races, or having come to terms with that division, than any other state. There's the South, and then there's Mississippi. However, so much has changed for the better in the last few decades. The Jim Crow dichotomy is the stuff of museums, but racial issues will always be the cobwebs that exist in dark corners."

"Have you ever heard of a man named Zachariah Belmont? He lived around here from the Civil War up through the nineteen twenties."

Atticus leaned back in his chair, the springs squeaking. "I have. From what I recall, he was active with the Klan before the Great Depression. He was one of the leaders in a lynch mob on the Shubuta Bridge. He may haven been party to more. Mississippi led the nation with its history of lynchings from 1882 through 1968. At least 580 people were lynched. Most were black. Outside of Belmont's Klan affiliation, he had a small, but devoted, following. They had a campground of sorts—a church, few out buildings, shacks and a sawmill."

"What made people follow him?"

"What makes anyone follow a charismatic charlatan who believes he has all the answers? He played the weak links, fears and insecurities in people. He was a fiery orator who believed Canaanite Jews and blacks were evil. It was all about keeping the white race pure. The irony is that, in his time, as it is today, the DNA of the human race is a mix of tribes and blood from all over the world. Sex, like pollen in the winds of time, travels beyond borders and ethnicity. We've all descended from tribes leading back to Eden." He touched his bowtie, his eyes far away for a moment.

"Do you know where Belmont ran his campground?"

"I knew of the location only because it's a ghost town that abutted the river. Saw it years ago. My brother and I were on a fishing trip. In a remote area near where the Chickasawhay River and the Leaf River converge is a very primitive old shantytown. Nothing much left there. Lots of weeds and undergrowth. It might not even exist today. Belmont abandoned it when his health got bad. His followers drifted away. Elizabeth, do you mind if I ask why the interest in Zachariah Belmont?"

"I think there's a connection, maybe it's very distant, but I have a feeling there's a link—maybe biological or philosophical, between him and the serial killer."

Atticus leaned forward in his chair, his snowy eyebrows raised. "Really? How?"

"I'm not sure. Do you know any more about him or his followers...or anyone today that may be following whatever doctrine he spouted?"

"Let me think...you might try Anna's Antiques. Anna Lawrence runs the old place. Before she retired to run an antique shop, she was the state archivist in Jackson. She's a walking encyclopedia or Wikipedia when it comes to Mississippi history. She has a section somewhere in her store that deals with the history of civil rights. Lots of posters, certificates, degrees, pamphlets, out of print magazines and whatnot. I read that Belmont had published a few things, extremist hoopla most likely. If anybody in Mississippi has access to it, Anna Lawrence would know."

FORTY-TWO

Elizabeth left the university and drove toward an appointment she wasn't sure that she should keep. Running a few minutes late, she considered going straight to the sheriff's station. Maybe Bradford had discovered something else when he returned to the crime scene. But she told the reporter she'd do the interview, and maybe…just maybe…she might be able to draw the killer out.

She thought about what Julie Lassiter had said concerning the man who'd approached Cindy at the demonstration near the Confederate monument. *Was he simply an upset onlooker, or was it something more dangerous? Could that guy have stalked and killed Cindy? Then what about the middle-aged executive who was killed and left with a wooden bowl on his body?* Elizabeth's mind played back images from Cindy's funeral, the boot prints, wooden cross leaning against Zachariah Belmont's headstone, the honeysuckles.

She slowed at the intersection, pulled into the parking lot and drove toward the Channel Four News van in a remote section of the lot. The cameraman had set the camera on a tripod, reporter Bill Keelson pacing near the van, a notepad in one hand, cigarette in the other. Elizabeth could tell he was nervous.

She parked and approached the news crew.

Keelson greeted her like a 'we finance' used car salesman. Shark's grin. Firm handshake. Direct eye contact. "Dr. Monroe, thank you for coming. I appreciate your time."

"You're welcome. I only have a few minutes, and I can only respond to the question we discussed, what the general public should be aware of in terms of their safety. Anything related to the investigation would be theoretical at best on my part, conjecture, and those questions should be addressed by the police."

"No problem. If you don't mind standing right about here." He pointed to the pavement. "Just look toward me." He turned to the cameraman. "How's the shot, Simon?"

"Good. We're rolling."

Keelsen faced Elizabeth, microphone clutched in his hand. "Doctor Monroe, as you know, there has been a second murder in Forrest County with nearly the same bizarre clues left behind by the murderer—the word *wrath* on this victim's forehead, and also a wooden bowl set on the body. As a forensic profiler, what does this tell you about the killer? Is he the guy next door, some guy operating a backwoods cult, or just a loner – someone you'd never suspect in a million years?"

"He, or she, could be all of those things. If we assume a man is the person responsible for these two murders, he believes he's smarter than the police and investigators. He thinks he's infallible and has a godlike agenda to kill for his perception of the greater good. But it's really all about him. Another thing, he will hate to be challenged…to be called out as wrong or a phony. And he will retaliate toward anyone who does challenge him. It might not happen immediately, but once marked, this killer will lie in waiting, and he'll try to ambush the unsuspecting person."

"Police say both victims had evidence of stun-gun burns on their bodies. What does this tell you about him?"

"That he ambushed them. That he stalked them. That everything he does is carefully planned. He's a sociopathic weakling with deep-seated anger problems that go back to his parents—or a parent. He has a grandiose sense of self, thinks he's entitled since he believes it's his right…because in his mind, he's superior to others. He may appear to be glib and even charming, but he's truly a wolf in coward's clothing. I believe he's got severe repressed issues, but he can't feel the same way caring people can. Which means he can't change, because to change, he'd need to feel remorse, something he's incapable of doing." She glanced toward the camera and said, "This weakling is a parasite, and he will be caught."

— —

Elizabeth drove to downtown Hattiesburg toward the Justice Center building, the tall statue catching her eye. She slowed passed the stately red brick courthouse, concrete steps leading up to an entrance supported by six massive white columns. Next to the courthouse was a marble statue towering fifty feet into the air. Elizabeth stopped her car. The statue had replicas of a Confederate soldier and a Confederate *heroine* at the base, and another Confederate soldier on the top tier. The inscription read: *To the men and women of the Confederacy 1861 – 1865.*

She thought about what Julie Lassiter has said: *'Shut up or the wrath of God will take you down.'* Elizabeth looked up at the soldier atop the memorial, the sky darker than the marble sculpture. She pulled away and arrived at the sheriff's department fifteen minutes before the interviews were to begin. She parked and walked toward the three-story building.

When she got to the steps, she saw someone out of the corner of her eye.

Two students she'd seen at Cindy's funeral were walking down the sidewalk, coming toward her.

FORTY-THREE

The last thing Elizabeth wanted was to speak with them. She picked up her gait and walked quickly toward the entrance to the sheriff's department.

"Hey, Professor Monroe," Gerald Simpson said. "My friend, Cameron Bosky, is in your psyche class. He says it's one of his best."

Elizabeth stopped at the top step, turned around. Gerald Simpson and Alex Davidson grinned and walked up the steps. Elizabeth thought Simpson had the slow measured pace of a predator. She said, "Cameron tells me he wants to go into investigative work, maybe apply to the FBI. What do you two want to do?"

Simpson grinned. "That's a good question. I've had two NFL scouts express interest. We'll see. My dad thinks I should play for the team that makes the best offer. But if the Miami Dolphins come knocking, I'm there."

Alex Davidson cleared his throat. "I'm leaning toward environmental biology."

Simpson looked over Elizabeth's shoulder and then at her. "So if you don't mind me asking, what brings you to the sheriff's office?"

She blinked once and then held his gaze, looking Simpson in the eye. "You do." She let the two words register for a few seconds. Simpson grinned, looked down at Elizabeth, his smile gone. Davidson folded his arms. "I'm working with investigators in the death of Cindy Carter. You both knew her well." She stopped, looked at Davidson. His jawline hardened, and then he forged a smile.

Simpson said, "We're not suspects. We're here to assist the detectives. We want to know who killed Cindy as much as you do, Doctor Monroe."

Davison nodded. "Maybe even more. You were only her teacher. Cindy and I had talked about getting married one day. Gerald and I have nothing to do with Cindy's death."

Elizabeth smiled. "Then you have nothing to worry about. Now, if you will excuse me."

Another man approached. He was in his early fifties, silver hair, and an expensive charcoal gray suit. His face haggard, suspicious, eyes blinking as if they were inflamed. He carried a briefcase. Gerald Simpson smiled and said, "Doctor Monroe, I'd like to introduce you to my lawyer. This is Bill Peterson. He's from the law firm of Peterson, Becket and Johnston in Jackson, and he's an old family friend."

Peterson extended his hand, "Pleasure to meet you, Doctor Monroe. Your name rings a bell. Are you one of Gerald's professors?"

"No."

"May I ask what you teach?"

"Criminal forensic psychology."

"Oh, now I remember where I heard your name. This should be interesting."

— —

Elizabeth sat behind a one-way mirrored glass panel. Her area was in the shadows, barely enough light for her to write. She looked into the interrogation room. Detective Bradford sat with his back to Elizabeth. Alex Davidson sat opposite Bradford. Under the lights, Elizabeth could observe Davidson well, close enough to see him blink.

A high-resolution camera was at eye-level, recording the interview. His image was projected on a flat screen to the right of the one-way glass, about six feet from Elizabeth. From that perspective, she could see the pupils in his blue eyes. She now assumed the high-priced lawyer was there to represent only Simpson. *So they're throwing Alex under the bus,* she thought as the interview began.

Detective Bradford had Alex state his name and the fact that he was a student. He told him that he was there to help investigators sort through some of the hazy details surrounding Cindy's death, and he was there through his own volition. Should he at anytime want to request legal services, all he had to do was to let them know.

Bradford started off tossing softballs: *How'd you meet Cindy Carter? What was Cindy like to be around? Where'd you go on dates?* And, after a few minutes, he asked, "Who do you think would have a reason to kill Cindy?"

"Nobody, really. Cindy wouldn't hurt a fly. She didn't have any enemies, at least not any that I ever heard her talk about."

"How about Larry Tucker?"

He shook his head. "Larry might be an odd dude, but he didn't know her that well. He met her at a couple of parties, but that's it, I guess."

"Do you know if Larry is into satanic sacrifices...you know, killing small animals?"

Davidson shook his head. "I heard he keeps a pet vampire bat. He's into some pretty dark stuff. I don't know about animal sacrifices."

"Do you think Gerald Simpson killed Cindy?"

Elizabeth watched closely. Davidson sat a little straighter. He glanced toward the camera for a second, nostrils flaring slightly, chest swelling. "No, Gerald may be a jock, but he's not the violent type."

Elizabeth looked at the monitor. She watched Davidson's pupils grow larger. He looked up at Bradford and said, "I thought we came down here to talk about places Cindy went, people she knew, that sort of thing. I didn't think I'd have to answer questions about whether or not I thought one of my fraternity brothers killed my girlfriend."

"Wouldn't you want to know? If someone in the Kappa house killed her, if the same guy is overpowering others, grown men, and killing them, wouldn't you want to know? You could be next."

Davidson pursed his lips. "Yeah I'd want to know, but no one in my fraternity is a murderer."

"But you can't be sure of that, can you. Last question—did you kill Cindy?"

"No! Why do you even ask me that? I loved Cindy."

"A lot of guys love their wives or girlfriends, get drunk and beat them to a pulp…or put a gun to their heads."

The door to Elizabeth's far left opened and Detective Ed Milton entered the room. His tie was loosened, white dress shirt wrinkled, sleeves rolled up on his beefy arms. He nodded at her, eyes puffy, looked at the interview for a moment. "So, Doctor Monroe…what do you think? You believe the boyfriend did it? As far as we know, he was the last person to see Cindy Carter alive."

She looked up at the detective. "No, I don't think Alex Davidson did it. But I do think he knows more than he's telling Detective Bradford."

Milton folded his arms. "Well, the other guy, Gerald Simpson, was the victim's first boyfriend when she came to college. He's all lawyered up. Let's see what he has to say."

FORTY-FOUR

L ess than five minutes after Alex Davidson left the interrogation room, Gerald Simpson arrived. And he entered with his lawyer at his side. They sat across the table from Detective Bradford, Simpson taking the same seat that Davidson had sat in, the attorney making small talk about two cases he defended in Hattiesburg a few years ago.

Detective Milton stepped into the room, glancing at the one-way mirrored glass, sitting down next to Bradford.

Bradford said, "Okay, let's get started. Thank you for coming here today. Detective Milton and I appreciate your willingness to help us as we work to solve these murders and try to prevent the perpetrator from killing again. Gerald, how would you classify your relationship with Cindy Carter?"

Simpson looked at his attorney. Peterson nodded and Simpson said, "Good...real good. We dated in our freshman year. That seems so long ago. Anyway, Cindy was a great girl. Her death is a horrible loss."

"Yes, it is. I saw you at the funeral. Did you have time to speak with Cindy's parents?"

"No, I saw them, but they were in pretty bad shape. Didn't talk to her sisters either. I just wasn't sure if I could come up with anything to say to help comfort them, considering what was going on that day."

Elizabeth cut her eyes from watching Simpson through the glass to the TV monitor. She leaned closer, watching his every move.

Bradford nodded. "I understand. Funerals are difficult. Why'd you stop dating Cindy?"

He raised his shoulders. "Well, you know, sometimes stuff just doesn't work out. We had some good times together, but I think our goals were different."

"In what way?"

"I can't say specifically. She'd be like hey, 'what's your idea of a perfect marriage?' That kind of talk sort of put the breaks on the relationship, least for me." He grinned. "We just drifted apart. I hardly ever saw her on campus, you know—different majors. And then she started dating my friend, Alex Davidson."

Detective Milton asked, "Do you think they had a good relationship?"

Attorney Peterson raised his right hand. "Detective, I need to interject here. That question will cause for my client to offer pure speculation. We'd rather not go there. Please stick to the facts."

Detective Milton smiled, his eyes leveled at the attorney. "Often times, the facts rise up like cream to the top once you stir the milk."

"But not at the sake of my client. I'd suggest you stick to the facts or this interview will end."

Elizabeth watched Simpson as he listened to his attorney, Simpson trying to bury a loftier look on his face. She made a note.

Bradford leaned back in his metal chair. He smiled. "I understand, Mr. Peterson, but this is not a deposition. It's not a hearing. The nature of the investigation, at this point, has a lot to do with speculation because that often leads to the facts or leads away from them. This includes the supposition and opinions of witnesses and people who were in Cindy Carter's inner circle. They're the ones who have the greatest insight into her life, and maybe what caused her death. So if you'd bear with us, I'd like to know what Gerald thinks in addition to the facts as we know them because here are the facts: two people are dead. Both had their throats slit. Both had the word *wrath* written across their foreheads and each victim had a wooden bowl set on their body. And the fact is the guy won't stop killing until he's caught."

Elizabeth smiled, pumped her right fist in the air and whispered, "And that's the way it is."

Bradford leaned forward in his chair. "As of late, Cindy was spending more time at the Kappa house. She and Alex did homework together, hung out. As part of that inner circle of friends, did you see anything out of character…something odd, maybe an intense argument? Maybe Cindy getting upset and leaving?"

"Sometimes. Usually after Alex knocked back a few. He's got a temper, or maybe he just got tired of her nagging. I'd see Cindy and Alex sometimes, but between sports, school, and working a part-time job, I'm not at the house as much as I used to be. I'm graduating in a few months."

"You told me you were there the night Cindy disappeared. Run through that, again, if you would…exactly what were you doing when she went missing?"

FORTY-FIVE

Simpson looked at his attorney. Peterson said, "Detective, again you are assuming my client knew or knows exactly when Cindy Carter vanished. He does not."

Bradford nodded. "Fair enough. Let me rephrase. You were at the same party Cindy attended the day she was last seen. What'd you see?"

"Well, so you want me to tell you what I already told you?" He leaned forward, placing his hands on the table, touching a bottle of water in front of him.

Bradford said, "If you don't mind."

"Like I said earlier, I was just hangin' out at the house. I don't drink much 'cause of football season, so I remember things pretty clearly. I saw Cindy off and on. She seemed fine, having fun. Drinking with everybody else."

Elizabeth could hear her Uncle Hal's soft voice. '*Most of the conscious moves are an act—the player trying to throw off the others. It's the subconscious ones that give way to deception.*' She watched Simpson close on the monitor. He didn't blink for most of his answer, his eyes dilating slightly. His voice a slight pitch higher as he spoke.

"I remember Cindy getting pissed at Alex for some reason. There were a lot of girls there that day. I thought it was some jealousy thing on her part. She was kinda like that with me. But with Alex, I think the jealousy went into some kind of possession, you know? Almost clingy, you know what I mean with chicks, right?"

162

Bradford ignored the question. "Did you have a pet as a kid?"

"Huh?"

"You know...a pet? Cat? Dog?"

The attorney said, "Why is that relevant?"

Bradford smiled. "Cindy's mother told me she had a dog back home. A golden retriever."

Simpson said, "She always talked about that dog, almost like he was her brother. Yeah, we had a dog. His name was Buster. He was an Irish wolfhound."

"How long did Buster live?"

"Huh? You mean like how many years?"

"Yes."

"I can't remember. We had him awhile and one day he ran away. We never saw him again. The whole family, especially my sister, was pretty tore up about it."

"What do you think happened to Cindy?"

"Some jerk killed her."

"Who killed her?"

"Wait a minute," said Peterson.

Elizabeth watched Simpson's body language.

Bradford leaned closer. "Again, counselor, we want to know what Gerald, Alex and the rest of Cindy's friends think may have happened. It doesn't mean there will be any real validity in what they say, but it gives us possible investigative avenues that we otherwise might not find. It's called running down leads. Most are dead-end roads."

Peterson rubbed his chin with his thumb. "I'll allow it, but with the conditional acceptance that this is all purely hypothetical and has no bearing on the facts." He nodded at Simpson.

Simpson half smiled and said, "Like Mr. Peterson says, I don't have any facts to prove it...but I know that Larry Tucker made a weird comment one time about Cindy."

"What comment?"

"He'd been smokin' a lot of weed, and he said it was too bad Cindy probably wasn't a virgin because she'd make a good sacrifice in a video game. He mumbled some crazy stuff about a darker link between modern society and ancient societies; something about how ritual killings helped destroy any democratic systems of government and just simply added to the tyranny of a class system. The dude's out there, a philosophy major. Good luck with that."

Bradford made a note on the pad in front of him. He looked up at Simpson and asked, "Why are you a ride-share driver?"

"Excuse me?"

"Your family can afford the services of Mr. Peterson. Looks like you may be drafted into the NFL. Why drive around and pick people up as a Uber, Lyft or Kars driver?"

"Just a way to make some spending money. I can work when I want to, off the clock or on, to fit my schedule. Besides, I'm a people person. I enjoy hearing what my customers have to say sittin' in the backseat of my SUV." He glanced at the one-way glass and then looked at Bradford. "I'm not a psych major, but you'd be surprised at how many people let their hair down and talk about all kinds of stuff when they're being chauffeured around."

"No doubt. Gerald, you're a top athlete. What, you're close to six-three, pushing two hundred pounds? I bet you can take care of yourself."

"I do all right."

"Then why carry a stun-gun?"

"Wait a minute!" fired Peterson. "There is no law to prevent the possession of a stun-gun any more than carrying a can of pepper-spray or mace. Where are you going with this, Detective?"

"Just curious. Gerald looks like he can definitely take care of himself, why carry a stun-gun?"

Simpson shook his head, smiled. "I grew up with guns in the family. I don't have a gun here at school or a permit to carry. But with such violence in the world, it doesn't matter if you can bench press two hundred pounds. A stun-gun just offers a level of defense without permanently injuring or killing a person."

Elizabeth took a note, studying Simpson. No one said anything for a few seconds, and then Bradford asked, "Is there anything else you want to add at this time?"

"No, nothing I can think of right now. I do want to commend you and Detective Milton. I know you have a hard job. I hope you find the person who killed Cindy and that man?"

"Did you do it?" asked Bradford.

"Did I do it?" repeated Simpson. "I can't believe you asked me that question."

Milton leaned closer. "Are you going to answer it?"

Attorney Peterson shook his head. "Of course my client had nothing to do with these murders."

Bradford sat back. "Then let him answer the question."

Simpson said, "Hell no! I'm an honest person. I didn't kill Cindy. I can't believe you—"

"It's our job to ask these questions," Milton interjected.

"We're done here," said Peterson, standing.

Elizabeth looked at the monitor closely, a slight smile at the corner of her mouth.

FORTY-SIX

Through the one-way glass, Elizabeth watched Larry Tucker enter the interrogation room like a human shadow. His lithe body had a feline tempo, a catlike tread, almost as if his feet didn't touch the tile floor. Dressed in black jeans and a dark hoodie, he strolled in with his hands in his pockets, scruffy gaunt face, dark half circles beneath his impassive, blood-shot hazel eyes.

Detective Milton stood and motioned for Tucker to sit opposite him and Bradford. "Please, take a seat," Milton said.

Tucker nodded and sat, slouching in the metal foldout chair. He crossed his arms. "Do I need a lawyer?"

Elizabeth leaned a little closer to the glass. She could see that his suspicion was guised as indifference. But Larry Tucker was very much afraid. He licked his thin, red lips.

Milton said, "If you want a lawyer, that's entirely up to you. At this point, we're simply questioning you again for clarification. There's no need for us to read you your rights because you haven't been charged with a crime. You are simply a witness, someone who knew the victim and her friends. Understand?"

"Sure, I understand a lot more than you think I do."

Elizabeth made a note.

Bradford said, "No need for push back. We appreciate you taking the time to come down here. We know you're busy. You're a full-time student and you work a job. Probably doesn't allow for much free time."

"That's for sure." Tucker looked at the camera and the one-way glass. "Who's on the other side of the glass?"

Bradford didn't offer a response. "Let's concentrate on what's in this room and we'll knock this interview out quickly. How's your pet bat?"

"CD's fine?"

"CD?" asked Milton.

"Stands for Count Dracula." Tucker didn't blink, staring at Milton before cracking his knuckles.

Bradford said, "Let's move on. When was the last time you saw Cindy Carter?"

"It's been a couple of months. It was at one of the keg parties at the Kappa house."

"How well do you know Gerald Simpson?"

"Gerald the jock? We don't have a lot in common. He's like 'hey let's go kick ass and take names,' figuratively speaking. I'm like let's just chill, dude. Smoke some medicinal marijuana; take the testosterone erection edge off the nervous world. No need to charge with bayonets. That's not how the art of war is won or waged."

"Your college major is philosophy. Going to graduate school or will you be looking for a career?"

"I'm not exactly sure what a career means today. I see myself as a consultant."

Bradford glanced at his notes. "Gerald tells us that you told him, and I'm quoting here, it was too bad Cindy probably wasn't a virgin because she'd make a good sacrifice in a video game. What did you mean by that?"

Tucker grinned, scratched the tip of his nose, nostrils red at the rims. "Like I said, the dude is a little heavy on the testosterone pills and it sort of clouds his cognitive ability. What I actually said was that I wondered if Cindy was still a virgin because she reminded me of a character in the video game Hellsblade."

"Since Gerald had dated Cindy, were you looking for confirmation that Cindy was or was not a virgin?"

"Naw, man. I could give a rat's ass whether she was or wasn't. I don't have stats, but based on a small sampling, I'd bet every chick that comes to this university, by their senior year, has had sex...and with multiple partners."

167

Elizabeth looked at the monitor, trying not to feel repugnance for the student on the other side of the camera.

Bradford and Milton took turns questioning Tucker, most of the line of inquiry directed toward timelines relative to Cindy's death and the murder of Charlie Lehman. "Did you know Charles Lehman?" asked Milton.

"No, never heard of the dude."

"The dude's dead, the second victim after Cindy."

"Heard about that. Seems like you guys got a serial killer running around Hattiesburg."

Bradford said, "The killer left the bodies in a gruesome display. It was as if they'd been through some kind of pagan ritual. You told us you aren't part of a satanic cult here in Southern Mississippi. Who is? Who might be someone who's moved from animal sacrifices to human sacrifices?"

He shook his head, pulled at his shoulder. "I have no clue. Like I told you guys, back at my house—I'm not into satanic rituals. I don't have time."

Bradford jotted down a note. "Alex Davidson said he's played video games with you...some pretty-off-the-charts dark stuff."

"Yeah, well you dudes have already typecast me, but how about Alex... what does that tell you about the son of a preacher man? He's not all he appears to be, especially after knocking back his beverage of preference— tequila. I might be a philosophy major, but I got nothing on Alex when it comes to the Bible, especially Revelation. He likes playing video games with the apocalypse theme. He said he plays better after seven shots of tequila because it's all about sevens. Seven trumpets. Seven seals. Seven angels." Tucker picked at his long thumbnail, lifting his eyes to the detectives. "And one beast."

FORTY-SEVEN

After watching the three interrogations, Elizabeth was ready to leave the room. Her palms felt moist. She took three pages of notes—one page for each interview. She stood as the door opened, Detective Bradford and Detective Milton entering. Bradford asked, "What'd you think?"

"I think I need to get out of this room. That was thorough."

Detective Milton said, "Yeah, there was a lot of knee-deep bullshit flowing in there."

Bradford said, "Let's go into the office. We can grab some coffee or water and hear what you think."

Elizabeth followed them through a hallway and across a short expanse of offices. They entered a conference room. Bradford asked, "What can I get you to drink?"

"Water would be good, thanks."

He opened the door to a small refrigerator and pulled out two bottles of water, looked over to his partner and asked, "Ed, you want some water?"

"Cup of coffee for me." He stepped to the counter and poured coffee into a paper cup. They sat at the conference table. "Well, Doctor Monroe," said Milton, holding the steaming cup. "What do you think?"

She looked at her notes for a few seconds. "They know more than they're telling us, especially Gerald Simpson."

Milton grinned, then sipped his coffee. "I could have told you that, and I don't have a Ph.D. behind my name."

Bradford said nothing, giving Elizabeth time to review her notes. She said, "Alex Davidson was the only one of the three who didn't try to throw one of the others under the bus. Gerald Simpson certainly did, making his BFF, Alex, out as a hot-tempered girlfriend beater. Larry Tucker volunteered more information than you asked…basically saying Alex has a Jekyll and Hyde personality after drinking too much. So the question begs…why didn't Alex have any negative comments about the other two?"

Milton swallowed a sip of coffee. "Maybe it's because what they say is true and the boyfriend, Alex, is not the mild-mannered son of a preacher man."

Bradford said, "Or maybe Gerald Simpson and Larry Tucker are in this together and made a pact to cover each other."

Milton nodded. "Tucker is a guy who's been bullied most of his life. He's developed a bizarre defense by going so Goth that people pretty much leave him alone…unless they want something. This was the case with members of the fraternity. They befriended Tucker and then summarily rejected him when they didn't need him anymore. Kinda reminds me of that old Stephen King novel, Carrie. Her rage came out like a bat outta hell. Speaking of bats, who keeps a pet vampire bat in his room? Maybe these deaths are Tucker's ultimate fantasy…his definitive video game where he stalks and kills real people."

Bradford replaced the cap on the water bottle, considering what his partner said. "That's not out of the cards. His house certainly has the Halloween feel of spiders and snakes. You'd expect bodies to be buried out back. But our killer isn't hiding bodies—he's displaying them. Granted, it fits with some crazy kind of satanic ritual. The word *wrath*, the wooden bowls. It's as if the playbook was taken from some dark video game…but something in my gut tells me Tucker isn't our guy."

Elizabeth said nothing, listening.

Milton pulled a wrinkled handkerchief from his pocket and wiped his glistening forehead. "Okay, let's consider Simpson's history. He was charged with date rape in his freshman year. Beat the rap with his big money lawyers. He recently bought a stun gun. Both vics were hit with a stun gun before they were killed. Simpson drives around as a ride-share driver picking up people in his new SUV. He's on a full football scholarship. If I were wagering money, Gerald Simpson is the most likely suspect. He's an asshole who believes he's entitled to things he will never earn. He was raised to believe he's superior to everyone else."

Bradford leaned back in the hard plastic chair. "But all of that doesn't make him a murderer. Why would he want to kill her or Charlie Lehman? We couldn't find any DNA or skin cells on his stun gun. We haven't found any physical evidence in his SUV. He definitely fits the profile but, as we all know, we can't take it to the prosecutor without something physical to tie him to one or both murders."

"That's because he didn't do it," Elizabeth said.

Both detectives turned toward her.

"How do you figure that?" Milton asked.

"Simpson's a pathological liar. When you asked him if he killed Cindy, he repeated the question. Most people, if innocent, simply say no to a question like that. It doesn't mean he actually killed Cindy, but he's being very evasive."

"No shit," Milton said, leaning back in his chair.

Elizabeth continued. "Larry Tucker has deep psychological issues. I'd bet he was abused, probably sexually, as a child. As far as a possible killer, Alex Davidson would fit the profile closer. Cindy was breaking up with him. His world was wrapped around her. He was raised in a strict regime of fundamentalist religious doctrine where he toed the line between coming of age and sinning. With an authoritarian, perhaps messianic preacher for a father, a man who may have been unyielding in his strict application of his literal interpretation of the Bible, Alex could be in a frightening place."

Milton cleared his throat. "How's that?"

"Sometimes, in an environment like Alex was exposed to, love was probably conditional. It would be earned by performing in dictated ways... almost like a puppy is rewarded for becoming housebroken. Alex leaves that world and enters college. He's popular. He pledges to a fraternity and the brotherhood of like-minded friends. And when he meets someone like Cindy, he locks into love that's no longer conditional. But when she puts conditions on his behavior and eventually breaks up with him, when his reality crumbles, he falls deeper into the fantasy of dark video games and the darker façade of alcohol abuse. It can be a lethal combination. When we factor in his fascination with passages from the Book of Revelation about the end of times, it makes his psychological mix even deeper...darker."

Bradford jotted a note on a legal pad. "So you think Alex Davidson is the strongest suspect...he may be the killer?"

"I wish I could answer that with a better degree of confidence. Oh, something I almost forgot...one of my students, Julie Lassiter, was Cindy's close friend. She told me that Cindy was approached by a man at a protest rally downtown at the Confederate Memorial."

Bradford nodded. "That was a couple of months ago. How was Cindy approached, and what did the man say?"

"Cindy and Julie were there, with a hundred other like-minded demonstrators to rally for the removal or to relocate the monument. Not unlike a dozen other cities across parts of the South, the activists were met with counter protestors. In this case, white supremacists, a few neo-Nazis, and others who had their own reasons for being there. Julie told me that Cindy said the man was a counter protestor, and he somehow picked her out of the crowd, walked up to her and said, *'Shut up or the wrath of God will take you down.'* What concerns me is that he used the word *wrath*. This person was most likely not a student at the university."

Milton said, "I saw the interview you did live on CNN—how you more or less profiled hate groups, Neo-Nazis and Klan members." He paused, picked at a callous on his left hand and raised his eyes up to Elizabeth. "Maybe this guy who approached Cindy—his choice of the word *wrath*—was purely coincidental to the same word used two months later on Cindy's body. I'm betting Charlie Lehman wasn't at the rally and wrath was written on his forehead, too."

The phone on the table buzzed. Bradford answered. He listened and then said, "Great, please bring the report to the conference room. Thanks."

"What was that?" Milton asked.

"The lab got a match on wood used to make the wooden bowl...and the white paint used to write *wrath* on the victim. The paint is the same stuff they use to make the white lines on sports fields, like football or baseball—"

"That'd be easy for Simpson to get. He's spent a lot of time on a football field."

Bradford nodded. "The lab thinks the perp used his finger to scrawl the word wrath on the vics. But there's no sign of a fingerprint anywhere on the bodies or near them. That paint's easy for anyone to get. But the wood's different. The stuff used to make the bowls comes from a fairly rare tree in Mississippi…the spruce pine. You can find them in the De Soto National Forest."

Elizabeth said, "The same forest where Cindy's body was discovered. Did the wood on the cross we found on Zachariah Belmont's grave match the spruce pine?"

"No."

"Maybe it'll match the planks on that old bridge over the Chickasawhay River."

FORTY-EIGHT

Alex Davidson walked slowly up the wooden steps leading to the front porch of the Kappa house, his mind playing back the interview the cops did with him. *They freakin' believe I did it,* he thought. *Lots of innocent people are in prison for crimes they didn't commit.* At the top step, he reached in his shirt pocket, pulled out a cigarette, slipped it in the corner of his mouth. He patted his jeans for the lighter.

Gerald Simpson stepped out from behind one of the columns. He snatched the unlit cigarette out of Alex's mouth, crushing the paper against his forehead, slivers of tobacco raining down on Alex's nose and lips. Simpson sneered. "I started to wait for you to light it. Then I could burn your forehead. Leave a little brand right in the center."

Alex swatted Simpson's hand.

Simpson grabbed Alex's wrist and pulled his hand behind his back. "What'd you say to the cops?"

"Nothing!"

"You talked with them a long fuckin' time, and when they got to me, they basically accused me of killing Cindy. I warned you, Bible boy. I'm not gonna let you mess up my NFL draft opportunities. Got it?"

"Let me go!"

Two members of the fraternity came out of the house, both with ear-buds wedged in their ears, faces glued to their phones. One student, lanky and a baseball cap on backwards, said, "What's goin' on, dudes? We're sup-posed to be fraternity brothers, not freakin' enemies."

Simpson let Alex loose, grinned. "We're just having fun—doing some horseplay. Ol' Alex thinks he can take me 'cause he wrestled back in high school. Right AD. He likes being called AD because it takes him back to biblical times…after death."

The student pulled out one ear-bud, angled his head like a cat watching a bird in a tree. He said, "I don't think it stands for after death. But AD's got a good vibe to it." He looked at Alex. "Later bros. Peace."

Alex said nothing, spitting out a flake of tobacco, and massaging his right wrist.

The second student, wearing a football jersey, half smiled and added, "Hey, Simpson, you get hurt in horseplay, you can't play in Saturday's game, coach will be like breathing fire." The two students left, ear-buds back in, walked under a magnolia tree, unaware of a cardinal singing from a low limb.

Simpson turned to Alex. "If anybody killed Cindy, it'd be you. You were so pissed every time you two had a fight. One time I saw the veins pop out on your forehead, like you were about to have a friggin' coronary. Maybe you took her out in the woods, raped her, and you and crazy Tucker did some kind of sacrificial killing. All that crap is in those games you two played together. You smoke enough weed and the boundaries get a little blurry." He used his open fist to tap Alex on his shoulder. "Your secret is my secret. Stays with me, buddy. But don't you ever point the finger at me again."

Alex stared at him a moment, the odor of damp tobacco lingering in his nostrils. "You're an ass and a bully. As of right now, I'm no longer a member of this fraternity. Never felt like I belonged here anyway. One final thing, Cindy told me what you tried to do to her. The same sick crap you did with Sandy Edwards. You put something in their drinks, and you rape them. Then say it was consensual. You should be in jail." Alex turned to leave.

Simpson bolted down the steps and placed his hand on Alex's chest. "Listen, dickhead, I didn't rape anyone. Don't need to. I have more women in a month than you'll have in a lifetime." He lowered his hand and started a slow smile. "Hey, look what's really going down…the forensic psyche teacher, Professor Monroe, she's manipulating us."

"What?"

"You, me, and weird Larry Tucker. The professor is playing us all off on each other. It's mind games. And she's damn good at it. When I talk to her, I'm like wanting to say, stop trying to read my fuckin' mind, prof. She's got some crusade goin' on in her head. It's all over the news—somebody killed her daughter a while back and the professor is hell-bent on pinning that on one of us or somebody she *feels* did it." Simpson made the sign of quotation marks with his fingers. "She's pretty—got a great body for a woman that old, but she seems anti-men, like she's a lesbian."

"I gotta go."

"Wait...she's gonna keep twisting things around, using her psychological garbage to paint pictures of us as frat boys with a murder complex. You see it happening every year. I watched a YouTube video of her testifying at the trial of that casino killer. That dude didn't stand a chance after that bitch was done. She had the jury hanging on every word. If we're not careful, one of us is gonna be next on her hit list. I'm hoping she zeros in on Tucker. He'd be an easy conviction. But if she comes for you or me...we need to be ready."

"What do you mean...ready?"

"Whatever it takes. It's like football...when you get knocked down, you need to get back up and hit harder. It's called self defense. You do what you gotta do. The art of war, bro."

Alex looked him straight in the eye. "Professor Monroe's not playing us against each other. She's inside your mind, and she's playing you against yourself. But since you don't have a conscience, it doesn't seem like much of a mind game." Alex stepped around him, walked under a canopy of live oaks to his car parked on the street, cottonwood blossoms floating down around his slumped shoulders.

—◆—

Elizabeth stood from the conference table. She stepped to the window, gazing outside, watching a robin hop on the fresh-cut lawn. She turned around, looked at the detectives and said, "After reading your report of the last crime scene, there is a close similarity to what happened to Cindy. After listening to the interrogation of those three students and reviewing the evidence, I really don't think any one of them committed the murders. Even if there was a pact between Simpson and Tucker, I'm not convinced they did it."

Milton said, "Simpson didn't have an alibi for the estimated time of death for Charles Lehman. The jock said he was working, but there was no client in his car during that period to back up his story. Again, for my money, Simpson is a cold blooded killer."

Bradford sipped from his water bottle, his eyes partly bloodshot. "Elizabeth, in the text you received, the perp used the word *he* to imply that someone else left that plate on Cindy's grave. Larry Tucker is susceptible to follow a charismatic cult leader. Maybe he didn't kill for the perp, but he could have delivered that plate."

"Possibly. But you said you didn't find prints on the plate or Cindy's earring. I think our killer's a middle-aged white man. He's probably divorced. Honorably discharged from the service. He'll be neat in appearance. If he has long hair, it'll be in a ponytail. He does things with an air of precision. He's a builder—a carver, someone who has the mind of an architect and the hands of a craftsman. His hands will be calloused, probably scarred or even missing a finger from a saw blade. And that might be why you can't find a print even though he used a finger to write *wrath* on the bodies. What if the tip of a finger is missing?"

Milton took notes and smiled out of one side of his mouth. "Are you psychic, or just throwing out random stuff that will cover about half the working men in Mississippi?"

Elizabeth turned and touched the window with the open palm of her right hand, the glass cool to her skin, white clouds motionless against a deep blue sky. "He'll drive a pickup truck because he hauls logs from the trees he fells to make things from wood, like bowls and crosses. Most serial killers strangle or bludgeon their victims to death. This guy uses a knife because he's comfortable around knifes. He probably will have a collection, attend knife and gun shows. He may have left his church due to a disagreement over policies or even the interpretation of scripture. He'll either be an active member of the Klan or certainly have a white supremacist's philosophy. And he'll blend in to Southern Mississippi like a pinecone on a tree. However, as vanilla as he appears, he has a deep-seated disgust for the system, the law, and the judicial process. He reacts to challenges. He must have seen my television news interview and retaliated with the honeysuckles just to let me know he's watching." She touched the conference table, looked at Bradford. "And it will escalate further. He's just getting started."

FORTY-NINE

Elizabeth left the justice department playing back the interrogations in her mind. She walked down Main Street, past the old brick courthouse, an American flag popping in the breeze atop a tall metal pole. A thin man with a wild gray beard, faded jean jacket with cut-off sleeves, blurred tats on forearms, walked toward her. His eyes had a distant, flat stare, mouth set down, a slight limp from his left leg.

Elizabeth approached the Confederate War memorial. Two plump pigeons waddled near the base, angling for food scraps visitors threw their way. An old black man, hair cotton white, sat on a park bench. The shadow of the memorial fell across half of his creased face, his right eye drooping. He reached into a Ziploc bag, slowly lifting out a boiled peanut, removing the moist shell with fingers from both hands and placing the peanut in his mouth. He chewed unhurriedly, tossing a peanut to a small brown sparrow near his worn boots, one boot unlaced.

In her mind, Elizabeth played back segments of the three interviews. *What am I missing?* Her thoughts kept returning to what her student, Julie Lassiter, told her about the unknown man and what he'd said to Cindy: *Shut up or the wrath of God will take you down.* Elizabeth reached in her purse for her phone and looked up Julie Lassiter in her contacts. She made the call. It went to voice-mail: *"Hi, this is Julie. I can't answer my phone right now. Please leave a message. Thanks!"*

"Julie, this is Elizabeth Monroe. I've been thinking about what you mentioned to me. It's in reference to what Cindy Carter told you about the man who approached her at the demonstration. Please call me when you get this. Thank you." She disconnected and placed the phone back in her purse. And then she walked five blocks downtown to Anna's Antiques.

The exterior of the store was roughhewn, the paint peeling. Aged black shutters faded to the color of weak coffee. The only thing that looked fairly new was the sign, *Anna's Antiques*, hand-painted with perfect lettering on the glass door. Elizabeth entered and bells jingled, similar to the Salvation Army kettle bells. The string of chimes was attached to the interior door handle.

Elizabeth softly closed the door and stood on the old wooden floor for a moment. There was no one. No customers. No store clerks. No Anna. The interior was filled with vintage furniture, yellow price tags hanging stationary in the motionless air. Wicker baskets hung from the ceiling. Framed paintings of Mississippi landscapes, paddleboats and beaches, took most of the wall space.

Elizabeth could see a winding path between copper pots, spittoons, Coca Cola signs, Tiffany lamps, tube radios, ceramic dogs and cats. She thought of Jack, paused for a moment, and took a step. The wooden planks creaked under her weight.

She stopped and listened, wondered if she should take her phone from her purse and call the store. If someone answered, she'd follow the conversation. She walked slowly through the open path as it led to another larger room with more antiques. A cracked and chipped mannequin of a woman stood near the aisle, the figure draped in clothes from the Gilded Age—a hat with a tapered blue feather, and a long, ghost white dress with ruffles, its fabric pale as a slice of aged wedding cake in the back of a freezer.

Elizabeth stepped around the mannequin, inhaled deeply through her nostrils. The smell was beyond the musty aroma of old books. It was an invisible link to past lives through things they owned, wore or kept close. The possessions of the dead, now made lasting by the lingering smells. Delicate scents more enduring than the people. It was a composite of odors—the whiff of perfume in the pages of books, the subdued fragrance of dried flowers, cigar boxes, turpentine, gun oil, yellowed newspapers, layers of antiquity all displayed in a building that itself was a time capsule.

Elizabeth heard the sound of movement.

She looked up at the wood beam ceiling. Someone was walking upstairs across the second floor. Moments later, she heard the sound of hard shoes against wooden steps behind a closed door. Then the door to the second floor opened and out stepped a diminutive woman dressed in jeans and a beige blouse.

Anna Lawrence was spry for her early seventies. White hair pinned up loosely. Her gentle face was that of a woman whose maternal instincts were unconditional. She carried a figurine, a marble angel not much larger than one of her hands. The angel held a horn to its lips. Anna looked across the room, saw Elizabeth standing there, and said, "Oh heavens, I hope you haven't been in the store too long. I didn't hear you come in."

Elizabeth smiled. "No, not long at all. I just got here. Didn't even have time to browse. And I do enjoy finding treasures in antique stores. It's one of my favorite things to do."

Anna held up the figurine. "This is a little treasure. It's believed to be at least two hundred years old. A tiny part of the trumpet is cracked. Other than that, she looks great for an angel two centuries old."

"Where'd you find it?"

"Italy, on one of my last buying trips. This is the type of antique that will attract a special buyer—someone who isn't looking to trade it, but rather enjoy it."

"What makes it so different?"

"Age for one thing. It's from the sculptor, Andrea Bilini. Part of the collection he sculpted called *Day of Judgment*. There are seven of these, each one a little different."

Elizabeth said nothing. She stared at the statuette carved from marble the color of thick, white smoke.

Anna smiled. "Please feel free to browse around the place. If you have any questions, I'll be at my desk up front."

"Are you Anna Lawrence?"

"Yes."

"Atticus Ward sent me to see you. I'm Elizabeth Monroe."

Anna stopped, tilted her head. Buttery light from a smudged window fell across her lined face. She smiled. "Thought I recognized you. Tell me, how is Atticus? I haven't seen him in a few months?"

"He's well. His second retirement, one that he says will be final, is coming up soon. He suggested that you might have information on a man, long dead, named Zachariah Belmont."

Anna's smile faded just as the natural light from the window dimmed when a cloud passed overhead. "Let me put this down. Please, follow me." She led Elizabeth back toward the front of the building, set the figurine on a glass counter near an old cash register. "It's in here." She walked to a closed door, unlocked it, and motioned for Elizabeth to follow her. "If the history of Mississippi were displayed as a long tapestry, or a multicolored mural, some of the darker parts would, justifiably, be hidden away as they are in here. The story of Zachariah Belmont is one of them. I'll show you why."

FIFTY

The room had it's own peculiar ripened hint of vanilla in the air. It was the decayed spores of old paper, text, ink, glue and mildew mixed like a stew—the pot liquor of things forgotten but rekindled by scent. Two walls of the large room had floor-to-ceiling sagging shelves, lined with hundreds of books. Most were hardback, their spines bruised by hands and time. The rest of the room was filled with file cabinets and a small desk and chair.

"This is where I've archived and stored some of our state's good, bad and ugly history," said Anna, stepping to a file drawer marked with the letter B.

Elizabeth followed her as Anna opened the cabinet and pulled at a long drawer packed with file folders, all neatly labeled and all in alphabetical order. Anna said, "The Civil Rights Museum in Jackson really covers the spectrum in Mississippi. As a former state history archivist, I formed my own collection over the years. I've made plans to donate it to the museum."

"What's here?" Elizabeth asked, looking at the wide cabinets filled with files and photos.

"I've tried to chronicle, or account for, much of the history of Mississippi as it pertains to civil rights, from deporting the Choctaw and Chickasaw Indians out of the state and far west of the Mississippi River to the colonists who came here, set up cotton plantations and bought slave labor to operate the farms. It extends from there through the journey of civil rights and to headline cases, such as Emmitt Till, Medgar Edwards, to the Klan bombing of black churches and Jewish synagogues." She paused and lowered her voice. "Two hundred years of bullying and bigotry."

Elizabeth nodded. "Why'd you do it? Why take the time to make and keep these files?"

Anna glanced across the big room. "I grew up in Hattiesburg. I was just a girl when a local grocery story owner, Vernon Dahmer, was killed in 1966. He was simply helping people register to vote when they came into his grocery store. I used to go in there and get a Coke and a moon pie with my brother. Members of the Klan, the White Knights, came to Vernon's home in the dead of night, fired shotgun blasts through his windows and tossed gasoline canisters inside. Vernon, his wife, and kids were in bed when the firebombing started. He somehow managed to hold off the Klansmen long enough for his wife and children to escape out the back door. But for Vernon, the damage was done. His lungs were scorched. He died a slow, painful death in the hospital the next day." She looked over at Elizabeth. "They burned his house, car and store. Two days before he was murdered, I came in his store to buy a Nehi Orange Soda after school. I took it out of the cooler, opened it and walked to the counter to pay. I searched my jeans pocket and realized the quarter I had was gone. He looked at me from behind the counter, grinned that big smile of his, and told me not to worry about it and that I could pay next time. He was a kind man. He and his wife raised all their kids in the church. His older sons were in the Army, fighting in Korea or Vietnam as their dad was working for voting rights back home."

"I remember reading about that in high school. I'm so sorry."

The leader of the Klan, the man who ordered the murder, Sam Bowers, was tried four times. Each time it was a hung jury. Four mistrials. Finally, thirty years later, he was tried again and sent to prison for life. He was quoted as saying that he could justify the murder and other murders because he interpreted the Bible to say it was his mission to do so and that archangels, such as him, were empowered to do it for the greater good."

Elizabeth said nothing for a moment. "Do you know if Bowers was influenced by Zachariah Belmont?"

"I don't know. I'll pull what little information I have collected on Belmont." She leafed through the folders, lifted one from the drawer and opened it. There was an aged pamphlet inside. "I remember this. It's a newsletter of sorts, if you will, that Belmont wrote. It's really more of a flyer he distributed. It's almost as if it were his manifesto. As you can see, he called the title, *Retribution*." She opened the two-page pamphlet, scanned through it. "I remember some of this. Belmont had his followers refer to him as Prophet Zachariah. A lot of what he writes in here could be a manual for hate groups today."

"May I read it?"

"Absolutely. There are two copies in the file. You can have one."

"That's very generous of you."

"If you'd like to read it while you're here, you can sit at the desk. I need to package an order and get it ready for the UPS man."

"Anna, do you know if Zachariah Belmont had children?"

"I believe that he did. I can do a check for you. By the time you finish reading that pamphlet, I might know." Anna handed her the file and left the room.

Elizabeth sat down and read. She bit her lower lip slightly, her mind seeing glimpses of Belmont's headstone, the wooden cross, the boot print, Nellie Culpepper—the word wrath on Cindy's forehead. Elizabeth finished reading and slowly stood. She examined both pamphlets and the rest of the folder looking for a picture of Belmont. There were none. She replaced the file, closed the drawer and took her copy back into the main part of the store.

Anna looked up from addressing a package at the counter. "Did you find what you were looking for?"

"Maybe more. Belmont's ranting is extreme, to say the least. Similar to what you said about Sam Bowers and his archangel comments. Are there any pictures of Belmont?"

"Not that I know about off the top of my head. Not a lot of cameras back in his era. I'll do some research for you, see what I can find."

Elizabeth smiled. "Thank you." She held the pamphlet in both hands, the paper shaking slightly.

Anna noticed it. "Let me put that in something for you." She picked up a folder from a shelf, removed an envelope from it and placed the pamphlet inside, handing it back to Elizabeth. "May I ask why you're interested in Zachariah Belmont?"

"When, as a little girl, you walked by the charred remains of Vernon Dahmer's house and store, the smell of gasoline and ashes, it sticks with you, like the smell of death. I don't know if the people who killed Vernon had any link, beyond hate, to Zachariah Belmont. But I believe someone today—the person responsible for the recent serial killings, might. Maybe it's a genetic link. Maybe it's only a philosophical connection. But I think it's there. And I need to find it."

"I've been following that in the news. And that's where I recognize your face." Anna stepped from around the counter. "You lost your daughter to a killer."

"Yes. I did."

"I hope the police can find the person responsible."

"They haven't yet."

Anna nodded. "Can I give you a hug?"

"Yes."

Anna felt small in Elizabeth's arms. She could touch the woman's jutted backbone beneath her shirt. "Thank you for giving me the pamphlet. But I'll make sure to get it back to you—it should remain part of the archives."

Anna folded her arms. "Thanks, and you're welcome. Oh, I found more information about Belmont's family. I discovered he had one son and two daughters. The son died in his teen years. Not sure how. The girls married." Anna lifted a piece of paper from the counter, her handwriting on it. "One daughter married Thomas Greenwood. And the other married Rhett Clements. All were men from Mississippi."

The daughter who married Clements…what was her first name?"

Anna glanced down at her notes. "Harriet…Harriet Clements."

Elizabeth said nothing, looking at the paper in the woman's hands.

Anna said, "I can tell you're on your own quest, too. I want to believe that the old ghosts of Mississippi in 1966 are gone. But I have no illusions. Be careful, Elizabeth."

"I will. Thank you." She looked at the fresh-cut red roses in a glass vase on the counter. "The roses are lovely. Did you buy them?"

"No, I grow them."

"Would you sell one to me? I want to take it to a grave."

"There are more than two dozen in the vase. Just pick as many as you'd like."

"Thank you. One will be fine." She lifted a rose from the center. "How much?"

"I suspect this would be for the young woman—the student, who was just killed?"

"Yes, it is. I just felt a longing to take it to her grave."

"There's no charge."

FIFTY-ONE

After Elizabeth left the antique store, she got in her car and drove across town, thinking about the pamphlet and what she'd read. She gripped the steering wheel with both hands, knuckles bone white. Feeling the sudden, overwhelming urge to buy security cameras for her house, she turned left toward the Best Buy store. After exiting the store, she thought of Jack and decided to backtrack, going to each place she'd left a poster of him and removed them. A rangy clerk in the pet food store asked, "Did you find a home for the cat?"

Elizabeth smiled, looked up from the picture of Jack on the flyer in her hands to the man's curious eyes. "Yes, I did."

— —

When Elizabeth entered into the cemetery parking area, there were half-dozen cars in the lot. She pulled up beside a Chevy Malibu that had a University of Southern Mississippi decal on the upper section of the back window. She parked, picked up her purse and the rose, and got out of the car.

She glanced across the cemetery. There didn't appear to be anyone standing next to Zachariah Belmont's grave. And there were no pickup trucks in the lot. She looked to the left, toward Cindy's grave and saw some-one. From the distance, the person appeared to be a man. He was sitting on a wrought iron bench near Cindy's gravesite.

Elizabeth quietly locked her car door and approached the grave, right hand just inside her open purse, the grip of the gun at her fingertips. The closer she got, the more she began to recognize the person—the rounded shoulders. The haircut. The look of burden he carried in his body language.

Alex Davidson sat alone.

He was less than fifteen feet from Cindy Carter's headstone. He slowly turned as Elizabeth walked up to him. She said, "I didn't expect to see you out here."

He made a reluctant attempt to smile. "Oh, hi, Professor Monroe. What are you doing here?"

"I was about to ask you the same thing. I didn't see you at Cindy's funeral."

"I was there...at least for part of it. But when they set Cindy's picture up near the...grave. When I looked at the coffin...when I saw her parents...her sisters...I just sort of lost it. I thought I was gonna throw up. I didn't want to make a scene, so I went back to sit in the car."

"Alex, I don't want to infringe on your private time out here, but it looked like you were speaking to Cindy when I walked up. Could you share with me what you were saying to her? I'd really like to know."

"What difference does it make? You were at the sheriff's office. I know you heard them question us."

"And I heard your answers."

He looked up at her, not sure what to say. His eyes welled. "I didn't kill Cindy. I loved her. I'd made up my mind to stop drinking. And I stopped. I quit the fraternity. I wanted to change my life around, and I wanted to do it because she mattered to me...she mattered a lot. And I know, at least for a while, she loved me, too." He wiped his eyes with the back of his hand.

"If a relationship doesn't make you a better person, maybe it's the wrong one. Sounds to me like Cindy made you realize who you really are... but you had to find it."

He nodded, inhaled deeply. A robin hopped on the ground and chirped.

Elizabeth extended the rose to Alex. "Why don't you put this on Cindy's grave?"

He slowly stood, his face flush, lips tight. Elizabeth handed the rose to him. He tried to smile and stepped closer to Cindy's grave, kneeling to gently place the rose next to her headstone. He stood, a deep sob coming from his chest.

Elizabeth said nothing, leaving him with his thoughts. After a minute she said, "Alex, I know you didn't kill Cindy."

He turned toward her, tears on his face. "You do?"

"Yes, I do. A psychopath can fake or mimic someone with a conscience, but he or she can't forge something they don't have. And that's a heart—true compassion and love for someone. It's beyond empathy or even sympathy. It's the capacity to feel deeply, to love profoundly…touch the spirit and be touched by someone's soul, it's a fire that burns in our hearts, and it's reinforced when that love is returned. There are not always happy endings, but deep and true love is worth the risks."

He stepped closer and lifted his arms. Elizabeth embraced and hugged him—his tears wet against her skin. "Thank you," he stammered.

—◾ ▬—

Elizabeth sat on a bench near a large fern in a hanging basket on her front porch. Jack stretched out beside her, purring. He ignored a blue butterfly flittering around the flowers less than six feet from his nose. Elizabeth unpacked one of the five small surveillance cameras she'd bought, read the instructions, and placed batteries in the first camera. She climbed a small stepladder and used a screwdriver to mount the first camera on an inconspicuous place in one corner, aiming the lens toward the front door.

She moved the ladder to another area of the porch, looked out at her long front yard, the street in the distance and her mailbox. She mounted the second camera under an eave and focused it to capture the image of her yard, driveway and mailbox. She climbed down and said, "Okay, Jack, two down, three more to go." She went inside, Jack leisurely following her. She placed the box of cameras down on her kitchen table, set her gun next to the box.

Jack rubbed his face against the side of her jean pants. She squatted down to pet him. "Let's put a camera outside to monitor the deck and back door. We'll put one in here and the steps leading upstairs. These are all activated by motion. If they get inside and get to the steps, headed to our bedroom, they'll be met with a brass band coming out the barrel of my nine-millimeter. Maybe it'll never get to that."

When she finished installing and testing the cameras, looking at the images on her computer and phone screens, she let out a deep breath. She made a call to an old friend. "Please be there," she whispered. "I don't know where to turn."

On the seventh ring, Otto Emmerson answered his phone. "My dear Elizabeth…it's been too long. What do I owe the honor of your call?"

FIFTY-TWO

Elizabeth paced her back deck for a moment. She said, "I wish I could just say, hey Otto, let's do a catch-up lunch, but that's not the case, at least not right now."

Otto Emerson sat in a chair under an umbrella on his back deck overlooking the languid Mississippi River, a freighter plowing the water half-mile away, sea gulls sailed in the air behind the ship. "Is it because of the travel logistics, I live outside of Natchez and you in lovely Hattiesburg or, as I sense, something else?" He sipped an ice tea, his lean face ruddy from a close shave, wrinkles around his ice blue eyes, a head of white hair, thick wrists, in good shape for a man who just turned sixty-five.

"I want to come visit you. It's only a couple of hours from Hattiesburg to your place, so I don't mind the drive. Do you have time on Wednesday? Maybe around noon—just in time for lunch?" She smiled and petted Jack. "The last time we saw each other was a year ago when you spoke to one of my graduate classes. Are you doing okay?"

"Better than okay. Greta and I are doing well. We've been married thirty-four years now. We're as comfortable as a pair of old shoes. I don't miss the FBI. Did at first, but that fades. Natchez is a fine place to retire. As you know, my brother and I grew up on the Mississippi River. The old river gets in your blood, and no matter how far I traveled around the world, it always was quietly calling me back home."

Otto folded a copy of the Wall Street Journal on his lap. "From my house, on this ancient bluff, I can look to my right and see toward the north, the river's birth. It begins more than twelve hundred miles away. I look to my left, and I can watch freighters head a couple hundred miles south into the river's wide mouth, the gateway to the rest of the world."

"It's lovely there."

"What's on your mind, Liz? Or do you want to wait two days to tell me?"

"We have a serial killer over here. I need some advice."

"I read about the murders. Seems like the same MO for both."

"Yes. I'm missing something, Otto. Maybe I can talk it out with you, and you'll have a better insight."

He laughed and sipped his ice tea, watched a ruby-throated humming-bird dart around trumpet flowers growing on the trellis mounted below the deck railing "Liz, you're the one with the visions. You're the one who some-how manages to climb inside a cold, dark place—the killer's mind, as you try to anticipate his or her next move. Me, on the other hand, well, I simply look at all the evidence that the agents or officers plow out of the farrows of the criminal mind, and I sort them out into discernible categories, always looking for some composite to finish the puzzle pieces. It's not unlike the old prospector, panning for specks of gold among the mud and grit. I try to wash away the dirt and look at what's left in the strainer."

Something caught Elizabeth's attention on her computer screen. It was the camera aimed at her front yard. A postal truck stopped at her mailbox, the postman leaning out his side window, placing mail in her box.

"Are you there, Liz?"

"Yes, I'm here. I just saw something on the new security camera I installed. It's just the postman. I'll see you Wednesday at noon. Thank you, Otto, for being there."

"No need for thanks, but I'll take it. Since you installed security cameras, I deduce that you aren't feeling safe. We need to talk about what's causing that. If it's this serial killer, we need to remedy it somehow. Stay safe." He disconnected.

Elizabeth watched the postman drive away. Her phone buzzed. She looked at the ID. Detective Bradford. She answered, and he said, "I need to get away from here for a while. My head's spinning. Ed Milton and I've been going around and around over the interrogations and what you had to say as well. Ed's convinced that Gerald Simpson is our killer. Hey, did you buy those security cameras? I can come over and hang them for you."

Elizabeth looked at her computer screen, the images from the five cameras displayed. "I had a little time, so I just did it. I didn't want to bother you in the midst of a double homicide investigation."

"It's not a bother, Elizabeth. Do you like Chinese food…I can pick up some and bring the food to your place."

Elizabeth started to decline, but decided not to. "That would be fine. Thank you."

"Great. I need some time away from my partner, Ed, to clear my head and regain some objectivity. He's a bulldog, and once he sets his bite, he doesn't want to let go. He's biting down on Gerald Simpson. Wants to put a tail on him, see where he goes, who he meets—maybe he's partnering with an older guy or even Larry Tucker."

"I don't believe Simpson killed Cindy and Charles Lehman. Mike, I think it's connected to the footprints in the cemetery. The old graves of Zachariah Belmont and maybe that man we saw standing near the graves. Who the hell is he?"

"I wish I knew. And I am tossing out a bigger net. Maybe there is a connection. We didn't get a plate number on the truck. Two people with the name of Belmont drive pickups in Forrest County, but one truck is a Dodge and the other a Chevy. The one in the parking lot was a Ford."

"Sounds like you've been chasing a few leads."

"Not a lot of chasing because there are so few leads. I just want to get this asshole off the streets before he kills again."

"We've got to go to that old bridge to see if those planks match the wood from the crosses."

"Even if it is a match, what that tells us is some nut job is leaving crosses on the graves of old ghosts—people who were part of a lynch mob in 1918."

"That's exactly a century ago. If these killings have a connection that goes back a hundred years, we have to find it."

FIFTY-THREE

Jack sat on his barstool and watched them eat, the big cat's languid, yellow-green eyes furtive. Elizabeth and Bradford sat at the kitchen table and ate slices of chicken, shrimp and scallops on beds of white rice. He poured a glass of chilled chardonnay for her and said, "I take it that no one's come forth to claim Jack."

She smiled. "Not so far. It may be because no one can afford to feed him. I'm convinced, if you'd picked up lasagna, he'd be sitting at the table with a napkin around his wide neck. Jack can pack down the food." She paused, looked at Jack's face. "And I'm hoping no one claims him. I removed all of the flyers I plastered across this part of town. Jack's been here more than a week, and he's a good fit. I've grown quite fond of him."

"I can see that. He let me pet him. If he puts on another few pounds, you can stick a sign in your yard that reads: Beware—attack cat on duty."

Elizabeth laughed and sipped her wine.

Bradford watched her a moment. "You have such a great laugh. I'd love to hear it more. I know we haven't had a lot to laugh about these last few days, but when this is over...maybe we can spend some time together. Off the professional clock. I like sunsets, reading, walks on the beach, margaritas—you know, the stuff you'd find on a dating website." He grinned wide.

She laughed. "I wouldn't know because I've never gone to a dating site. I prefer eye-to-eye communications, and sipping a glass of wine with dinner. And I enjoy making dinner. I had a small restaurant once. It was really more of a bakery and gourmet sandwich shop. I made most of what we served."

"Really?"

"Yes, really. And don't look so astonished. I'm pretty good in the kitchen. Molly used to help in the restaurant…that seems so long ago." She glanced at the framed picture of Molly on the shelf.

Bradford finished his wine. He ate in silence for a moment. "You're a remarkable woman, Elizabeth." He smiled. "And I'm a patient man."

She looked across the table at him and smiled. There was movement on her computer screen on the far right side of the table. "Look," she pointed to the screen. "These cameras are sensitive, and they pick up motion well. You can see a raccoon crossing my front yard."

Bradford leaned toward the screen, watched a large raccoon waddle across the yard, stopping at the sidewalk, sniffing, and moving on. "Beware, raccoon crossing."

Elizabeth smiled, finishing her food. "I'm so full. Thank you for bringing dinner. That was thoughtful. I'll do the dishes."

"I can help."

"Absolutely not." She smiled wide. "You brought the food and wine, the least I can do is a few dishes. Just sit there and bond with Jack."

"I can do that." He scratched Jack behind the ears. "This cat is pretty laid back. Doesn't seem like a stray or a feral cat. Look's like he's got Garfield's DNA."

Elizabeth smiled. "He's definitely a cool cat. I wonder if his owner was elderly. Maybe he or she died, and Jack just wandered away."

"His history is a mystery. Wish he could talk. He'd probably ask for a scotch. No ice."

Elizabeth laughed, cleared the table and started washing dishes. Bradford glanced at the computer screen, watched the sky darken. He said, "So these cameras work with the Internet. Can you get an alert on your phone?"

"Yes. Movement triggers an instant email, and I can click to see what happened or I can watch the live stream anytime. Gotta love technology."

"You did a great job installing these and getting everything online."

"I can follow printed instructions." She smiled.

Bradford got up, poured a little more wine in his glass, and walked from the table into the kitchen. He stepped up behind her as she dried the last dish. "I was teasing you—not about the margaritas—about the walks on the beach. I like the beach, but I prefer boating. But those are destinations. Most importantly, I appreciate absolute integrity in people. You have that, Elizabeth, and you have it in spades. Seriously, though, maybe we could spend more time together and—"

"Mike…I like you. I like you a lot." She turned around to face him, drying her hands on a towel. "You're a good man with a noble heart. You're in law enforcement for all the right reasons. You want to make a positive difference—to help and protect people…to right a wrong, if possible. And you're doing that. I'm just not ready to go in that direction, at least not now."

He nodded, took a small step backwards. "I can appreciate that. I also can appreciate that you're a vibrant, attractive woman with a keen mind, and you're human with human needs and desires. Like I said, I'm patient."

"My needs don't necessarily parallel with my desires. I don't feel I need a relationship unless it's the right relationship. God knows I've had my share of the wrong ones, from my father to self-centered boyfriends to a wandering eye husband who left Molly and I when she was in diapers." She set the towel on the counter. "Would you like some coffee?"

"Sure, thanks."

She put on a pot and hit the brew button. Jack dropped down from his barstool and sauntered into the family room, jumping up on the couch. Elizabeth put the dishes away and poured two cups of coffee. "I don't have any cream. Is black all right?"

"I can suffer though it." Bradford smiled and took the cup.

"Let's follow Jack into the family room."

They sat on the couch, Elizabeth picked up a file folder and legal pad. Her handwriting filled a page. "I've done some additional research on Zachariah Belmont. I was intrigued when the groundskeeper in the cemetery told us that Belmont's cult followers called him a prophet."

Bradford shook his head. "What else did you find?"

She opened the file folder and removed the pamphlet. "This. A former state archivist, who now owns an antique store, had it. It's a flyer or manifesto. In 1918 Belmont published this and called it *Retribution*. He predicted that, in a century, the nation would resemble a modern Sodom and Gomorrah. And he said someone would step out from beyond the shadows to show the sinners that the wrath of God was coming to destroy the wicked. Belmont said that, although he didn't know the name of the person, he would have the initials L...O...T. Remember the character in the Bible with the name Lot? He and his daughters were spared from the destruction of Sodom. I know this is going to sound bizarre, but what if whoever's committing these murders and leaving the bowls and the word *wrath* on his victims has the initials or the name Lot?"

"I've never met anyone in Forrest County with that name. The initials could apply to a lot of people, no pun meant." He smiled.

"Mike, the three students, Gerald Simpson, Alex Davidson...Larry Tucker...do you know Tucker's middle name?"

"Not off the top of my head. I have a copy of his driver's license in one of my reports. I can access that information on my phone." He picked up his phone and hit a few keys, waited and pressed a half dozen more. His eyes narrowed, reading. "You ready for this? His middle name is Owen... Lawrence Owen Tucker. It could be simply coincidental."

"Maybe. That's if you put any weight in coincidences when it relates to criminal investigations."

"Elizabeth, you're at the top of your game when it comes to criminal profiles, but we have to rely on evidence and a path that leads us to something tangible. Anything else and we might as well hire a psychic. But most of that stuff is pure guesswork and none of it, at least in my experience, results in physical evidence to take to a district attorney."

There was a *ping* on Elizabeth's phone. She lifted it from the coffee table, clicked on the email alert. "Let's see if our friendly raccoon is coming back." She opened the email and played a ten second video. "Mike... somebody's outside."

He looked at the video, the distant image of a man at the end of the driveway. Elizabeth stepped over and picked up her computer. She clicked on the live feed from the camera aimed down the front drive. "He's on my property and coming toward us."

FIFTY-FOUR

Detective Mike Bradford held his finger to his lips. He quietly stepped to Elizabeth's back door. She followed him. "Wait here," he said. "I'm going to circle through the side yard, into the front yard, and surprise him." He lifted his gun from the holster, chambered a round.

Elizabeth held her laptop, stared at the image of the man dressed in a dark hoodie. She said, "He's just standing in the middle of the driveway. Not coming further or turning around."

"The bastard is on your property, right?"

"Yes."

"He's trespassing. And considering the unwanted and unwelcome honeysuckles you've received, I'm going out there to nip this in the fuckin' bud."

"You can see he's wearing a dark hoodie. That's what Larry Tucker wore during your interview with him. Maybe you should call for backup."

"There's no time. This guy's nuts. He's damn dangerous. Look…he's moving again. I can't see if he's armed. But right now he might as well be. You watch the monitor. If something happens to me, call 9-1-1."

Elizabeth picked her pistol up from the table. "I'm your backup."

"Stay inside!"

"It's my house! I'll do what I have to do."

Bradford inhaled a chest full of air, slowly releasing it. He looked at the screen once more, opened the back door and stepped into the night.

Elizabeth licked her dry lips. She watched the monitor, the man stay-ing in the shadow of her hedge bushes, stopping and starting. He seemed hesitant. Unsure. She chambered a round in her gun. Jack sauntered over to her, sitting and looking up at Elizabeth. She said, "I told you it wouldn't be a good idea to hang out with me. You're in jeopardy here."

Movement caught her eye. She could barely see Bradford coming up behind the intruder. Elizabeth held her breath. Hoping for the best. Fearing the worst.

— —

Bradford leveled his 9mm, aimed at the back of the man's hoodie. He walked softly behind the intruder and said, "Police! There's a gun pointed at you. Don't give me a reason. Raise your hands slowly! Now!"

The man did as ordered. He held a file folder in one hand. Bradford said. "Lie down on your stomach! Arms out!"

The man complied, dropping to his knees and then lying prone in the driveway. Bradford approached. He seized the man's arms, pulling them behind his back, handcuffing him. Bradford pulled down the man's hoodie and looked into the angry eyes of Gerald Simpson. "You got this wrong," Simpson said. "I was just delivering an essay my buddy wrote in Professor Monroe's class."

"Stand up!" Bradford gripped Simpson's arm, lifting him to his feet. He patted him down, removing a stun gun from his pocket. "You always make deliveries armed with a stun-gun?"

"Come on, Detective. You know I carry one."

"And I'm sure you know how to use it. Why are you here?"

"Like I said, I'm here to deliver an essay to Professor Monroe. My bud-dy's sick. He asked me to bring it over here. Matter of fact, he wanted to pay me. You've heard of Uber-Eats—delivering cooked meals to people. In ride-share, we aren't always with a passenger. We deliver stuff to places, too."

"You're under arrest."

"What for? C'mon!"

"For trespassing on private property for starters, but then the charges escalate to murder."

"Murder? I didn't kill anyone. I'm simply making a delivery. The paper's due tomorrow."

"Your friend could have emailed it."

"No, no he couldn't. The syllabus states it has to be turned in by hard copy. He doesn't want to jeopardize his GPA. He's got a 4.0."

"You have the right to remain silent. Anything you say can be used against you in a court of law. You have the right to an attorney. Do you understand your rights?"

"I understand that you're making a big mistake, and it might cost you your job."

"Don't threaten me, punk." Bradford lifted his hand-held radio and called for a police cruiser.

The front door opened and Elizabeth stepped onto the porch. She'd watched the handcuffing and decided to leave her gun inside. She approached the men. Simpson grinned and said, "Good evening, Doctor Monroe. I'm afraid there's been a misunderstanding. I was delivering an essay from Cameron Bosky. He's very sick. Says he can't be in class tomorrow, but he didn't want his essay to be marked late."

Elizabeth stepped closer. "That's very conscientious of Cameron. But if he's ill, he's excused until he returns to class."

"I guess he didn't know."

"I make that very clear at the beginning of the semester. How did you know where I live?"

He grinned in the light from the floodlights at the corner of her home. "The contact information for all the of the university professors is online on the college's curriculum management system. Also, I'm a ride-share driver, and I can find locations almost as good as GPS."

Bradford said, "What he's not telling you is that he was packing a stun-gun. It's one of the most powerful I've seen, and it was in the pocket of his hoodie."

"I told you, I only carry that for protection. You never know who's climbing into your car."

The flashing blue and white lights from a cruiser raked across the tall pine trees as backup approached. Simpson looked over his shoulder at the approaching vehicle. Elizabeth watched him closely, looking for signs of fear in his eyes. He half smiled, turned toward Bradford. "I'll be out within an hour. You have nothing to hold me. Just making a delivery. There's no law against that. If there were, you'd be arresting the UPS drivers all day long."

The cruiser pulled into the driveway. Bradford signaled for the driver to come closer. He stopped less than twenty feet away. Two officers got out and approached. Bradford explained what happened. He added, "Take him in, and book him for murder in the deaths of Cindy Carter and Charles Lehman."

One of the officers said, "Be our privilege, Detective."

"Let's get a tow truck out here. We'll put his SUV in the compound and have forensics go over it. I'll follow you guys back to the station."

As they took Simpson away, Bradford said, "Give me a few seconds. I want to look in his SUV." He walked to the Lincoln Navigator, opened it and looked through the front and back. He walked back to Elizabeth. Touched her arm. "Are you okay?"

"Do you believe him?" She picked up the file folder and looked at the essay paper.

"No. He's a sociopath. Too bad he's so dumb that he's willing to throw away a potential career in the NFL because his criminal gene is more dominate than his competitive sports gene." Bradford removed a small plastic bag from his pocket and dropped the stun gun inside, sealing it. "This is so powerful it could stop a grizzly bear. Imagine what it could do to someone as small as Cindy Carter."

"I don't have to imagine that. I've seen it." She hugged her arms in the cool night air. Seconds after the cruiser left, tree frogs chirped. She said, "You're right, Gerald Simpson is a sociopath. His hand is always in the cookie jar. He believes he's entitled to people opening doors for him because of his athletic talents and the way he was raised."

"I need to get back to the station to deal with this punk." He glanced toward the security camera. "Get a good night's sleep, Liz. Simpson won't be coming back here."

"Something's not right, Mike." She glanced at the file folder in her hand. "After my class tomorrow, I'd like to go with you to that old bridge over the Chickasawhay River."

"Even if the wooden planks match the crosses on Zachariah Belmont's grave, what does that prove?"

"That the student you just arrested for murder didn't do it. And the real serial killer is out there somewhere in the dark of night."

FIFTY-FIVE

Elizabeth reached in the in-basket at her faculty office, counting the essays. All stapled. Neat cover pages. The title: *The Abused Becoming the Abuser – Handed Down or Learned.* She turned the cover page on the essay written by Julie Lassiter and read the opening thesis statement. Elizabeth smiled, reaching for a paper cup filled with coffee.

Dean Harris stepped into her office. "Elizabeth, the news media are calling the university. Our star football player, Gerald Simpson, was arrested at your home. What the hell's going on here?"

"Good morning to you, too."

"The time for pleasantries is gone. We have news media camping outside our institution. The NCAA's public relations people are calling. The cable news networks want to know if Simpson is a suspect—a serial killer."

"Then have them call the sheriff's department for a statement."

"Your last statement on Channel Four has done nothing but add fuel to the fire. To paraphrase you—you called the killer someone who's entitled since he believes it's his right; because, in his sick mind, he's superior to others. You called him a weakling and a parasite—"

"What would you call him, Jim? He tortures before he kills. Police asked me to help profile this psychopath. If he's not caught, the slaughters will continue."

"And now one of our students is being held at the county jail as a suspect. What does this say?"

"And one of our students is dead. It tells me that you're more interested in PR bullshit than you are about getting a killer behind bars." She stood. Picked up the file folders with the student essays. "Now, if you'll move out of my way, I have a class to teach."

He stepped aside, arms folded. Lips tight. Mouth bent. As she stepped to her door, she turned back to Dean Harris. "Simpson will, no doubt, make bail. Here's the good news, Jim...your star athlete will most likely not be tried for murder, although I'm convinced he's capable of it. The bad news is that someone even sicker than that prick is out there. And it's just a matter of time and circumstances before he kills another one of our students. So ask yourself this: Would you rather speak to the media about theory and supposition, or would you prefer to look another set of parents in the eye and tell them their daughter or son won't graduate because they've been murdered?"

— —

Elizabeth stood at the front of the class, watching her students arrive. Within a few minutes, the door closed and everyone had taken his or her seat.

Except two people.

She looked at the spot where Cameron Bosky always sat. Vacant. The impassive words from Simpson echoing through her mind: *I was delivering an essay from Cameron Bosky. He's very sick. Says he can't be in class tomorrow, but he didn't want his essay to be marked late.*

The second vacant seat was that of Julie Lassiter. Elizabeth thought of the message she'd left on Julie's phone: *I've been thinking about what you mentioned to me. It's in reference to what Cindy Carter told you about the man who approached her at the demonstration. Please call me when you get this.*

Elizabeth stared out the classroom window, students hurrying to classes, the American flag drooping from a pole. She turned to her class. "I know that Cameron is ill today. But has anyone seen or heard from Julie?"

No one lifted a hand. Blank faces. Shrugs. Then one girl, a brunette wearing her hair in a ponytail, raised her hand. "Julie told me she got her car out of the shop, but something was wrong so she took it back. And she lives off campus. Want me to text her?"

Elizabeth nodded. "That'd be great. Thanks."

The student used both thumbs to send a quick text. Elizabeth lifted the file folders. "I've been reading your essays. Very impressive writing. You guys are either extraordinarily bright or paying lots of attention in class and I'm a darn good teacher. I think it's the former more than the latter." She smiled and read one of the opening thesis paragraphs and said, "What I like about that is the way it really sets up what's to come next and how it made me curious to read more—to find out how she will measure the hypothesis."

The student in the ponytail raised her hand. Elizabeth, recognizing she was the one who reached out to the missing student, called on her. The girl said, "Julie's not answering my text. And that's strange for her—especially when it comes to anything about school or your class. Julie works hard to get A's." The girl leaned back in her seat. "Maybe somebody should go by her house."

Elizabeth set the folders down. "Do you know here she lives?"

"Yep. I've been there a couple of times."

"Do you have a class after this one."

"No. I can go there."

"Great. Please call me when you find her."

FIFTY-SIX

E lizabeth wasn't expecting the ambush. She placed her purse strap over her shoulder and stepped out of the university administration building into the bright sunlight and a waiting mob of news reporters. They sprang into action—a pack of wolves, as the reporters and camera operators surrounded her. They formed a moving half circle, cameras aimed at her, questions fired with rapid speed while she tried to walk from the building toward the faculty parking lot.

One tall reporter asked, "Doctor Monroe, did your profile of the serial killer in any way indicate that a student from your own university—a star football player, could be a suspect?"

She ignored the microphone thrust in her face, the lens of the camera less than five feet away. Another reporter, the same one that questioned her near the crime scene when Cindy's body was found, asked, "Doctor Monroe, is it true that Gerald Simpson was arrested in your home last night? If so, can you tell us what he, as a student, was doing there?"

Elizabeth stopped walking, looked at the woman and said, "He was trespassing. And he wasn't in my home. He was in my driveway. I don't care for the inference you guise in your line of questioning. Please get your facts straight so you can ask accurate questions."

"Does Gerald Simpson fit the suspect profile?"

"That question is better addressed to the sheriff's investigators."

Another reporter, a burly man, perspiring ruddy face, dressed in wrinkled khakis and a golf shirt, asked, "Are you surprised Gerald Simpson was released?"

"No, I'm not."

"Why is that, professor?"

"In my estimation, he doesn't fit the profile. Now, if you folks will excuse me."

"Was that the reason he was released without being charged?"

"That's a question for the police." Cameras flashed. And a dozen questions were torpedoed at her. Elizabeth continued walking, ignoring the barrage of questions, the clicks of cameras.

Detective Bradford arrived in an unmarked car, intercepting Elizabeth from the mob and chaos. She got in the passenger side of his car. The reporters continued to ask questions as she closed the door. Some recognized the detective and ran around to his side, tapping on the window.

When they'd driven from the parking lot, Bradford glanced in his rearview mirror and said, "They smell blood. In the first appearance, Simpson made bond. This time two partners from the law firm in Jackson, as well as Simpson's father, showed up threatening to sue the county for false arrest. They asked that the charges be dismissed."

"What did the state's attorney say?"

"She acquiesced and refused to file a formal murder charge against Simpson. This comes even after forensics found a hair in the front seat of Simpson's SUV that matched Cindy's DNA. His attorney argues that since she was his girlfriend at one time, a hair follicle in his car didn't suggest anything. That, of course, is bullshit. So Gerald Simpson is facing a charge of trespassing."

Elizabeth said nothing, watching students walk and bicycle down the sidewalks aligning the university property.

Bradford glanced over at her. "And you still think he's a sick puppy but not the perp, right?"

"He fits a lot of sick puppy profiles, but not the framework of the person who killed Cindy Carter and Charles Lehman."

Her phone buzzed. She recognized the caller ID. It was one of her students. "Hi, Charlotte."

"Professor Monroe, I went over to Julie's apartment. I knocked pretty hard on the door and even the window. No one came to the door. You think I should call her mom? I met her once. Maybe I could find her phone number."

"Does Julie have a boyfriend?"

"No, at least not a steady one that I know of, and we're pretty close. She's all about grades and the future."

"If you can find her mom's number…just to see if Julie has checked in with her. Maybe she's sick and called her mother."

"Okay…but Julie would have to be in the hospital not to return a text. She's that responsible."

"Thank you, Charlotte. Please call me if you hear something—"

"Get her address," Bradford said, interrupting.

"Charlotte, what's the address to her apartment?" She paused and repeated. "Okay, that's 3398 Quincy Street, Apartment 3-A. Great. Thank you. Bye."

"I'm assuming that was one of your students?"

"Yes. She was checking on another student, a girl who, like Cindy, has never missed one of my classes. Her name's Julie Lassiter. I'm worried about her. She and Cindy attended that rally to remove or relocate the Confederate Monument. And, like Cindy, Julie is a passionate young woman with a strong moral compass, someone who will stand up when it comes to doing the right thing and helping others. In a world where far too many kids feel entitled, she's not. Neither was Cindy."

"Want me to call and get a unit to her place?"

"That would be good, thank you."

Bradford nodded, made the call, disconnected and looked at the map on his screen. "Let's head up to Shubuta."

Elizabeth saw the rusted water tank first. It was the tallest structure in Shubuta, Mississippi. She lowered her window on the passenger side of Bradford's unmarked car as they entered the small town. They drove down Eucutta Street, the Mt. Zion Methodist Church on the left, an abandoned building across the street. A hand-painted sign on one boarded up window read: *Jesus Loves You.* They drove past a medical and dental clinic. A man in a John Deere cap, a hunter's camouflage jacket and jeans stared at them before slowly getting into a rusted pickup truck.

Bradford lowered his window, continuing down the street past a Dollar General Store and half a dozen empty buildings, paint cracked, peeling and faded by time and neglect. The heat shimmered off the hoods of parked cars. A balding mailman in shorts, sweat stains on the back of his shirt, entered the open screen door of a grill, the scent of fried chicken and approaching rain in the humid air.

They left Shubuta, heading northeast onto East Street for a few miles. Elizabeth watched the sky in the distance. Clouds the shade and weight of wrought iron moved in an ominous conga line, building in the north. Bradford said, "Looks like we're in for a soaking."

Elizabeth watched the road change from pavement to dirt. She reached into her satchel for her tennis shoes to switch from her high heels. A large vulture circled, riding the air currents, its wings blacker than the clouds. "Is this place on GPS?" she asked.

He glanced at his phone. "Sort of, at least until the dirt road ends. We'll be on foot for a hundred yards or so."

She was silent. A second vulture joined the first one in a corkscrew rotation. "I'd say we're about to reach our journey's end…at least for now."

Lightning flashed in the distance, the sound of thunder coming within three seconds. Bradford stuck his left hand out the open window. "Air temperature has dropped dramatically. Could be a big one heading our way. I hope we'll have time to lift up one of the planks on the old bridge and get it to the lab."

Elizabeth said nothing, lost in thought.

Bradford cut his eyes to her, and slowed as he approached a large *No Trespassing* sign on the left side of the dirt road. The road ended, nothing now but a wide trail. Bradford parked and turned to Elizabeth. "If the wood from the planks matches the cross on Belmont's grave, what then? There was no cross left on Cindy's grave or Charles Lehman's grave."

"Because some psychopath has made it his mission, exactly one hundred years after the hangings on the Shubuta Bridge, to carry out a prediction that he believes is an order directed at him—all stems, I think, from the paranoid writing that Belmont left in the pamphlets he circulated before his death. If we can find how the perp is connected to Belmont or his cult teachings—I think we might be closer to solving the murders and stopping the next one. He, most likely, was at the protest rally attended by Cindy and Julie. We know that Charlie Lehman was on the editorial board of the Hattiesburg Times. He wrote an editorial piece that spoke against the hate groups. And he singled out Neo-Nazis and members of the Klan. So, our links to the two deaths point or center on the protest rally in the shadow of the old Confederate Monument."

Bradford shook his head. "There were hundreds of people there—on both sides. Many were from out of town."

"But very few, if any, would have some kind of link to Zachariah Belmont, or his cause. At this point, maybe we can find his relatives, if there are any living today in Southern Mississippi."

Bradford pursed his lips. "That's like suggesting the distant relatives to Joseph Stalin, his great, great grandchildren could have inherited his psychotic DNA and become killers today."

"It happens, but vendettas and missions get passed down, too."

Bradford parked under the limbs of an old oak. "Looks like this is where we get out and walk the rest of the way to the river and the bridge."

FIFTY-SEVEN

They walked down a crooked path, the soft shadows cast by tall pines fading into shades of gray as a storm neared. Elizabeth's purse felt heavy, the pistol inside it. Bradford looked at the sky. "Maybe I should have brought an umbrella. I have one in the trunk. I can go back and get it."

Elizabeth shook her head. "We've already gone at least a hundred yards. I'll be fine. Let's keep going."

The path was wide enough for them to walk side by side, an occasional downed tree lying across the trail, the scent of decaying wood and damp pine straw in the air. They entered a small clearing. Elizabeth could see the rusted steel girders through the opening in the trees and undergrowth. She pointed. "Looks like we've reached our destination."

"I wonder if we can cross from one side of the river to the next, or will the boards be rotten?"

"We'll soon know."

They wound their way through a few remaining pines and scrub oaks. The Shubuta Bridge looked its age. The girders were the shades of fall leaves, a calico mismatch of burnt orange and brown painted by the ages and the earthy, iron oxide palette of nature. The tarnished trusses and crossbeams looked as if a leviathan died trying to cross the river, its blotted skeleton spanning a dark water and darker history. Green tendrils of kudzu snaked around the beams closest to land.

Elizabeth stopped. "I smell honeysuckles."

Bradford said, "I do, too."

Lightning popped in the distance. Elizabeth looked up and saw a vulture rotate in a clockwise spiral. The gusts quickened and the bird flapped its large wings, sailing into the abyss of the darkening sky.

Elizabeth paused near the entrance, the mouth of the bridge gaping in an ominous call to enter, framed by rusted pillars. She looked at honeysuckle vines wrapped around the joists, the creamy white flowers in contrast to the eroded metal and wood. Most of the planks leading into the entrance were still in place, a few gaping holes, but passable.

Black clouds swelled overhead, the entire sky dark. In the dim light, Elizabeth stood at the entrance and tried to look across the bridge to the far side.

Something was in the center.

She stared at the object in the distance—her mind refusing to go there. "Oh dear God," she whispered.

Bradford looked in the direction she stared. "What the…hell?"

A body was lying in the prone position. Face toward the sky. Elizabeth dropped her purse, walking quickly across the wooden planks. She slipped and got up. Lightning splintered in white, marbled bursts, molecules in the air charged with energy. Thunder exploded, the effect rocking the unsteady bridge. Rain moved upriver with the noise of an approaching waterfall.

"Elizabeth!" Bradford shouted. "Don't go there! It's not safe!"

She disregarded him, stepping on and over the old boards, some spongy with rot, some missing. Others splintered, giving way under her feet. She held on to the corroded tresses, the rain pelting her face. She wanted to run. Wanted to scream. She could tell the body was that of a young woman. Her hands were folded on her chest—a wooden bowl on her stomach.

Bradford stepped across the planks behind Elizabeth. One cracked and broke under his weight. He caught himself on a strut and kept walking. "Elizabeth!"

She didn't turn back as she had come close to the body and looked down at the pale face. She stared at Julie Lassiter's body—the word *wrath* scrawled across her forehead.

Elizabeth's legs felt weak. She knelt down beside the girl, her hands shaking, nausea rising in her throat. She placed one hand under Julie's head, wanting to lift her. Wanting to hold and comfort her.

Her body was cold, her eyes open, frozen on the turbulent sky. Elizabeth cried out. "No…God…no…please…." She looked at the lifeless face, tears spilling from Elizabeth's eyes, mixing with the rain. She knelt there, slightly swaying in the wind, holding one of Julie's small, lifeless, hands. Elizabeth bit her lower lip and wept, the rain pelting against her face. She looked up at the dark sky through the tarnished crossbeams, the clouds moving like angry black smoke, rain falling horizontally in the wind.

Lightning struck a tall pine on the other side of the bridge, a flash of greenish-white fire exploding in the branches. Rain poured, the droplets causing the word across Julie's forehead to dilute, white paint running into her hair, dripping through the spaces in the boards and down into the dark river flowing below the hanging bridge of Shubuta.

FIFTY-EIGHT

B y the time the sheriff's deputies from the Clarke County Sheriff's office arrived, the storm had passed. Elizabeth and Bradford answered questions and gave statements to the deputies and one investigator, a straightforward, husky detective in his late sixties, with close-cropped gray hair. White dress shirt. Sleeves rolled to the elbows. Detective Earl Clements scratched his wide jaw. "So you came here lookin' for a board and you found a body?"

Bradford said, "And it fits the same MO that I've had down in Forrest County, Detective, with the two other bodies I told you about. Now, you got it here. The perp knows no boundaries."

Elizabeth said, "No, but the common link is this old bridge, its morbid history, the wooden planks, and some psychopath who's made it his mission in life to kill people who he thinks violate the grain of his long-held beliefs. These are beliefs that go deep into the heart of the Klan and every backwards racial inequity before and since the Civil War."

Clements jotted down notes, looked up from his notebook to Elizabeth, studying her. "Sounds a bit farfetched, but we'll take all that into consideration as we investigate this murder."

She stepped closer to him. "The girl the coroner is loading into his van was nineteen years old. She was a student in my class, just like one of the other victims. There are three deaths now associated with this freak of nature. And the common link is that two of the victims attended a rally at the Confederate War Memorial in Hattiesburg. The third, a newspaper columnist, wrote an editorial in which he said the monuments are not so much historical markers as they are memorials to the Confederate States of America and all they stood for then and now."

The detective grunted. "Sounds like this fella, the killer, has a hell of an ax to grind. But it doesn't look like it's about race 'cause he's not killing blacks."

Bradford nodded. "Maybe not, but in one way or the other, it's usually about race in Mississippi. We're the only state that has five separate Klan groups. They're almost like franchises down here. Maybe he feels we should require passports to enter the state."

The detective stopped writing, clicking the top of his ink pen and placing it in his shirt pocket. "Well, this is definitely an inter-agency investigation. Let's share information. I'll keep y'all abreast of the investigation from this end." He handed Bradford a card.

"Likewise, Detective Clements. I'll email reports to you."

"If we're workin' together, I go by Earl."

"All right, Earl. Where do you begin?"

"We'll do as much forensic samples as we can, send it all out to the state lab. I'm like an old birddog. I just keep sniffin' and lookin' for a scent. I usually get on point when I start talkin' to folks. It's been my experience that most murders happen within what I call the sphere of influence...meaning somebody knows somebody and the victim is usually somehow associated with one or more of 'em somebodies." He winked and turned to walk back to his car.

Elizabeth said, "Detective...Earl...."

He turned around. "Yes ma'am."

"Within the last few months or so, someone was found removing planks from sections of the bridge. He was using them to make small crosses. And he was putting them on the graves of the men who hung those teenagers off this bridge in 1918. Do you know who was removing the planks?"

Earl ran his tongue on the inside of his left cheek, looked back in the direction of the bridge and then eyed Elizabeth. She flashed back to her Uncle Hal in the casino: *'See him moving his tongue on the inside of his cheek...he's got a strong hand. It's a subtle display of swagger.'*

Earl said, "Well, I don't know of anyone removing the boards. But this ol' bridge attracts its share of weird folks. Souvenir hunters, ghosts hunters, psychics and a suicide jumper or two have all come up here through the years. The hangin' bridge has some kinda damn eerie cult following. It wouldn't surprise me in the least if somebody pilfered a few boards to cut 'em up into crosses." He nodded and started to turn.

"Earl...the lynch mob that hung those teenagers...where are those people buried?"

"I got no idea. That was a hundred years ago. Shubuta Cemetery has been here since the early 1800's." He cut his eyes over to Bradford. "Y'all got anymore questions before I leave."

Elizabeth shook her head. Bradford said, "No."

Earl walked back to his county car, a slight limp on his right side.

Two deputies remained, walking the perimeter, looking for evidence on both sides of the bridge. Elizabeth and Bradford walked to his car. He carried a wooden board from the bridge in one hand. He opened the truck and placed the board inside. They got in the car and sat in silence for a moment as he checked his phone.

Elizabeth looked over at him. "I think Earl knows more than he's telling us."

"What do you mean?"

"I think he knows who has taken boards from the bridge. Maybe its more than one person...but he knows. Gerald Simpson didn't kill Julie and leave her body on that damn bridge."

"You think the perp picked the bridge because he's been carving miniature crosses from the wood?"

"That's part of the reason."

"Okay...what's the other part?"

"I'll read it to you. I have to go online." She lifted her phone and tapped the keyboard. "Remember what Revelation said about the bowls? The one found on Cindy's body—the first. It says the first angel poured the contents of his bowl on land. Hence the dirt and small plant in the bowl. The second, found on the body of Charles Lehman, with the seashell in it, represented the second angel pouring out his bowl on the sea. And now, the third bowl, found on Julie's body." She read from the screen. "It says the third angel poured out his bowl on the rivers, and they became blood. Julie was placed above the river. There was water in the bottom of the bowl when I got to the body, before the rain started. It looked like riverwater. Even though it rained, when the water is tested, it should confirm some of water came from the river."

Bradford started the car. "That sick fuck...I almost don't want to ask what the fourth angel poured out."

"We have to stop it from happening." She glanced down at her phone screen. "It says the fourth angel poured out something on the sun which in turn allowed the sun to scorch sinners with fire." She looked at Bradford. "The next bowl will have something in it that the killer believes represents fire. It could be anything from a book of matches to hot coals."

Bradford made a half circle with the car, backed up, and drove out from the area under the trees. He said, "Right now, all we really have, in terms of a common link between the three victims, is that rally held two months ago around the monument next to the courthouse. I'll pull video, talk to news stations and see if they still have clips of the event. That protest up in Charlottesville, Virginia, turned damn bloody. One person died and there were news clips running for days afterward. You could see many of the white supremacists or whatever they choose to call themselves, and many of the university students. I'm glad the rally in Hattiesburg was peaceful."

Elizabeth looked at him. "We just found the body of the third victim. The monster doing this was there. We just have to find him."

"Where the hell do we begin to look?"

"Let's start in Shubuta."

"Where in Shubuta?"

"The city cemetery."

FIFTY-NINE

Something about the gate to the old cemetery reminded Elizabeth of the entrance to the bridge. Bradford parked the car on a patch of grass and dirt near the entry. A wrought iron gate, made in the shape of an arch and supported by two worn brick pillars, served as the entrance. Elizabeth and Bradford walked beneath the arch. A large crow cawed out twice and then flew from a maple tree across the graveyard.

They entered the city cemetery and headed toward some of the taller monuments. Large granite and marble headstones, discolored from the elements and inattention, stood under the boughs of red cedar trees. Elizabeth walked slowly, reading the inscriptions. Many of the deceased had lived before, during, and after the Civil War. She wondered if any had fought in the war. And then she looked up at a Confederate War memorial less than thirty feet away.

Bradford used a stick to knock down a thick spider's web that extended from a headstone his height to a smaller one that was waist-high. A spider, almost the size of Elizabeth's hand, descended from a low-hanging branch, suspended in the air by a strand of web that caught sunlight breaking through the clouds. The spider's yellow and black legs moved sluggishly, like an old man flexing the fingers of his swollen, arthritic fist.

There were a few graves behind a small wrought iron enclosure. Bradford pushed open the gate, the sound of rusted hinges screeching, the musky smell of rotten cedar in the motionless air. He pointed to an old grave. "Take a look at that." A small cross was propped up against the headstone. "I'd bet that came from the same hand, the same person who left one of those on the grave of Zachariah Belmont."

"And maybe it came from the same wood that's in the trunk of your car."

"There's only one way to find out. He slipped on a plastic glove, lifted the cross and placed it in a small paper bag. "I don't feel any better than when I removed a cross from Belmont's grave. It's like I'm stealing from the dead."

Elizabeth read the inscription on the headstone. "Theodore Dexter. Born 1850…died 1920." She looked across at Bradford. "I'd bet that Theo here was, in fact, a member of the lynch mob."

"I wouldn't take you up on that bet. Let's see if there are any more of these mysterious crosses in here."

They stepped out of the wrought iron enclosure and scouted the other graves, Walked around headstones with the same family surnames: Archer, Crawford, Watkins, Baldwin, Clements, Pickett, Jones and a dozen more. Most left unattended in recent years. There was no indication that wooden crosses had been left on any of the gravesites.

Elizabeth approached one headstone that stood alone, almost tucked away in a corner of the cemetery and beneath the canopy of a sprawling live oak, leaden clusters of Spanish moss drooped from a low-hanging limb like steel wool, almost touching the top of the tombstone. She moved to the face of the stone. A second wooden cross was leaned up against it. She turned toward Bradford. "Here's another one."

Bradford came forward, pulling a small paper bag from his back pocket. "The woodcutter gets around."

Elizabeth read the inscription. "Edward Thompson…born 1849… died 1927. Zachariah 14: 3-5: The Lord will go out and fight against those nations as he fights on the day of battle." She paused, studying the gravesite. "There's a boot print to the right of the grave. The tread markings look similar, if not identical, to the print near Zachariah Belmont's headstone and Cindy's grave."

Bradford stepped around the burial site and took a close-up photo of the print. He lifted the wooden cross. Elizabeth raised her right hand. "Before you put it in the bag, I want a picture of it."

He held the cross in his gloved hand as she snapped a photo using her phone. Then he placed the cross in a paper bag. Bradford said, "We're lucky the rain didn't wash the print away. If it weren't for the thick canopy of limbs from this old oak, probably would have."

Elizabeth turned, looked at the tree in the mottled light. A breeze blew from the direction of the river, jostling limbs and moving shadows across the tree trunk, bark gnarled and thick. Her mind flashed back to the evening she stood alone near Cindy's grave. She saw the image of an old man in the tree trunk as a fading sunset cast dark purple shadows. Elizabeth blinked hard. The face faded. She hugged her arms, staring at the tree.

"You okay?" Bradford asked.

She turned to him, not sure how to answer his question, the cawing of crows echoing across the cemetery. "I'm okay...it's just this image I see sometimes. I saw it that evening in the cemetery not far from Cindy's grave. You had already gone, a fog was building, and not much sunlight was left in the shadows of the woods behind her grave. I saw what appeared to be the face of an old man in the trunk of an oak tree. And just then...when I turned around and looked at the trunk of that oak tree, for a split second, I saw the same image in the knotted bark." She half smiled. "Creepy...maybe I'm finally losing my mind."

"No. It's called sleep deprivation and stress. Two people close to you, two of your students, were slaughtered. These deaths carry some of the pain associated, I'm sure, with the murder of your daughter, Molly. I'd say you, Doctor Elizabeth Monroe, may see a mirage or vision because of all the cumulative stuff you're going through right now."

Elizabeth touched her hair, still damp from the rain. "Mike, how do you tell another set of parents that their daughter has been butchered?"

"There is absolutely nothing you can do, no training you can get, that'll ever make it easier. No one wants to deliver that news...and no one wants to receive it. An accidental death is bad enough—a murder is...off the emotional pain charts. It's simply a senseless or non-processing blow to the heart that will last the rest of the parent's life. Not to mention siblings and other family members. When I called Ed to give him a report after we left the Shubuta Bridge, he was pretty distraught. He has two kids. One is a daughter about the age of your students."

Elizabeth looked around as the sun went down. "Let's get out of here."

They walked around the graves, neither one talking.

In the car, Bradford said, "The news media will be all over this...the networks and cable channels. We've got to find this sick prick. I'll put a rush to see if we can get the wood analysis back tomorrow. It's, no doubt, the same pervert. We have three bodies, no eyewitness, and we're no closer to finding this guy than we were when he killed Cindy. I wish I could read Detective Clements good ol' boy mind. If he's not coming clean with us, if he knows the trespasser or trespassers lifting boards off that bridge, we need to know."

"He might operate on some backwoods 'as need to know' basis, and he determines the conditions. Maybe I'm wrong...it could be that he doesn't know who's stolen wood from a bridge with one, if not, *the* most tragic histories in the nation. We're missing something, Mike. It's right near us. I can feel it, but I can't see it. We're close."

"Unfortunately, close never counts in a murder investigation."

"I have a dear friend in Natchez, someone who basically set up the FBI's behavioral profile division. He's been retired for three years. I'm going to visit him. If I can present the evidence and the correlating theories, he'll look at it with fresh eyes. And that could be the difference."

SIXTY

E lizabeth almost didn't want to press the button. If she did, she knew
she might have a harder time than usual falling asleep. She stood next
to her couch, Jack lying on a comfortable chair looking at her through half
closed eyes. She pointed the remote at her television and pressed the power
button.

The screen faded up from black as the 11:00 p.m. newscast began. Two
news anchors, a man and a woman, both early forties, sat a little straighter.
The man said, "Good evening everyone. We have breaking news. Police are
searching for the serial killer who has taken a third life here in Southern
Mississippi."

The woman said, "We have a crew in Clarke County where the body
was discovered. Next of kin has been notified and police say the body is
that of nineteen-year-old Julie Lassiter. She was a student at the University
of Southern Mississippi. Her body was found in the center of a long-
closed bridge with a gruesome history in Mississippi. Channel Two's Jeanne
Sanders has the story."

The video image was of the Shubuta Bridge shot from an angle near
the river, looking up, showing the bridge in silhouette against the backdrop
of a gunmetal gray sky. A reporter's voice said, "The body was found in a
place that's no stranger to authorities for finding dead bodies. This is the
Shubuta Bridge." The image cut to one of the entrances to the bridge where
the reporter stood. Her auburn hair was shoulder length, the wind blowing
it. "In the last century, six people were hung from the bridge, two of them

were pregnant teenage girls. And now there is another victim. Police say the body of Julie Lassiter was found lying on her back at near the midpoint section of the bridge. They say the death scene is almost identical to two others recently. Officers found a wooden bowl on the victim's lap and the word *wrath* had apparently been written across her forehead. Some of it washed away in the rain. The Clarke County Sheriff's office is working in conjunction with Forrest County authorities to apprehend someone police say could wind up becoming the worst serial killer in Mississippi history if he or she isn't stopped."

The image cut to Detective Earl Clements standing in front of the sheriff's office. He said, "This is one of the worst, if not the worst murder, I've seen in a thirty-five year career. The killer staged the body in a morbid fashion. No one deserves the fate that this girl suffered. We'll find the perpetrator."

The reporter asked, "Was the victim killed on the bridge?"

"We're still investigating that. But, at this time, it appears she was killed elsewhere and her body was simply left on the bridge. Whoever did this planned it out and carefully executed it. It's a damn shame."

Elizabeth stepped closer to the screen, watching Clements' body language, his eyebrows lifting as he finished. The images cut back to the bridge and scenes of sheriff's detectives and forensic investigators looking for evidence on and below the bridge.

The reporter's voice said, "Detective Clements tells us that the body was actually found by a Forrest County detective who was in the area. We spoke with Detective Mike Bradford."

The picture cut to Bradford standing in the parking lot of the Justice Center building in Hattiesburg. "We were looking for additional evidence in connection to the deaths of Cindy Carter and Charles Lehman when we found the victim."

"Why were you specifically at the Shubuta Bridge?" the reporter asked.

"We go where the evidence trail leads us. Some are dead-end streets. Others aren't. This one obviously was not."

"How is the old bridge, especially with its rather tragic history, connected to these murders?"

"We're not sure it is connected. That's why we investigate."

"So the latest murder victim found on a bridge with a malicious past is a coincidence then, correct?"

"As these murder investigations proceed, I'm not in a position to speculate or release what evidence we have or don't have. We are moving as quickly as possible to get this person off the streets."

The interview ended and the reporter stood at the base of the bridge near the river. She said, "Whether the fact that the body of Julie Lassiter was placed, after her death, on the Shubuta Bridge is coincidental or not, remains to be seen. What is known is that the young woman was a university student studying forensic psychology. The first murder victim was her classmate, also majoring in criminal psychology. One of the professors teaching them was, coincidentally, Doctor Elizabeth Monroe, a well-known and respected authority who has testified as an expert witness in two of Mississippi's most heinous murder trials. Doctor Monroe lost her only child to a murderer who has never been apprehended. Some in law enforcement have speculated whether there may be a connection between the death of Doctor Monroe's daughter and the recent victims of this bold serial killer. But that, too, like the discovery of the body on the bridge behind me, remains a mystery. Reporting from the Shubuta Bridge in Clarke County, Jeanne Sanders, Channel Two News."

Elizabeth lowered her body to the couch. She felt drained, her pulse slow, energy seeping from her pores. Jack slinked from the chair and jumped up on the couch, sitting next to Elizabeth. She looked at him and half smiled, his large eyes somehow discerning. She petted him, and he lowered his chin to her leg. "Jack, I feel a strong need to visit Molly. I don't bring her flowers. I bring her something for the birds."

Jack looked up. Elizabeth smiled. "Now I have your attention. I hung a bird feeder near Molly's grave. I fill it from time to time because she so loved birds, butterflies…all of God's creatures. She would certainly fall in love with you…as I have." She leaned down and kissed him on top of his head. He purred.

"A very evil man is taking lives. And unlike you, we frail humans only have one life. It's not something to be taken for granted…because all time is borrowed and most precious because you can never bottle it. I have three stops tomorrow. One, as you know, is with Molly. The other two are old friends who couldn't have had more polar opposite careers. One man hunted evil for a living—profiled it. The other didn't hunt it…but he pursued it in other ways to change dark hearts. The question is, could he do it now with the evil I feel is coming closer to us each night."

SIXTY-ONE

As Elizabeth drove through Natchez, she remembered the time when she believed in fairy tales—believed in innocence. It was before her father's illness, her mother's suicide, and before her brother was killed. It was before a dark curtain closed around the weakened leftovers of her family.

They'd taken a steamboat trip through time up the Mississippi River, the big wheel slapping the river, the steam engines churning, smokestacks belching, passengers aligned along the decks. People smiled in the glow of fireworks over the river.

She remembered Natchez at night, her father pointing toward the Natchez-Vidalia Bridge, its lights twinkling across the black water, fireworks exploding high above the bridge, a big Ferris wheel on the shore seemingly turning in sync with the paddlewheel. She remembered the smells of fried catfish and pipe tobacco—the weathered captain clenching the pipe stem between his false teeth. She loved the sound of the paddleboat's whistle in the night air as another paddle wheeler, the Delta Queen, passed them, heading to New Orleans.

But, most of all, she remembered the fireflies.

The captain had pulled the steamboat close to shore so the passengers could see the Victorian houses and hear the history of Natchez. One massive bluff was nearly covered in a green wall of kudzu. And the fireworks here weren't manmade. To Elizabeth, as a seven-year-old girl, it seemed like there were millions of fireflies crawling on leaves, their lights twinkling, giving the illusion of a giant glowing wave cascading down from the bluff and spilling into the mighty Mississippi River.

She remembered the captain telling the passengers about the legend of the fireflies and the fairies in Natchez. "It started not far from the Devil's Punch Bowl," he said, lighting his pipe, the flicker of fireworks in his pale blue eyes. "The trolls didn't like the fireflies. The trolls preferred the light of the stars. This was when fireflies kept their light on all the time, mind you. So the trolls made it their mission to get rid of all the fireflies along the river. They almost got 'em, too."

Elizabeth remembered the grandfatherly captain winking at her brother, Nathan, who hung on to every word. "But one elf named Kismet and a little fairy named Dawn came to the rescue. They were told by their great grandma, Mother Dove, where to find the fireflies. The trolls had 'em locked in a cave on the bluff. So Kismet and Dawn had to sneak up the riverbank past other troll guards until they got to the cave. Once there, they found the lone guard fast asleep. So they quietly opened a wooden door, entered the cave and told all the fireflies they were free to go. And they delivered a message from Mother Dove. They told the fireflies to always fly high above the reach of the trolls and to turn off their lights when they saw them. So that's why, to this very day, fireflies flash, and the gazillion you see all along the bluff are thankful descendants of those that escaped."

Elizabeth's cell phone rang, bringing her out of her childhood memories as she approached the home of former FBI profiler, Otto Emerson. She saw Mike Bradford's name on her caller ID and answered. He said, "The wood from the crosses matches the wood from the Shubuta Bridge. So now we know that whoever was pilfering wood off the old bridge was making crosses from the boards and most likely, he is the one responsible for the murders."

"I'd think that someone with the Clarke County Sheriff's office ought to know if one person or more had been taking boards off the bridge."

"I don't think anyone really cares. You saw the shape of the bridge. It'll probably be torn down eventually because the bridge is a potential liability. It's not like there's any value in rusted steel, iron and old boards, some of which, have just about turned to petrified wood. Deputies have run teenagers off the bridge who've gone there to smoke pot and make out."

"Somebody up there knows something. Maybe it's not Detective Clements, but Shubuta isn't Jackson. Everybody knows everybody. Maybe the perp isn't from the area, but he feels a connection to that heinous bridge and all of the people in the lynch mob. We'll just have to figure out why."

"Did you meet with Otto Emerson yet?"

"No, I'm pulling up to his house now. I'll let you know what he says."

"Thanks, be careful, Elizabeth, on the way back home. Oh, by the way, if you need for me to run by your place and feed Jack, just let me know."

"Thank you, Mike, but you don't have a key."

He chuckled. "Not yet. Please call me when you're done." He disconnected.

Elizabeth parked in the circular driveway, the old Victorian house sitting on a bluff overlooking the Mississippi River with all the grandeur of the Gilded Age. The home, with its four white columns, had been restored and remodeled. Otto Emerson and his wife spared no expense. The spacious lawn was well manicured, grass dark green. A robin in the center almost seemed to be a prop until it moved, hopping towards a large sweetbay magnolia tree to the right of the house, the tree's blossoms creamy white.

Elizabeth walked up to the front door and rang the bell, chimes ringing inside the house. Within seconds, Otto Emerson opened the door, wide smile, white hair perfectly parted. He wore a blue polo shirt and beige shorts. Boat shoes. "Elizabeth, give me a hug." They hugged and he said, "Come in. Ruth fixed one of her lunches right out of the pages of Southern Living Magazine. She had to go into town to pick up our oldest granddaughter for a doctor's appointment. But she put everything out for us."

"She shouldn't have."

"But she did—that's just how Ruth does things." His thick eyebrows lifted with his smile. "Come, let's go on the back deck and visit."

She followed him through the home, much of it decorated with a classic edge, but with a southern nautical theme related to the Mississippi River and the coastal areas. As they walked by a large framed lithograph on one wall, Otto stopped and pointed to it. "That's the *Sultana*. It would become the center of the greatest maritime disaster in U.S history…right up to today. But very few people have heard of it. Doesn't have the sex appeal of *Titanic*."

Elizabeth looked at the image of a large steamboat, partially on fire, in the center of a river, people, trying to escape the heat. "What happened?"

"It was in 1865. The Civil War had ended. Lincoln had been assassinated. They were hunting for John Wilkes Booth. So the press coverage was on other things at the time. Almost two thousand soldiers, Union, were being transported from New Orleans back north when the boilers exploded near Memphis. A witness said the heat was so intense, that flames and steam could be seen for more than thirty miles in any direction. The *Sultana* chugged upriver right outside my back door. Come, say hello to Old Man River, at least that's what I call him. Maybe it's because I watched the movie Show Boat one too many times. Paul Robeson singing *Ol' Man River* still gives me the chills, especially when I hear the line...*I'm tired of living but scared of dying.* Come, Elizabeth."

She followed him out the back door to a large wooden deck. It overlooked a high bluff and the Mississippi River. In the center of the deck was a round table and chairs with a large, red umbrella. Hanging baskets of blooming petunias and ferns adorned the eaves and parts of the deck. Food had been set out with two plates. Chicken and rice casserole. Southern-style collard greens and cornbread. Elizabeth looked at the river, stepped to the railing and inhaled deeply, the scent of magnolia blossoms and Confederate jasmine in the breeze. "What a magnificent view."

Otto stood next to her, the wind rustling his hair. "What I love about it, in addition to the vast panorama, is the constant change. The colors of the river change with the seasons and the time of day. Ruth and I enjoy the arrival of the migratory birds. The boat and barge traffic on the river has its own sort of Mark Twain sense of slow rhythm. Let's eat. It's time for me to shut the hell up and hear what you've come here to share with me. The third murder is all over the news. Now I want to hear your insight into what's happening."

SIXTY-TWO

Elizabeth looked from the bluff to the Mississippi River, a container ship heading downriver, the big diesels pushing the cargo, the movement creating a long V in the water behind the stern. She glanced over to Otto who sipped a German pilsner. Elizabeth explained in detail what had happened up to the wood from the bridge matching the wood used to make the crosses.

Otto used a white napkin to wipe his lips. "You most definitely have, shall we call it, cross pollination between suspects. In other words, the three young men from the university all have issues. The loner, Larry Tucker… you mentioned that he'd mumbled some things about a darker link between modern society and ancient societies and something about how ritual killings helped destroy any democratic systems of government, which simply added to the tyranny of a class system."

Elizabeth nodded. "Yes."

"That intrigues me. He, in his mind, has justification and cause. But that, as you know Elizabeth, doesn't make Tucker a murderer. When I was with the FBI, we often found that psychopaths fell into one of the following three distinct categories: the mission-oriented killers commit murder to rid the world or society of those who they feel are immoral, unworthy, unclean, and lower class. These killers roll up their sleeves like they're going to work in the killing fields."

"Hitler and Stalin would be good examples."

"Indeed, but these men had the means to kill on a scale of genocide. The common psychopath next door doesn't have the power or position to do that, so he or she systematically kills when the urge meets opportunity. The second group is the visionary killer. These offenders say that they receive commands from a higher authority…voices…if you will…and they're simply fulfilling a calling from the gods or other imaginary beings that demand the psychopath kill. The third group is the hedonistic killer. For them, it's all about the thrill of the hunt and the kill. These offenders can be divided into two sub groups: the lust-oriented murderers who kill people for sexual gratification and the thrill-oriented offenders who kill for their own pleasures. They get very excited—like riding alone in the front car of the ultimate roller-coaster ride. For them, it's a power or control type of kill, which gives them dominance over another human being."

Elizabeth sipped her coffee, a breeze coming across the river and causing wind chimes to tinkle. She hugged her arms. Otto looked at her. "What are you thinking?"

"I'm thinking this perp has all of those traits. Which makes him deadlier, if that's even possible."

"It is indeed possible. It's highly unusual that a psychopath has all of the aforementioned anomalies, but it can happen…and he will exemplify evil."

"I gave you an assessment of my profile, the one I shared with police. Do you agree? What am I missing that I don't see?"

"At this point, it's always a theory based on proven case studies and analysis. I think your profile is as accurate as it can be considering the circumstances. However, let's look at the common links between all three murders, the evidence…and you. Had he not sent you the text message, left honeysuckle flowers, I would have ruled you out of the equation. But that's not the case."

"Why me?"

"A number of reasons, but there's a primary one. The offender is a man who holds the mission of the South's lost cause deep in his gut. When you combine that with what he believes is an even higher mission from God— or what he perceives as his god, it becomes a binding contract in his mind. He's essentially a follower of doctrine preached a century ago by Zachariah Belmont. You mentioned the pamphlet Belmont wrote called *Retribution*. Maybe the prime clue will be the letters L – O – T. There is a connection there. Find it, Elizabeth. The perp culled the two girls, your students, from the herd at that rally. He followed them, systematically hunting them down. He killed Charlie Lehman because Lehman had written strong editorials admonishing the white supremacists hate groups and Neo-Nazis at the rally. And you stood out when you did the live interviews on national television, essentially deconstructing the mind of hate groups. You referred to it as a dark triad that includes extreme narcissism, Machiavellian or opportunist and psychopathy or personality disorders associated with callous, manipulative behavior. You used the allegory of snakes in the garden. For this perp, you waved a red flag in his face."

Elizabeth set her napkin down and drew in a deep breath. "I forgot I used that term."

"I remembered it when I watched the TV interviews with more than bated breath." His white eyebrows rose. "It's always a powerful study in psychology to see how some groups, such as the Klan, can use the shadow of the Civil War as a central place and theme to light fires of hate. The war wasn't as much about slavery as it was about commerce, what some perceived as a dictatorial and partial federal government, and a way of life on either side of the Mason-Dixon line that was out of sync with business and cultures. It doesn't justify war, but sometimes the whole picture is reduced."

"There was a passage in the pamphlet, *Retribution*—the entire thing was only two pages. I pulled it from the archives of the library and copied it to my phone. I'll read it to you." She picked up her phone and tapped the keyboard. "On the second page, Belmont wrote: '*Fear not the serpent. Invite the serpent into your place of worship. God will protect you from its wicked bite. Fear not an eye-to-eye encounter with the serpent for those truly filled with the Holy Spirit cannot perish from the serpent's bite. There were snakes in the Garden of Eden, and you brothers and sisters, never have to crawl on your belly like a reptile as long as you remain true to the mission and never forget that retribution is your birthright. Sip from the cup of wormwood, raised in a toast to the heavens in one hundred years by the eighth angel on the eighth day.*' She put her phone down, the blast from a tugboat whistle in the distance. "Are they bizarre ramblings of a zealot who thought of himself as a prophet…or are they instructions."

"Could be both. Depends upon who's reading it and the interpretation. Man has a propensity to twist the Bible for personal convenience."

"So my comment on national TV about hate groups being akin to snakes in the garden struck a nerve with this guy."

"It struck more than that. You drilled down to the core of his beliefs that, in his mind, are non-negotiable and beyond reproach. You've struck out at his *identity*."

"I believe some of the group psychosis boils down to a fear factor. Fear of the unknown, fear of change or what might happen if anything is different than you or falls outside your definition of what's supposed to be normal. Some people establish themselves as part of a tribe, and they say this is the group with which I identify. I believe what I choose to believe, regardless of facts or logic that may point otherwise."

Otto nodded. "Many of these people are not the loner type. This guy, I believe, is the head of the snake. The posing of the bodies, the word *wrath*, the wooden crosses. He's making bold and very deadly statements to uphold his point. He knows your history, the death of Molly, and your nationally recognized position as an expert witness in criminal insanity defense trials. He sees you interviewed on TV, peeling the layers of the onion into his mind, and he's watching you."

He paused, glanced across the vista to the river. He watched a tugboat push a flat barge, black diesel smoke curling from the boat's exhaust pipes. "Elizabeth, the more I drill down on this with you, the more I'm seeing a common thread you're weaving in this killer's open and festering mental wound."

"What's that?"

"You are, no doubt, searching for Molly's killer. You're doing and saying things that subtly cross over into a challenge with a psychopath—"

"He left one of Cindy's earrings on her grave. As I mentioned, the text message said—*Did you find the earring? He left it for you.* Otto, Molly's killer took one of her earrings as a souvenir, too. Maybe there's a connection."

"We don't know if the serial killer took Molly's life. If he's caught and can be interviewed, you may know, but only if he feels in the mood to confess. And that's assuming there's evidence or personal knowledge to connect him."

"To me, the earring is close enough."

Otto finished his beer, placing the bottle over a damp napkin on the glass table. He looked at Elizabeth, his eyes kind but probing. "I doubt he's Molly's killer. But if he can play to that ruse, he can get closer to hitting you where you're most vulnerable. Be very careful, Elizabeth, that you don't let that happen. You're at war. Not in intermittent battles here and there like most normal folks in society. But you are in a sustained war, because the hunt for Molly's killer is a constant strategy in your mind. You think about it trying to fall asleep. It wakes you at night, and I'd bet it's the first thing on your mind in the morning when you open your eyes—"

"Otto, please, I don't need—"

"Hear me out. I'm an old lion who's lived and witnessed more Shakespearean tragedies than many people, most from my own profession. Please allow me to be allegoric to war. In sustained ground combat, the soldier's instincts to live may keep him or her alive, but something inside dies on the battlefield; and, in the end, it's the dead who live to see the close of the physical war. The third act will follow them back home. If they're fortunate, the epilogue will be a surrender that doesn't happen on the battlefield, but must happen in the heart of mercy."

"I can never offer mercy to the man who killed Molly."

"I'm not suggesting that. By heart, I mean your heart, Elizabeth. Have mercy, compassion, on yourself. That doesn't mean that you ever stop searching for Molly's killer. It means that you give yourself permission to live…to not allow someone's evil to steal your joy of life itself and to further define you the rest of your life."

Elizabeth pushed her plate away, the wind chimes grew silent, the breeze across the river gone. "Thank you, Otto. You're right, and I needed to hear that. But it's not just me finding the man responsible for killing my daughter. I looked into the eyes of Cindy Carter's desperate parents and said I'd do my best to help them. And now there are Julie Lassiter's parents—all numb from inconsolable pain. All needing partial closure because I know they'll never find complete closure. There are no happy endings. Just endings."

He reached across the table and placed his right hand on the top of her hand. "Still, of course, remain vigilant in this case because it's now coming into your wheelhouse. The perp, no doubt, saw your interviews on national TV, probably saw some of the ones you did regionally, too. You have become his nemesis. He has you in his target. He's killed three people. Left three bowls. If it's tied to Revelation and God's wrath, and it appears to be, he'll kill at least four more times. One of those times, he will target you."

SIXTY-THREE

Three hours later, Elizabeth drove up to St Patrick's Catholic Church in Hattiesburg, playing back in her mind the conversation with Otto. She parked in front of the aged, red brick church, the front entrance and windows trimmed in white. A tall brick bell tower was to the right, large white crosses on either side of its castle-like turret. She thought of the first wooden cross they'd found, the one that was set against the headstone of Zachariah Belmont.

Elizabeth arrived twenty minutes before her appointment with Father Gregory MacGrath. She sat in her car, checked her phone, looking though the lens of the cameras around her home. She looked for Jack. The only movement was a red cardinal in the bird feeder on her deck. She closed her eyes for a moment; Otto's words ricocheted inside her head. *If it's tied to Revelation and God's wrath, and it appears to be, he'll kill at least four more times. One of those times, he will target you.*

She locked her car and walked up the brick steps to the cathedral. Elizabeth tried to remember the last time she had attended mass. When Molly was growing up, she brought her here every Sunday until they moved away. Coming back to the area after Molly's death, Elizabeth attended one mass, sat in the back pew and tried to make sense of her detached state-of-mind. She lasted a half hour in mass before getting up and leaving. That was four years ago.

She opened the center door and cool air billowed onto her damp face. She stepped inside, memories of attending the parish for fifteen years flooded her thoughts. The weddings she had seen. The funerals. She inhaled deeply, the faint scent of incense in the texture and heart of the church. No one was in the cathedral.

Elizabeth walked slowly past the wooden pews, candles burned in every corner and along the dais. Afternoon sunlight turned the stained glass windows into rich colors and scenes depicting the life of Christ. Soft lights illuminated statues of Jesus and some of the disciples.

Elizabeth walked quietly up to the front near the pulpit. A statue of Mother Mary was to her far right, a large stained-glass window behind the podium depicted Jesus feeding the hungry. She knelt down and made the sign of the cross, remembering when Molly, as a little girl, was baptized on the very spot. Elizabeth looked up, sunlight illuminated the face of Christ in the stained glass, her eyes welled. She slowly rose, stepped back, and sat in the first pew. The only sound was from the whir of the air-conditioning through the vents.

She thought about the horrific scene of Julie's body lying lifeless on the bridge. And she reflected on what Julie had told her in the classroom. *'Cindy said when she tried to give her opinion, the man told her to shut up or the wrath of God will take her down. I don't know if what he said about the wrath of God has anything to do with the word wrath left on Cindy and the man who was killed...or is it coincidental?'*

The sound of heavy shoes jarred Elizabeth from her thoughts. She turned in the pew and watched Father MacGrath approach. For a man in his early seventies, he walked straight, good pace, his body language made a presence. As he got closer, Elizabeth could see a wide smile spreading across his welcoming face. His hair looked more silver than gray, cleft chin and eyes the tint of jade. Even in retirement, he wore the priest's collar.

Elizabeth stood and smiled. "My dear Elizabeth," he said embracing her and then stepping back. "Let me look at you. You never age. Must be the good genes and a glass of wine now and then." He beamed, slightly rocking on the balls of his feet.

"Just a little. Thank you, Father, for agreeing to meet me here today."

"Wild horses or a free trip back to Dublin for a short stay wouldn't have kept me away. Let's sit. I played a gentleman's game of soccer yesterday; the blokes almost turned it into rugby. My knees are a little sore."

They sat in the pew, crimson light from the stained glass soft against one side of the priest's face. Elizabeth turned to him. "Father MacGrath, sitting here, I thought about some of the sermons you'd delivered in mass."

"I'm delighted they stayed with you through the years."

"They have, and I'm grateful."

"Since you returned to the area, I've not seen as much of you as I would have liked. I know Molly's death left you devastated and questioning your beliefs. I hope you're returning to the church. In my heart, I know you never left God. How can I help you, Elizabeth?"

"I'm working with the police to profile and find the person responsible for three murders in the last few weeks. What I've seen has shaken me to my core. With all of my training in criminal psychology, I can usually put evil in a specific box. But how do you box a monster with multiple personalities?"

Elizabeth's phone buzzed with an incoming text message. She looked at the caller ID—Detective Bradford. The message read: *Call me. The boot prints from the grave at Shubuta Cemetery match the print from Zachariah Belmont's grave.*

SIXTY-FOUR

Elizabeth looked up from the phone screen into the sea green eyes of Father MacGrath. He glanced at her phone, a wry smile on his face. "Is it good news?"

She gave him a summary of what had happened thus far and added, "I want to show you something." She turned the screen toward the priest. "This is a picture of one of the wooden crosses police have removed from the graves. It came from a grave in the Shubuta Cemetery. This cross is very similar to one found on Zachariah Belmont's grave. The wood used to make the crosses was from lumber on the Shubuta Bridge—the infamous hanging bridge. The killer is placing these crosses on the graves of people who were believed to have been members of the lynch mob that hung four teenagers off the bridge. Two of the girls were in their last trimester of pregnancy. And this month is exactly one hundred years after the teens were hung from the bridge."

"So, if all this ties to the person responsible for killing the three people recently, two of whom were your students, are police any closer to apprehending the person?"

"Not as much as we'd hoped. The killer is trying to justify his heinous actions, at least covertly, by writing *wrath* on the bodies of his victims and placing something in each of the wooden bowls that is symbolic of the seven bowls of God's wrath in Revelation."

"Interesting. Very sad, but interesting in that someone would use that ploy in order to justify his own wicked decisions."

"I remember, one time in mass, you spoke about the eighth angel in the Book of Revelation. You said something to the effect, this angel will be chosen by God to deliver his final message—fire raining down on earth. Something in my gut tells me this killer thinks he's destined for that role because he's playing all the parts."

Father MacGrath nodded, his thoughtful eyes studying her face. "I've tried all my life to put Revelation in prospective. At this point, I don't believe it's humanly possible. John of Patmos wrote those words not long after he'd seen Roman soldiers leveling destruction on Jerusalem. He was in exile to the Greek island of Patmos. John said that the eighth angel would reach into a massive incense cauldron and use the hot coals to rain destruction on earth. If the killer believes he is the eighth angel incarnate or in human flesh, he would think he's the one ordained by God to rain fire on whom he perceives as a sinner. This person, Elizabeth, would personify evil." He crossed his legs and looked at the statue of Mary, the light above creating a soft shadow on the face.

Elizabeth said, "What I've seen recently is difficult to quantify in terms of serial killers that fall in certain groupings. This killer appears to be a hybrid of evil, if that's possible."

"More people abandon their faith because of evil than any other reason. It's certainly the greatest test of faith."

"Father, I'm weary of being tested."

He nodded. "St. Aquinas once wrote that we can't have full knowledge all at once. We must start by trusting in God and believing that God is within us. Afterwards, we may be led to master the evidence for ourselves." He paused and blew out a breath, looking back at her. "Elizabeth, our beloved God is good, and you come from that good as surely as a pinecone comes from within the tree. You will gain insight and direction to defeat darkness."

She half smiled. "It's interesting that you mentioned a pinecone. I just had this discussion with a friend. We talked about the symbolism of the pinecone through the ages. The primary correlation is the pineal gland in the brain. It's there where our insight, perception or vision is created."

"It's there where the hand of God placed it. It's up to you to use your gifts wisely."

Elizabeth was quiet a moment. Beyond the stained glass windows, the distant sound of a train horn came closer. "What if…I'm not sure how to say this, but as a little girl, I used to get feelings—warnings if you will when danger was close. It's continued through most of my life. Sort of comes and goes depending on what I'm going through at the time. This was especially true as a teenager."

"I remember your intuitive insight when you were a girl." He smiled. "You were always an old soul, Elizabeth."

"I don't know if I have an overactive pineal gland, or if there's some kind of divine intervention…but I've seen things."

"What kind of things?"

"Visions might be the best way to describe it. One is a carving of a face in a tree somewhere. It's an image of an old man. Flowing beard. Wide eyes. Like some Greek philosopher's face carved in the heart of a tree trunk or maybe it's the image of an angel, at least my perception of an angel, and I don't know what it means or where it will lead."

"If you continue to trust in God, you will be shown more of the path."

"I've shared with you some of the excerpts from the pamphlet, *Retribution*. I appeared on a national TV news program where I referred to hate groups as snakes in the garden, a term I heard my grandmother once say. I don't know why this stuck with me, but it did." She pressed keys on her phone, reading from the screen. "Zachariah Belmont wrote that there were snakes in the Garden of Eden, saying that *'you brothers and sisters, never have to crawl on your belly like a reptile as long as you remain true to the mission and never forget that retribution is your birthright.'* I think the killer is following some rigid edict or purported biblical mission."

"Many people identify snakes in the Garden of Eden as Satan or symbolic of the presence of evil. So, to a follower of Zachariah Belmont's declaration, he or she could think that you called them Satan, while diminishing their mission in the same breath. And that mission, based on what you've shared, is their belief of superiority over others or certainly over other races. Something Belmont apparently preached. Systemic evil is one of the worse kinds, Elizabeth, because it needs a group of like-minded people to identify with and to fervently believe in regardless of facts that are contrary to their belief system and group identity. This is what creates lynch mobs."

He looked up at the image of Jesus on the cross in one of the stained glass windows. "And it's what nailed the Son of God to a wooden cross."

Elizabeth's phone vibrated in her hand. She glanced down at the alert. "Excuse me Father, I just got an alert from one of my cameras." She looked at the image of her front porch. She could see Jack curled up on one of the three rocking chairs on the porch. And then his head moved. He stood in the chair. A gloved hand reached into the frame of the camera, ripping the camera from its mount. Elizabeth saw the blur of the green ferns. The welcome mat. The wind chimes. Blue sky. Concrete steps.

A man's boots.

Jack. His back arched. Mouth open. Lips curled in a defense posture.

And then the image went black.

SIXTY-FIVE

Elizabeth took her 9mm from the glove box and squealed tires leaving the church. She drove fast through the perimeter roads toward her house. She started to call Bradford, tapping his name on her contact list, but decided to put the phone back in the console. She checked the side and rearview mirrors. No one appeared to be following her. She accelerated, taking her car up to ninety in a fifty-five zone.

She thought about Jack. *Lazy, lumpy ol' cat with the big eyes and heart. What had he seen just before the camera was hit? Was he okay...or was he harmed or dead?* She held the steering wheel with both hands, knuckles white. She sped past trees and houses—the exterior of her car a blur, her mouth dry.

Elizabeth was nearly to her home. No sign of a car or truck in the vicinity of her property. She stopped at the entrance to her driveway. Not afraid to enter, but fearful of what she may find. She grabbed her pistol from the console between the seats and chambered a round. And then she drove with her left hand, holding the 9mm on her lap.

She came up to her front porch, scanned the yard and surroundings for any sign of Jack. There was nothing. She'd turned her front porch light on after she'd left early in the morning. The yellow light appeared muted, subdued in the late afternoon sunshine.

She parked her car. Something on the porch caught the light, an odd reflection where there was never one. She left her purse in the car. Elizabeth held the pistol in her right hand, trigger finger ready. She approached her front door.

One of the two cameras was on the floor of the porch, glass lens popped out, like it had lost an eye in battle. She looked at the rocking chair that Jack had been in when the trespasser approached. There was no sign of blood or fur. She checked her front door. Turned and looked toward the street, glancing at the remaining camera. The breezed picked up, causing the single wind chime to tinkle. A bumblebee hovered near purple lavender flowers she'd planted near the porch.

"Jack!" she shouted. "It's safe to come home. Jack!" Nothing moved except the wind chimes.

Elizabeth stepped back and walked around her yard. She entered the back yard and scanned the area for her cat. She checked outside the doors and windows for any sign of a break-in. Everything looked in order, except for the broken camera on the front porch. She walked up to her back deck, studying the area. She checked her phone for any other surveillance camera alerts. She watched the brief recorded video of herself, moments ago, park her car and approach the porch.

Then why didn't that camera pick up an image of the intruder before he took down the other camera, the one aimed solely at the front porch and front door? Someone must have known there were two cameras. Who?

Elizabeth called Bradford and told him what happened. She added, "The camera pointed toward the driveway didn't detect motion. And it's working fine because it just recorded me arriving. How did the trespasser know there were two cameras mounted in front? And he removed only one."

"The camera aimed at the drive is visible, barely, from the street. Maybe he did a drive-by, saw it and decide to approach your house from the left or right. Nothing but woods either way."

Elizabeth was silent for a few seconds. "I'm worried about Jack. I've become very attached to him, and he certainly attached himself to me. On camera I saw him snarl, something I've never seen him do. So he had to be very frightened." Elizabeth unlocked her back door, disarmed the alarm, and walked through the house, phone in one ear, the gun in her right hand.

"There's no sign of entry into my home." She told him about her conversation with Otto Emerson and Father MacGrath. "The perp might as well have the word retribution, from Belmont's pamphlet, tattooed on his arm. I must have cut deep to the bone in those interviews. He's stalking me. Baiting me, Mike, and he's doing it on the one hundredth anniversary of the hangings from the Shubuta Bridge. I think the only reason he hasn't tried to kill me yet is that he wants to make me his seventh victim. In the meantime, it's a cat-and-mouse game of contrived attack, at least toward me while he's summarily killing others he deems unworthy."

"Why would the perp use the word *'he'* when he texted you, as if he was talking in third-person and someone else delivered the earring to Cindy's grave."

"Some psychopaths speak about themselves or their criminal deeds in third-person. For them, it's as if they're outside their own body, watching things unfold, often supplying the narrative in third-person. Maybe this was the case with his text."

Elizabeth walked into her family room, looked at the framed photo of Molly. Bradford said, "I got a court order to pull every pair of boots and shoes from Alex Davison, Gerald Simpson and Larry Tucker. I know these three don't fit your profile, but we simply do not have another suspect. What we do have are boot prints from Belmont's grave matching the print from the grave of Edward Thompson in the Shubuta Cemetery, and we have a match from wooden crosses to boards on the bridge."

"Otto Emerson believes that the perp was in the crowd at the rally—one of the white supremacists. The hate group is the killer's apparent family—the cause is his mission carried over from Zachariah Belmont. Father MacGrath calls it systemic evil—the kind that is shared by a like-minded group, often covert, like the Klan." She thought of one of the passages she'd read: *Sip from the cup of wormwood, raised in a toast to the heavens in one hundred years by the eighth angel on the eighth day.* "Mike, can you hold a second? I want to look up something?"

"Sure."

She sat at the table and typed on her computer keyboard, her eyes scanning the page. "In Revelation it mentions a large star called Wormwood. Also, it's said to denote a mighty prince...or the feeling of supernatural power in the air. And it will be used as an instrument in its fall to earth. Down here on earth, wormwood has been used for centuries as medicine or as a hallucinogenic. Its properties have an effect on the human brain similar to THC in marijuana, but stronger. It's best known use is in the making of absinthe, the liquor distilled from wormwood."

"Maybe the perp is mainlining the junk into his arteries."

"This person doesn't need a chemical for motivation. He gets it from his quest. I think he'll kill at least four more people to total seven and then, if he really fantasizes he's the eighth angel, he may do something horrific on a much larger scale. Maybe similar to the massacre in Las Vegas or the bombing of the federal building in Oklahoma City."

"I remember studying the bombing, in-depth, when I went through the police academy. Almost 200 people killed. Scores more injured. Limbs lost. Eyesight gone. Timothy McVeigh is the only homegrown terrorist to be put to death because of what he did. He was said to have been inspired by the white supremacist, William Pierce, who wrote a novel called the *Turner Diaries*. Some of the pages from the book were found in McVeigh's car. The story dealt with a violent revolution in the nation, followed by a world war. You think our perp is planning something on the scale of what McVeigh did?"

"Maybe even more devastating since he seems to be using Revelation as his guide. Back in McVeigh's day, there was no Internet. No way to watch a video online to see how to make a bomb. Today, it's a few mouse clicks away. Remember that line inscribed on Edward Thompson's headstone? It read, *The Lord will go out and fight against those nations as he fights on the day of battle.* This is all coming together in a frightening way, it's almost like a century-old covert splinter group is rising up from Belmont's grave. Or at least one of his followers is, and I'm hoping it's only one."

"You should have seen the rally and counter protestors downtown. Their anger is seething, palpable. Will we ever learn to simply live and let live? When you're a cop, you know the answer every day you put on the badge and go to work."

Elizabeth heard the beep from an incoming call. She looked at her screen. The ID read: Nellie Culpepper. "Mike, Nellie is calling. She rarely uses the phone. I've received only a few calls in my life from her, and I've known her since I was a baby. I mentioned that we have dinner together every Wednesday. That's tonight. I should call her back—make sure she's okay."

"I hope Jack shows up. Call me, Elizabeth. Just…stay in touch, okay?"

"Okay." Elizabeth returned the call to Nellie Culpepper. It took her nine rings to answer. "Hello…." Her voice sounded drained, as if she needed to clear her throat.

"Hi, Nellie, it's me. I was on the line when you called. You're not cancelling our dinner date are you?"

The old woman stood by the small table on her porch, her swollen arthritic fingers holding the phone Elizabeth had bought for her birthday two years ago. "No, I'm not fixin' to cancel. Wednesdays with you, Liz'beth, is almost my favorite day of the week. Sunday's with the Lord's my favorite. But I do love seein' you. That's why I'm callin,' it's on account of the nice gift you brung me."

Elizabeth paused. She stood from her kitchen table, glanced out in her back yard. "Nellie, I didn't get you a gift. What are you referring to?"

Nellie reached her left hand down, extending her brown fingers, the dull gold on her wedding band catching late afternoon light. She touched the rim of the bowl with her fingers. "I thought it was you, child, who brung me a beautiful wooden bowl. In the very center, is a candle. And when I got home a little while ago, I could smell somethin' lovely. Smelled like honeysuckles in June. But when I stepped up on my porch, opened the screen door and seen it sitting on my table…it's not flowers, but it is a lovely bowl and inside is a burning candle. It's one of 'em scented candles that smells once you light it. I'm lookin' at it now. The candle has the smell of sweet honeysuckles, like I remembered when I picked blackberries on the side of the road in the hot summers."

"Nellie…listen to me. Get off your porch!"

"Why, Liz'beth? You sound upset."

"Step away from that bowl! Leave your front porch! Leave your house! Now!"

"Why, child?"

"Just do it! Don't hang up! Stay on the line. I'm coming to your house right now. I have to hear your voice."

There was a pause, the sound of the phone changing hands. "Liz'beth, my bat'tree is gettin' low. For heaven's sake, I cain't hardly 'member to charge it up no mo'e. Can you hear me child?"

SIXTY-SIX

Elizabeth wanted to call Detective Bradford, but she didn't want to lose Nellie on the phone line. She picked up her gun, locked the front door, stepped over the broken camera and ran to her car. She started the engine. "Nellie, don't touch that bowl. Are you off your porch and out of your house?"

"I'm standin' on the brick steps leadin' up to my porch. Liz'beth, I'm an old woman. I need to sit my body down. Tell me why you sound so scared, baby?"

"Can you go to a neighbor's house until I can get there?"

Nellie stood on the worn brick steps, looked around her small yard like it was the first time she'd see it in years. Her thoughts going back to the time she and her husband had stood side-by-side and planted the magnolia trees on both sides of her home. She tried to remember her husband's face.

"Nellie, where are you?"

"I'm in my yard. The magnolia blossoms smell like heaven on earth. Liz'beth, you are what folks used to call a steel magnolia. A woman who's beautiful on the outside and tough as steel on the inside. Now, that don't mean you got a heart hard as steel. It means you can be a lady and a woman to reckon with 'cause you got gumption. Yes you do. Gumption and grit."

"Nellie, I want you to walk to your closest neighbor's house, okay?"

"Are we havin' chicken 'n dumplins tonight?"

"Yes, Nellie. Just go to your neighbor's house." Elizabeth heard odd sounds, as if Nellie's phone had fallen or had been tossed into a bag and shaken. "Nellie, can you hear me?"

Nothing. Dead silence.

"Nellie! Can you hear me? Nellie!" She looked at the phone screen and could see Nellie was gone. Elizabeth drove fast, slowing for stop signs and traffic lights. She called Bradford. "Mike, the perp left a bowl at my dear friend's house. She's Nellie Culpepper, the elderly black woman I told you about that helped raise my brother and me. She found the bowl on her front porch. A candle was burning in the center of the bowl. In Revelation it says the fourth angel pours out fire on the earth. I'm heading to her house. Can you meet me there?"

"I'm on my way."

"It's a small house, wood and cinderblock, with a screened front porch. Rows of magnolias planted on both sides of the property at Sandy Run Road. I don't remember the address but—"

"Elizabeth! Slow down…I'm en route. Is she home?"

"I was talking with her minutes ago before her phone died. She was in her yard. Hurry, Mike, she's seventy-nine with the onset of dementia. I told Nellie to walk next door to her neighbor's house. I'll be there in five minutes." She disconnected and held the wheel with both hands, the speed-ometer pushing one hundred.

— —

Elizabeth arrived first. She pulled into the driveway and parked under the thick limbs of an oak. The house and yard were cast in dark shadows, the last rays of sunlight filtered though the magnolias. She lifted her pistol and got out of the car. There was no sign of Nellie in the front or side yard. Elizabeth stared at the screened front porch. She held her pistol with both hands and walked down the right side of the house into the back yard.

Nellie had two hard plastic chairs on the small concrete back porch. A large green fern in a hanging basket was attached to an eave. A bird feeder hung from a low limb on a red maple tree, a blue jay pecking at seeds in the feeder.

Elizabeth wanted to call out—to shout Nellie's name. To hear her voice. *Be at your neighbor's house, Nellie.* She could hear sirens in the distance, the bark of a dog somewhere on the next block. She walked around the perimeter of the house, back to the front yard. She held her gun in her right hand, used her left to open the screened door to the porch. There was the slight squeak of a rusty hinge.

The smell.

It was artificial. Manmade. The fragrance of summer—honeysuckles—embalmed in a scented candle. It stuck in Elizabeth's nostrils. She stepped inside, stared at the bowl on the table, the single flame rose in its slow, steady burn at the bottom of the bowl. *He was here. The bastard stepped into the inner sanctum of family…of Nellie's small house.*

She stood by the front door as Detective Bradford arrived. He parked next to Elizabeth's car. Three patrol cars, blue and white lights flashing, came up behind him and parked. Bradford, pistol in one hand, huddled with the four officers. All of the men had pistols drawn. Bradford looked toward the house and shouted, "Elizabeth!"

"On the porch."

He signaled for two of the officers to go into the back yard. The other two fanned out in the side yard. Two followed him onto the porch. They looked at the bowl and candle. Bradford nodded at Elizabeth, stepped up to her and lowered his voice. "Where's Nellie?"

"I hope she's at her neighbor's house."

"Have you been inside?"

"No."

He tried the door handle. It was unlocked. He turned to the two officers. "Let's check it out."

The men nodded and followed Bradford inside, guns drawn, sweeping through the shadows of the dimly lit home. Elizabeth followed, held her gun at her side.

"Clear!" shouted one officer.

"Clear!" came the second.

Elizabeth stood in the small living room as they searched the house. She looked at the mantle above the fireplace; the tick of an antique clock filled the room with a painful rhythm of loss—an elderly woman missing. Time to find her alive, measured in heartbeats. Elizabeth could feel that the perp was no longer in the house. He was physically gone, but yet lurking on the fringes of her thoughts, taunting, daring to invade her life again. She turned, stood in the doorway, watching the candle flicker in the bowl.

She could hear Bradford and the officers talking, their voices muted, sounding far away. She stepped onto the porch, looked at the small wooden table with a blue tablecloth. It was a special little spot in the world where she and Nellie would have had dinner later tonight. She wanted to throw water into the bowl—to drown the fire, the smell—to take an ax and splinter the bowl into hundreds of pieces and make a bonfire from all of the wooden bowls and crosses they'd found. Her thoughts raced. *How did the perp know about Nellie? Was I followed?*

"Elizabeth," Bradford said, voice loud, the two officers standing near him.

She turned toward them.

Bradford nodded. "I had to raise my voice. You were staring at the bowl…my men are going to knock on the neighbor's doors. We'll find Nellie." The officers left, meeting with the others in the yard, the men nodding and forming three search parties, the snap of police radios like military orders at the beginning of battle.

As they fanned out and began their hunt, Elizabeth moistened her thumb and forefinger with her tongue and smothered the candle flame.

SIXTY-SEVEN

The wait was excruciating. Elizabeth wanted to run to all the homes in the block, pound on doors with bleeding fists until she saw Nellie's smiling face safe in a neighbor's warm home. She and Bradford waited on the porch. He walked back to his car, picked up a paper evidence bag, and used a glove to lift the bowl from the table and place it in the bottom of the bag. He turned toward Elizabeth. "We're getting quite a collection. None have had any prints. Maybe there's something on the side of the candle. Maybe he finally made a mistake."

"He doesn't make mistakes, Mike. He kills people with impunity because he believes he has a license to do so. He thinks he has permission, no...a mandate...from Zachariah Belmont to carry out a repulsive, aberrant goal that's anything but biblical. It's sacrilegious, blasphemous, and it violates the absolute core and sacred heart of do unto others as you would have them do unto you."

"Psychopaths, as you've said, have no conscience. Taking a life to them is like trimming a rose bush."

"Nellie is ninety pounds. She's lived through generations of racial strife and hatred in Mississippi. But yet, I never saw her bitter. Never heard her utter a negative word about anyone—white or black. I never heard her complain about how life can be unfair or hard. Entitlement isn't in her vocabulary only because she doesn't believe in it. She worked the fields. Worked as domestic help. One time she picked cotton for a week to buy a wind-up clock that's above her fireplace. She and her husband, Rudyard, never had

252

children of their own. Yet they treated my brother and me as if they'd given birth to us."

"We'll find her, Elizabeth."

"If he killed Nellie, he'll transport her body elsewhere for his macabre ritual because that's what he does. He kills, transports, and puts his victim on display. I swear to God…if she's dead, I will…." She stopped, leveled her bloodshot eyes over to Bradford. "When I called you and told you to meet me here, you said I'm on my way. You didn't ask for directions. I never told you Nellie's address—"

"Elizabeth, what's going on here? I said I'm on my way and was about to ask you for the address when you mentioned the street name, Sandy Run, and described the house. That's all we needed, okay? And I'm a detective for Pete's sake—we can pull names and addresses easily from our database."

"You are the only person who knows I have two cameras on my front porch. One pointed at the door and the other aimed at the street. Whoever was on my porch, whoever Jack saw, somehow knew the other camera was there."

Bradford shook his head. "Do you really think I came to your house and frightened Jack? You can see the camera from the street. And do you think I put that damn bowl on Nellie's table? Elizabeth, please. You're exhausted. The whites of your eyes are almost bleeding. When's the last time you got more than a couple hours of sleep. If you're not up late grading papers for your classes, you're traipsing around the state, talking to people."

"I'm looking for answers. I'm looking for a way to keep at least four more people from dying…maybe a hell of a lot more."

"We're doing everything we can. Following every lead. Each day we chase down tips—most go nowhere. We took Gerald Simpson off the street for a while. Maybe we were wrong, but everything pointed to him at the time. Ed Milton and I are knocking on doors. We don't stop, we won't stop until this perp is caught." He looked at the paper bag in his hand, the acrid scent of the candle smoke seemed trapped in the porch. "Elizabeth, it's very important to me that you believe what I'm telling you. I'm just a guy trying hard to do his job in an understaffed, under budgeted department where the faucet of crime is always pouring."

She looked over at him, her eyes burning from fatigue and anxiety. Out of the corner of her eye she saw movement. Two officers came from a small pathway through the trees among the houses. Nellie was between them, walking slowly. Each officer supported her by the arm, approaching her house.

Elizabeth flew from the porch and ran across the front yard, stopping in front of Nellie. She bit her lower lip. "I was so worried about you." She hugged Nellie, the old woman gently caressing Elizabeth's back with her small hands.

"I was fine, Liz'beth. When I walked down the path to my neighbor, Joe Hutchins'—he'd just got back from the sto'e. He wanted to know if I'd be stayin' for supper. I tol' him no thank you 'cause I got a Wednesday night dinner with my sweet Liz'beth." Next thing I know'd was these po'leece men come there to bring me back home." She smiled at the officers. They nodded and returned her smile.

Elizabeth held Nellie's hand and walked her the rest of the way to her front porch. "Nellie, this is Detective Mike Bradford. He's my friend."

Nellie smiled, dipped her head. "Pleased to meet you, suh."

"It's an honor to meet you, too, Mrs. Culpepper. Can you tell me what you saw before you spoke with Elizabeth on the phone."

"I'd just come from Doctor Baker's office. The bus lets me off right at the end of my driveway. Mr. Haney, the driver, don't have to do that on account that it isn't a city bus stop. But he does. Anyway, I come up my driveway. When I opened the porch do'r, I saw the bowl with the candle inside." She looked at Elizabeth. "I thought Liz'beth brung it 'cause we was gonna have dinner."

Elizabeth smiled. "We're still going to have dinner. But now it'll be at a restaurant. I know you love the food at Captain's Table."

Bradford asked, "Did you see any strange cars or trucks parked near your place? Anyone walking you can't identify?"

"No suh, cain't say I did."

"Okay, thank you Mrs. Culpepper."

Elizabeth asked, "Where's your phone, Nellie?"

The old woman dug deep in a large pocket on her cotton sundress and lifted out her phone. Elizabeth reached for it. She looked at the screen. "Nellie, the battery has died. We can recharge it in my car. Does your brother, James, still live on the north side of town?"

"Yes. He stays there with his wife Bessie. Their chillens are grown and left outta Mississippi."

"Maybe you can spend a couple of nights with James. It's not safe here."

Nellie looked up at Elizabeth. There was no further explanation necessary. The old woman blinked hard, like she was clearing something from her eyes. "When my bat'tre is back, I can call him." She glanced at the empty table on her porch, touched a large silver crucifix cross on her neck, the cross hanging from a silver chain. She looked at Bradford, a bead of sunset through the magnolias on her face, her left eye partially closed. "Liz'beth tol' me y'all are huntin' for the fella who was takin' wood off the hangin' bridge and makin' crosses."

"Yes ma'am. We've been searching. So far we found two teenagers who used some of the wood to make a fort. That's about all. Do you know anything you can share?"

"My family had kinfolk kilt on that bridge. The two girls hung that day in 1918 were my grandma's cousins. In my brother's church, an old man, name was Samuel Estes, was fishing in the river below the bridge when he seen a fella take wood off the bridge. Samuel died of a heart attack recently. Funeral was 'bout a week ago. I knew Samuel, too."

"Was he married?" asked Bradford.

She nodded. "His wife died a long time ago. He never remarried. They didn't have chillen."

Bradford pulled out his small pad of paper and a pen. "Did Mr. Estes ever say who the person was that he saw taking the lumber?"

"Don't think so. It's probably on account he didn't really know the man's name. Knew more of his reputation."

"What was that, Mrs. Culpepper?"

She tilted her head and looked up at Bradford. "One thing you won't see in a church with black folks is a snake. Samuel said the man was lifting boards and out crawled a big rat'ler. Samuel said the man caught the snake with his bare hands. Put it in a croaker sack and tho'd it in his truck. Samuel said he walked a lil' ways up the river bank and asked the man what he gonna do with that rat'ler." She paused, as if she wasn't sure how to say what she'd heard. "The man laughed and hollered back that he was gonna carry the snake to church."

"What kind of truck was it?" Bradford asked.

"Don't know." She shook her head, looked down at her hands, fingers bowed from arthritis. "Samuel said the man had a sign on the side on his truck. It was sorta like a drawing of a lumberjack wit' an ax."

Just as Bradford was about to ask something, a TV news truck from Channel Four pulled into Nellie's driveway. A second truck from a Fox News station followed the Channel Four crew onto the property. Within seconds, the reporters and camera operators were out, cameras rolling. They shot video of the police cars, the officers filling out reports, and aimed their lens toward the house.

Reporter Bill Keelson and his cameraman came closer, Keelson holding the microphone in one hand like a man ready for a knife fight.

SIXTY-EIGHT

A third TV news truck entered the property. Elizabeth turned to Bradford. "We need to get Nellie out of here. I don't want her face splashed all over the news. It's bad enough that the perp knows where she lives."

Nellie held onto the back of a wooden chair to steady her balance. She watched the reporters and camera operators emerge onto her property as if they were stealth invaders. She looked at Elizabeth. "Why 'em news folks be comin' here, Liz'beth?"

"They monitor the police radios, Nellie. It's not a news story now because you weren't lost and wandering around the city. You're home. Detective Bradford will tell them that and they'll go away." She looked at Bradford and didn't blink.

He nodded, blew out a breath, opened the screen door and walked outside to greet the media. A half-dozen reporters and photographers formed a near circle around him, microphones extended. Reporter Bill Keelson asked the first question. "Some of the radio traffic indicated that another wooden bowl was found on the property, Detective Bradford. Is there a dead body here, too?"

"No. We did find a wooden bowl. It will be examined by forensics techs to see if it was made from the same wood as the other bowls."

"Where did you find the bowl?" asked another reporter.

"In the residence behind me. On the porch."

A tall reporter asked, "Do you think this is where the bowls are being made?"

"Absolutely not. It's the home of an elderly lady."

Bill Keelson looked at the cars. "I recognize that car. Professor Monroe owns it. Is she here?"

Bradford glanced back at the house. "Yes. The elderly woman is a close family friend."

"So that's the connection, right? Two of Professor Monroe's students are dead and now a bowl is delivered at the home of an elderly friend. Is this killer sending a fatal message to Professor Monroe, Detective Bradford?"

"I didn't say that it was delivered. There has been no foul play here today. No one was hurt. Obviously someone trespassed on private property, sort of like you folks are doing with all your trucks on the lady's grass. The investigation here today is over. I told you all everything I know. We should have the forensics results in a couple of hours. I'm happy to take more questions in the sheriff's office at that time. Now, everyone, the homeowner would like for y'all to leave. She's going to have her dinner in quiet. Thank you."

— —

Two hours later, after dinner at a restaurant, Elizabeth drove Nellie nine miles away through the northwest section of Hattiesburg to her brother's modest gray house, vinyl siding, rose bushes around the house. A leafy dogwood tree grew in the front yard. A battered and rusted pickup truck sat in the driveway. Dried mud on the tire walls.

Elizabeth parked and walked around her car to open the door for Nellie. She helped her out, gently supporting her forearm. Nellie stood and smiled. "When I was your age, I could run around this car a dozen times and still have my wits 'bout me. Now, oh my...the upholstery is wearin' thin."

"Let me get your bag." Elizabeth opened the back door and removed a suitcase. "I'll carry it up for you."

Nellie nodded and shuffled slowly up the sidewalk to the front door. Elizabeth pushed the doorbell, the sound of a TV coming from inside. The door opened and a rail thin black man, gray whiskers, bifocals, white T-shirt and jeans grinned. James Hatfield stepped outside and hugged his sister. "Lemme take your suitcase."

"James, you remember Liz'beth Monroe. I worked for her mama and daddy 'til they died."

James lowered his chin, looked over his bifocals—jigsaw pieces of the past and present coming together in an opaque picture. His wet mouth pursed, a slight whistling sound coming from his lips. "Well, I'll be…it's been a long while, Elizabeth. Think the last time I saw you in person was right after your mama's funeral. I picked Nellie up from your home. And now, all these years later, I see you on the TV news. Heard one of the reporters speak about your daughter. I'm so sorry. Hope you find the person responsible."

Elizabeth nodded. "Thank you."

"It's horrible, the killin' that's goin' on. Now, my little sister ain't safe neither."

Nellie said, "I'll be just fine. It's Liz'beth that I'm scared for. She's by herself and darkness seems to be fallin' all around her shoulders."

Elizabeth smiled, "Wherever darkness goes, it's met by light. I'll be okay, Nellie. Don't worry." She kissed the old woman on the cheek and stepped back as her brother picked up the suitcase. "James, Nellie told me about Samuel Estes—what he saw recently while fishing in the river near the Shubuta Bridge. The man who was taking boards off the bridge…does anyone know his name?"

James set the suitcase down on the steps, glanced around the neighborhood. "Step inside the house. I'll tell you what I heard."

SIXTY-NINE

The house was decorated in warm earth tones. Overstuffed couch. A brown leather recliner chair. Pictures of family on a far wall, the smell of fried pork chops coming from the kitchen. Elizabeth could hear someone washing dishes, a TV sitcom on in the kitchen area.

James said, "Have a seat. Would you like something to drink?"

Elizabeth smiled. "No thanks."

Nellie sat on the couch. Elizabeth took a seat next to her, James settled in the recliner. He said, "Samuel Estes wasn't sure who the man was 'cause the sun was comin' up over the river and bridge. So the fella was in silhouette. Couldn't get a good look at his face. They spoke briefly, but from a little distance. Samuel was just amazed that a grown man would or even could catch a rattlesnake with his bare hands. Said the man squatted down on the bridge, waved his left hand to get the snake's attention, and used his right hand to snatch the snake up behind the head. Said the man stood and the rattlesnake, e'ver bit of six feet, wrapped around the man's arm and looped his thick body around the fella's neck—the rattle sounded like a mess of angry bees. Then he put the snake in a burlap sack, tied it, and set it in the back of his truck."

Nellie shook her head. "James, you remember when Papa used to say don't mess with nature 'cause it's always hungry."

James grinned. "Specially in the bayou. He had a sayin' for most everything. He used to say weeds don't grow in rows like flowers, but they know how to endure. Papa knew Samuel Estes, too. Daddy hep'ed him butcher hogs and salt hams and fatback for winter." He crossed his feet in the chair. "Samuel said the man had a sign, like a decal hangin' on the side of his white pickup truck."

Nellie said, "I tol' her and the detective 'bout that?"

"Samuel said it was like a cartoon. The picture was of a big man favorin' Paul Bunyan, maybe, with an ax in his hand standin' next to a cut down tree."

A small black woman in a sweatshirt and cotton pants stepped from the kitchen, an apron around her tiny waist. James said, "Elizabeth, this is my wife, Ava."

Ava entered the living room. "Pleased to meet you, Elizabeth. Hi, Nellie."

Elizabeth said, "It's nice meeting you. Something smells delicious."

She smiled. "We just finished dinner. Pork chops, yams and some greens, too. You hungry? I can fix you a plate."

"No thank you. Nellie and I just ate."

Nellie said, "I used to work for Liz'beth's mama." She patted Elizabeth's arm. "This child is the closest I ever had to a daughter."

Ava nodded. "I remember you talkin' about her. It's good to finally meet you. Would you like some coffee?"

"No thanks. I need to be going." She kissed Nellie's check. "Keep your phone charged. I'll call you, okay?"

"Okay." She touched Elizabeth on the knee. "You need to get your rest, you're lookin' wore out, Liz'beth."

As Elizabeth drove away from the property, she glanced in her rear-view mirror, the front porch light on at James' house. Nellie with family. Elizabeth headed south, going back to her house. She lifted her gun out from the glove box and set it in the console between the seats.

She drove for a moment, looked at the lights from the homes, the flicker of color from windows as people watched television. She looked in the rearview mirror again. There didn't appear to be a car following her.

After a mile, she pulled into a convenience store parking lot, edged up to the gas pumps. She turned off her car and sat there for a moment, rubbing her eyes with her fists. Two Hispanic men came out of the store with a case of beer. Elizabeth filled her tank with gas, thinking about the day's events.

A pickup truck entered the lot and pulled up to the pump opposite her. She heard the radio. Could smell a whiff of cigar smoke. The radio host was talking about traditional American values and taking calls from the audience. "I agree with you," said one caller. "I'm not Irish-American. I'm just an American. Anytime you got a hyphen in a ethnic name, something identifying somebody from a different place other than America, I say that's a big damn issue." The sound from the radio faded down, the noise of the cars on the highway was what Elizabeth could now hear.

She took the receipt from the pump and got back in her car. She checked her phone—looked at live streaming images from her home and studied each camera angle. No sign of Jack. She felt a lump in her throat, stomach burning, fatigue like fog behind her eyes. "Jack…where are you? Please come home…you've grown on me."

Bam – bam – bam.

There was a loud pounding on her driver's side window. Instinctively, Elizabeth pointed her gun at the window. An older man in a black T-Shirt, dirty jeans, unkempt long reddish beard, raised both hands and stepped back. "What the fuck! You crazy, lady, or what?"

Elizabeth slid her window down about halfway, the pistol still in her right hand. "What do you want?"

"Not a damn thing. I was gonna ask you if you had a dollar for a bite. But I don't want to get my ass shot off doin' it."

Elizabeth looked at him through drained eyes. The image of the bearded man she'd seen in the tree trunks abruptly superimposed over the stranger's face. She blinked hard—the image not going away. She raised the gun, removed her seatbelt. Elizabeth opened her car door, started to get out. She cut her eyes up to a security camera on a metal pole, the camera pointed toward the gas pumps.

She set the gun down on the seat, reached in her console for money, finding a five-dollar bill. She opened the car door. The man shook his head, stepping backwards. Elizabeth shouted, "Wait! Here's some money. Take it, please. Just go eat." She walked toward him, holding out the money. The man raised both hands, nails long and impacted with black dirt. He looked around the convenience store lot, turned and ran toward the road.

Elizabeth felt a sense of anguish that she'd pulled her gun on the homeless man. She stood there in the lot, the smell of gasoline in the cool evening air, the sound of a semi-truck entering the highway. A chill ran through her body, almost as if someone was watching her.

She turned. Her car was at least thirty feet away—her gun on the seat. The pickup truck door slammed, the diesel rumbled and the truck eased away from the gas pump. Elizabeth could see the lights from the convenience store reflecting in the dark windshield on the driver's side.

The truck pulled out of the lot as Elizabeth got back in her car. She strapped her seatbelt over her lap, fastened it. She looked out her window, the pickup now on the street, moving.

Under the dull yellow glow of a streetlight, she saw something on the side panel of the truck as it drove away. It was the exaggerated image of a lumberjack, a caricature holding an ax over a felled tree. Her pulse quickened. Elizabeth rubbed her eyes. *"Hallucinating…."* she mumbled. "Keys… where'd I put them?" She thought they were on the seat next to her gun. She moved her hands quickly around the seat and console in the dim light. Nothing.

She looked back up, the pickup truck's taillights were a small glow in the night, the driver heading for the Interstate highway. She found her keys on the floorboard. Her mind raced—thoughts fast like a time-lapse film. She called Bradford. "Mike, I'm in a gas station at Richburg and Highway 98. I just saw the pickup truck—on the side panel was a sign depicting the caricature of a lumberjack holding an ax."

"What make of truck?"

"What?"

"Ford? Chevy?"

"I don't know! That's a guy thing! It's white, okay? The driver's going north on Highway 98."

"I'll send deputies and alert the highway patrol. Elizabeth, do not—I repeat, do not chase that truck."

Elizabeth disconnected and started her car. She squealed tires out of the lot, driving fast toward Highway 98 and the northbound entrance.

SEVENTY

Elizabeth glanced down at the speedometer. The needle was crossing the 100 mph mark, her car beginning to vibrate in the wind. She accelerated, both hands on the wheel. She passed dozens of cars and semi-trucks, eyes scanning beyond her headlights and the oncoming traffic across the median center. She passed two exits. *Did he turn off the road?* She looked at exit ramps. Overpass bridges, the moon nearly full in the east.

She accelerated. The car shook harder. Engine whining. She looked in her rearview mirror, Nellie's voice reverberating in her thoughts. *Samuel said the man had a sign painted on his truck. It was like a drawing of a lumberjack wit' an ax.*

Blue lights flashed.

"Shit!" she said, eyes in the rearview mirror. The patrol car was behind her, coming up fast. She slowed down, moving into the right-hand lane and pulling off the road. She stopped, opened the glove box and set her pistol inside. She removed her registration. The patrol car stopped close behind her, blue and white lights pulsating against a bridge overpass.

Elizabeth hit the redial button on her phone and touched the speakerphone key. The call went directly to Detective Bradford's voice mail. She set the phone on the dashboard, opened her purse and removed her driver's license. And then she lowered the window and put both hands on the steering wheel.

A Hattiesburg city police officer approached. One hand was on the grip of his gun, the other held a long, black flashlight. He looked around the tires, stared at the reflection of her face in the side-view mirror, stepped up to her door.

He was in his early twenties. Close-cropped military haircut. Jowls pink and slick from a fresh shave. He moved the flashlight beam around the interior of her car. His face pinched, suspicious and edgy.

He cleared his throat. "Slowly, let me see your license and registration."

She handed it to him.

"You know how fast you were goin' out here?"

"No officer." She looked at his nametag. *R. Lewis*

"Just a tad more than a hundred and seventeen miles per hour. Where you headin' in such a hurry?"

"Officer Lewis, I was trying to find a man who I believed killed at least three people. He's getting away as we're talking. Did you get an alert to be on the lookout for a white truck with a figure of a lumberjack on one or both sides? The Forrest County Sheriff's Office issued—"

"I'm asking the questions tonight, all right?" He looked at her picture on the license and then studied her face. She knew he recognized her. "I know you, or I know of you. Your picture has been all over the news lately. They're calling you the vigilante professor. You need to step out of the car, ma'am."

Elizabeth complied. She got out and stood, facing him. "Ma'am, have you been drinking tonight? Using drugs? You don't look so good."

"No to both of your questions. I don't look so well because three people have died in the last month by the hands of a serial killer. I am assisting the Forrest County Sheriff's office and prosecution to catch a killer—the same murderer that's on this highway tonight. And the longer that you detain me here, the more miles he puts between us."

He stared at her like she was an alien. "Let's move to a safer area. I need to give you a sobriety test."

"Officer! Please call Detective Mike Bradford with the sheriff's office. I have his number."

"You don't look so good, ma'am. Are you using opioids?"

"No!"

The police radio spluttered in his open car and a dispatcher said, "Forest County SD issued a BOLO for a late model, white pickup truck. Make and model unknown. There is a decal or sign on the side panels with an image of a lumberjack."

She looked at the officer. "Please, may I leave now? You know what I'm telling you is the truth." Elizabeth looked at the watch on her left wrist.

"Not 'til I write you a ticket for going a hundred 'n seventeen in a sixty." His phone buzzed. He looked at the screen. "You wait here. I'll be right back." He stepped over to his car and took the call.

Elizabeth could see him nodding. She heard him say, "I understand. But speeding was speeding." He looked at the northbound traffic, back at her, and then at the camera on his dash. The interior light from his car was pastel in the dark and the near constant streak of headlights behind him. He nodded and disconnected, walked back to Elizabeth.

"Miss Monroe, far as I'm concerned, there's no excuse for your speeding. I understand the circumstances, but I've investigated too many fatal pileups out here to justify your heavy foot on the gas. You get a warning tonight." He dipped his head for a second, shutting off his flashlight.

"Thank you, Officer Lewis."

"This fella will get himself caught. No use in killing yourself or others on the road to chase some mean loser. He'll get what he sows. Good night and be careful, Miss Monroe."

He walked back to his car and got inside. The rotating blue and white lights throbbed against Elizabeth's face, a sharp ache growing behind her left eye. She turned and got in her car, started the motor and pulled onto the highway.

After she'd gone a mile, her phone buzzed. She looked at the screen: Bradford. She answered and said, "Thank you."

"I heard some of that, at least until he escorted you away to do a sobriety test. I had to call the shift commander, who was in the radio room. He made the call to the officer. I should have let him write you the ticket. I warned you not to chase the suspect because—"

"Mike, please. Now is not the damn time or place. Some madman in a white pickup truck is, or was, traveling northbound on Highway 98. All I did was try to ensure he didn't circle back, tried to keep my eye on southbound traffic, too, and some of the exits until I was pulled over."

Bradford sighed into the phone. "That officer might have accidentally saved your life, either from a horrific crash or at the hands of a psychopath with you in his sights."

"And I might have caught up with the truck and had a license plate number for you. What do you have?"

"Nothing yet. We have seven cars converging on Highway 98 from points north of the original entry location. The highway patrol has many units on the road at exits, gas stations, rest stops. Anywhere we can look on and off the highway. We'll find him."

"Remember the truck in the lot after we went back to the cemetery where Cindy is buried?"

"Yes."

"It was white."

"I didn't notice a sign on the side."

"We were probably too far away, and the truck wasn't facing us in a profile position."

"Now that you mention it, that's right."

Elizabeth drove in silence, squinting at lights and exit signs.

Bradford asked, "I'm assuming Nellie Culpepper is with her family."

"Yes. She's…in a safer place…."

"Go home, Elizabeth. I don't know if you've noticed it, but I've had extra patrols ride by your house every night."

"Thank you."

"You sound shattered. I'll call you if we find this guy?"

"If you find him…and if you find Jack dead and stiff in the back of that pickup…just tell me." She disconnected and took the next exit off the highway.

She drove down a back road toward her house. She looked at the phone screen at the live camera feeds. No indication of motion at her home. Nothing had been recorded.

And no sign of Jack.

She glanced up in the night sky, a cloud covering the moon, and Elizabeth thought about what Nellie had said earlier, *"It's Liz'beth that I'm scared for. She's by herself and darkness seems to be fallin' all around her shoulders."*

— • —

Elizabeth sat on her couch in the dark. All her blinds closed. She set her pistol on the coffee table and opened her computer, looked at the live feed for all of her cameras, the glow of the screen in her bloodshot eyes. The only movement was moths flying in and out of the floodlights.

Her head pounded, the pain in the center of her forehead. She thought about her pineal gland, wondered if it had simply shutdown from over-use. She wanted to smile, but even that felt like an effort at 3:29 a.m. She used the flashlight on her phone to reread the pamphlet, *Retribution*, looking for clues—looking for something that she may have missed. On the back of the three pages, toward the bottom of the page, Elizabeth read words that Zachariah Belmont had written: *'You, my brothers, will always be welcome at Polemo. We may have lost the Civil War, but we did not lose the battle that is Polemo.'*

Elizabeth keyed in the word, Polemo, looked for a definition. She whispered, "Polemo…Greek for a battle that is a sustained cause over time. The Greek deity Polemos, both the king and the father of all with the capacity to bring all into existence and to annihilate as well." Elizabeth looked up from her computer screen, her thoughts racing.

There was a sound.

A *thud* on her backyard deck.

She lifted her gun from the table and walked quietly to her back door, moved the drapes slightly, and looked outside. She saw another pinecone on the sundeck, looked at the limbs of a sycamore tree near her deck. The leaves weren't moving. No wind. She stared at the lone pinecone. *Did it fall or did someone throw it on the deck?* She stepped back, picked up her computer and looked at the camera live feeds. Moths orbited the floodlights. On the kitchen table was the flyer with Jack's picture. She picked it up and looked into the cat's big eyes. "I miss you, Jack. So much. Will I ever see you again?"

SEVENTY-ONE

T he next day Elizabeth stood in front of her class, not sure what she was going to tell them. She wore no makeup. No lipstick. Her hair pinned up. She looked into their worried faces. "I can teach you forensic psychology. I can teach you how to profile criminals based on evidence and patterns of behavior, and how to compare that to hundreds of behavioral analysis cases. This data, along with your trained eye for human psychology as it applies to body language, and much of it does apply in this business, will help leverage your education and hard work into a career."

She moved to the left for a few steps, looked at the empty seats that once were occupied by Cindy Carter and Julie Lassiter. She scanned the sorrowful faces of her students, wanting to give them the answers that they needed to hear—but she couldn't.

She didn't have the answers.

Elizabeth glanced out the classroom window, the morning sky battleship gray. A lone blackbird perched on a power line. "I can teach you these things—the psychology of competency exams in relation to the criminal mind, the way to use your knowledge and skillsets to assist law enforcement in everything from profiling a suspect to testifying in criminal trials. But there is one thing I cannot teach you."

Some students sat a little straighter. Some shifted in their seats. Others folded their arms—faces filled with grief and mistrust.

Elizabeth inhaled deeply and said, "I can't teach you what evil is…I can tell you the results of evil. I can tell you what the anatomy of evil is in terms of psychopathy labels, such as heavy narcissism mixed with aggression. I can point out places where evil thrived. Auschwitz, as an example. It's a one-word Cliffs Note for the combined atrocities of World War Two—maybe all the wars. To explain evil is to truly understand it. It's root. It's motivation. Maybe even its source. Some say a person can be born evil. Does that mean he's not culpable because he came out of the womb with a defective, evil gene, as if the baby was born with a disease for life?"

She paused, stood next to the lectern. "Is the evil card something we pull from the deck when dealing with a mind so aberrant, so wicked, that we can't prescribe therapy or rehab…but we're consigned to lock it away until it dies? But evil never dies. Not in the physical sense. It simply finds a new host, like a hermit crab locates a shell. The constant in evil is it reinvents itself to resurface in all veins of society, like tainted blood. From the massacres in Las Vegas, Orlando, Sandy Hook…to evil's old standby of pedophilia, rape and murder."

None of her students spoke. No one took notes. Some glanced down at their desks or their hands. Others stared at her—trying to comprehend what Elizabeth knew was incomprehensible in an absolute sense. "Evil has nothing to do with natural disasters or acts of God, as some people label hurricanes or earthquakes. Evil has everything to do with the moral disaster of the human heart. And a truly evil act leaves a scar on a victim for life. It may be a small, almost innocuous, scar. But the *mark* of the perpetrator is there. No, I can't teach you to define evil, or to categorize it in a neat box. There's no online app to help you identify or destroy it. I hope I can teach you to better recognize its subtle transgressions—which are too often the prelude to a deadly storm. I can't define evil, but I can tell you that until we come up with a better word, we're stuck with it for life. When there are heinous crimes from one person against another person—perpetrator to victim—when traits of greed, narcissism, and hate raise the head of a hydra to cannibalize good, let's use the ugly and encompassing word we have. Let's call it what it really is…evil. The total absence of good."

Elizabeth touched the lectern with one hand, her eyes moving across the students' faces. "Any questions or comments."

A student wearing a New Orleans Saints jersey, unshaven, raised his hand. "Professor Monroe…although evil is the absence of good, sometimes hard to see at first glance, can we actually feel it?"

"You mean in the presence of others, correct…or somewhere else?"

"Around others. If someone is inherently bad or evil, can't we sort of sense it, like some little alarm bell going off as a warning?"

"Sometimes. Other times, not so much initially. It depends on the people or person and the circumstances. People can put on deodorant to mask body odor, but it's still there, only covered for a short period. Some people, who do harm to others with no conscience or remorse, can disguise that as well…at least for a while. But like a dark shadow, it follows them. And, when they make a wrong turn, we can glimpse it."

"I think evil is when somebody makes the decision to do something morally wrong against another person and the transgressor feels good about what he did by hurting the victim."

Elizabeth smiled. "That's one good definition for evil."

A blonde in a ponytail said, "It feels so weird to look over and see the two seats left empty by some pervert who made the decision to kill Cindy and Julie. Do you know if the cops are any closer to an arrest?"

"Not much has changed since I sent everyone in this class the email. My urgent suggestions, and that of the police, remain the same until this person is caught. Always walk in pairs across campus—even if you're just going to the restroom. Always check the backseat of your car before you get behind the wheel. Carry your phone, and be ready to call 911 if needed. Be vigilant using ride share. Let a friend or parent know what company you're taking and the name of the driver. Police don't know if the killer was working for a ride-share company, but they suspect he may be a part-time driver. Bottom line is just be very aware of your surroundings. College is supposed to be a great time—a fun time. I'm so sorry that someone…someone evil, is manipulating this time and experience for you. He will be caught soon." She smiled. "I'm dismissing class early today."

As the students left, one girl with shoulder-length red hair approached. "Professor Monroe."

"Yes, Angela."

"Are you okay? You look like you haven't slept much. I can see why, but I'm worried about you, just like I'd worry about my mom." The girl smiled.

"I'm fine. Thank you for asking, and thank you for elevating me to a mom level. I haven't felt like a mom in quiet a while. Be safe out there." Elizabeth smiled.

"I will." The girl turned and left the room.

Elizabeth glanced out her window and spotted a TV news truck in the parking lot. She thought about the white pickup truck with the lumberjack sign on the side panel. She could hear James Hatfield sitting in his brown recliner, '*Then he put the snake in a burlap sack, tied it, and set it in the back of his truck.*'

Elizabeth rearranged the papers in her briefcase and looked at the manila file marked *Wrath*. She waited for the last student to leave the room and went to her office to call Detective Bradford.

SEVENTY-TWO

E lizabeth closed and locked the door to her office. Through the glass, and beyond the receptionist's desk, she saw Dean Harris pause in the hallway. He looked back at Elizabeth's office before turning to walk away. She placed a call to Bradford. "Thanks again for calling the watch commander at the police department and having him call the officer. No sign of the pickup truck, I gather?"

Bradford leaned back in his chair in the homicide division of the sheriff's office. "We crisscrossed half the county. Found nothing. Plenty of white pickups, but none with the image of a lumberjack on the side panels. Did the officer write you a ticket?"

"He gave me a warning."

"Maybe you'll listen to him."

She said nothing.

Bradford rested his elbows on his desk, sleeves rolled up. "Elizabeth, right now it's all about your safety, the safety of your students and anyone else this perp believes has some weird kind of skin in his depraved game." He paused, looked at some notes on his desk, and glanced across the room at his partner Ed Milton who was working the phones. Other detectives were coming and going, some stopping to exchange information or share a joke to lighten the mood of a tough day. The smell of burnt coffee from a stained mug on Bradford's desk hung close in the air. "Elizabeth, did Jack come home?"

"No."

"Well, he's known to have a wandering eye. Maybe he'll show up. I wish I could put out a missing persons or missing cat BOLO for you."

She smiled. "I wish you could, too. Thanks."

"Ed has been calling all morning, looking for some kind of connection to that truck. Woodcutters, guys who are tree surgeons, people who pretty much make a living with a chainsaw. Lumber yards. Sawmills. So far, we haven't found anything. We've looked at employee records with all the area ride-share companies, trying to match names to Zachariah Belmont's name, and even the name on the tombstone of the Shubuta Cemetery, Edward Thompson. So far nothing. But we did find the manufacturer of the boot that made the print at the graves. It was made by the Wolverine brand, a company in Michigan."

"Where are they sold in Hattiesburg?"

"Just about everywhere shoes and boots are sold. You can get them from Amazon and probably other online stores, too."

"Although it's difficult to track the sale of boots, and they could be an older pair, we do have wooden bowls made from a fairly rare tree, the spruce pine, and crosses made from planks off the bridge. Maybe, somewhere in the middle…in somebody's garage…or woodshed, or barn, we'll find wood-working tools, spruce pine and the boards from the bridge."

"And if a white pickup is parked outside, I'd say we have our guy."

"Mike, the light was low and I was tired, but it looked like the image I saw on that truck last night was drawn on side panels or some kind of boards—something that could be removed."

"Between Forrest County and Clarke County, there are a lot of white pickup trucks on the road."

Elizabeth said nothing. She played back in her mind what Otto Emerson said, *'You used the allegory of snakes in the garden. For this perp, you waved a red flag in his face.'*

"Elizabeth, are you there?"

"Yes, I was just thinking about something Otto Emerson said. He'd suggested that since I used the metaphor of snakes in the garden, I'd waved a red flag into the perp's face. Basically placing him in the category of Satan. Hold a second." Elizabeth opened the file marked *Wrath* and read from her notes. "In the pamphlet, *Retribution*, Belmont wrote, *'we believe that there are children of Satan in the world today. They are the descendants of Cain, and this was a result of Eve's original sin. We know that because of this sin, there is a battle and a natural hatred between the children of Satan and God.'* Remember the inscription on Edward Thompson's headstone?"

"I took a picture of it. I can pull it up."

"I have it here. The inscription was a quote from Zachariah 14: 3-5 and read, *"The Lord will go out and fight against those nations as he fights on the day of battle."* She looked through her notes. "The word *battle* is used in both references. What battle?"

"I'm hoping it's not some vigilante group bent on blowing up a courthouse or federal building."

She read from the file. "One hundred years ago, Belmont talked about retribution and wrote, *'Remain true to the mission and never forget that retribution is your birthright. Sip from the cup of wormwood, raised in a toast to the heavens in one hundred years by the eighth angel on the eighth day.'"* Elizabeth closed the folder. "The exact anniversary of the hangings from the bridge is in two weeks. We believe the killer will murder at least four more people to match his view of the bowls and the wrath of God. And maybe in two weeks, on the one hundred year anniversary of the deaths on the bridge, he'll be doing something even more horrific. In his sick mind, he believes he's fulfilling a mission. And he wants to deliver fire and brimstone. The only way that can happen is from a bomb—an enormous explosion or using automatic weapons to shoot into a crowd of thousands of people like the Vegas killer did. "

"I have no idea how all the tea leaves are coming together in the bottom of this cup of wormwood. But it sounds something like Ruby Ridge, Waco or the Oregon standoff could be brewing if this guy's not acting alone. Or maybe he is alone and wants to go blow up a building and kill a lot of people. I have a friend with the FBI in Jackson. He has his ear on the door of hate groups, black, white, Hispanic, Asian…they're all in the state. Maybe he's heard something. I'll check with him."

"At this point, we can use all the help we can get." She looked out her office window and spotted another TV news truck entering the parking lot. "Something else, in the pamphlet, *Retribution*, Belmont calls his commune or settlement Polemo. It's Greek and basically means a sustained battle for a cause. The Greek god Polemos was pretty much in charge of waging war. Oh, another thing…the professor emeritus of the university's history department told me Belmont's community was on some land where the Chickasawhay and Leaf River converge to form the Pascagoula River. The area has been a ghost town for a century." She watched another TV news truck arrive, this one from Fox News. "Mike, has something else happened? I see more news trucks around the university. Have you received a missing persons call referencing any of our students?"

"No, not that I know of, and I'm in the direct loop on all MP calls in the county."

"You said there are a lot of white pickup trucks in the area between here and Clarke County, no doubt. But I'd bet there are very few, if any, churches where you'd find snakes handled during the services." She opened the file, silently read from her notes.

"I'd agree. What are you thinking, Elizabeth?"

"I'm thinking there's a connection. Just like there's a connection with the wood used to make those handmade bowls and the wood used to make the crosses. In Belmont's pamphlet, *Retribution*, which now reminds me of the Unabomber's manifesto, Belmont wrote, '*Invite the serpent into your place of worship. Fear not an encounter with the serpent for those truly filled with the Holy Spirit cannot perish from the serpent's bite.*'" She looked up from the paper. "Maybe… just maybe…there are some of these churches somewhere in Mississippi where the preacher handles snakes."

"That sounds a little farfetched to me." Bradford looked over at Ed Milton who tossed two extra-strength aspirins into his mouth and washed them down with Dr. Pepper.

Elizabeth said, "No, it's not as farfetched as you might think. There are churches like that scattered around the South, including in states, such as Kentucky, Virginia, West Virginia, Alabama, and so forth. There are a lot of psychological issues when the preacher, sometimes looked at as a prophet, uses the Bible as a kind of weapon towards the congregation, presenting God as a God of harsh judgment and condemnation rather than as a God of love and deep mercy. Some of these fundamentalist preachers strongly thrust their literal interpretation of the Bible—snake handling on Sunday, as part of it. If we find a church like that here, maybe we'll be one step closer to finding the white pickup with a lumberjack on the side of the truck."

"Alex Davidson's father is some kind of fundamentalist preacher. Ed has the file on that. I remember we found out the father runs a primitive church outside of Florence. Ed and I'll ride over there and speak with the man—see if he drives a white pickup and see if he has a pair of Wolverine boots. Maybe Alex is following his father's bidding. What if the apple didn't fall too far from the tree…or what if we go back to what the perp wrote when he sent you that text that read, *Did you find the earring? He left it for you.*"

SEVENTY-THREE

Elizabeth hoped she wouldn't run into Dean Harris before she could leave the building. She picked up her briefcase and purse, locked the office door and headed down a large hallway. As she approached the exit, her phone buzzed in her purse. She didn't want to stop and check it there. *Later. Keep walking. Eyes straight ahead.*

She almost walked into him.

In her peripheral vision, she saw Alex Davidson turn, the smell of cigarettes on his clothes. He stopped and stared at her for an awkward moment and said, "Hi, Doctor Monroe." He turned and walked down the hall, blending in with dozens of other students. Elizabeth heard Bradford's comments in her mind, *What if the apple didn't fall too far from the tree…or what if we go back to what the perp wrote when he sent you the text that read, 'Did you find the earring? He left it for you.'*

She hurried past more administrative offices along the large foyer and exited the main entrance.

A hoard of news media met Elizabeth.

Video cameras pointed toward her. The dark glass in each camera seemed to be black holes—one-eyed monsters with the steely nature of Cyclops. Microphones moved toward her in jagged unison, a small rolling wave like the synchronized movement from the legs of a centipede in motion.

A tousled newspaper reporter asked, "Professor Monroe, is it true that police have taken your friend, Nellie Culpepper, into a witness protection program—a safe house, because they think she's possibly the next victim of the *wrath* killer?"

"Is that the label you're using? *Wrath killer?*" Elizabeth looked at him and continued walking.

Cameras flashed and another reporter, a woman from Fox News, asked, "Doctor Monroe, with the word wrath left on three bodies and something different found in each bowl, what message do you think the killer is sending? What do you think is the meaning of those things—are they symbolic of something?"

Elizabeth kept walking.

The reporter continued, "We heard that these bowls are somehow related to the killer's interpretation of the wrath of God found in the Book of Revelation. Is this accurate, and if so, how do you profile this type of killer?"

Elizabeth stopped and looked the reporter in the eye. "He's a descendent of Cain."

"What does that mean?"

Elizabeth cut her eyes from the reporter into the lens of the camera. "He handles snakes because he is one. Always will be." She stepped around the woman. The horde followed with more questions.

An investigative journalist from a Jackson TV station, dressed in a dark sports coat, black T-shirt and jeans said, "Doctor Monroe, two of the three known victims were students in your criminal psychology class. Nellie Culpepper is said to be an old family friend of yours, what do you think is the connection in the mind of the killer?"

Elizabeth stepped around the reporter, his cameraman almost running to keep up. The reporter shook his head, jawline hard. He asked, "Could this be related to the death of your own daughter?"

Elizabeth stopped. Started to use the moment to further bait the killer, but changed her mind and said, "All of your questions need to be addressed to law enforcement. They are handling the investigation. Thank you." She walked quickly across the parking lot.

Two university security officers caught up with the pack of reporters as they jostled to ask more questions and shoot pictures and video. One tall officer said, "You folks need to give Doctor Monroe some space, all right?

We don't want her, or any of you, tripping over something and falling on the concrete, busting your head wide open. Please, move back."

The herd thinned somewhat. Elizabeth took keys from her purse, quickly unlocking the car door. She got inside and started the motor, put the car in gear, and pulled forward, one cameraman stepping hurriedly out of her way. As she drove through the lot, she resisted the urge to look towards the third floor corner office window. If Dean Harris was there looking down, *enjoy the show.*

Elizabeth drove out of Hattiesburg, toward a place she had wanted to visit for the last three weeks—her daughter's grave. It was a half-hour drive from the city. Elizabeth thought about the questions the reporters had shotgunned at her. *'How do you profile this type of killer?'*

'He's a descendent of Cain.'

Elizabeth knew her comment would be broadcast and seen online almost immediately. He would, no doubt, see it or hear about it. Her smear would drip through his sick mind down to his soulless, dark heart.

And then he would come for her.

Seething. A bowl in one hand—a knife in the other.

Maybe he'd skip the other three killings she felt he had planned and come straight for her. Possibly she could save the lives of three more innocent people. She thought of her students and of Nellie. And she thought of Molly. *'Could this be related to the death of your own daughter?'*

Yes…it could.

Come find me, asshole.

Elizabeth leaned over and removed her gun from the glove box, setting it between her seat and the center console. She looked up in the rearview mirror as she drove farther into the country, tall pines on each side of the winding road. There was no traffic behind her, or in front of her.

She glanced in the back seat at the bag of birdseed she'd bought a few weeks ago. She remembered the time a baby bluebird had fallen from its nest just before it was ready to fly. Molly was ten years old. Dark shoulder-length hair—wide smile. And an imagination that knew no boundaries.

Molly had handfed the fledgling bird for six days, and then on the seventh day, Molly knew it was time. She took the bird back outside, perched on her finger. They stood on the hill in their back yard, Molly holding her hand up to the sky, and in a puff of wind, the bluebird leapt off and flew. It circled Molly, chirping, and then alighted near the top of a cottonwood tree. "Look Mom!" Molly's voice radiated confidence. "I knew she could do it." The breeze changed directions and the bird flew from the tree, across a wide creek, into the horizon and a sky as blue as its new feathers.

Elizabeth smiled, remembering the times with Molly. After another mile, she looked up into her rearview mirror. A vehicle was in the distance.

A pickup truck.

The color was white.

SEVENTY-FOUR

Elizabeth lowered her right hand to the grip of the pistol. She lifted it, setting the gun on the center console. She looked in the rearview mirror—the truck closer. She accelerated, going from forty-five to fifty-five.

The truck gained speed. Coming nearer. Elizabeth thought about calling Bradford. But, he could never get to her in time. No, the line in the sand was drawn. If the driver of the white pickup was coming for her, come on. She thought about turning down a spur road. See if he'd follow. She looked on both sides of the road. Nothing but thick forests, saplings and undergrowth.

Elizabeth increased her speed. Looked in the mirror. The driver followed, staying about one hundred feet behind her car. But it was close enough for Elizabeth to see some of his physical traits. Wide shoulders. He wore a baseball cap. Face partially hidden in the reflection of trees and sky off his front windshield.

She tried to see the sides of the truck as they drove through the winding road. She looked in her side-view mirrors each time the road made a twist. Elizabeth couldn't tell if there was a sign or signs on the side panels of the truck. One thing she could see was a gun rack in the truck's back window.

And there was a rifle or a shotgun cradled in the rack.

She licked her dry lips and thought about reaching for the lip balm in her purse. Thought about the truck she'd seen with the lumberjack panels. *Was it the same?* She couldn't remember a gun rack, but then again, she only spotted the truck from the side for a split second. She thought about the conversation she'd heard from the radio in the truck when the driver pulled opposite the gas pumps at the convenience store. She remembered the whiff of acrid cigar smoke.

But she couldn't remember him buying gas.

Think. She had been so exhausted. Had he been following her the entire time? Was he following her now? She knew that if the gun in the rack behind his head was a 12-gauge shotgun, loaded with double-aught buckshot, all he'd have to do is drive up closer and fire out his widow. One, maybe two blasts, and her car would have the back window blown out. Maybe the gas tank ruptured. Maybe her head shattered.

The winding road straightened for at least a half-mile. No oncoming traffic. Just her and the man in the white pickup.

And he was coming closer. Her heart raced.

Elizabeth lowered her driver's side window, the wind whipped through the car. She gripped the pistol with her right hand. Drove with her left. The truck was now about fifty feet behind her. She tried to see if he'd removed the gun, but the reflection in the window from the sun and tree line covered most of his windshield.

He pulled out to pass.

She watched him in her side-view mirror. *Was the damn gun in the rack?* She couldn't tell. She'd wait a few more seconds before slamming on her brakes. Catch him off guard. He'd either fly by her, or try to shoot her through his passenger-side window.

Elizabeth watched the truck start to pass. Coming closer. She lifted her pistol, finger on the trigger, the tip of the barrel just hidden behind the door.

In three seconds. One…two…three….

She hit the brakes hard. The truck driver made a slight swerving motion. She held her gun up, the barrel fully displayed. She looked at the truck as it passed. The passenger window was down. The driver's face pinched, confused and angry. He saw her pistol and gunned his big diesel engine, flying by her.

Elizabeth looked at the side panels. No indication of a sign or where one had been. As the truck passed, she could see that the gun was still in the rack. And she could see that it was definitely a 12-gauge shotgun. Pump-action. Within seconds, the truck was down the road, moving fast. Elizabeth guessed the driver had hit more than ninety miles per hour after he saw her pistol.

And she guessed he was on his phone calling the sheriff's office. She'd call Bradford before the troops were dispatched. Elizabeth set her gun back between her seat and the console. She watched the truck disappear down the highway. Her mind raced.

She thought about the one hundred year anniversary of the deaths from the Shubuta Bridge coming up in just a few days. Thought about what Otto Emerson had said, *'Maybe the prime clue will be the letters L – O – T. There is a connection there. Find it, Elizabeth.'*

Shaken and distracted, Elizabeth realized she had missed the road where she was supposed to turn. Because she would have to backtrack a few miles, she kept driving—there was another grave she'd visit.

For a second time.

SEVENTY-FIVE

Mike Bradford and Detective Ed Milton studied the gravel parking lot as they approached the Shiloh Baptist Church a few miles south of Florence, Mississippi. There were three cars and one white pickup truck in the lot.

The church was made of wood, thick timbers milled more than one hundred years ago. Its white paint was in need of a new coat. Small steeple. Green shutters and a wooden entrance porch. A large live oak cast one part of the church in shade. Bradford could see a small cemetery to the far left of the building.

Detective Milton said, "That's gotta be the church."

"And we have an old pickup that's white."

"Let's check it out before we see if Pastor Davidson is in residence."

They parked in the shade and walked over to the pickup truck. It was a Ford, at least ten years old. Bradford and Milton moved slowly around the truck, looked at the side panels. They eyeballed for traces of nuts, bolts, brackets or rusty screw holes where a sign could have been mounted. They studied the dented truck bed.

Milton used the tip of his pen to lift something caught in a rusted bolt in the bed. It was thread of course cloth. "Mike, look at this. You said Nellie Culpepper's brother said the fella who saw someone toss a rattlesnake in a truck put the snake in a burlap sack. This looks like burlap to me."

Bradford glanced up at the church to see if anyone had come to the windows. "We have a white truck and a shred of what appears to be burlap. Let's go meet the minister."

"I wonder what shoes or boots he's wearing."

They walked up the four steps leading to the porch and the front door. A woman was coming out of the door. She was near fifty. Hair pinned up. Blue sundress, straps, simulated pearl necklace. Her white purse slung over a freckled shoulder. "Oh, excuse me," she said, caught off guard.

Bradford smiled. "Is Pastor Davidson here?"

"Yes sir. He's in his office. Was on the phone just a minute ago. I'm Polly Henderson. I help with Sunday school, and I write up the church bulletin. We have a funeral tomorrow. I'm just tryin' to help out. Y'all go inside, and it's the door on the left. Right after the bathroom."

Milton nodded. "Thank you, ma'am."

They entered and approached the open door to the office. Pastor Davidson looked up from an old oak desk. He was writing a note. A painting of Christ on the cross was directly behind him, a view of the cemetery from the only window in the office. He stood. Salt and pepper hair gelled and combed straight back. He wore a flannel shirt and jeans. "Can I help you fellas?" He stood and extended his hand. "I'm Pastor Davidson."

"I'm Detective Bradford and this is my partner Detective Milton. We're investigating serial murders in Forrest County."

The pastor's smile melted, his mouth now bent downward. "It's the devil's work. Signs of the end of times are everywhere. Las Vegas. Orlando. Paris. We're not that different from Sodom and Gomorrah with its debauchery." He paused and tilted his head back, eyes narrowing a notch. "I almost recognize you both from the description my son, Alex, gave me after y'all interrogated him for two hours. He had nothin' to do with the death of that girl."

Bradford studied Davidson. "That girl was your son's girlfriend. Did you not meet her?"

"No sir. Can't say I did."

Milton said, "It was an interview not an interrogation. There's a difference."

Davidson set his wide hand down over a large black Bible on his desk. "In my book, which is the Holy Bible, it's about treating people like Christ taught us. Y'all fellas should have learn't that back in Sunday school."

Bradford said. "We're conducting a murder investigation. In that situation, there are other influences at work. Just like it was when they killed Christ." Bradford looked up at the painting and then cut his eyes to Davidson. "When was the last time you were in Forrest County?"

"Been months."

"You sure you weren't visiting your son the last couple of days? Maybe just a quick trip down Highway 98, right?"

"Sir, I do not tell lies. It's in God's commandments. What is this about?" He sat back down.

Milton watched Davidson's hands. "As we said, we're conducting a murder investigation."

"If my son is not a suspect, why are you here?"

Bradford said, "Everyone in Cindy Carter's inner circle is a suspect until we find and prove who killed her. But he didn't stop at Cindy. He killed another student, Julie Lassiter, and a man, Charlie Lehman, who had written an editorial for the newspaper condemning hate groups for what they really are…cults of loathing, fearful people."

Davidson set his arms on the chair's armrest, touched the tips of his fingers together in a steeple, glanced out the window for a moment before looking at the detectives. "Why y'all here?"

Bradford said, "You mentioned end of times. Lot's of that is mentioned in Revelation. Something your son, Alex, knows well."

"If a man don't know where he's going, he can't live his life in preparation of that journey. You fellas need to take a hard look at Deuteronomy. Read it slowly."

Bradford nodded. "After the killer murdered each of his victims, he wrote the word *wrath* across their foreheads. And he placed wooden bowls on the bodies. Why do you think the killer is taking his interpretation from Revelation, paralleling the seven bowls of God's wrath."

"Probably on account that somebody's fed up with all the sin on earth, and he's taking it into his own hands to make a statement. Now, that don't make it right, okay?"

"Last time I checked, murder was a sin."

Davidson scratched the tip of his bulbous nose. "I hope you find the feller doin' these killin's before he takes another life."

"Are you familiar with Revelation 14: 3-5?" Bradford asked.

"Yes sir. It says the Lord will go out and fight against those nations as he fights on the day of the battle." Davidson nodded, pleased with his quick narration.

"Is that battle one big one…or is it one sustained effort?"

"It's an on goin' battle to fight wickedness. But come judgment day, it's the last battle, Armageddon. You boys ready for that? God's got a good ear."

Milton stepped closer to the oak desk. "Pastor Davidson, we noticed shards from a burlap sack in the back of your truck. Any idea how that would have caught on a rusty bolt in the bed of your truck?"

"Yeah, I got an idea, 'cause I know why. I run twenty head of cattle. And I have close to forty layin' hens. I haul feed in the winter, seed in the spring." He stood. "Unless there's somethin' else y'all want to discuss, I need to get some lunch. My blood sugar is low. I wait much longer, and I could fall out. It happened twice before. I'm sure y'all don't want to have to dial 9-1-1."

As he walked around his desk, Bradford and Milton looked at his shoes. He wore soft brown loafers in need of a shoeshine.

"We'll walk outside with you," Bradford said, following Davidson.

Outside the church, Davidson turned and locked the door. "Y'all have a nice day. I'll tell my boy, Alex, we had a nice chat."

As he started to leave, Bradford said, "On the farm, I bet you have some fine work boots. A friend recommended the Wolverine brand. You ever own a pair?"

"Naw, sir. Can't say I can recall."

"You ever bring snakes into your church?"

Davidson stopped at the bottom step and twisted around, as if he had a slight back spasm, the sunlight partially on his face.

Bradford continued. "You know, snakes to handle during the service. You ever use them?"

"No sir. Serpents don't belong in the house of God. We welcome sinners 'cause all of us sin. Some more than others. A person's got to know when to repent. How 'bout you fellas…ready to repent?"

A red-tailed hawk cried out as it rose up from a field and flew over the woods. A small snake twisted in the hawk's talons. Davidson cocked his head, used one hand to shield his eyes from the sun, the hawk a silhouette as it vanished beyond the tree line. "Snakes don't come around my church. No sir. Y'all boys have a good day."

SEVENTY-SIX

Elizabeth parked her car near the wrought iron gate leading into Shubuta Cemetery. She sat there for a moment as the motor cooled and ticked in the shade of a live oak tree. There were no other cars or trucks, no one visiting the cemetery. She thought about the inscription on one headstone. She remembered the name of Edward Thompson and the engraving on his headstone: *Zachariah 14: 3-5...The Lord will go out and fight against those nations as he fights on the day of battle.*

Elizabeth thought about the word *battle* and its connection to Belmont's commune: *Polemo.* She recalled another surname from the day that she and Bradford were here: Clements. *Was there a connection to Clarke County Detective, Earl Clements? And was there a connection to Zachariah Belmont?*

Elizabeth put her pistol in her purse, locked the car and strode across the cemetery toward the headstone that she wanted to read again. As she approached the gravesite, she heard a rifle shot echo from somewhere in the distance.

Two mourning doves flew from their perches on the tarnished gate that surrounded Edward Thompson's grave. Elizabeth resisted the urge to look at the massive oak where, in her state of exhaustion, she had seen or hallucinated the image of the man's face in the gnarly tree bark.

She stood next to three graves that were inscribed with the last name Clements. The first was Harriet. She was born June 1926, and she died September 1999. The second was Rhett Clements: 1925 – 1995. A third grave was inscribed as Timothy Clements, 1949 – 1951. *Just a baby,* Elizabeth thought. She looked in her purse and found the card that Anna Lawrence had given her and made the call. "Anna, it's Elizabeth Monroe. The name, Harriet Clements, one of Zachariah Belmont's daughters—"

"Yes, what about her?"

"In your notes, does it say when she was born and when she died?

"Yes. Hold a second and I'll get them."

As Elizabeth waited, she watched a black pickup truck slow at the entrance to the cemetery, the passenger side window rolled down. Elizabeth could see a younger man in a hunter's green camouflaged shirt, scruffy beard, staring in her direction. The truck stopped.

Elizabeth unzipped her purse, rested her right hand on the pistol grip. The passenger said something to the driver and the truck slowly pulled away, brake lights flashing once and then the truck exited the cemetery for the road. Elizabeth could hear it accelerating and then the silence of the grave-yard returned.

Anna came back on the line and said, "Harriet Clements, born Harriet Belmont in June of 1926, and she died Harriet Clements in September 1999. Computers and good county and state record keeping make all the differ-ence. I found some more information for you."

"What'd you find?"

"Harriet and Rhett Clements had two children, Timothy who died at age two. And the other son was…or is Earl Clements. According to his birth records, he's in his sixties. I couldn't tell you where he is, though."

"I know where to find him."

"Oh, I almost forgot. I managed to dig up a picture of Zachariah Belmont. It wasn't easy. He apparently didn't like having his picture taken because he wrote that he believed it harmed the soul."

"That's assuming he hadn't traded it to the devil in some Faustian pact. Maybe the Shubuta Bridge was Belmont's crossroads at midnight. Can you email or text the photo to me?"

"Of course. An old college friend of mine at the Civil Rights Museum had it in their archives. She sent the digital file to me. I'll just forward it to you."

"Thank you, Anna. You've been a great help." She disconnected and started walking to her car. When she got inside and closed the door, her phone buzzed. Anna had sent the photo. Elizabeth opened it. Staring at the face of Zachariah Belmont, prominent nose, dark eyebrows, beard, brow furrowed. He looked directly at the camera, mouth tuned down.

She could see the subtle resemblance to another man.

Elizabeth searched her purse for the card that Earl Clements had given her and made the call. When he answered, she said, "Detective Clements, this is Elizabeth Monroe."

"Well, hello, Miss Elizabeth. Now, I told you to call me Earl. What can I do for you?"

"Maybe it's something I can do for you?"

"Pardon me?"

"Meet me at the Shubuta Bridge in an hour, and I'll show you."

"Is it related to our murder case?"

"Very much so."

SEVENTY-SEVEN

Elizabeth drove down the dirt road, past the *keep out* signs, and parked at the dead end. It was near the same place where she and Bradford had parked when they came to the Shubuta Bridge. She lifted the gun from her purse, chambered a round, and set it back in her purse. She called Bradford and asked, "Did you meet with Alex Davison's father?"

"Yes. He's a fundamentalist preacher and then some. He drives a beat up old, white pickup truck. We found a thread of burlap that was caught on a rusty bolt in the bed of his truck. He tells us he hauls feed and seed in burlap sacks."

"What's your gut telling you?"

"That he sees things in an extreme black-and-white world through his narrow lens. I don't think he colluded with his son or anyone else for that matter. Although he might be empathic in some areas, he's mostly pretty rigid in his beliefs but not crazy out there, so to speak. So I don't think he rounds up rattlesnakes and murders people. Ed and I met with Ben Dixon of the FBI. He gave us an updated rundown of some of the hate groups in Mississippi. These include all ethnicities. He said the bureau has been following a very covert group that's been more active in the last few months."

"Who are they?"

"Members call themselves STA or Trans-Am for short. Their longer title is Sons to Transform America. Ben said they're believed to have about seventy-five active members in Mississippi. The FBI isn't sure who's leading this group. Rumor has it that he's a former philosophy professor from Old

Miss who lives in Vicksburg. But that can't be corroborated. Ben knows of at least five members of the group who live in Hattiesburg. He said that the bureau suspects that more than a dozen members of the group were part of the counter-protests at the rally near the Confederate memorial. Just maybe one of them had that brief conversation with Cindy Carter."

"And that person, assuming he has the serious religious mission drift in terms of his interpretation of Revelation, could be our killer."

"Maybe. Ed and I will interview the five known members, primarily to see if we can get a reaction that might lead us further. Where are you now?"

"Near the Shubuta Bridge."

"What the hell are you doing back up there?"

"Meeting Detective Earl Clements."

"May I ask why?"

"I found out that he is the son of Zachariah Belmont's youngest daughter. Belmont is or was his grandfather."

"Whoa…run that by me again. How the hell did you find that information?"

"The woman who runs Anna's Antiques in Hattiesburg, Anna Lawrence, was a state archivist before she retired. She keeps Civil Rights history inside a back room in her store. I found out that Earl Clements mother's name was Harriett Belmont. She married Rhett Clements and they had two sons. One died at age two. And the other is very much alive. He's Earl Clements. Mike, I felt that this guy wasn't all he appeared to be that day when we found Julie's body on that bridge."

"Do you think he killed her?"

"I don't know. But I believe that he knows who was taking wood from the bridge. Maybe it's only the guy who catches rattlesnakes with his bare hands. Maybe it's someone else…or all of the above. Regardless, I'm going to find out."

"Elizabeth, if there is a family connection to these murders, you can't meet Clements on that damn bridge alone. I'll be your back up."

"Where are you now?"

"We left Florence, headed to Hattiesburg. We can take Highway 84 and go towards Laurel and over to Shubuta."

"You're two hours away. You'll never make it in time."

"Then reschedule. You don't have to meet this Clements—"

"Mike, I can't reschedule when three lives have been taken, and we suspect he'll take at least four more before he tries to spread his own warped brand of apocalypse on earth."

"If Clements is part of this hate group, considering his heritage, and somebody in the group is targeting you, he might know that and tip the guy off. Or it might even be Clements himself. You're walking into a potential ambush."

"I won't be caught off guard. He doesn't know what I discovered about him. I'll play it by ear."

"I'm afraid that you might be blinded because you think this guy could be Molly's killer, too. And somehow you'll let your guard down because you want him so damn bad."

"I've thought about this day for a long time. There is no such thing as letting my guard down. I need to go, Mike. I want to be near the bridge before he shows up."

"Elizabeth, we're headed your way. You need back up and—"

"Okay. Gotta go." Elizabeth disconnected, picked up her purse with the pistol and extra rounds. She locked her car door and walked down a sandy path leading to the Shubuta Bridge.

SEVENTY-EIGHT

Elizabeth stopped walking at the entrance to the Shubuta Bridge. She looked straight down the center of the bridge across to the other side. The view narrowed by the long symmetry of steel, wood and leafy green vines wrapped around crossbars. Shafts of sunlight poured through rusted girders. It was a man-made structure broken and reclaimed by nature, creating a forced perspective through distance and time—through pain and suffering. At the far-side opening, a bare branch moved in the breeze, as if it were beckoning for Elizabeth to cross.

She took a step onto the bridge and looked down at areas where boards had been removed, the silent river flowed beneath the open slats. A snake had shed its skin, leaving the ghostlike membrane on the timbers. The breeze blew across the water and came through the open holes on the floorboard. She turned and looked in the area behind her. No sign of Detective Clements.

Elizabeth adjusted the purse strap on her shoulder under the added weight of the gun. She walked across the bridge, stepping over spots of rot and missing timbers. She watched the river below her, the briny smell of algae, mud, and wood rot in the air. And then she approached the place where Julie had been found. Dried blood spots the size of quarters were soaked into the timber. She knelt down, stared at the stains, touching the largest bloodstain with one finger. Julie's voice was a whisper in the wind. *Cindy's funeral is tomorrow. I don't think I can go. I want to remember her when she was alive. I want to remember her smile and how she laughed at my dumb jokes.*

Elizabeth slowly stood, looked at the discolored trusses. She was exactly midpoint on the bridge. *Was this where they hung the teenagers in 1918? Was it the same spot where they hung two more teens in 1940?* She stepped to the side of the bridge and looked down at the muddy river. A swirl of eddies formed in a clockwise pattern across the water where the current recoiled off an overhung bank.

She felt someone looking at her.

Elizabeth turned her head to see Detective Earl Clements standing at the entrance to the bridge. "You won't find any more evidence there," he said, coming her way. "We picked it clean to the bone, lookin' for threads, hairs, semen...you name it."

"Julie wasn't raped. That's not his MO."

"We didn't know that 'til the autopsy report was done."

"Cindy Carter, as we mentioned, wasn't raped either. The next young woman he kills won't be raped. But he will slit her throat, write the word *wrath* on her forehead and leave a wooden bowl on her body."

"There won't be a next victim, least not in Clarke County."

"How can you say that?"

"Because the victim wasn't from here. Looks like she had been killed somewhere else and left on the bridge. He won't be back."

"Why do you think he brought her here?"

"Ma'am, I'm just a detective. Who knows? If we catch the son-of-a-bitch in my county, I'll damn sure ask him. Now, you mind sayin' what it is you want to show me?"

"He brought Julie here because of the bridge's sick history. He brought her here because he was taking boards from the bridge to make crosses that he left on the graves of the men who hung those kids off this bridge in 1918." Elizabeth paused, studying Clements' face. "One of those crosses was left on your grandfather's grave...Zachariah Belmont."

Clements said nothing. He half smiled, and then his mouth turned down, a muscle twitched near his left eye. He took a step closer to Elizabeth. "I hope you got a point to your veiled accusation."

"There's nothing veiled about it, Detective. Your mother was Harriet Clements, the second daughter of Zachariah Belmont—the Klan leader who led the lynch mob out to this very spot one hundred years ago and hung four teenagers—two pregnant. And they did it without a trial or due process of law."

Clements pulled at his left earlobe. He looked at the river running south and then turned his head to Elizabeth. His eyes were flat. Jawline hard. Elizabeth slowly slipped her right hand in her unzipped purse, the pistol within her grasp. Clements said, "Lots of folks in this county and down in Forrest County, too, have had relatives in the Klan at one time of the other. It don't mean much. That was a long time ago."

"Oh you're wrong. Lots of people down here wear that lineage like a badge of honor."

"Granddaddy Belmont died way before I was born."

"But his influence lives on today. His merry band of followers were white supremacists before there was an official label to describe their hate and terror toward poor blacks, Jews, and any other group that didn't look like them."

"Unless you got something to say that's not an insult to my family, we—you and me, Doctor Monroe, are done here." He started to turn around.

"Who took some of the timbers from this bridge? Who drives a white pickup with a woodcarving sign on the panels? You can't miss it because there's a caricature of a lumberjack on the side. In a small county like this, a truck like that will stand out."

"If I see it, I'll be sure to let you know."

"The killer is taking his direction from your grandfather's grave. Zachariah advocated a one hundred year Armageddon after the lynchings on this bridge. In your grandfather's pamphlet, *Retribution*—catchy title, he's all about the last judgment. He writes, and I quote here because I read it more than once. He says that someone will step out from beyond the shadows to show the sinners that the wrath of God was coming to destroy the wicked. Belmont said the name of the person would have the initials L...O...T. Does the woodcarver have those initials?"

"Let me put this in words that even a psychologist like you can understand...you're fuckin' crazy, lady. Word around here is you're tryin' to connect these killin's with your own daughter's murder." He smiled. "Maybe that's affecting your reasoning."

"The man taking boards from this bridge killed a girl we found on this very spot. There are three known deaths so far. But since he's following your grandfather's instructions, using the seven bowls of God's wrath in Revelation, we know there will be four more before his grand finale. Is he going to blow up a federal courthouse or just shoot from a high-rise building into an open-air concert? Which is it?"

"You better watch your accusations or—"

"Or what? Are you going to shoot me and throw me off this bridge a century after your own grandfather and his mob threw four people off after tying ropes around their necks?" She held up her phone, the screen facing Clements. Zachariah Belmont's image was on the screen. "There's no denying the bloodline. You even have his nose."

Clements glanced at the screen, his eyes on fire. "Where'd you get that?"

"It's in the state archives inside the Civil Rights Museum in Jackson with other pictures and stories of terrorists who fire-bombed churches, synagogues and homes. Who was Edward Thompson?"

Clements looked at the river and shook his head. "Never heard of him."

Elizabeth heard her Uncle Hal's words: *'When a liar is asked a direct question, the poker tell is the pause.'*

She took one step closer to Clements and said, "He's buried in the Shubuta Cemetery not too far from your mother's grave. There was a wooden cross set next to his headstone, and you're standing on some of the wood that was used to make it. Where's the Thompson family live in Clarke County."

"I'd suspect that there are a few folks here with a common last name like that. But can't say I know any of them. You can take your theories, Doctor Monroe, and shove 'em up your sweet ass. I'm leavin' and this conversation is over. Be careful walking across these old timbers. Some are pretty rotten. Be a real shame if you fell through. River's shallow below the bridge. Be like divin' into the kiddie pool from ninety feet up. It'd probably snap your neck." He turned and left.

SEVENTY-NINE

Elizabeth walked around her car, half expecting a tire to be sliced. She glanced through the windshield into the back seat and spotted the birdseed she'd brought. "Molly," she whispered. She closed her eyes for a few seconds, inhaled deeply, glanced about the remote area and unlocked her car.

She got in the driver's side and checked her phone, checking the live cameras at her home. She could see the breeze blowing the ferns on her front porch, and she could see most of her front yard and her back deck. "Where are you, Jack?"

Elizabeth called Bradford and told him about her conversation with Detective Clements. "Mike, there's no doubt in my mind that he knows who took the boards from the bridge, which means, unless there is more than one person stealing the timber, he probably knows who drives the lumberjack truck."

"I'll do a trace on all of Clements known relatives and see if we can come up with something."

"Maybe he's related, or good friends with any family member of Edward Thompson, assuming there are some in the area. For that matter, graves adorned with a wooden cross from bridge timber are suspect or at least the living members of the family are suspicious."

"Elizabeth, if Clements is somehow connected to this, you've poked the bear in his cave. He will speak with the perp or someone in the perp's inner circle, and he or they might come for you."

"Let them."

"I'll add extra patrols in your neighborhood. A visible police presence will help until we get this guy. Maybe staying in a hotel for a couple of nights would be a safer bet for you."

"I'm not going to let this perp keep me from my home. I'd rather have him come for me than another nineteen year old college kid." Elizabeth looked up and saw a Clarke County Sheriff's cruiser coming toward her car parked in the dead end. "Speaking of police presence, it looks like Clements is sic'ing one of his deputies on me. A sheriff's car is heading my way." Elizabeth removed the gun from her purse and placed it in the glove box.

"Are his lights flashing?"

"No."

"Just drive away slowly. Keep me on the phone. Don't even make eye contact with him."

"I'm putting my phone on hands-free mode."

Elizabeth started her car and pulled out of the cul-de-sac. She drove about fifty yards and glanced into the rearview mirrors. The deputy turned around and began following her. "He's tailing me, Mike."

"Just stay at the speed limit."

She drove another mile, the deputy following close behind her car. Elizabeth glanced up in her rearview mirror just as the deputy turned on the cruiser's lights, blue and white flashing in her mirror. "He's forcing me over."

"Okay, keep me on speaker phone."

Elizabeth pulled off the road, parked and lowered her window. She watched in the side-view mirror while the deputy approached. She recognized him as one of the deputies who'd worked the crime scene on the Shubuta Bridge when Julie's body was found.

He stepped up to her window, his right hand resting on the grip of his pistol. "Driver's license and registration, please."

Elizabeth nodded. "Okay, why did you pull me over?" She removed her license and registration, handing it to him."

The deputy studied her picture for a moment, looking back at her face. Elizabeth read his nametag: J. Grover. She said, "Deputy Grover, I saw you working the Julie Lassiter crime scene. She was one of my students."

"That's what I hear."

"Any leads in Clarke County?"

"That information is above my pay grade. I need you to step out of the car?"

"Why?"

"Step out of the car, ma'am. I want to take a look inside here."

"Not without probable cause. I was going below the posted speed limit. My brake lights and turn signals are all in proper order."

"I'm gonna ask you one more time. Get out of the—"

"Doctor Monroe is correct, Deputy Grover," said Bradford on the speakerphone. "This is Detective Mike Bradford with Forrest County SO. I, too, met you working the crime scene. You seemed thorough, so I'm surprised to hear you slip investigative protocol and demand to search Doctor Monroe's vehicle without probable cause or a warrant. Our agencies are working as a joint taskforce in the Lassiter murder investigation. I'm sure that Detective Clements made you aware of that. It would be best to allow Doctor Monroe to be on her way."

The deputy looked around the area, his face tense, dark eyes hard as black marble. He saw an old man sitting on his front porch holding a fly swatter, staring at him. A woman walked her mixed breed dog, coming in their direction. A crow cawed from the top of an aged water tower. The deputy handed the license and registration back to Elizabeth. "Be careful on the roads out here in Clarke County, Doctor Monroe. Have yourself a nice day." He turned and walked to his car.

Elizabeth pulled back on the highway, glanced in the mirror as the flashing lights turned off. "All clear, Mike. I owe you another one. I'm the psychologist but you understand the psychology of police talk better than I do."

"I don't understand it better, I might talk the game a little better because I'm in the game. Are you on your way back to Hattiesburg?"

"You go ahead and head back, I have to make a stop first. The anniversary of Molly's death was three days ago. This is the first time since she died that I haven't gone to her gravesite on the anniversary. I feel bad about that."

"I'd say you've had some horrific distractions get in your way."

"Before I visit Molly, I want to get a cup of coffee and go online. Maybe I can find an address?"

"For who?"

"For any members of the Edward Thompson family that might be in the area."

"Let's do that together. You don't want to trespass on private property in Clarke County."

"I don't plan to. I just want to drive by and see if a white pickup truck is in the driveway."

EIGHTY

Elizabeth drove for ten miles, checking her mirrors, before breathing easier. She entered the parking lot of Millie's Diner, a 1960's low-slung wooden building with a brick chimney. Three cars and one red pickup truck were in the lot. The weathered sign on a pole near the building proclaimed the diner has sold its *world famous* fried chicken since 1989. Elizabeth parked in the shade cast from the roof of the diner, lowered her car window and used her tablet to go online.

She searched the county genealogy records for births and deaths, finding the death of Edward Thompson. He and his wife, Grace, had five children. Four died in the decades since, but one survived. The Reverend Jerome Thompson. He and his wife had two daughters and one son, Lance Thompson.

Elizabeth did a series of cross-references checks, looking for property registered in their names, deaths or divorces—looking for addresses. There was no public record of Lance Thompson's property. *Probably doesn't live in the area*, she thought. But there was an address for Reverend Jerome Thompson. Elizabeth entered the information into her phone, got the GPS location and pulled out of the parking lot, driving north toward the town of De Soto.

The road ran a twisting path parallel to the Chickasawhay River for a dozen miles, the river on one side, woods with thick slash pines on the other. There were brief glimpses of white siding through the woods, the few homes barely visible from the road. Elizabeth slowed at a curve and saw a doublewide trailer down a dirt road scattered in pine straw. A little girl on a bicycle stared back at her.

Elizabeth glanced at her phone screen. The destination was now less than three miles away. She slowed her car, reached in the glove box and removed her pistol. She looked toward the river and saw a man in overalls sitting in a johnboat, removing fish from a trotline, the white belly of a flopping catfish reflecting the sunlight.

Elizabeth drove another mile and braked. According to the map, the home of Reverend Jerome Thompson was just up ahead on the left. She searched for something—a landmark or a store beyond the Thompson address. She found it. The Calvary Cemetery less than a mile beyond the entrance to Thompson's property.

She looked at the satellite image and estimated that the house was about one hundred yards off the road. The driveway appeared straight except for a curve midway between the road and the house. *Maybe there will be a clear view from the road*, she thought.

She pulled her car up next to an old black mailbox. The last name *Thompson* on the side in hand-painted letters. The mailbox leaned slightly forward, the door wide open, honeysuckle vines wrapped around the wooden pole supporting the mailbox. Elizabeth could suddenly smell the scent of the honeysuckles left in her mailbox, the whiff of them from the wreath on her porch, and the odor of death and honeysuckles at Cindy's murder scene.

Elizabeth glanced inside the mailbox. It was empty. She set her gun on the console and entered the dirt driveway. She stopped and looked toward the concrete block house in the distance, a vintage Ford tractor was parked to the left of the house, a camper RV in the driveway. She couldn't see what car or truck may have been parked on the other side of the RV, closer to the house.

Elizabeth drove slowly up the driveway, past a rusted keep out sign nailed to a pine tree, the dried pinesap below the sign resembling intersecting trails of opaque mucus slime left by slugs. She thought about calling Bradford. But he was now traveling in the opposite direction, heading back to his office. She would simply drive up the driveway and knock on the door. Beyond that point, she would deal with whatever situation developed.

She lowered her window, the drone of cicadas in the pines, the mottled shadows of the tree line falling across her windshield. She could see a trampoline to the far right, a Confederate flag on a pole near a red maple tree and a black barbeque grill. A half dozen metal chairs, all painted Army green, made a near circle around the grill.

In the distance, to the left of the tractor, was a large metal barrel. It stood upright, a trace of white smoke drifted up from the barrel. Elizabeth assumed someone had burned trash. She could see a clothesline hung between two metal poles, jeans, overalls and T-shirts hung straight down from the line.

The driveway made a short curve around a strand of live oaks. One tree looked to have been hit by lightning long ago. It had no leaves. The branches had the appearance of atrophy, limbs skeletal, twisted and bent. But the trunk was massive.

Elizabeth hit her brakes.

The face. The one she'd seen in her state of sleep deprivation.

It was carved into the base of the dead oak.

And it seemed to be staring directly at Elizabeth.

EIGHTY-ONE

Elizabeth could feel her pulse pound in her fingertips, blood rushing under the skin through her arms and legs. She stared at the carving in the tree, her mouth abruptly dry. Her thoughts raced. It was a carving of an old man, his hair long, full beard, a wide, prominent nose. But it was the eyes that drew her into the image. Intense eyes. The figure reminded her of statues and paintings of angered Greek deities, such as Zeus or Poseidon.

She drove a few feet further and used her phone to snap a picture. She texted it to Bradford, looked at the house, and then she called him. "Mike, I just sent you a picture of a carving in a tree that's looks like the image I saw twice—both times in trees. I thought I was hallucinating from sleep deprivation or exhaustion, combined with the twilight play of shadows in the tree trunks. Somebody carved the exact image into a dead oak tree. I can't believe—"

"Elizabeth, where the hell are you?"

"I just pulled into the driveway of Reverend Jerome Thompson. He's apparently the only surviving child of Edward Thompson. Maybe Reverend Thompson placed the wooden cross on his father's grave."

"What's the address?"

"It's in a very rural area off Riverside Road. The address is 1217 Riverside." Elizabeth looked at the house. The front door opened and a woman stepped out on the porch. She stared at Elizabeth's car, waved nonchalantly, and then went back in the house and closed the door.

Bradford said, "Do not approach the house."

"Too late for that. A woman came onto the porch. She waved at me and went back inside. Maybe she's the preacher's wife. Maybe she can tell me something. I can't sit in my car in her driveway for an hour until you can get here. I'll make her acquaintance. Tell her I'm lost and looking for someone—which I am."

"You're playing with fire, Elizabeth. We can start back in your direction but it'll—"

"I have to go." She disconnected.

Elizabeth parked behind the RV and got out of her car. Somewhere behind the house, a rooster crowed. There was the scent of burnt garbage and pinesap in the air. She shifted her purse strap to her shoulder and stepped around the RV, walked down the drive toward the front door. A Ford Explorer was parked in front of the RV.

There was a series of cages, similar to chicken coops on stilts, to the left of the closed garage door. The cages were partially covered in burlap. As she walked near them, there was musky odor of something dead.

And then the brief buzz of a rattle.

It sounded like the short burst of a tambourine. A high-pitched rattle. A warning.

Elizabeth stared at the cage on the far right, the thick midsection of a rattlesnake was just visible in an area not covered by burlap. She walked away, stepped onto the brick front porch, wind chimes barely tinkled in a slight breeze. She knocked. A rooster crowed again as the door opened and the same woman stood in the threshold. She had a turned down mouth. Suspicious brown eyes. Early sixties. Her hair was died black, a slight line of gray hair near her scalp.

"Hi, I'm looking for directions. I hope that you can help me. I saw the name on your mailbox. Are you Mrs. Thompson?"

"I go by Ruth." She paused and studied Elizabeth's face. "Are you lost, child? I can see a weight in your eyes…maybe your soul." The woman spoke with a heavy southern accent.

"Yes. As a matter of fact, I am lost."

"What's your name?"

"Elizabeth Gardner."

"What you lookin' for? God? Salvation?"

"The Calvary Cemetery."

She lifted one arm and pointed northwest. "At the end of the driveway, go left. You're less than a mile from it."

"Thank you."

"You got family buried in there, child?"

"No." Elizabeth said nothing else, watching the woman closely.

"Best to my recollection, there hasn't been a burial in the cemetery since the 1960s." She took a step closer, studied Elizabeth's face. "I believe you're a woman with a gift."

"Gift? What to you mean?"

"Prophecy…maybe. I was born with it, too. Seein' things don't always make understanding things any easier."

"How do you mean?"

"I delivered two sons into this world. After the first boy, I had a vision that if I conceived again, my second son wouldn't live to see his twenty-first birthday. Does a woman become pregnant knowin' she'll eventually bury her child? Is that the ultimate love…give a child two decades to be loved… or was it selfish on my part?"

"I can't answer that. Visions don't always parallel reality."

"Depends on where they come from. Did you lose a child?"

"Yes. My daughter died."

"It wasn't an accident or natural death, was it?"

"No."

Ruth looked at the woods across her driveway, wind chimes tinkling, a taste of smoke in the air from the things smoldering in the upright drum. "I'm sorry to hear that."

Elizabeth nodded. "I couldn't help but notice the remarkable carving in that tree near your driveway. It's truly a work of art. Looks like a chainsaw was used. May I ask, who's the artist?"

"Name's Henry Griffin."

"Does he do work for hire?"

Elizabeth could see the woman cut her eyes to the far right. "I believe he does. My husband would know more about that."

Elizabeth looked over her shoulder. A tall, medium-built man stood there. He wore a flannel shirt, dungarees, work gloves and boots. He was mostly bald, his weathered face was deeply lined, his head shiny with sweat.

The Reverend Jerome Thompson removed his gloves and approached Elizabeth.

She rested her right hand on her unzipped purse.

EIGHTY-TWO

A rooster crowed again. Ruth Thompson said, "Jerome, this is Miss Gardner."

Elizabeth said, "Pleased to meet you. I hear a rooster. Do you have chickens?"

"Yes ma'am," he said in robust voice. "We have, what I like to call, a gentlemen's farm. Some of this and some of that. Odd that our rooster is crowing this time of day." He glanced at his watch. "Kinda reminds me of the Bible verse, found in Mark fourteen that says...*before the rooster crows twice, you will deny me three times...and Peter broke down and wept.*" He grinned and came closer to Elizabeth.

His eyes were pale blue, dark rings around the irises that shimmered in the changing light. He looked at her, glanced at her purse, her fingernails. His manner was examining, like that of a man who undresses women with his eyes. His fingers were long, almost delicate. Nails perfectly manicured. Elizabeth could smell cigarette smoke on his clothes. He said, "Pleased to meet you, Miss Gardner. I'm Reverend Jerome Thompson." He reached out with his right hand, took her hand and held it in a soft greeting.

Ruth Thompson said, "She was asking for directions to the Calvary Cemetery, and she noticed the carving in the old oak. Wanted to know if the Henry Griffin does custom woodwork."

Elizabeth smiled, placing her right hand back on top of her unzipped purse. "Nice to meet you as well, Reverend Thompson. As your wife said, I'm enthralled by woodworking. People who can take a tree trunk or a block of wood and carve a work of art…well I find it so fascinating. The carving of the face in the tree on your property is truly art. Did you commission it?"

"No. After a sermon one Sunday in the spring, Henry visited us. Said he saw the two hundred year old live oak that had been struck by lightning. Told us he felt God callin' him to carve a face in the tree."

"Who's face did he carve?"

"Henry says it's the image of the eighth angel in Revelation…in Armageddon. He said God revealed it to him."

Elizabeth studied the preacher's craggy face and asked, "Does Henry do custom pieces for customers?"

"Far as I know he still does, if he finds something that inspires him. He doesn't do it for an income. He does it as a sort of therapy…because he loves it."

"How's he make a living then?"

"Henry's a big man with a big appetite for life. He left Mississippi for a few years and cut timber in Alaska and parts of Montana, too. Came back here with a long, gray ponytail and a tattoo of the eighth angel on one arm. Says if he cuts his hair, he loses his strength. He trims trees. Takes down diseased trees. He'll make stuff from trees when he can. Henry said that way the tree lives on but in a different form. He told me when he carves deep into the rings of an old tree, into the heart, it's like goin' back in time. He says he can feel the nation's history in the palm of his hands. Like before the Civil War, and even all the way back to the Revolutionary War."

Elizabeth smiled. "So does he mark our nation's history with its wars?"

Thompson's eyes widened and became veiled at the same moment. He tilted his head back, looked at Elizabeth as if he wanted to check her for parasites. "I was just using that as an example."

"I suppose it's a good example, considering that after a war or a revolution, things change, sometimes for the better."

"If it's fought for the right reasons. As a minister, I can cite many examples of that from the Bible."

Ruth said, "Jerome, I'm sure Miss Gardner doesn't have time for that." She cut her dark eyes at Elizabeth. "Once you get him started, there's no such thing as a short story. If you're in these parts, you are always welcome at our church. You can hear him preach 'til your heart's content."

Elizabeth nodded. "That's very thoughtful. I might just do that. Where's your church."

Ruth raised her arm and pointed. "It's sort of out of the way. Seven miles north. First dirt road on the left past Black Creek. Ten years ago, we found an old abandoned church. It is on property that had been a big plantation—the Butler plantation. The owner took in Confederate soldiers who'd been injured in the war. Lot's of 'em boys died there. There's a Confederate cemetery on the north side of the church. Most of the plantation, except the church, cemetery, and an old barn, is gone. We heard a fire took the main house down. It was built originally as an Episcopal church. Erected like they did in parts of Europe. It's remained intact all these years."

Elizabeth looked at Reverend Thompson. "Are you an Episcopalian minister?"

He shook his head. "No ma'am. We don't define our religion by a specific denomination. Some folks say we lean toward the Pentecostal beliefs. I like to say that we take our direction plainly from the pages of the Bible. We believe God gives us tests in life…He tests our faith. And because of that, God protects us from evil. He allowed the serpent into the Garden of Eden. The beginning of man failed that test. We don't aim to fail no more."

"Does that mean you permit snakes in your church as part of your service? Maybe to display your faith in God…faith that you won't be bitten."

Ruth Thompson crossed her arms. Reverend Thompson pursed his wet lips, used two fingers to subtly twist the gold wedding band on his left hand. He said, "That's part of the reason. You come to our little church in the woods, and you'll witness the others."

"Do you go in the woods and swamps to catch your own snakes?"

Reverend Thompson said, "No, never. That's seeking confrontation. The serpents are always donated to us. And they aren't in short supply here in Mississippi. We keep 'em in a coop beyond the garage. I had a big cottonmouth brung to me. The fella told me it was called a preacher killer on account the snake had bit a preacher up near Tupelo."

"Did he die?" Elizabeth asked.

"The Lord takes us when it's our time to die. It was his time."

Elizabeth inhaled deeply, shifting her gaze between the pastor and his wife. "Thank you for the invitation. Oh, before I go…do you know how I might get in touch with Henry Griffin?"

Ruth said, "He doesn't have a home phone or a cell phone. Not sure where he lives 'cause I haven't been to his house."

Reverend Thompson said, "He may be in our church Sunday."

"He's a member of your church?"

Reverend Thompson grinned. "I'm not sure Henry is much of a joiner. He comes to church often. Listens to the sermons. And then he leaves."

Ruth said, "He always sits in the same place. He sits in the seventh pew. Our son, Lance, knows him 'bout as good as a body can."

"How's that?"

"Lance has done some tree trimming work with Henry. That was when Katrina come through and debris was everywhere, from Hattiesburg to the Gulf coast."

"Lance is a nice name," Elizabeth said. "Who chose that?"

"My brother did," said Reverend Thompson. "My brother, before his death, always liked the story of Sir Lancelot in medieval times. How Lancelot was noble, strong and fair. Ruth was about to give birth when Jeremiah died. He asked us to name the baby Lancelot if it was a boy."

Ruth smiled, "I shortened it to Lance. But Jerome calls him Lot, because it makes a reference to the role Lot played in the Bible. Sometimes Lance sits with Henry in the seventh pew."

EIGHTY-THREE

Elizabeth took a series of deep breaths as she drove off the Thompson property. She looked in the rearview mirror, Ruth Thompson still on the porch. No sign of her husband. Elizabeth glanced at the carving in the oak tree as she drove by, the preacher's words reverberating in her head. *'Henry says it's the face of the eighth angel in Revelation...in Armageddon. He said God revealed it to him.'*

After Elizabeth entered the highway, she drove past an open field where she could pull onto the shoulder of the road. She called Bradford and told him what she saw and heard. She added, "I think that Henry Griffin and the son of the Thompson's, Lance or Lancelot, or as Reverend Thompson calls him, Lot, are in this together."

"Elizabeth, hold just a second. I have the FBI list of known or suspected members of the group, STA. Something is ringing a bell." He paused for a few seconds. Elizabeth looked in her mirrors. A Jeep was coming down the road in her direction. Bradford said, "Henry Griffin is on that list. No known address. Lance Thompson is on the list as well."

"How about his father, Jerome, is he on there too?"

"Yes, and remember, I have thirty-seven names out of a suspected seventy-five or more. We have another puzzle piece that is now coming together in the picture."

"What's that?"

"The name Griffin...I did a background check on Detective Clements. His sister married a guy by the name of Donnie Griffin. I'd bet you that

Donnie and Henry are probably brothers. I can find out. So it appears that if Henry is pulling boards off the bridge, catching rattlesnakes with his bare hands, and carving wooden crosses…Detective Clements might turn his head if his sister married into the Griffin family."

"What do you do now to apprehend Henry Griffin?"

"We find out where he lives, and we bring him out."

"What if Lance Thompson is involved and he hears about the arrest and flees?"

"We'll take one down and then the other."

"What if you could get them both at once, and get them in a place where they won't be armed and their guard will be completely down?"

"Is that in their sleep?"

"No. It's in a church. Ruth Thompson said Henry Griffin always sits in the seventh pew. Her son attends the church. Tomorrow is Sunday. Maybe both of them will be there."

"You're suggesting we raid the church?"

"Yes. But I'll go in first—"

"No. You—"

"The Thompson's invited me. There won't be any suspicion."

"If Griffin is the serial killer, he'll recognize you."

"I'll go in late, sit in the back row and watch. I doubt that he'll be carrying a gun in the church. He's described as a big man who wears his hair in a gray ponytail. There can't be that many people of that description sitting in the seventh pew. From the back of the church, I can be wearing a wire and whispering to you and your team. I can fully describe the suspect for you, maybe ask someone if Lance is in attendance, and then prompt you when to enter."

"Meet me in my office. We need to go over this with Ed, the captain, and the rest of the team. How soon can you be here?"

"Maybe in a couple of hours. I'm close to the old church. I want to go there so I'll be more familiar with the place tomorrow."

"What if Henry Griffin happens to be there, or Lance Thompson?"

"It's Saturday. I'd say the odds are very low that anyone is near the place. If the church is unlocked, I'll go inside to get familiar with the layout."

"Elizabeth, text the address to me so I know where you are."

"I don't have an address. I have a location. I'll text it to you. It's past Black Creek on the property of a former plantation. A cemetery is near the church. Confederate solders are buried there. I'll see if there's a wooden cross on any of the graves."

EIGHTY-FOUR

Elizabeth looked in her rearview mirror after passing Black Creek. There was no oncoming traffic. She turned onto the first dirt road on the left and followed it through a majestic forest of two-hundred-year old live oaks, their massive limbs enveloped in swathes of Spanish moss. A flock of blackbirds flitted among the branches. She passed remnants of a foundation to a house covered in weeds. An old outbuilding looked swayback from time and nature. Half the structure was covered in a green blanket of kudzu vines.

Elizabeth rounded two curves in the dirt road and came upon something that looked like it has been transplanted from a medieval forest in England or Scotland to rural Mississippi. Nestled in a small grove and under the limbs of a mammoth live oak was a small church that reminded Elizabeth of the time she visited Rosslyn Chapel in Scotland. The church here in the woods had a remarkably similar Old World design inspired from Camelot, just on a lesser scale.

Elizabeth slowed her car and parked about one hundred feet from the entrance. She sat for a moment and stared at the church. It had the look of a small, noble fortress with the elegance of Arthurian design standing in the deep shade of Mississippi oaks.

She counted a dozen ornate turrets almost as high as the steeple and sharp-pitched roof. The front entrance had the stately appearance of an elegant church on a grand manor. Elizabeth almost expected to see a coat of arms somewhere near the doors, as well as feudal banners and flags with the family crest hanging on either side of the entrance.

There were no cars or trucks to be seen on the property or near the church. She could see a cemetery to the left, behind the church. Elizabeth intuitively touched the grip of the gun in her purse. She got out of the car, the purse on her right shoulder, her hand on the unzipped opening. She walked quietly across a hard-packed dirt path that led to the front entrance.

As Elizabeth stepped onto the portico, she turned to look back at her car and the primitive road she'd just traveled. No cars. No trucks. No sign of anyone. No engine noise. Only the sound of a crow cawing in the distance.

She stopped at the wooden front door and turned the handle. It was unlocked. She slowly pushed the door open, the hinges creaking, sunlight spilling into the dark recesses. The interior was simple but yet elegant in the use of light and space. Stained glass windows were on all four walls. The largest window, depicting Christ with his disciples, was behind the pulpit, the deep cues of red, blue, white and green were warm from sunlight.

She counted fourteen wooden pews, her eyes stopping on the seventh pew. Ruth Thompson's words resonated in her mind, *'He always sits in the same place. He sits in the seventh pew. Our son, Lance, knows him 'bout as good as a body can.'*

Elizabeth walked between the pews, the worn timber floor creaking under her shoes. The old church smelled of antiquity—the musty odor of aged stone, candle wax, and generations of human sweat and tears soaked deep into the pews. She could see a cobweb under one of the back pews. She walked toward the front of the church. Something moved. A mouse scurried toward a roll of carpet in one corner.

Elizabeth stepped toward the pulpit. She looked at the old stained glass window, the bottom section was square, the top was arch shaped, and the center point tapered into at slight apex. In the two corners above Christ and his disciples were two angels looking down, wings folded behind their backs. Elizabeth studied the eyes of both angels. One had an uncanny resemblance to the carving in the tree. Reverend Thompson's voice almost seemed to come from behind the pulpit. *'Henry says it's the face of the eighth angel in Revelation…in Armageddon. He said God reveled it to him.'*

Elizabeth heard a sound from outside the church. A vehicle was approaching. She walked toward the front entrance. Through the partially open door, she could see a pickup truck.

And the color was white.

EIGHTY-FIVE

Elizabeth wrapped her hand around the grip of her gun. She stood in the shadows of the alcove and looked outside the church. The pickup truck driver parked under the shade of a large live oak. She watched as he opened the door and got out. He was an old man. Elizabeth thought he was in his late-eighties, maybe older.

He wore pressed blue jeans and a white collared shirt buttoned at the top. He didn't look to be carrying a weapon. But he was carrying flowers. Red roses. She eased her gun back inside her purse and stepped onto the entryway.

The old man glanced at her car and then saw Elizabeth standing near the doorway. He lifted his left hand to shield the sun from his eyes, thick fingers swollen from arthritis. His shoulders were rounded, hair the color of new snow, face deeply lined, jowls and neck sagging. He cleared his throat. "How you doin' ma'am?"

Elizabeth smiled and stepped down from the porch. "Fine, thank you. Are you a member of this church?"

"For the last sixty-five years. I've seen a dozen preachers come and go. Outlived three of 'em."

"It's certainly a beautiful old church. You must be very proud of it."

"Yes ma'am, I am. It's been here twenty years before the Civil War. Lots of people have come to know Jesus in our little church. It's a good place for a wedding." He glanced toward the cemetery. "And it's seen plenty of folks buried on these grounds. Earle Butler built it from the design of an old church he'd seen in Scotland or England…can't remember which."

"Maybe the Rosslyn Chapel in Scotland?"

The old man lifted his head back, both unkempt white eyebrows raised. "Yes ma'am. That's the one. He had some of the stones used to build the church imported from Scotland. Took 'em five years to finish it on account of the distance and whatnot. The tales of King Arthur always fascinated Earle Butler. He wanted this place to look like something out of that world." The old man laughed, his laughter more of a high-pitched chortle. "Mr. Butler had jousting contests out here. He even had a round table in one room of the plantation. Yankees took it before they burned the place."

Elizabeth thought about what Reverend Thompson had said, '*My brother, before his death, always liked the story of Sir Lancelot in medieval times. He asked us to name the baby Lancelot if it was a boy.*' She said, "Maybe some of the locals joined him at the round table back in those days."

"They did. My great granddaddy was one. There were a couple of dozen through the years leading up to the war. Fellas like Crawford DuPont, Wyatt Porter and Travis Thompson." He grinned. "Most were cotton farmers or business owners who came out here to the plantation for some kinda reenactments they did. As a boy, I heard that Earle Butler even had a sword partially encased in a stone and put in his garden. The old folks said he called his black stallion horse Excalibur, too." He paused, his eyes taking in the strand of oaks, the church, outbuildings and the cemetery. "Yes, this is a special place."

"Who owns it today?"

"God does. I actually have the deed to it. But, upon my death, the church gets the remaining property. Are you wantin' to attend a service?"

"I thought about it…if that's okay? I heard about the old church and wanted to take a look. I hope you don't mind."

"Of course not. That's why we don't lock the door. God doesn't lock the door to Heaven. It's people that lock themselves out."

Elizabeth walked closer to the old man. He clutched the roses with both hands. She glanced at the side panels of the truck and then looked over at him. She could see cataracts in his hazel eyes, one eye slightly discolored. Elizabeth smiled. "May I ask…are the flowers for the service in the morning?"

He shook his head. "No, ma'am. They're for my wife. I lost her two years ago. We'd been married sixty years. Today is the anniversary of her death. She's buried here in the cemetery."

"I'm sorry."

He nodded. "She was a good woman. She tried to live her life according to the Bible. We had a fine life together. Raised two boys…at least we raised one to manhood."

Elizabeth looked across at the cemetery, waiting for the old man to elaborate. He didn't. An acorn fell from the oak, hitting the bed of his pickup. She asked, "You mind if I walk over to the cemetery, too? I've always found old cemeteries fascinating and a chronicle of local history."

He nodded. "Follow me." The old man led Elizabeth under the live oak, around the left side of the church and into a cemetery that covered at least an acre. There were no fancy monuments, just dozens of simple headstones beneath the trees. Many of the inscriptions on the markers were barely readable from time and wear. He stopped and used his left hand to point. "Over there, under that big pine, are twenty seven graves of Confederate boys. Most of 'em died during the war. One, my daddy, lived on 'till the new century but wanted to be buried back here when he passed."

"Where's your wife's grave?"

He pointed to the far left, near a red maple tree. "Georgina is over there. If you'd excuse me, I need to go speak with her."

"Of course." Elizabeth watched him walk through the cemetery, careful not to step directly on a grave. She looked back toward the Confederate burial site and approached it. Most of the headstones were still legible. She read many of the names. The average age of the solders appeared to be nineteen. One was not.

She read the inscription: *Jackson Griffin Born 1846 – Died 1935*

A small wooden cross was set next to the headstone.

Elizabeth didn't have to pick the cross up to know it had been made from the aged wood of the Shubuta Bridge. She heard the chants of a mourning dove in the trees.

Elizabeth looked back across the cemetery. The old man had placed the bouquet of roses next to his wife's headstone. He clasped his hands behind his back for a moment, his head bowed. And then he looked at the headstone. Elizabeth could tell he was speaking.

She watched him, an old man deeply missing his wife. An old man who's own father was buried thirty yards away surrounded by Confederate dead who shared a departed mission and a lost cause that helped usher an early death. She thought about the carving in the tree, the angels on the stained glass window in the old church, and she knew that she had to ask an elderly man a question that might be difficult for him to answer.

EIGHTY-SIX

The old man looked up as Elizabeth approached. She smiled. "The roses are lovely."

"They were always Georgina's favorite flower. She used to grow them, grew some of the finest in Mississippi."

"I never got your name. I'm Elizabeth Monroe. Pleased to meet you."

"My name's Shelby Griffin."

Elizabeth said nothing for a moment. Two squirrels chased each other around the girth of a wide oak tree. "You mentioned that you and your wife had two sons. May I ask their names?"

"Our oldest boy was Winston. The youngest is Henry." He paused and pointed to a grave marker next to his wife's headstone. "Winston's buried there. He died before his eighteenth birthday. As a parent, you never get over something like that."

"No…you never do. No parent expects to bury his or her child."

"Did you lose a child?"

"Yes…my daughter."

"I'm so sorry to hear that."

"You're right…a parent never gets over it. May I ask how Winston died?"

He glanced down at his wife's headstone, and then slowly raised his eyes to Elizabeth. She could see abrupt sorrow in his face, mouth turned down, his thoughts buried deeper than the dead in the cemetery. "Those boys, Henry and Winston, were like Cain and Abel. Georgina died from cancer…but her heart carried a sickness, a burden, for years." He paused, his eyes moist.

Elizabeth was silent, letting the old man continue when he could. After a few seconds, he said, "Winston died from a bullet to his heart. He and Henry had been cleaning guns in our basement. We heard the shot. Henry came running up the steps to the kitchen and told us his gun had accidently gone off and hit his brother in the chest." He looked at his son's headstone. The birdsong ended and a hush bore down on the cemetery like heavy air.

Elizabeth said nothing.

Shelby Griffin turned his head to her. "Those boys could never get along. It wasn't for the lack of trying on Winston's part…but his brother, Henry, never seemed to have the interest or ability to sincerely apologize for anything. He could act the part, though. Damn good at that."

Elizabeth waited a moment, gauging whether she should ask the question and how to phrase the question. "Do you think the shooting was an accident?"

He exhaled, a wheezing sound coming from deep in his chest. "I wanted to believe it was an accident…but even after all these years…I have my doubts. The seed of hate goes back earlier than Cain and Abel, the world's first murder. Before Georgina slipped the bonds of earth, she said one last prayer…and it was for Henry. She asked God to soften his heart and take out the hate…take out the darkness and the evil that always led him astray."

"Where is your son today?"

"I wish I could answer that. He comes and goes as he pleases. At one time, he lived in a trailer somewhere in the De Soto Forest. He pulls an Airstream trailer behind his truck and lives off the land. He likes to be by rivers. He hunts and fishes down on Pascagoula River."

"How does he earn a living?"

"He's a carpenter by trade. He can build a house from trees he fells. He cut trees in Montana and Alaska for a spell. He's got talent with his hands. As a boy, he'd climb trees like a squirrel. Used to stay way up in the tops of trees for hours. After the death of Winston, Henry got real quiet for long spells. He carries a worn Bible with him everywhere he goes. He was influenced by an older preacher we had here at the church for two years. Pastor

Ramsey knew the Bible, especially the Old Testament and Revelation, like nobody I've ever seen before or since."

"Where's Pastor Ramsey today?"

Shelby pointed to the right side of the cemetery. "He's buried not too far from the Confederate boys. Pastor Ramsey's death is a sort of a mystery. He was found dead in his garage, next to his tool bench. The coroner said he died from snakebite. But there was never any sign of a snake in that garage. Odd thing though, he was good with snakes. Used to catch 'em as a boy and sold 'em to zoos in Mississippi. He taught Henry how to catch snakes with his bare hands."

"When was the last time you saw Henry?"

"It's been about three weeks. He comes here to church if he's in the area." Shelby paused and glanced toward the church. "Maybe he'll be here tomorrow. I just never know."

"I was chatting with Pastor Thompson and his wife, Ruth. She'd given me directions to find the church. I want to take some photographs of it when the sunlight is lower in the sky. The Thompsons said they have a son named Lancelot. I was wondering if there was any connection to the story of the this place, the plantation and how Earle Butler tried to have his own version of Camelot out here."

Shelby nodded, considered what she said, his thoughts far away for a moment. Finally he said, "Since you asked, I'll tell you a story. Lance, that's what he really goes by, had an uncle that was in deep cahoots with the Klan. Kinda odd since his brother, Reverend Jerome, is a man of the cloth who leads by trusting in God. Many people believe the Klan was founded up in Tennessee. I'm sure what eventually became known as the KKK was started up there. But here in Mississippi, we've had our own versions of the Klan before there was a national name. And it began right here at this plantation."

"How? Was Butler the founder?"

"He was the original leader. Him and a fella named Zachariah Belmont. Before titles like Grand Wizard of the Klan and whatnot, they called themselves knights…like knights from King Arthur's time. Then they grew into names, such as the White Knights. And in the early 1920's, it wasn't only about the oppression of the Negro…it was about defying groups like Jews, Hispanics, just about anybody who immigrated here and didn't look or act like they did." He stared at the Confederate graves. "My heart is heavy for the boys in Confederate uniforms who are buried here and elsewhere. I know they died fighting for what they believed in, but what I believe in is the Holy Bible. And it tells us to seek good in others by displaying it ourselves. Those without sin cast the first stone…or fire the first minie ball, cannon or nuclear bomb. The result is the same…and for the most part…so is the cause. It just doesn't make it right, at least not in the eyes of God."

He stepped next to his wife's headstone, removed one rose and laid it beside his son's memorial. "Elizabeth, it was a pleasure talkin' with you. I need to be going. I feel a little vertigo comin on. It happens when I get tired."

"Can I help you back to your truck?"

"That would be fine, thank you."

She moved her purse strap to her left shoulder and used her right hand to hold the old man by his forearm, her right hand on his back to steady him. Together they walked slowly to his truck. She opened the door and helped him get behind the wheel. She said, "Looks like you left your keys in the ignition. Are you able to drive? I'd be happy to drive you home."

He sat a little straighter, looked at her through the open window, late afternoon sunlight behind Elizabeth's head. He made a weak smile. "I'll be fine. I hope you don't mind reminisces of an old man. I don't have much of an opportunity to talk to folks nowadays, especially a pretty lady like you. God never granted Georgina and I the blessings of a daughter. I often wish He had. I bet your father's very proud of you, Miss Monroe." He reached out and took her hand in his. "On my way home, I'm gonna say a little prayer for you. I think you're in need of one." He glanced at the church, deep purple shadows cast in the setting sun. "I hope you can get a nice photograph. The light looks like butter over the church."

"Thank you. I do appreciate you speaking with me today. I know some of the things you shared weren't easy to discuss."

He nodded his head. "You're a good listener. Not many folks are anymore. It's a dying art. People are too busy with their own thoughts, not wanting to hear others. And their eyes are glued to their phones and their short attention spans are disjointed. I got no use for cell phones. If you decide to visit for the Sunday sermon, and if Henry's here…I'll introduce you to him. He drives a truck like mine, except he has a tree trimming sign on either side. It's got a drawing of a lumberjack, and that's what he was in Montana." He squeezed her hand gently, started his truck and drove down the dirt road like he'd done so many times in the past.

Elizabeth called Bradford and said, "We need to talk right now."

"Where are you now?"

"Maybe standing on the crossroads between good and evil. I'm outside of an old church on land where the Klan was apparently born in Mississippi."

EIGHTY-SEVEN

Detectives Ed Milton and Mike Bradford listened intently to Elizabeth in a sheriff's office conference room. They sat at the table, drank black coffee from Styrofoam cups and took notes. She told them about her conversations with Reverend Jerome Thompson, his wife, Ruth, and her talk with Shelby Griffin in the church cemetery. "Henry Griffin drives that lumberjack truck. Now we just have to find him. Maybe he'll be at the church service, pretending to be a good churchgoer."

Bradford nodded. "That's the place to pick him up if he shows."

Detective Milton put his pen down, leaned back in his chair and said, "It sounds to me like Henry Griffin, the Reverend Thompson, Lance or Lancelot Thompson and maybe others in the church are not too far removed from Zachariah Belmont and his crazy spewing about hate and wrath."

Bradford said, "What we do know is that, according to the FBI, the three you just mentioned are part of the group, STA. FBI intelligence tells us that, according to video and pictures shot on the scene, the STA members were not only at the recent protest rally and demonstration in Hattiesburg, but they've attended the ones in Jackson, Macon, Memphis and Charlottesville. Henry Griffin apparently wears a ball cap, dark glasses and hair back in a long ponytail. He appears to be the size of a NFL linebacker. We just gotta find him."

"We can take a dozen guys from SWAT to the church tomorrow. Like Elizabeth said, she can be wired and give us the cue to take him down...best bet will be after the service when he's outside and heading to his truck. My goal is to take him, and this guy Lance, if he's there, without firing a round. No threat to bystanders. Just a clean fast takedown."

Bradford nodded. He clicked a few keys on a computer and a satellite image of the church was displayed from a projector onto a white wall. "I agree. This is the satellite imagery of the church and surrounding property. In the close-up, you can see the areas our men can enter. With the underbrush and heavy woods, officers and vehicles can pretty much be unseen until you cue us, Elizabeth. You said the service begins at 10:30. We'll set up a perimeter force way before that time. You go in the church, take your seat in the last pew and keep us apprised of what's happening and who's there. Describe Henry Griffin—clothes he's wearing, features. Same for Lance Thompson, if he's there, too."

Elizabeth said, "What happens if they don't show up?"

"We track down Lance Thompson. Bring him here, see if he'll turn state's witness for a reduced charge, and go hunt for the mountain man, Henry Griffin."

Milton said, "Unfortunately, at this time, we don't know if or how complicit Lance Thompson is or is not with Griffin. All we have to go on is the information you got today from Thompson's parents. Lance helps Henry Griffin in the tree trimming business. What we want to learn is the answer to this question: Does Lance help Griffin in the sick matter of homicide?"

———

On her drive home, Elizabeth looked at her phone screen when she stopped for a traffic light. She stared at the live images of her home, indoor and outside. She could see the ferns moving in the breeze on the front porch. She saw a leaf, pushed by wind, flop across her back deck.

But she couldn't see Jack.

Maybe he was killed by Henry Griffin, she thought. *Maybe Lance Thompson took him from the porch.* She thought about the images she'd seen on screen. The look on Jack's face as someone came up the porch steps. Sweet Jack, trusting and unruffled, quickly moving into attack mode. Ears back and flat. Fangs barred. Body tense.

And then the gloved hand removed the camera. Followed by a burst of white light and dark, the lens destroyed. Elizabeth thought about the image. She pulled into her driveway, the lights blazing, no sign of Jack in the drive or on the porch. She opened her purse, touched the pistol grip, locked her car and entered her home. She disarmed the alarm and reset it. In the kitchen, she flipped through the archive of the security camera images, looking for the date that Jack went missing.

She found the image of the glove. She played it. Less than two seconds. Almost a blur, but enough time for her to freeze the frame and study the picture. The glove appeared to be a burnt orange color. Somewhere she'd seen a gloved hand like it or very similar to it.

But where? Think. She closed her eyes, trying to draw mental pictures to match it to the image on the security camera.

The groundskeeper.

The man at the cemetery the day she and Bradford first saw Zachariah Belmont's grave and the first wooden cross. *What was his name?* She clenched her fists, the conversation returning to her. He'd worn work gloves the color of a persimmon and he'd said, *'Pleased to meet y'all. Most folks call me LT. Kinda like lieutenant. I served in Iraq, but I damn sure wasn't a lieutenant.'*

"No, you creep, you weren't," Elizabeth mumbled. "But I'd bet the LT stands for Lance or Lancelot Thompson."

She picked up her phone to call Mike Bradford.

EIGHTY-EIGHT

wo SWAT snipers looked through their riflescopes. One focused on
the front door to the church in the woods. The other man looked
through the scope at the back door. Both men were dressed in camouflage
and dark face paint. Both were approximately seventy yards away from their
potential targets. They found clear paths to shoot through the canopies of
trees. The men wore radio gear—ear and mouthpieces.

From the nearby perimeter, Detectives Bradford and Milton directed
the operation. They'd arrived in Jeeps and four-wheel-drive trucks, parked in
the scrub bush and woods surrounding the property. All the deputies were
heavily armed, Kevlar bulletproof vests on each one. They watched and
waited for instructions.

And all eyes were on Elizabeth.

She parked her car under one of the live oaks and got out. There were
more than two dozens cars and trucks near the church. The parishioners
had gone inside. The church doors wide open in a yawn, piano music and
singing coming from inside.

Elizabeth touched the small microphone under her blouse and asked,
"Can you hear me?"

Bradford, standing with Ed Milton and two SWAT deputies near a
strand of trees, said, "Yes. We hear you clearly."

"I'm going inside. I only see one white truck, and I think that's the truck
that Shelby Griffin drives."

"Maybe his son has another vehicle or is running late."

"I'll soon let you know. Henry Griffin shouldn't be too hard to spot. And I know what LT, AKA, Lance Thompson looks like, so do you, Mike." She glanced toward the woods. Every person in the operation was hidden. Elizabeth knew they were there, but if she didn't know, there would be no visible indication that more than a dozen deputies were watching her every move.

The minute she stepped inside, the visuals would end. And the oral communications would be it, assuming she could speak without drawing suspicion. *The great thing about a church,* she thought, *was that you could whisper prayers and no one would be suspicious.* When she arrived at the open door, it was easy to hear the congregation singing *How Great Thou Art.* Just before she entered, she turned and glanced at the surrounding woods, the dirt road leading up to the church. She said a silent prayer and stepped inside.

An overweight woman, with thick glasses and a yellow sundress, played the upright piano in the corner of the area near the pulpit, the loose skin of her upper arms bouncing. Reverend Thompson led the congregation in song, his voice slightly off-key, but still singing at the top of his lungs. Most of pews were filled with people. They used hand fans to circulate stale air around their heads. The church smelled of sweat and plywood.

Elizabeth wanted to sit before the singing ended. Reverend Thompson spotted her. He nodded, smiled, and continued singing. A younger man, tall and beanpole thin, white shirt, black pants above his ankles, gelled brown hair, was near the pulpit singing. Elizabeth assumed he was an assistant pastor. She saw two wooden boxes to the right of the stage. Both were about the size of large suitcases, and both had glass tops. Locked.

She looked at the seventh pew, the right side and then on the left side of the center aisle. There was no sign of a large man wearing a long, gray ponytail. She did see Shelby Griffin in the third row. He didn't appear to be singing. He wore a plaid Western shirt and looked toward the largest stained glass window.

Elizabeth stood next to the rear pews, nodded and smiled at those seated. There was some space to the far right side, enough room for her to sit and speak softly into the microphone without being understood by those sitting nearby. She made her way there and sat just as the song was winding down. She lowered her head, lips as close to the mic as possible and whispered, "No sign of either subject."

Through her earpiece, she heard Bradford say, "Understood. We'll wait."

Reverend Thompson stopped singing as the song ended, and he placed his hymnal on the lectern and picked up a worn black Bible. He looked out into the congregation and said, "I feel the presence of Jesus here tonight!"

"Amen!" shouted someone in the congregation.

Thompson smiled, opened his Bible, read silently for a second, the hand fans fluttering, a mother hushing a child. Thompson stepped from behind the podium, nodded at the man in the short trousers and said, "Jesus didn't need the trappings of his society during his time. He concentrated on healing and helping. Ask yourselves this: do you really need to consult Google for answers to your questions when the answer is here. Right here!" He held up the Bible. "The answer is and always will be in God's Word!"

"Yes, Lord!" shouted a woman in the second pew.

Thompson nodded. He paced the stage like a caged animal and said, "Our society today is heading in the wrong direction. It's an abomination of the Word. We have got to unite or we'll be enveloped in a Sodom and Gomorrah that will dwarf the original by billions of people."

He preached for a few minutes about the downfall of mankind, his hair becoming soaked with sweat. "It all started in the beginning in the Garden of Eden. Everyday since that time, mankind has been tempted by evil. But when you trust in the Lord, the temptation can be defeated. There is a shield against evil!" He stepped closer to the locked boxes.

There was a sound that caused a hush across the church. It was the sound of a rattlesnake. People sat straighter. The odor of perspiration flowed from the hand fans. The man near the podium stepped over to the boxes. He fished in his tight pockets for something. He pulled out two keys on a ring, squatted down and then unlocked the first box.

Thompson stood next to the boxes, facing his congregation. "The power of belief…the power of the Holy Spirit will keep the serpents from inflicting harm if you truly believe. What happened in Eden can be defeated here today and tomorrow if you do not fear evil on account of the power of God."

"Amen, Pastor," shouted an older man.

Thompson opened the glass covering of the first box and lifted out a large rattlesnake. He held the snake by its thick midsection, lifting it over his head and stepping to the center of the stage. "Believe!" he shouted. The sound of the snake's rattle bounced from all four corners. The big snake's triangular head staring out at the people, it's black tongue flickering—tasting the fear in the air. Its eyes like black pearls. "This is the power of the Holy Spirit!" cried Thompson. His wet hair hung like seaweed.

His wife, Ruth, stood from the front row and yelled, "Amen! The Spirit is here today!"

Elizabeth could barely hear Bradford over the noise in the church. He asked, "What the hell is going on in there?"

EIGHTY-NINE

Reverend Thompson's upper lip curled up in an edgy grin. He nodded at his wife, stepped over to the box, set the rattlesnake back inside and locked the glass. His assistant licked his red lips and unlocked the second wooden box. He stepped back as Thompson watched the snake for a moment, said a prayer, reached in and grabbed a large water moccasin behind the head and picked it up. The snake hissed. Mouth gaping. Head twisting. Gums ghostly white. The entire mouth the color of cotton. The snake hissed again, louder.

There was a collective gasp from the congregation. This snake was different from the rattler. Somehow more sinister. Aggressive. Dark olive green. Thick body. Muscular. Opening its mouth wide, the fangs like opaque daggers. Reverend Thompson watched the moccasin closely. He used two hands to handle it.

Some people raised their hands, palms out. Others rocked slightly in their seats and whispered prayers. The woman behind the piano touched her sagging neck with two fingers, her mouth turned down. A baby cried on its mama's hips.

Thompson stood in the center of the stage, both hands still on the moccasin. He looked at his flock. The parishioners clasped hands together in prayer. One woman spoke in tongues. The air in the room was hot from body heat, breathing and the lack of air conditioning. The moccasin added the odor of fear. Thompson stood under a small ceiling mounted spotlight.

His eyes were wide as silver dollars. He looked at his people, each one ready to see him handle the snake and set it back inside the safety of the box.

"Believe!" he shouted. "I feel the protection of the Holy Spirit in here tonight. The serpent will be denied its desire to inject evil in us. Believe!"

"We believe!" yelled a man with a skinny wife and two blond towhead boys, the boys looked up in fear and awe as the snake's black tongue flickered from its white lips.

Thompson said, "The Lord protected Daniel in the lion's den and Jonah in the belly of the whale. Tonight he protects me." He released one hand from the snake's head and kept the other hand on the reptile's midsection. For a moment the moccasin did nothing. It stared into the crowd of people, its eyes following the back and forth motion of hand fans.

Thompson smiled, his eyes now wild, sweat rolling from his forehead under the light. His shirt soaked at the armpits. He said, "The serpent may have been in the garden but he's not here tonight."

It happen so fast that most of the congregation wasn't sure they saw it.

The moccasin twisted and struck. It sank its fangs deep into Thompson's forearm, the snake's muscles pumping venom into his bloodstream.

Thompson looked dumbfounded. His smile melted. He stared at the snake for a moment before dropping it onto the stage. People stood. One woman screamed. Ruth Thompson rushed to her husband's aid. The snake slithered toward the boxes. Thompson looked at his forearm, blood dripping from two holes down his arm and onto the old hardwood. His mouth twitched.

He gazed down at his shocked congregation and said, "Don't be scared. This is not the first time I have been bitten. It's been six times over twenty years, and I'm still standin' here preaching." Sweat poured down his face. People were standing. His assistant tried to capture the moccasin, the snake coiling and striking at him, hissing. He jumped back, swallowed dryly, the snake holding its ground.

"Everything is gonna be fine brothers and sisters," Thompson said, the blood now spurting out of his wound each time his heart beat. "I defy your poison! God defies you!"

Ruth stood next to her husband, not sure what to do. She reached for his injured arm, now beginning to swell. He pulled away. "No! Believe! Have faith, Ruth."

Elizabeth stood. She stepped around the pew and walked toward the center aisle, people standing, praying, and some crying. Thompson saw her and smiled. "Miss Gardner," he said. "I'm delighted you could visit with us tonight." She looked over at Shelby Griffin who had a perplexed expression on his face, as if Reverend Thompson had made a mistake with her last name.

Elizabeth approached the stage. She looked up at Thompson. The blood from his arm had formed a puddle the size of a saucer next to his shoe. She said, "I'm calling 9-1-1. You must get to a hospital immediately."

"No! God only takes us when it's our time. He still has a lot of reform work for me to do on earth."

In her earpiece she could hear Bradford, "We have a snakebite kit on one of the Jeeps. I'm coming inside."

She wanted to respond but felt a dozen people watching her. She stared at Thompson's left hand, the fingers swelling, bloating. He looked down at her, his eyes wet with perspiration and tears, soaked hair like seaweed on his head. He raised his injured arm and pointed to her. "Mark 16:18…says and they will pick up snakes by their hands, and they will drink their poison… and it will not hurt them…."

His eyelids fluttered, and he collapsed to his knees. He stared at Elizabeth, his face confused, in disbelief. He looked toward the stained glass window, his breathing shallow. He mumbled, "Then the eighth angel took the censer, filled it with fire from the altar, and hurled it on the earth. And so is the wrath of God for the sin of man."

Reverend Thompson shuddered once. He fell on his back, head against the wooden stage. He mumbled, "It's so dark…why…." He took one final breath and the blood stopped dripping from the two holes in his swollen arm. He died with his eyes wide, frightened.

Elizabeth stepped to the corner as three men ran up to their fallen preacher. They openly cried, tears running down red, hot faces. Ruth buried her face in her hands and sobbed. Shelby Griffin stood slowly, stared at the fallen preacher, two men trying to catch the loose snake. The old man's eyes somehow incapable of any more tears.

Elizabeth whispered into the microphone, "Forget the snakebite kit. Thompson's dead. No sign of Lance Thompson or Henry Griffin. His father, Shelby, heard Reverend Thompson call me Miss Gardner, the name I used when I spoke with them. And Shelby is heading for the exit."

Bradford said, "Got it. Maybe he'll tell us where is son is."

"I'm worried that he'll tell his son we're looking for him."

Elizabeth walked around the shocked crowd and followed Shelby Griffin out the door.

NINETY

A half-dozen people looked like they were going to vomit. They stood outside the church, crying and trying to comfort each other. One middle-aged woman, with short, mousy brown hair, sat on the steps and tried to light a cigarette. Her thin lips clamped around the cigarette butt, her hand with the lighter shaking uncontrollably. Two small children played tag. A man in a blue shirt buttoned to his neck was on the phone speaking to a 9-1-1 operator. He told them what happened and to send an ambulance immediately.

Shelby Griffin stopped to hug one woman, patting her on the back and trying to console her. The woman's round face was flush, cheeks wet, hair flat from the heat inside the church. "There's nothin' we could do," she said through sobs. "It happened so fast. Reverend Thompson didn't want nobody to call the ambulance. Now, it's too late." She used a damp tissue to wipe her tears, dark eyeliner makeup smeared like raccoon eyes.

Shelby said, "It never should have happened. I feel real bad for him and deeply sorrowful for Ruth and Lance. I never thought we should have snakes in the worship service. Reverend Thompson was the only preacher who ever brought serpents in our church. I told him I didn't think it was a good thing, downright dangerous. I hate being proven right like this. It's horrible…a senseless death." The woman nodded and blew her nose in a wadded Kleenex, a tattoo of Daffy Duck on her thick left wrist.

Shelby walked slowly toward his truck parked under the shade of a tree. He glanced up as Elizabeth approached. "Mr. Griffin, I'm so sorry that happened in there. I didn't know Reverend Thompson or his wife Ruth well, but they were kind and considerate when I was lost and stopped by their house for directions."

He looked at her, spattered light breaking through the trees and falling on his weathered face. He tilted his head, eyes empty, as if he was having a hard time hearing her. He swatted at a blowfly. "I'm glad they invited you to our church. I feel awful that he was bit by the snake and died so quickly. He always told us if it happened, not to interfere because it was simply his time, and God was calling him home. I've seen too much death, especially in the Korean War."

"Do you believe that God was calling him home...or do you believe he was careless and took risks he didn't have to take?"

— —

Detective Ed Milton and Bradford listened closely to the conversation from their earpieces. Milton looked over at Bradford, three SWAT officers standing close, and said, "Emergency dispatch is heading our way. And they have no fucking idea we're standing in the woods like a bunch of eagle scouts. Jerome Thompson, one of the guys on the STA list just died. His son isn't there, according to Elizabeth. And Henry Griffin could be cuttin' trees back in Montana for all we know."

Bradford held up one hand. He used the index finger on his other hand to steady the earpiece in his ear. "Wait a sec, Ed. Elizabeth is trying to get the old man to tell her where his son is...."

— —

Shelby Griffin looked down at the back of his left hand. A one-inch cut was partially scabbed, inflamed, an old wound that looked like a split in upholstery. He raised his faded eyes up to her. "I've made it a habit never to second guess the Lord. He gives us free will and choices. Evil is always there in the shadows. I don't think Reverend Thompson was right or wrong. It was his decision, and he felt right about doin' it." He paused and swallowed, looked at Elizabeth through probing eyes. "Let me ask you something, Elizabeth. Why did the preacher look at you and call you Miss Gardner?"

"Maybe he forgot my name. Maybe I reminded him of someone named Gardner."

"One thing he was real good at doin' was remembering the names of folks. He had it down to an art. He wouldn't see someone in the congregation for months, and when they came, he'd greet them after the service, look them in the eye and remember their first and last names. He never missed. Why'd he miss with you?"

"Perhaps it was because he'd just been bitten by a highly venomous water moccasin and was dying, hallucinating or both."

Shelby looked back toward the front of the church, more people gathering but yet lost—lost for words, looking for a reason tucked somewhere in the gospel of Reverend Thompson and his final impasse with a deadly snake. "Miss Monroe," said the old man, "Did you really come here to partake in our church service…or is there another reason?"

"I wanted to see what the service was like. To get a feel for the history of this property and the church with a history that predates the Civil War."

"What are you looking for?"

"What do you mean?"

"I don't think you're looking for salvation or redemption. I think it is something even deeper, if that exists."

Elizabeth said nothing, the sobs of the parishioners coming from the front of the church. She asked, "What do you mean?"

"By the grace of God, I've lived a long time. What I saw in the Korean War…the forgotten war…I can never forget. What evil man is capable of doing to his fellow man defies sense and moral consequences. It just is… like some parasite that can't be extracted from the human heart. I've thought long and hard about all that, and I'm no closer to understanding it today than I was seventy years ago. I told you how my son, Winston died. May I ask what took the life of your child?"

"It's not what…it's who? Molly was murdered. Shot in her head and buried under the carcass of a deer in the woods."

"I'm so sorry to hear that. But I'm not surprised at what you just told me because it's part of you now. Probably always will be, and that's sad. Did they ever find the person responsible for her death?"

"No."

"Is that why you're here? Did you hope to find him in our house of worship?"

"I think you believe your son Henry killed your son Winston, and it was no accident."

The old man said nothing. His nostrils opened wider, breathing quicker, chest expanding up and down. Elizabeth said, "And I can tell by your reaction that you think I'm right."

"I have to go now."

There was the wail of sirens in the distance, growing closer. "Mr. Griffin, in the last month, someone has murdered three people. Two were students in my class at the university in Hattiesburg. One was a man who wrote an editorial for the newspaper highly critical of hate groups...groups like the Klan. And according to you, we're standing where it was formed in Mississippi. No Camelot here, only an abyss of fear and hate. I think your son killed those people, and he will kill at least four more—a total of seven to match the seven bowls of God's wrath. And after that he may try to kill hundreds if not thousands more, either in an attack he does by himself or with others from the STA. Please, for the love and grace of God...tell me where I can find Henry."

The old man looked like he'd been hit in the gut. He shuffled toward his truck, fumbled with his keys to open it. Elizabeth was right behind him. "Please, Mr. Griffin...Henry's sick. We can get him treatment. Get him off the street, protect his life and save the lives of others."

He stood next to the open truck door, holding the frame with one bent hand. His eyes narrowed. "You think Henry was the one who killed your daughter?"

"I don't know. Maybe."

He grabbed the steering wheel and slowly pulled himself up onto the seat, like an old cowboy trying to get in the saddle for the last roundup. He turned and looked at her. "I don't know where he is. But If I were lookin' for him, I'd start at Lance Thompson's place. He lives in a trailer on nineteen acres of land south of here. It's past Clara on Highway 63. Go beyond Mill Creek to Pine Grove Road. Take a left and its down at the end of the road. You won't see the trailer from the road. There's no mailbox. Look for a steer head—the kind you'd find in the desert out West. It's nailed to a big pine tree. His driveway is dirt. Henry, Lance and a dozen or so others meet there from time to time. I warned them all to end this vendetta they have for groups they don't like."

Elizabeth touched his hand on the doorframe. "Thank you, Mr. Griffin."

"If you're callin' the law, and I know you are, please don't kill my boy. Maybe he'll seek salvation, repent and truly ask God to forgive him for his sins." He looked across the cemetery property just as an ambulance and two fire trucks rumbled up to the church in a cloud of billowing dust. He stared at the cemetery and said, "It was Georgina's last prayer…she prayed that Henry would find deliverance and redemption through knowing the love and grace of Christ."

Shelby started his truck, wiped a single tear from his sunken cheek, and he drove past the paramedics who bolted into the church, clutching bags of lifesaving gear. They would soon carry Reverend Jerome Thompson out on a metal gurney with a white sheet over his stark face. It would cover eyes that were locked into a fright he saw coming as he took his last breath on earth.

Elizabeth watched the old man drive slowly down the dirt road. She almost looked away just as he followed the road to the left. From that angle, she could see his silhouette. And she could see him put a phone to his ear.

NINETY-ONE

Detectives Bradford and Milton gathered the SWAT team around one of their black Range Rovers before they left the church property. Elizabeth removed her hidden microphone and watched as the detectives and the SWAT team looked at satellite maps and discussed their options.

Bradford studied topography maps of the land and trailer that Lance Thompson owned. He considered the best ways to enter and exit at the lowest probability of detection and retaliation. Milton used another computer to search for any arrest records that Thompson might have had.

Milton looked up from the laptop and said, "Lancelot Calvin Thompson...is his full name. Served six months in the county jail for assault in a bar fight. He's had a string of different grunt jobs, including that of a gravedigger and a ditch digger. He's worked as a bouncer. Arrested for B&E in 2016. He beat it because the homeowner refused to testify. Thompson has worked as a tree trimmer and a ride-share driver."

Bradford said, "Maybe he's the one using the stun gun on the victims and delivering them to Griffin."

"We need to get to Thompson's place stat. I can call in and have Judge Wallace's assistant send a digital warrant to us. Ike can print it in the van."

Bradford glanced around. "Do it! Lance Thompson's mother or someone else from the church will call him, if they haven't already, to tell him his daddy's dead. The property is forty-five minutes from here with blue lights and no sirens."

They made tactical reconnaissance plans and issued orders to the members of the SWAT team. Within five minutes, they were ready to leave.

Elizabeth said, "I think they've already been alerted."

"How?" Bradford asked.

"Shelby Griffin. When I spoke with him in the cemetery next to his wife and son's graves, he told me he had no use for cell phones. When he was driving off the church property, I saw him hold one to his ear. I think he called Henry and warned him. So the last place they might be, since Shelby gave me directions, is Lance Thompson's trailer out in the woods."

"Maybe," said Bradford. "But right now that's all we have. And that's where we're going."

"I want to go with you."

"I'm sorry, Elizabeth. You aren't trained for this, and I don't have an extra vest for you. So the answer is no. It's too dangerous." He turned to leave. "Let's go guys!"

Elizabeth gripped his forearm. "I need to speak with you for a second."

He looked at the team and said, "You men head out. Follow Ed. I'll catch up."

Elizabeth watched them jog to their vehicles. She looked at Bradford. "I've been part of this since the beginning. I know I don't have tactical training, but I'd go toe-to-toe with any man on your team at the range—"

"The answer is no."

"Mike, I don't expect you to have me approach the trailer with a SWAT team. But I can stay back in your car on the perimeter, be another set of eyes for you in case someone approaches while your guys are going through the house and property. I have a pistol in my purse. So I'll be fine sitting in the car, and it might keep your men safer."

Bradford looked at her, watched his team pull away. He took a deep breath, the Kevlar vest tight around his chest. "Okay, Elizabeth. Get in. I may be fired for doing this, but it won't be the first time. It could be very dangerous...I just don't want to risk anything happening to you. "

She smiled and touched the back of his hand. "Thank you."

NINETY-TWO

The sheriff's convoy stopped at the end of the country road deep in a rural section of Wayne County. Tall pine trees lined on both sides of the rustic road. Detective Milton stopped his black Jeep and looked at a steer head skull and horns attached to a large pine. He held his radio microphone near his mouth and said, "X marks the spot, and here the X is what's left of a big ol' steer that's seen better days."

Bradford pulled up in his Range Rover opposite Ed Milton. Elizabeth watched Bradford use his radio to give final instructions to his men. When he finished, he looked at her and said, "Remember, stay in the vehicle. Got it?"

"If I see someone approaching, slowing down near the driveway or turning in, I'll call you."

He nodded as his phone buzzed. He looked at the ID. The captain was calling. Bradford answered and the captain said, "We got another homicide. Body was found with the damn word *wrath* on the forehead. The victim was a twenty-year-old male. He was found in an alley off Front Street."

"Was there a wooden bowl on the body?"

"Yes."

"What was in it?"

"A candle. You need to get down there as soon as you can."

"We're just about to go on a SWAT raid at the house of one of the perps who we think is responsible for these deaths."

"Milton's with you, right?"

"Yes."

"Okay. Tell him what happened. I'll send Bud Peterson to the scene on Front Street. Be careful, Mike."

Bradford disconnected. He looked over at Elizabeth. "You heard at least half of the conversation. "We have a fourth body."

"Where."

"Alley behind Front Street. Vic's male. Young. Probably a college kid. And he probably attended the rally. Pissed off the wrong people, the Sons of the Transformation of America, which might as well be the sons of anarchy." He paused and exhaled. "I'll tell Ed and the rest of the team." He spoke into his microphone. "Let's go in, just like we planned it."

The SWAT team pulled far off the road on the opposite side of the entrance to the property. They parked beneath trees and tried to hide their vehicles in the scrub oaks. Within seconds the team unloaded gear, clutched assault rifles and began infiltrating the property.

A doublewide trailer, faded from inattention, sat in a small clearing. There was a wooden porch built onto the front of the trailer, two plastic chairs and a faded red umbrella, the canvas sagging like a limp birdwing. Scrawny chickens strutted around weeds that managed to sprout in the hard-packed dirt yard. A yellow cat sat under one of the chairs on the deck.

Two chicken coops were near a small metal, barn-like structure. There was a large shed behind the trailer. A windmill rotated in the breeze, water guzzled up through a PCV pipe and emptied into a big galvanized tank near an enclosed fence. A malnourished brown and white horse stood beyond the fence. Black flies darted near the horse's wet eyes.

The SWAT team made a half circle around the property. Bradford studied the trailer through a pair of binoculars. One dark blue Toyota Camry sat in the driveway. He spoke into his radio microphone. "Let's roll!"

The team converged in a tight circle. Three larger members of the group ran to the front porch, other men covered the sides and back of the trailer. One sniper looked through the crosshairs of a riflescope, waiting for any sign of movement or a hostile target.

The tallest SWAT deputy kicked open the front door with one strike of the combat boot on his right foot. The door flew open and the men entered. "Police! Down on the floor!"

No one was there.

They quickly moved from room to room. "Clear!" from the kitchen "Clear!" from the bedrooms. Within a minute, they had done a preliminary search of the doublewide.

"All I could find is a mess," said one deputy to Bradford.

"No pictures of a wife or kids," said another deputy with wide shoulders. "Looks like this guy lives alone."

Bradford nodded and began taking a closer look at the interior of the home. He turned to Milton and said, "There are out-buildings scattered around the place. Have some men check them out."

Milton nodded. "He turned toward two deputies and said, "Jake, you and Ricardo give it a look. Let's keep Roy in sniper position." He followed Bradford into the kitchen. Dirty dishes in the sink. Three empty Budweiser cans on the table stained from cigarette burns.

Bradford put on gloves and looked through junk mail on the table, and flipped through old newspapers. A manila file folder was under a stack of tactical weapons and gun magazines. He leafed through the file, stopped and read a handwritten letter. He let out a low whistle.

"What do you have?" asked Milton.

"This guy's nuts. In this unfinished letter or manifesto, he's giving examples of Hitler's greatest achievements and other rambling hate group stuff." He picked up a second piece of paper. "Oh shit. Here's a receipt for one ton of ammonium nitrate. It indicates the delivery was picked up three weeks ago in Jackson. You can make a hellava big bomb with that."

"The question is…where is it now?" He peered out the window, watched his men approach the shed.

Bradford shook his head. "Elizabeth thought they might try something on a grand scale. We gotta find these perps, and now."

— —

Four deputies walked around the perimeter of a small barn. The door almost fell off the hinges as they entered. There was nothing but three bales of hay and an engine block from a car sitting on two sawhorses. They continued searching the property. They kicked opened the door to the shed, which was almost as large as a barn. A rat ran behind some burlap sacks in the far back corner. There was an older model tractor parked inside near bags of fertilizer and farm tools. The men used flashlights to look through some of the items stacked on the lined metal shelves.

One deputy said, "Nothing except lots of dull tools, small motors, grease and dirt. It's clear. Wherever the bad guys are, it's sure as hell not in this place."

The deputy nodded, keyed his radio microphone and said, "All clear."

Ed Milton heard the call and said, "Maybe it's time to head back."

Bradford nodded. "We need some help from the feds to run all these STA guys down. Roust 'em. Somebody knows where Griffin and Thompson are hiding out. Now that there's a fourth vic, they're probably in some dive bar celebrating their mission and the latest killing of another kid."

Bradford's phone buzzed. It was Elizabeth. He answered and she said, "Mike, a black pickup truck drove slowly by the entrance to the driveway. The guy hit his brakes, almost stopped and then drove on down the road."

"Did you get his plate number?"

"No...sorry. I didn't think to get it. Did you find anything?"

"Nobody's here. Found a receipt for a shit load of ammonium nitrate and a rambling letter. I'm not sure who wrote it because it's not signed. I left it on the table."

"What's the premise of the letter?"

"Religion. Philosophy. The genius of Hitler and Stalin. Nothing tied directly to the killings."

"It's the indirect stuff that worries me. Can I see it?"

"Sure. I'll go back inside and get a phone shot of it before the evidence team swoops in and packs some of this stuff up."

"May I join you? If you've cleared the area, I'd just like to see the environment in which Lance Thompson lives. For a psychological profiler, that often speaks volumes."

"Okay, but make it quick. We need to call it here and go find these guys."

NINETY-THREE

Elizabeth put on gloves, stood in the dirty kitchen, and read the letter. Bradford and Milton waited, the sound of police radios popping from SWAT members standing on the porch. Elizabeth set the letter down on the table and snapped a picture of it. She turned to Bradford and Ed Milton. "I think this letter would be good to include as evidence."

Milton said, "All right. What do you read between the lines? Seems to be a lot of verbiage about nothing."

"For the most part, it is just that. However, if Thompson wrote it, the letter shows a parallel kind of reasoning with the writings we found in Zachariah Belmont's manifesto, *Retribution.*"

"What the hell's that?"

Bradford said, "I mentioned it to you. Elizabeth found some of the propaganda in a pamphlet Zachariah Belmont wrote back in 1918…right after the Shubuta Bridge hangings."

Elizabeth said, "It's a dangerous philosophy that mixes the Bible with Belmont's own brand of hate for people who don't look or think like him." She glanced around the kitchen and walked into the living room. She looked at cigarette butts in an ashtray on the coffee table. Newspapers and magazines stacked in one chair. A paper plate with dried barbecue sauce smeared on it sat on top of the stack. A beer can was on the glass coffee table. No coaster under the can. She looked at Bradford and Milton, and said, "The serial killer is what behavioral profilers would call organized. Almost methodical. Lance Thompson is the opposite. Disorganized. He may be playing a role in the killings, but his hand—his unique signature, is not there. That, I think, belongs to Henry Griffin.”

Bradford nodded. “Let’s get out of here. The place stinks. We’re ready to let forensics in here to go over the place”

They exited the house with two members of the SWAT team following them. Milton said, “Maybe Lance Thompson is at his job.”

Bradford shook his head. “It’s Sunday. I doubt if he’s working at a cemetery on Sunday.” He looked over at the newer model Camry parked in the dirt driveway; a rooster was sitting in the shade beneath the car. “If he’s doing his ride-share job, you’d think he’d use his Camry. You said the county records show he owns the Toyota and a Chevy truck.”

Milton folded his arms across his chest. “Maybe he and Henry Griffin are sitting somewhere churning out the wooden bowls for their next kills.”

The men watched one deputy carry a bolt cutter. Bradford asked, “Where you going with that?”

“Jenkins needs it. Said they went back in the shed to take a closer look at the bags of fertilizer. He cut open a couple of them. They’re good ol’ black cow manure. But the guys pulled up a bail of hay on the floor and found a trapdoor. There’s a padlock on it. We’ll cut it to see what’s stored in there.”

Ed Milton lit a cigarette and paced on the deck, the yellow cat watching them complacently from under one of the plastic chairs. Bradford said, “Let’s take a look around to see if we can find any bomb-building material. Elizabeth, you want to stay out here?”

She shook her head. “No, I don’t.”

The men stepped off the porch, Elizabeth following them. The three deputies walked behind them. Bradford paused to look at a small cardboard box. The three deputies passed them. Bradford said, “Looks like it was delivered from Amazon. We’ll open it in a minute.” He, Milton and Elizabeth walked around the trailer, the men getting closer to the shed. From the distance of one hundred feet, Bradford could see inside the open shed. One of his men snapped a lock and bent down to open something.

The burst was like a small sun. Bright white. Ear-splitting noise. The explosion roared with the power of a category five tornado. The shockwave blast obliterated the shed. Molecules sucked from scorched air. Severed arms and heads flew like shrapnel. Blood, bone and tissue rained down on Bradford, Milton, Elizabeth and three deputies.

One deputy was knocked to the ground, clutching his throat. Elizabeth fell on her back from the powerful concussive force. A ball of fire reached up into the sky, the sound of the explosion echoed across the hills and woodlands like booming mortar shells.

Bradford stood there staring at the singed ground, the smell of charred flesh in the air. His mind almost couldn't process what he felt, heard and smelled. It was a warzone with pulverized bodies after heavy artillery fire. One of the younger deputies stumbled to the side of the trailer and vomited in a withered flowerbed. The windows were blown out of the side of the trailer that faced the explosion.

Bradford ran to Elizabeth. He dropped to his knees down beside her. She bled from a cut to the forehead. He used his hands to wipe the blood and hair from her face. "How bad are you hurt?" he asked, his eyes frantic.

She sat up, the reflection of orange fire in her eyes. "I'll be okay." She coughed and spat out blood.

Milton was on his radio calling headquarters. "We got an emergency! Officers down and injured at the subject's address. Send every ambulance you can spare. Call Wayne County and get them to do the same thing."

The rest of the SWAT team came running, each man stopping as they rounded the trailer, their minds having difficulty grasping the scene. Arms, legs, heads and torsos were scattered like garbage. Fire burned from the site where the shed once stood.

Elizabeth stumbled over to the deputy on the ground holding his throat. He made a gurgling sound as she struggled to stabilize him. A large piece of metal had impaled his neck, like a jagged arrow protruding out the opposite side. His body flopped, arms flailing. The other deputies knelt down to help her.

"Hold on, Carlos," said Milton. "Keep you heart rate down. The paramedics are on their way."

The injured man moaned, tears on his face. "Tell Marie…I love her. His breathing was fast and then his chest stopped moving. Elizabeth stared at the lifeless man a moment, his blood covering her hands. She looked up and Bradford shook his head.

The deputy who was serving as the sniper came running up to Bradford and asked, "What the fuck happened?"

"It was a trap. The damn shed was booby-trapped. Jenkins, Morris, Rodriguez and Holton are gone."

The deputy looked at the man's body as Elizabeth and the others stood, blood splattered on their clothes. He whispered, "Carlos…you were one of the best, brother." The man choked up, wiped his eyes and looked out into the woods. "I saw this kind of hell in Iraq. Never thought I'd see it back home."

Bradford, knees weak, steadied himself against a wrought iron hand railing on the back porch. He looked at his phone, hands shaking, wiped a film of blood from the screen. "I'm calling Ben Dixon with the FBI. They need to assign agents to question every son-of-a-bitch that they know is a member of the STA. This is much bigger battle than what our department can fight."

The sound of sirens filled the air and ambulances and emergency personnel came running. Elizabeth stared at hundreds of small spots of blood on her arms and clothes. She heard the sound of a medevac helicopter in the air. It came closer, circling, and then positioned itself to land in the front yard. Compared to the explosion, the blast from the prop felt like a summer breeze against Elizabeth's face.

She closed her eyes for a moment, Bradford's words stinging deeper than the bleeding cuts in her skin. *This is much bigger battle than what our department can fight.'*

NINETY-FOUR

Elizabeth checked her phone screen, looked through all of her home security cameras before she drove the last mile to her house. She parked and entered, disarming the alarm and resetting it. She took the pistol out of her purse and walked upstairs, her body physically and emotionally drained to nothing. In the bathroom, she set the gun on a small table next to her shower. As she undressed, Elizabeth looked at the spots of blood on her shirt and pants.

She stepped to the mirror over the sink. She almost didn't recognize herself. Her hair was matted with dried blood. The bandage the paramedics had placed on her forehead was the color of a dark strawberry. She slowly removed it and looked at the one-inch cut. Her eyes were red and swollen. Her bottom lip cut.

She entered the shower and stood under the steaming water, the blood in her hair poured over her stomach and between her feet before going down the drain. She scrubbed her body, closing her eyes, the images of the explosion playing back in her mind. She felt something in her hair. She used her fingernails to pull the small object from her scalp. She held it in the palm of her hand. It was a bone fragment, maybe part of a tooth that had landed and stuck in her hair.

She set the fragment in her soap dish and held on the shower handle on the door for a moment, her head feeling light, the stench of death not seeming to come out of her hair and skin. She stepped back under the shower-head, hot water pouring over her body. Mike Bradford's voice reverberating in her mind. *'I'm calling Ben Dixon with the FBI. They need to assign agents to question every son-of-a-bitch that they know is a member of the STA. This is much bigger battle than what our department can fight.'*

Elizabeth opened her eyes, water streaming over her face. She remembered what she'd read in the pamphlet, *Retribution*, the words Zachariah Belmont had written, *'You, my brothers, will always be welcome at Polemo. We may have lost the Civil War, but we did not lose the battle that is Polemo.'*

'This is a bigger battle that what our department can fight.'

Battle.

She stepped out of the shower, wrapped a towel around her body, and called Bradford. After he answered, she said, "Mike, it may be a long shot, but I think I might know where Henry Griffin and Lance Thompson may be hiding."

"Where?"

"Remember what I told you about something Zachariah Belmont had written in the pamphlet *Retribution?*"

"He wrote a lot of bull shit. Which section or topic are you talking about?"

"The stuff about Polemo. He wrote *'You, my brothers, will always be welcome at Polemo. We may have lost the Civil War, but we did not lose the battle that is Polemo.'* Professor Atticus Ward told me about the remnants of the old camp down on remote land near the place where the Chickasawhay River and the Leaf River form to make the Pascagoula River. I want to go there in the morning."

"Elizabeth, my department is helping the families plan funerals for four good men. Three of them don't have enough body parts to bury. I can't do another SWAT operation until I get—"

"You don't have to. There may be nothing there. Like I said, it's a long shot but it's worth checking the area out. What if just you and I run down there? The driving time is less than an hour. We can leave at daybreak and be back by nine. That includes stopping for coffee."

Bradford said nothing.

"All right," Elizabeth said. "I'll go by myself. Maybe I won't find anything but ticks in the woods. I'll let you know." She started to disconnect.

"Hold on...you're right. Probably nothing back in there but weeds growing through rotten wood. But it's worth taking a look. I'll see if Ed wants to join us. He's not in a good place. He was a mentor to one of the deputies, Carlos Rodriguez. And right now Ed would do anything to find the perps that took Carlos' life."

"Do you want me to meet you at the station in the morning?"

"I'll pick you up. Are you in a hotel?"

"No. I'm at my home."

"I'll have a patrol drive by a few times tonight. Sleep lightly, and if you need me…call."

NINETY-FIVE

Elizabeth sat in the backseat of the Range Rover and sipped a large black coffee from McDonalds. Bradford drove and Ed Milton sat in the front passenger side. Milton had said very little through most of the drive, the sun just now coming over the tree line in the east.

Bradford glanced at the phone mounted in a holding bracket on the dashboard. He looked at the digital map and said, "We're heading in the general direction. But there's no physical address near that remote part of the state. So there isn't a guidance system to take us to the edge of the property. The satellite maps indicate lots of dense woodlands and a small clearing tucked somewhere inside."

Milton cleared his throat. "Wish we had access to real-time satellite images. I'd like to know if there's any sign of life in that old camp. Maybe see if vehicles are in there. The feds ought to pull that off for us."

Bradford nodded. "I haven't heard back from Ben Dixon yet. I know he was in court testifying in a sex trafficking trial. In my message, I told him about the explosion and fatalities. And now it's all over the news. Everybody in the nation will know about it today."

Elizabeth looked at her phone screen. "It seems like the best way is to go south on Merritt Road, and then take an unmarked dirt road that appears to lead right where the two rivers form the Pascagoula. It's similar to the letter Y. We may have to walk the last half mile or so."

They drove a mile down a dirt road only wide enough for one car. The road ended near fenced property with two *no trespassing* signs on a locked gate. Bradford said, "I'll move the car off the road behind that thicket." He parked and they got out. They walked toward the gate, Milton looked up in the trees for any sign of surveillance cameras. Cicadas hummed in the trees.

Bradford knelt down near the locked chain. He touched tire tracks in the dirt. "These are fresh. Before we left, I checked the weather history for this area in the last three days. It hasn't rained."

"You think somebody is in there?" Milton asked, stretching his fingers and touching the grip of his gun in his belt holster.

"I don't know. But I can tell that those tires fit a large vehicle, probably a heavy-duty truck."

Elizabeth looked at the two faded red and white *no trespassing* signs and said, "The fence is full of barbed wire at the top. How can we get in there?"

"Bolt cutters," said Bradford. "I have some in the vehicle." He walked back to the Range Rover.

Milton shook a cigarette from the pack, offered one to Elizabeth. "Smoke?"

"No thanks. I don't smoke."

He grinned, used a Zippo to light his cigarette. He took a deep drag. "I'm not a profiler, but I could have figured that." He looked beyond the fence, trying to peer through the thick woods. "I don't know if anybody's in there. But if they are, and if it's Griffin, Thompson and God knows who else, they won't greet us with flowers and the community welcome wagon."

"I know."

"You don't have to go in."

"Yes, I do."

"You know, I didn't care for you at first. All that psychological profiling stuff. But you're pretty spot on with it. And you've kind of grown on me. I appreciate what you tried to do for Carlos." He took another drag of the cigarette. "I don't want to see anything bad happen to you."

"I'll take that as a compliment."

"Meant that way."

Bradford returned with the bolt cutters and a small pair of binoculars around his neck. He stood next to the chain, placed the padlock in the mouth of the cutters and chopped through the lock. It fell to the ground. He pulled the chain off the fence and opened the gate. He looked back at Elizabeth. "You want to stay here?"

She smiled. "Do you and Ed work from the same playbook? Do you think I sat in the back seat and came down here with you two if I wanted to stay in the damn car?" She unzipped her purse and lifted out the 9mm. "You might find I can have your backs. Not that you may need a woman watching over you." She walked around Bradford.

Milton stomped on his cigarette with the heel of his shoe, shook his head and went inside, Bradford closed the gate, looping the chain back in place and tossing the severed lock in the bushes. He glanced at his phone. "Looks like we don't have a cell signal out here. It's probably one of the last remote spots in Mississippi where you can't get cell service. We need to watch for trip wires and any sign of booby-traps. From this point on, it's just the three of us."

Elizabeth fought the urge to smile. She set her gun back in her purse and walked with the men into the woods.

NINETY-SIX

They followed a dirt road deep into the pines and oaks. Yellow flies zoomed in and out of the bush, orbiting around their heads. A large fly alighted on Milton's forearm, near a cut from the explosion. He swatted it. "Gotcha. These flies are ten times worse than mosquitoes."

Bradford knelt down and looked at the tire tracks. "So far we've seen four different sets of tire tracks. All are fairly fresh."

Milton said, "We know there are or were at least four different vehicles in here. Assuming there is only one driver per vehicle, we're outmanned by one. And if there are two or three guys per vehicle. We're in deep shit. That's guessing that there might be someone in here."

Elizabeth looked further down the trail, the sound of cicadas growing louder. She said, "If there is someone or some people in here, we have the upper hand for now—the element of surprise."

Bradford said, "We were the ones surprised at Lance Thompson's place. Somehow, I have the feeling that these perps know more about us than what we think." He looked at Elizabeth. "They certainly know about you. You've become their poster child for what they believe is everything wrong with people who call violent white supremacist terrorists on American soil."

She nodded. "I did say that, and it's true."

Bradford looked at his watch. "Let's go. If the place is vacant, maybe we'll find some physical evidence to tie this thing more together."

They walked another hundred feet, the trail made a bend to the left. Milton pointed to a sign nailed to a pine tree. "There's something that might be considered evidence." It was made from a board and the word *Polemos* was stenciled deep into the wood. He looked at Elizabeth. "I recognize that plank. Most likely came from the hangin' bridge. What'd you say that word, Polemos, means?"

"It's Greek. Roughly translated it deals with war…the capacity to bring all into existence and to annihilate."

Milton eased his pistol from the holster, looked around the thick woods and deep shadows. Bradford gripped his gun and continued walking. They moved another hundred yards. The chanting from the cicadas faded. Birdsong went silent. The morning sun was in their faces. Milton pointed, dropped his voice to a whisper. "There are old buildings and barns. Seems like somebody's been working around the place. From here I can see new lumber mixed with the old."

Bradford looked through his binoculars, scanned the clearing from right to left. "I don't see any sign of people, but there's an Airstream trailer back there near those old growth oaks."

Elizabeth stopped, Shelby Griffin's words replaying in her mind. *He pulls an Airstream trailer behind his truck and lives off the land. He likes to be by rivers.'* She said, "Henry Griffin's father, Shelby, told me his son pulls an Airstream trailer and pretty much lives off the land."

Bradford said, "Let's approach from the cover of the woods. Just watch everywhere you step. A vine could be a tripwire."

They left the dirt road and walked through the woods and undergrowth, Bradford in the lead followed by Milton and Elizabeth. They ducked under limbs and pushed through scrub growth. A large, brown wolf spider crawled across a low-hanging limb. She watched it for a second and continued walking.

They moved quietly through the woods. Bradford stopped and turned toward them. "Let's approach that trailer from the cover of the trees. We didn't see any vehicles so there might not be anybody here. And that would give us a chance to search this place."

Milton and Elizabeth nodded, and they continued, the earthy scent of leaf decay, pinesap and moss all around them. Twigs and small branches snapped under their shoes. After a few minutes, Bradford stepped closer to the clearing. He looked through the binoculars. "I still don't see anyone or a sign anyone has been here. No campfire smoke. No vehicles. We're less than fifty yards to the trailer. Let's just tackle it from the bushes, see if there's any vehicle on the other side. If not, maybe we'll see what Henry Griffin keeps inside his little home in the woods. At this point, eight people dead, maybe hundreds more in the crosshairs, we'll get a search warrant when we get back to civilization. "

Two minutes later they were there. Elizabeth could see the silver exterior of the trailer through the breaks on the foliage. She held her gun tighter.

NINETY-SEVEN

W hen they got to the outer edge of the trees and on the opposite side of the trailer, it was there. A white pickup truck. It was
parked less than fifty feet from the trailer. The sign on the panel facing them
depicted a caricature of a lumberjack holding an ax. The caption read: *Paul
Bunyan Tree Trimming.*

Elizabeth touched two fingers to her throat. She looked down on her
arm. A tick crawled near her elbow. She brushed it off. Her pulse quickened
as she stared at the truck.

Bradford said, "This changes the game plan. Looks like there is only
one door on this model trailer. Ed, let's approach the door together. If it's
unlocked, maybe I can catch Griffin off guard if he's in there. I'll enter to
the left and you go right. It's small so we ought to be able to cover it in
seconds."

Milton said, "What if it's locked?"

"We kick it off the hinges." He looked at his phone. "Still no cell signal.
Elizabeth, if you just keep us covered that would help. You can stay hidden
from right here and still get off a shot if you need to. Should, for some
reason, all go to hell in there…you run outta this shit hole until you can get
a cell signal and call for help."

She looked at the truck and the perimeter of the clearing. "I've counted
five outbuildings to the rear of the trailer. Do you think you should check
them out before you burst in there?"

"No. Henry Griffin is the head of the snake. We cut that off and the body has nowhere to go. We've only seen his truck. Maybe there isn't anybody else here. He might be gone, too. Off to kill more college kids." Bradford's eyes narrowed in disgust. "Let's get this monster."

Milton followed him to the trailer, both men jogging quietly, moving stealth style, hunched over, staying close to the exterior, and avoiding windows. Elizabeth watched as they approached the door, pistols ready. They stood on an iron grate step, Bradford's hand on the door handle. Slowly turning. Elizabeth bit her bottom lip as the men opened the door and bounded inside.

"Police!" she heard Bradford shout.

Milton said nothing. She watched the trailer move slightly as the men searched it. Within thirty seconds there were done. They stepped outside. Guns still in hand. Bradford signaled for Elizabeth. She held her pistol at her side as she approached.

Bradford said, "No sign of life. The place is spotless…almost sterile. The exact opposite from Lance Thompson's trailer. They could be any-where. But they don't appear to be here. A key hook is on the inside of the door. Nothing's hanging on it. If Griffin's keys were there, I'd say he's here somewhere. Maybe he's with Thompson."

Elizabeth said, "Good. That will give us time to call for backup. Have forensics go over the truck and trailer."

Milton said, "We're here so let's take a quick look around the place. But don't open locked doors."

They walked toward the first outbuilding. It was an old barn like struc-ture. Made from thick timbers that withstood time and insects. Bradford paused at the door. He looked at a large cast iron hinge lock. It was open, the padlock unlocked and a brass key at the base. Bradford, Milton and Elizabeth put on gloves.

Milton said, "Looks like somebody forgot to lock up."

"Maybe that's because they're still here," Elizabeth said, looking around.

Bradford slowly opened the wide door. It swung to the left, the hinges squeaking. Inside were hundreds of bags stacked to the ceiling. Bradford stepped inside. Milton and Elizabeth followed.

Milton let out a low whistle. "If this is what I think it is…it's enough shit to take down any courthouse or federal building in the nation."

Bradford read the label on one of the bags. "It's exactly what you think it is, ammonium nitrate." He stepped over to a long bench filled with woodworking tools, a jigsaw, circular saw, orbital sander, chisels and wooden mallets. There was a stack of aged boards. "I'd bet a paycheck these came from the bridge."

Elizabeth lifted the lid of a cardboard box with a piece of splintered wood. "Dear God…there are three more crosses and three wooden bowls in here."

Milton and Bradford walked further down the workbench. On top of it were wires, a soldering iron, tools and electronic pieces. Two had been assembled.

Elizabeth asked, "What's that?"

Bradford said, "Wireless detonators. Probably have a range of a couple hundred yards. And that's plenty of safe space for a terrorist to kill hundreds of innocent people from the comfort of his pickup truck. Let's get back to call in the troops. And we need the FBI to get their assess down here and do a manhunt for these perps. They're about to go from the horrific killing of college kids to the wholesale slaughter of hundreds, maybe thousands."

They walked back outside, the morning sunlight brighter. Elizabeth paused, thinking she saw a movement at the base of trees to the far right of the outbuilding. She continued walking, staring. Bradford and Elizabeth stepped ahead of Milton who stopped to light a cigarette. Elizabeth turned back toward him. "We need to go. Something doesn't feel right."

He nodded and took a long drag from the cigarette.

Ed Milton's head exploded.

Blood, teeth and brain matter rained down on Elizabeth and Bradford.

Bradford returned fire. The man in the shadows ran behind the outbuilding. Bradford grabbed Elizabeth and sprinted to the opposite side. He whispered, "I think I hit him. Stay right here. I'll work to the left of the building. If you remain at the corner, you'll have some protection, and you can get off a shot if he runs back this way."

She nodded, dropped her purse and stood at the edge of the building. Ready. Both hands on her gun, her heart slamming in her chest.

NINETY-EIGHT

Bradford stepped cautiously around the side of the building and was out of sight. Seconds later there was the sound of four gunshots. Close together. Separate guns. And then silence.

Lance Thompson appeared around the corner of the building. He held his gun in one hand. Blood poured down his arm from a deep wound in his right shoulder and thigh. He stumbled to his knees.

Elizabeth stepped around the edge and approached him, her gun aimed at this head. She could tell his shattered arm was almost useless, the gun dangling from his bloody hand. Bradford ran around the building, his pistol aimed at Thompson. He yelled, "Drop the gun! On your stomach!"

Thompson looked up at Elizabeth, sunlight in his eyes. He squinted and grinned. "So we meet again. I figured I'd be diggin' your fuckin' grave about now."

"You figured wrong."

"You got a big mouth, Doctor Monroe. You done pissed off a lot of people."

"Put the gun down!" shouted Bradford.

"Or what...you gonna shoot me? You already done that and I'm still here. There are hundreds...thousands...hundreds of thousands...maybe millions just like me. You gonna kill us all. You can't 'cause we're your next-door neighbors. And it's just a matter of time before we rise up."

"You tell me where Henry Griffin is and you'll live," Bradford said.

Thompson watched the blood pool near his knee. He lifted his eyes up to Bradford. "You'll only find Henry if he wants you to. That man can take a single ax and go off and live in the Montana mountains for years. He's a survivalist and then some."

Elizabeth looked at Thompson and stepped closer. "What did you do to my cat?"

He grinned, blood splattering beneath his limp arm. "You every hear the saying…curiosity killed the cat. Your fuckin' cat was a little too damn curious."

Elizabeth raised her pistol, her finger on the trigger.

Thompson grinned. "What's the matter? Cat got your fuckin' tongue."

She said, "Your father's dead. He played with fire. A snake in his garden, a snake just like you, bit him. I said it on TV, and I'll say it to your face. You and members of your STA are snakes in the garden. You're the deadly and fatal combination of evil mixed with stupidity. You kill college kids. You want to slaughter thousands of innocents. You think you're a warrior when the sad fact is you're a frightened wimp."

"Fuck you!" He raised his pistol.

Bradford fired once, the round hitting Thompson in his temple. Blood and sinew flew almost to the door of the building. Bradford ran to Ed Milton, his body crumpled, a cigarette wedged between his fingers. Bradford touched Milton's shoulder and slowly stood, eyes tearing. He glanced around the perimeter. "Let's get back to the car. We'll head through the woods. I don't want to take a chance and walk more than a hundred yards through the clearing."

"I feel horrible about Ed."

"Let's go." Bradford sprinted toward the adjacent trees, Elizabeth right behind him. Just before they entered the woods, she turned and looked back at the silver trailer under the oaks. She saw the sun wink from a riflescope. Before she could scream, there was a burst of fire from the muzzle, one round hitting Bradford in the back. He fell on the spot.

Elizabeth returned fire and ran to Bradford's side. He looked up at her, blood trickling from the right side of his mouth. "Go on," he said, coughing. "Take cover."

There was the sound of another round. The bullet whizzed by Elizabeth's left ear and hit a pine tree, knocking a large pinecone down.

"Elizabeth! Go! Take cover!" Bradford coughed, his head resting on the ground.

Elizabeth turned and fired two rounds back at the trailer. She bolted into the woods and began working her way toward the trailer. Within a minute, she was less than a hundred feet away. She could see the left side of Henry Griffin. Even from the distance, he looked large. A mountain man in every physical sense of the word. Wide shoulders. Long gray ponytail. He wore jungle camouflage clothes.

She stood behind a sycamore tree and raised her gun. Griffin looked her way and darted around the trailer into the woods. She moved in his direction. Slowly. Careful not to make a sound. Avoiding twigs and limbs on the ground. Two blue jays squawked from the top of an oak tree in the area where Griffin disappeared.

Elizabeth glanced up at the birds. They tilted their heads. Watching. Hopping from tree limb to tree limb. Fussing at the human somewhere below them. They flew to the top of another tree much closer to Elizabeth. The jays seemed to enjoy their mock chase. After a few more seconds, they flew away, over the clearing and into the distance.

And now Elizabeth was completely alone with a monster in the woods.

NINETY-NINE

She looked at the screen on her cell phone. There was a slight signal. One bar, but it was there. She hit the stored number. The woman's voice said, "Forrest County Sheriff's Department."

Elizabeth held the phone to her lips and spoke in a whisper not much louder than a breath. "Detectives Bradford and Milton have been shot. We're in an old hunter's camp between the forks of the Chickasawhay and Leaf Rivers. Need help now...."

"Ma'am...what is your name?"

Elizabeth disconnected. She heard a limb break in the woods. Not a natural sound of nature. It was the sound of someone approaching. She looked near her feet and lifted a rock. She threw it hard toward her left. The sound through the trees was as if she were running in the woods and then abruptly stopping.

Griffin gave chase. His burly body popped limbs like a grizzly as he ran toward the sound. And then he stopped. The only sound was that of a yellow fly near Elizabeth. It landed on her arm. She wanted to slap it, but dared not to. The fly bit into her skin, its jaws like tiny knives, its mouth drinking her blood.

She looked up. Henry Griffin stood twenty feet away. He held the rifle at his hip and pointed it at her.

Elizabeth instantly raised her pistol.

He laughed. "You think you got the drop on me? You might manage to get a round in me. But unless you're real good, girl, I'll keep coming. I won't kill you right away. Got big plans for you."

"Like you had for the college kids? Plans to kidnap them? Cut their throats, write your favorite word across their heads, and leave one of you're fucking bowls on their laps? You chose them from the rally at the Confederate monument?"

"I did. I'd dispatch Lancelot to catch them. Like netting butterflies. I understand your late daughter liked butterflies."

"And I understand you had a huge jealously problem with your brother Winston."

Elizabeth looked down the barrel of her pistol, the beaded sight on Griffin's forehead, his eyes hardening with hate. She thought of the word *Wrath* in blood on Cindy's forehead. Her finger rested against the trigger.

"You won't shoot me. It's not in you." He grinned. "Lancelot would be dispatched at my beckoning. He'd get the pathetic people and bring them to me for processing, following the instructions in the Book of Revelation."

"You're really sick, and you need help."

"Help? Come, Doctor Monroe. I'm not crazy. I know exactly what I'm doing. Deliberate. Methodical. I was going make you the seventh sacrifice. Now, it looks like you moved up the chain to number five. The fifth angel poured out his bowl on the throne of the beast and its kingdom was plunged into darkness. People cursed God but refused to repent for what they'd done. Are you ready to repent, Doctor Monroe?" He licked his lips. "Are you ready to go back in front of the TV cameras and recant all the garbage you said about us? Tell me! Are you?"

She looked at his hands, his middle finger on the trigger, the angle of the rifle muzzle. From her perspective, it appeared to be aimed at least a foot over her head.

"You can spout Bible verses all day long, Henry. Everything you and your sick members are doing has nothing to do with God or the Bible. It has everything to do with your own insecurities, prejudices and hate. You—"

"How dare you! Don't you enter my kingdom and utter blasphemous words! You will gnaw your tongue!" He raised the bore of the rifle and fired.

The round went over Elizabeth's head. Before he could get off another shot, she fired once. The bullet entered his thick chest directly in the center.

He grinned and charged toward her. She fired again. And again. One round hit his massive shoulder, shattering bone. The other entered his stomach.

And then he was on her.

His huge hands were around her neck. Fingers squeezing deep into her throat. Elizabeth managed to fire a fourth shot into his chest. This loosened his grip for a moment. She sucked in air, her head spinning, blackness descending.

He fell to his knees. Blood poured from four holes in his body. He looked up at her and said, "You can kill me…but never the cause." His eyes became distant.

Elizabeth reached over and grabbed him by the bloody shirt. "Did you kill my daughter? Tell me! You knew about the butterflies! Did you kill Molly Monroe? Don't lie!"

Griffin grinned, blood trickling from his mouth into the gray stubble on his wide face. He's lips tried to form words, his breathing labored. He whispered, "Lie? Well, why would I lie? Maybe she was my first…there must be sacrificial lambs." He smirked, his head bobbing like a drunk. "Molly had a little lamb…its fleece as white as…." He fell backwards and took his last breath.

Elizabeth slowly stood. She felt nauseous. Her hands shook. She looked down at him and saw that he was missing a third of his right index finger. She could hear the sound of a police helicopter approaching, the wail of sirens coming closer. As she turned to walk away, to walk out of this killing field, she could smell the fragrance of honeysuckles mixing with the odor of burnt gunpowder.

It was an odor she would never forget.

ONE HUNDRED

The following day, Elizabeth spent five hours speaking with FBI agents and a dozen state and county criminal investigators. They conducted the interviews in a conference room at the Forrest County Sheriff Office. FBI agent Ben Dixon ran his fingers through his gray hair and said, "This mission...this vendetta, you believe, began after a lynch mob hung the teens from the Shubuta Bridge?"

Elizabeth sipped from a bottle of water, her fingers sore, bruised and cut, lacerations on her hands and forehead. "I suspect it started long before that, Agent Dixon. How far in time do you want to go back? That was just one of the mile markers in the trek of evil deeds. When you have a psychopath who believes he's on a divine mission from God, there's no talking him off the ledge. He'll either jump or you have to shoot him down. It was that way with Zachariah Belmont and with his protégé a century later, Henry Griffin and his followers."

"The Bureau, based in Jackson, has been fighting these hate groups since we were formed. It's a deadly game of whack a mole, and it looks like we'll do battle with them forever."

Elizabeth studied the agent's lined face. "It is a battle, isn't it?"

"Yes. We rounded up nineteen members of the STA so far. Most are pleading the fifth or lawyering up. One fella, who wants to cut a plea, did tell us the big blast was to be detonated by Henry Griffin, and they'd targeted the Robert C. Weaver Federal Building in Washington. It houses hundreds of employees, the General Services Administration and the Department

374

of Housing and Urban Development. It's named for the man who was the first African-American member of a president's cabinet during the Kennedy administration." He paused and chose his words carefully. "Your diligence, Doctor Monroe, along with your psychological profiling, probably saved hundreds of innocent lives. Thank you."

— —

Elizabeth walked down a hospital corridor past an older man pushed in a wheelchair by a nurse. She could hear the beeps and electronic life monitoring coming from within the propped open doors, the smell of disinfectant and dysentery. She stopped at room 509 and knocked softly. There was no answer. She slowly opened the door. Mike Bradford looked asleep. He was propped up on pillows, white bandages wrapped across his chest, two IV lines in his arms. Elizabeth stepped in the room. The door made a sound when it closed. His eyes fluttered open, and he looked at Elizabeth standing at the foot of the bed.

He tried to smile, his facial muscles weak. "Are we in heaven together?" His voice was raspy.

"Not yet." She smiled and walked up to him. "How are you feeling?"

"Like I was shot by a high powered rifle." He paused, looked at flowers on a tray near his bed and cut his eyes back up to Elizabeth. "I feel so bad for Ed and his family."

"I do to. He was dedicated. He tried to make the world a little better place."

"What happened Elizabeth? After I was shot, everything went black. What happened?"

She told him the details leading to the shooting and death of Henry Griffin and added, "How these people develop into who they become is something we'll theorize over until the last of days, I imagine. Maybe it's supposed to lead us to the last days. Lines in the sand drawn. Black and white. Good and evil. Taking sides because, somehow, someway, we failed at the central human trait that is so important, so hardwired into our DNA, but somehow so conditional and illusive. It's love. We need it. Most of us want it. We all laugh, cry and bleed. It's the emotional glue. Why doesn't it stick to our conscience…why doesn't it hold the human race together?"

"I wish I could answer that, but with the pain meds I'm on, you really don't want to hear my interpretation." He made an effort to smile, closed his bloodshot eyes for a second.

"That's where you're wrong, Mike. I would like to hear it. Maybe not now because of your aforementioned condition, but over a glass of wine."

"You mean a real date?"

"Let's not label it. Maybe we should call it what my students call it: 'hanging out.' For me, it's a good dinner, a glass of wine, great conversation, some laughs and a Van Gogh starry, starry night on the back deck with an Irish coffee."

"I wish I could write this down so when I wake up I won't think I dreamed or hallucinated it."

"I'll remember."

He leaned his head back in the pillows, his face gaunt, gray stubble. "Before Griffin died…did you ask him if he killed Molly?"

"Yes. He was flippant. He said maybe she was his first. He spoke a mock nursery rhyme before he died. He said he knew Molly loved butterflies and added that he'd sent Lance Thompson to get the victims he chose…to get them like catching butterflies."

"I'm sorry, Elizabeth. I wish you had closure."

"When someone murders your child, no matter what revelation comes forth, you never have closure. That is a myth." She leaned over and gently kissed Bradford on his forehead. "Get some rest."

ONE HUNDRED ONE

The cemetery was one of the oldest in Mississippi. It was filled with mausoleums, statues and early graves. Sycamore trees and old oaks dotted the cemetery grounds. There were adjacent woodlands and vistas that allowed visitors to look out to the rolling countryside. The oldest graves dated back to 1798.

As Elizabeth drove through the cemetery, she remembered coming here as a freshman in college. It was for an art class project. She'd attended a funeral two years earlier. One of her best friends had died from a drug overdose. Elizabeth had seen a majestic statue of a winged angel. It marked the cemetery plot of the Fitzgerald family. They'd help settle Hattiesburg and Biloxi. Years ago she'd spent two hours sketching the statue. She'd watched the squirrel's play, the sycamores and oaks teeming with birdsong.

Twenty-five years later, it would be the place she chose to bury Molly.

Elizabeth parked at the southwest section of the cemetery, the morning sun was breaking over the tree line, an overnight rain left the air washed, the scent of moss, acorns and damp earth in the still air. She took flowers and birdseed from her car and walked down a winding path to Molly's grave. Elizabeth stood there for a minute, whispered a prayer and then set the flowers against Molly's headstone. "Hey baby," she said, her eyes watering. "I hope you like the flowers. They're fresh-cut magnolia blossoms, your favorite. I miss you so much. I have a lot to tell you Molly, but somehow I think you already know. Some bad people are no longer doing evil things to kids like you, sweetheart. Maybe the world is a somewhat better place for just a little while." She looked at the birdseed. "Thought I'd refill the feeder. I haven't had the chance to visit you and the birds in the last few weeks. I brought extra seed to make up for that."

Elizabeth stepped over to a wooden birdfeeder that hung from a branch of a sycamore tree. She filled it with seed and then sat down on a wrought iron bench near Molly's grave. Within half a minute, a bright red cardinal alighted in the feeder and began eating. A lighter colored female cardinal soon joined the bird. Elizabeth smiled watching them. She looked at Molly's headstone. "Two of your favorite birds are here."

The male cardinal flew to a limb about half way up the sycamore. He tossed his head back and sang, his head bobbing in his repertoire, his singing loud and resonating across the cemetery. He was soon joined by a wood thrush that sang from a pine tree. Elizabeth watched the bird, its body no larger than the pinecone next to it on the limb, but at that moment, the small bird was pitch perfect and sang volumes.

Three hours later, Elizabeth stood on her front porch reworking the soil in a planter box filled with petunias. She pushed a loose strand of hair from her eyes and planted a new flower in the box. As she was about to go back in the house to get more potting spoil, something caught her eye. She turned and looked down her driveway.

Jack sat at the top of the drive.

"Oh my God!" Elizabeth removed her gardening gloves. "Jack!" She stood there, almost dumbfounded. Jack got up and sauntered toward her in his usual slow cadence. Elizabeth held her hands to her face. She watched him for a few seconds and then bolted off the porch, running to Jack. She bent down and picked him up. "Where have you been? I thought you were… I thought you'd used up every one of your nine lives and were on borrowed time." She kissed him on the top of his wide head, tears rolling down her face. "Oh Jack, I was so worried." She carried him back to the porch.

She sat down in her wicker rocking chair, Jack next to her. She scratched him behind his ears. He purred and nuzzled her. Elizabeth wiped the tears from her cheeks. Jack looked up at her, tilted his head as if to say everything was going to be all right now. He placed a thick paw on her arm. She rocked in the chair, Jack on her lap, the fragrance of petunias in the late afternoon.

A gentle breeze caused the wind chimes to tinkle in a sweet song of nature. And somehow, at that point in time for Elizabeth, the world was restored as a fine place once again.

The End

9 781981 226290